NIGHT MAGIC

"Savannah, would you like to go out sometime?" Paul asked. "For dinner or something?"

"Oh, all right. I mean, that would be nice—" Savannah turned to find his face only inches away from hers.

Without thinking, she pressed against his body, gently rubbing her lips over his. She wanted to savor this closeness, to taste his sweetness a little at a time.

His arms folded around her waist. Then, burying his hands in her hair, he began softly kissing her face. Paul's lips etched a hot trail over her nose to her chin, finally caressing her neck.

Suddenly, the loud bang of a door slamming deep inside the house caused them to pull apart quickly. Savannah took a deep breath to steady herself.

"I'd better go in now, I need to get an early start in the morning," she said, moving further away from him, flustered by her lack of control. "Goodnight."

"Goodnight." Paul made no move for several minutes before going to his Jeep. He could still feel the glow of Savannah's touch. Her combination of beauty, courage, and sensuality packed a mighty punch that knocked his defenses flat. Staring into the night, he was determined to make her want him just as much.

NIGHT MAGIC
LYNN EMERY

PINNACLE BOOKS
KENSINGTON PUBLISHING CORP.

PINNACLE BOOKS are published by

Kensington Publishing Corp.
850 Third Avenue
New York, NY 10022

Pinnacle and the P logo Reg. U.S. Pat. & TM Off.

First Printing: September, 1995

Printed in the United States of America

10 9 8 7 6 5 4 3 2

Chapter 1

Savannah strode into the spacious professionally decorated office. Without a word she stood in front of the large oak desk. "Did you finish that report?" Bill Clayton did not look up from the file he was reading.

"Yes, sir. Now I'm through with everything." Savannah slapped down the report and in rapid succession another single sheet of paper with only one short typewritten paragraph.

"Resign? I don't think you really want to do this." Clayton held up the paper to someone who was behind her.

"That is exactly what I want." Startled to find Devin suddenly at her shoulder, Savannah tried to maintain her firm, calm exterior. She had thought Clayton was alone in his office.

"This is an overreaction. You should give yourself a chance to cool off before doing something so rash." Devin spoke in his celebrated measured tone. Handing the resignation back to Clayton, he stood beside the senior partner's large leather chair.

"He is right, St. Julien. I know things have been tough since that foul-up on the McNealy case, but—"

"The McNealy file was altered after I had completed and analyzed that research." Savannah could feel her self-control slipping.

"Stop and think, Savannah. Until now you've been doing some of the best work of all six associates. Why would you give up this kind of position in a firm where international reputations are made? It simply makes no sense." Clayton shook his head.

"Mr. Clayton, maybe a vacation would be an alternative. A break from the stress of keeping up here at the office." Devin was the picture of solicitude. His dark, handsome face wore the appropriate worried look of a concerned friend.

Savannah could not help noticing, as she had the first day they met, his impeccable taste in clothes. The pin-striped blue suit, light blue shirt, red-and-blue silk tie with matching handkerchief tucked just so in his coat pocket—all said here was a young man who was on his way to the top. What she had first found so appealing she now found appalling. He had pretended to be her friend and had even wooed her. Savannah had let down her guard, telling him about her deepest feelings. Tentatively, she'd shared her childhood hurt at losing her mother and feeling shut out by her father. She had begun to trust him and to believe they could be more than friends . . . that he would not hurt her.

But seeing him playfully pat Karen on the behind when they thought they were alone had proved his betrayal. Karen was blond, with the shape and walk of a model rather than an ambitious young attorney. She'd been cold and condescending to Savannah as frequently as possible, openly fuming when she was praised for good work. Karen, who lately had known as much about Savannah's assignments as Savannah had. Karen, who'd tried to convince the partners whenever they reviewed cases that Savannah wasn't quite up to the big ones.

"When I finished that report, it was perfect. You remember, Devin. I left the office at about seven that night. You and Karen were still here.'' She stared at him hard.

"That was weeks ago. Besides, with all the nights we've worked late, how would I recall—'' His voice trailed off lamely before he shrugged.

"Yes, all those nights working late. With Karen.''

"Never mind that now.'' Clayton glanced between them speculatively for a few seconds. "Listen, we have several important clients in the southern part of the state. In fact, one in your hometown, or near there, is having some trouble. You could go down. As Devin said, less pressure, a slower pace. A nice visit with the family.''

"I don't know.'' Savannah felt a sudden pang at the mention of going home.

"You people are too emotional, impulsive. Take my advice, give yourself time to cool off.'' Clayton wore a look of indulgence as he spoke in a placating tone.

" 'You people'? Just what the hell does that mean?'' His words cut through the pang of remembering, causing her to place both hands on her hips.

"Hold on, I meant you young people. Devin.'' Clayton nodded toward the door, a signal that he should go.

"Of course.'' He was obviously reluctant to leave them alone, but he had no choice.

"Listen to me, Savannah,'' Clayton started as the door clicked shut. "Don't junk a promising career. Take some time for yourself. Say, three weeks.''

"Don't think I'm not grateful for what you've done; I am. But this isn't just a whim. I've been thinking about going into practice on my own for a while now. This is just the kick in the butt I needed to really do something about it.''

"Take as long as you need—a month, two.''

"Come on, there are dozens lined up to take my place.''

"In this game, nothing is done out of pure altruism. You brought big money into this firm from some of the most successful minority- and women-owned businesses in this region. Frankly, why should I gamble on an unknown, when we already have a winner? Those two are amateur sharks. You can learn to deal with that and more. We both know it."

"That's just what I'm afraid of, learning to deal with them, then becoming one of them. No, it's better this way." Savannah shook hands with him.

"Some of our best clients may jump ship when they hear you're gone." Clayton's eyebrows came together.

"I haven't discussed this with anyone, but naturally, I won't turn down business." Savannah lifted a shoulder.

"I understand. Good luck, St. Julien." Clayton rose to shake her hand. "Don't burn this old soldier too badly when you set the world on fire."

"No promises, Mr. Clayton," Savannah called over her shoulder as she left his office. Devin appeared from nowhere, blocking her exit.

"So that's it. You're leaving behind an ugly accusation that may affect my future with this firm. After what I've done for you?" Devin spoke in an undertone, aware they were the center of attention.

"Not quite."

A loud crack rang out as her palm connected solidly with his face. With one motion, she scooped up her leather portfolio and pushed her way through the glass door toward the elevator. The sound of applause from the secretaries and legal assistants followed her. Before the doors whisked shut, the last thing she saw was the stunned, then enraged, expression on his face.

Savannah pressed the button, causing the car window to slide down smoothly. Glancing up, she frowned at her reflection in the rearview mirror. With one quick tug, the tortoiseshell barrette that held her thick mane of black hair in check opened with a snap. The feel of it tumbling about her shoulders brought a smile.

"Hmm, better. Much better." She winked at her reflection.

Savannah felt released—not just from the conservative hairdo she'd adopted, which had blended so well with the decor of the prestigious law firm she'd left behind, but from an invisible bond that had held her to a world far removed from her childhood in the Creole culture of south Louisiana.

The first two weeks after leaving the firm had been a vacation. Savannah had taken time to regroup and say goodbye to all her friends. The last week had been a blur of tying up loose ends. Packing up several years of her life proved harder emotionally than physically. Even though over a month had passed since her abrupt departure from Clayton, Briggs, and Schuster, she was still angry: angry at the way she had been treated; angry at Devin's betrayal. Sure, cutthroat competition was to be expected between associates, but what he and Karen had done had gone far beyond that. They'd used dirty tricks. She could still hear Devin's voice, making excuses.

"Lying, two-faced dog," Savannah muttered.

Yes, leaving was the right thing to do. It's over. Now relax. She flexed her fingers to relieve the stiffness in her hands. Loosening her tense grip on the steering wheel, she sank back into the bucket seat.

The warm breeze across her face felt so good. The September sun beat down on the countryside. Slowing down just a little, she let her eyes sweep the scene surrounding her. The two-lane highway snaked through a lush growth of palmetto and swamp willow. Mixed in with the shadows cast by trees, sunlight-dappled bayous could be seen on either side at intervals. The sky was cloudless, a brilliant blue framing the bright green foliage stretching up to it. A profusion of brown-eyed Susans swayed in the wind. They crowded right up to the paved road, their yellow heads bobbing. She breathed deeply, taking in the rich scent filling the car. How she had missed this vibrant growth, the kind that seemed to explode overnight. This was the enchanted forest of her childhood. During the summer months she had spent long, blissful hours roaming the countryside—with her playmates, occasionally with her father, but mostly with Tante Marie. How wonderful it had been to learn the names of all the wildflowers and herbs from Tante Marie. She could even see the affectionate, slightly sad smile Papa always gave her when she handed him a bouquet she'd picked just for him.

A flash of white in the corner of her eye drew her attention back to the present. A snowy egret began a graceful descent, its large wings flapping slowly as it settled beside several others among the tall reeds. Stinging tears blurred her vision. Convinced, now more than ever, that this was where she needed to be, Savannah pressed the accelerator. She felt an almost desperate need to get home.

Suddenly, a large four-wheel-drive vehicle pulled from a small dirt road leading out of the woods. Though she saw it coming, her car had already gathered so much speed she was sure they would slam together. Jamming her brakes, she jerked the wheel, sharply missing the front of the other vehicle by inches. She jumped out of her car, anxious to see if the other driver was all right. A dark-haired man wearing sunglasses leaned out his window.

"What's your problem, lady, you haven't gotten your quota of road kill today?" With an angry blast of his horn, he began to drive off.

"No, you idiot. I've got a few notches left for stupid country boys who can't read stop signs!" Savannah gave him a three-fingered salute. "Stupid jerk. Well, welcome home." She continued the ride home now feeling as tense as she had before.

The town looked pretty much the same, except more prosperous, now that tourism had taken off due to the current interest in the French-speaking bayou country.

Savannah turned the car down Rougon Street, cutting away from the center of town toward her old neighborhood. As she approached the large house, a lump rose in her throat. Sitting well back from the blacktop street, the spacious wood frame house looked as inviting as ever. The white paint gleamed in the sunshine, set off dramatically by the dark green trim of the windows. Climbing the porch steps, Savannah took time to get reacquainted with the beloved windowboxes of bright flowers, the cypress swing that she had shared with Tante Marie on summer evenings after supper. She was lost in memories, and it took awhile for her to realize that the Creole tune she heard came from inside the house, not her head.

"Tante Marie!" she called, her voice unsteady. She cleared her throat. The rich contralto voice stopped.

"That my baby?" Tante Marie came to the porch still wearing her apron. Her hair was pulled back in a bun, the way she wore it when she cooked. She laughed and squeezed Savannah, her full, round face glowing with pleasure.

"You look as fine as ever." Savannah pinched her aunt's cheek playfully.

"Go 'head now. You the one. Lord, Lord. You down to nothin', cher. But we gone fix that, yeah." Tante Marie held her at arm's length, looking at her niece's trim waistline. "Done lost all them fine hips."

"Not all, no indeed." Savannah chuckled, patting the full hips that curved to fill out the straight-legged jeans she wore.

For the next few minutes she carried in her luggage, all the while keeping up a steady stream of chatter with her aunt. Tante Marie brought her up to date on current events in Beau Chene.

"You seen your papa yet?" Tante Marie hung up several dresses in the armoire that stood in Savannah's old bedroom.

"Not yet. Is he all right? I mean, has he been doing

pretty well?'' Savannah didn't look up from the suitcase she was unpacking.

"Cher, he miss you. Go see him." Tante Marie took the clothes from Savannah's hands.

At this time of day, she knew exactly where to find her father. The once slightly shabby storefronts housing mom-and-pop businesses were now replaced by newly restored shops selling antiques, arts and crafts made by locals, Creole restaurants, and even a few art galleries. As she pulled into a parking space directly across from her father's store, Savannah sat in the car for a few moments to gather her courage. Seeing her father again was what she wanted most, yet dreaded. He was the big, strong, handsome man she had passionately adored. For as long as she could remember, she had wanted to please him. But would he welcome her now? Her mother's death had left an empty space between them that neither had found a way to fill. Talking was never easy. Somehow, what started out as a discussion always ended in conflict. Taking a deep breath, Savannah vowed to make this reunion peaceful.

A large, finely carved cypress sign that read "Antoine's" hung over the door. The tinkle of a bell over the door caused her father to look up from rearranging a shelf of small carved animals.

"Hello, Poppy." Savannah stood uncertainly just inside the door.

"Hello, sweetheart. Come give the old man a hug." Her father stood straight and reached out his arms.

Savannah dropped her large handbag on the counter and allowed herself to be swept up in his embrace. She buried her face in his shirt the way she had when she was a little girl seeking solace after some mishap. She breathed in the familiar smell of wood and his favorite old-fashioned aftershave, lilac vegetal. Any fear that he would still be angry or hurt that she'd left home dissolved instantly. She pulled back, hastily wiping the tears pushing at her eyelids despite her efforts at control.

"How have you been doing, Poppy?" Cupping his face in her hands, she tried to make the question sound casual. Yet she couldn't help but notice that he looked older. And tired.

"Can't complain, baby. Can't complain. Come on over here and tell me how you been doin'." He led her into his small office, where there were two old, comfortable chairs.

Savannah noticed he moved a little more slowly than before, yet he still cut a dashing figure. His six-foot-two-inch frame was as erect as ever. The broad chest and brawny arms were evident even beneath the old long-sleeved flannel shirt he wore. His skin, usually the color of walnut, was still the darker mahogany brown that came from spending days outside in the hot Louisiana summer sun. To her, the gray hair at his temples made him look distinguished. But there was more gray now than when she'd visited at Christmas last year. He eased into the swivel chair behind the desk after setting two steaming cups between them.

"More important, how are you?"

"I'm okay. No, really," she reiterated, at her father's stern look. "It was hard at first, but I'm just fine now. Besides, I wasn't that crazy about living in Shreveport."

"The way you used to talk, it was like you'd died and gone to heaven. Remember how we had to beg you to come home that first Thanksgiving after you'd moved? And then all you did was talk about that law firm." He sounded skeptical that she could give up her new life so painlessly.

"I'd have thought you'd be glad. When I decided to take that job, we got into a big fight. You said I was too young to be so far away." She stared into her coffee cup.

That was not all they'd said. The argument had become heated, until both had said things they later regretted. But it was too painful to repeat the bitter words they had exchanged.

"I'm so sorry for that. I was being selfish, too wrapped

up in my own pain to give you the support you needed. I never told you how proud you made me. But every time I looked into your eyes, I saw your mother. I just felt like I was losin' Therese all over again." He turned away, his voice breaking.

"I'm sorry, too, Poppy. I should have understood how you felt." She reached out and took his hands in hers.

"Well, now you're home." Antoine squeezed her hand once before letting go. "Guess you wanna just take it easy for a while, huh—get yourself settled?"

"I could use a rest. But it's got to be a short one. Finding a job is next on the list."

"You don't have to rush into nothin', cher. You know that. Like I told you before you left, my business is good, and what's mine's yours." Antoine got up to refill his cup.

"I like earning my own way. And I like being a lawyer." Savannah was beginning to feel the familiar tightness in her stomach.

"All right, all right. Let's not fuss. Do what you think is best." Just then the battered old rotary phone on his desk rang. Picking it up on the second ring, Antoine began taking a mail order. He handed Savannah a small color catalogue. "Look at that, we ship outta state now," he whispered. "Yes sir, that's right. It's five dollars off, a special sale 'til the end of the month."

"This is great." Savannah admired the photography. Her father's wood carvings of animals were set in reproductions of the natural bayou or forest habitats. She uttered a tiny delighted cry to see a selection of food items. Apparently, the years of nagging had paid off. Tante Marie, her father's older sister, had finally decided to share her wonderful dishes with the world.

"Say, what's the matter? Y'all don't want to make money today? This is no way to treat customers," a male voice boomed aggressively. The bell over the door jingled in the background.

Startled, Savannah dropped the catalogue. Hurrying

through the door, she almost upset a row of ceramic figures. Holding her breath, she gently rearranged them. After checking that none was broken, she turned abruptly and collided into a broad chest. Two large hands cupped her shoulders. Suddenly, she found herself looking up into a pair of eyes the color of almonds. For a moment she felt lost in them. Savannah gazed at the strong, smooth hands that held her. She took in the dark eyebrows that stood out so wonderfully against his smooth brown complexion.

"You okay? I was coming to save them, too." He smiled down at her, revealing a small space between his two front teeth.

"Uh-huh." That was all she could manage. For some inexplicable reason, that one small flaw in an otherwise perfect row of even ivory teeth set her heart to fluttering. She fumbled with the figures a little longer than she needed to, trying to regain her balance. But turning to see the tall, dashing man still smiling destroyed whatever composure she'd managed to gain. *Great, the first good-looking man you meet, and you stumble around like a dimwit.*

Paul stared at the dark hair that brushed his chest as Savannah turned her back to him suddenly to arrange the figures on the shelf. The smell of her perfume, a light floral scent, was so pleasing that he leaned toward her as almost a reflex action. When just as suddenly she turned back to face him, he stepped back quickly.

"Just making sure you didn't need any more rescuing." He smiled his best shy smile.

"Is that your Jeep?" The beginning smile on her face froze instantly. She pointed to the dark green vehicle parked outside. She suddenly found his smile too smug.

"Sure is. A real beauty. I'm sure you agree."

"You almost killed me today, fool." Savannah glared at him.

"Out on the old highway? That was you? Well, well. You were driving kind of recklessly, you know. But I'll forgive you for not yielding—this time, anyway."

"Say what?" Savannah's anger began to boil. She could not believe this. Did he think his charm would make almost smashing into her all right?

"Now I know I should have stopped to examine you closely for injuries." Paul gave her a sassy grin.

"You were too busy being an—" Savannah began.

"Hey, Paul. How you doin', man? You done met my little girl, I see." Antoine gave Paul a hearty clap on the shoulder.

"Oh, yes, I sure have. But we didn't formally introduce ourselves. Paul Honore." He nodded to her.

Savannah gave him a tight smile. "Mr. Honore—"

"Paul, please."

"Paul," she said. The smile became even tighter.

"Paul is an engineer with his own business." Antoine beamed at him.

"Well, actually, my partner Sam and I share ownership with the bank." Paul gave a short laugh.

"Came to get them decoys for your daddy, huh? Work goin' okay, I hear." Antoine took over. Finding them in the cabinet nearby, he carefully wrapped each meticulously carved decoy in old newspaper before putting it in a large box.

Savannah wore a careful mask of disinterest as she took his payment and handed him a receipt. Seeing the smooth brown hands reach out, she imagined what the skin on his chest and shoulders looked like. In an instant, she pictured dark, curly hair spread across his chest and reaching down to his navel. She became aware that their hands had brushed lightly. The place where contact had been made tingled. She snatched her hand back, placing it on her hip. Paul grinned at her, succeeding only in making her even more determined to resist him.

He, on the other hand, gazed at her in dismay. Things were not going well. And to make things worse, his reaction to her was not the animal attraction he usually felt when faced with a beautiful woman. Why was he so fascinated by the movement of her hair? Or thinking of her skin, comparing it to the color of dark honey? He actually cared what she thought about him. When she withdrew her hand as if she didn't want it to be soiled, his jaw tightened in irritation. Obviously this woman didn't think much of him. He turned abruptly to her father so she would not see the effect she was having on him.

"By the way, I ran into Kyle Singleton's foreman the other day. He says the plant is going to be fully operational in two months or less. Trosclair got the go-ahead from DEQ last week," Paul said.

"Don't matter, no. They gone hafta cross me to keep that thing right in our backyard, that's the truth. Jackson, he say we got a good case for to appeal that decision." Antoine nodded in the direction of the lawyers' office.

"Well, I'll be seeing you later, *Ms.* Savannah." He emphasized the Ms. and made as if to tip an imaginary hat.

"Whatever," Savannah said without looking at him, her tone suggesting that she'd forgotten he was present and certainly didn't care if he left.

"Coo!" Her father laughed. "What was that about? Y'all just met, an' you're already fussin'."

"He thinks a whole lot more of his charm than I do. But what is this about some plant you're opposed to?" Savannah was genuinely interested in their last exchange and eager to get away from the subject of Paul Honore, lest her father notice too much.

"Claude Trosclair put one of his Batton Chemical Corporation plants right near Easy Town. They gone burn toxic waste. We ain't gone let 'em, though. We got too many them things all along this river already. And mighty strange they is most time built next to our neighborhoods. All that land he own, he didn't sell near his fancy big house or over near no other white people."

"I read several articles recently about charges of environmental racism in different parts of the country. The big companies deny it. They claim to choose sites that make good business sense, like being near companies that need their services or have good access to water or rail transportation routes." Savannah frowned in concentration, trying to remember her limited knowledge of environmental law.

"Bull! They just figure we too poor to fight, or too dumb. But Mr. Trosclair wrong if he think we just gonna roll over this time." Antoine spit out the name as if it were something nasty he was trying to get off his tongue.

"Claude Trosclair is a powerful man in this state. He doesn't like having his plans blocked. The last time you tied in with him. Just be careful, Poppy." Savannah was worried now.

Her father had been nearly killed in an "accident" while he was fishing one day eight years ago, this during a dispute over property Antoine owned. The Trosclairs claimed it was originally part of the plantation, and thus rightfully theirs. Antoine had escaped serious injury when he'd fallen from his boat into the chilly waters of Bayou Teche. He'd managed to hang onto a floating log for a half hour. Another fisherman had seen him and gotten help. The accident was suspicious because it was well known that Antoine traveled in the bayou and knew it like the back of his hand. He knew the submerged log anchored between the large swamp cypresses the day before. The speed at which his motorboat was going made the impact hurl him several feet into the air. Though nothing could be proved, the unwanted scrutiny brought on by this coincidental event caused Trosclair to back off.

"Be careful. Promise, Poppy."

"Don't worry now, cher. Your papa, he can take care of himself." He hugged her to him.

Savannah nodded uncertainly. She knew her father was a strong man and not easily taken down, but he couldn't keep dodging danger forever. Despite his confident words, she felt a sense of foreboding. The mere thought of losing Antoine was more than she could bear. She tightened her embrace and pushed away the frightening image of him lying hurt in the swamp.

Chapter 2

"Galee, sha! You done got so pretty. Come give Nenaine some sugar." Nenaine Sherleen grabbed Savannah in a big affectionate hug.

"Humph, humph. You sho is somethin', yeah." Uncle Coy took his turn, giving her a big kiss on the cheek.

Savannah was a bit overwhelmed by all the relatives who descended on the spacious home. Even the wooden frame house seemed to be bulging, packed with family and friends eager to see if and how Savannah had changed. Like good-natured doctors, they poked and prodded for clues that she was still one of them. She endured teasing about losing her taste for down-home favorites like cracklings.

"Now, y'all just hush up. No matta how long she been 'way from here, she won't lose her taste for real food." Tante Marie set a large plate down in front of her containing a generous helping of fried catfish.

Savannah forced a smile. Looking down at the dish, she took a deep breath. The spicy aroma of traditional Creole seasonings made her mouth water. It would take all her strength not to stuff herself on everything on the plate and then accept seconds. She picked up a golden brown hush puppy. She broke it in half and a thin finger of steam rose from the center. Nobody could tempt her like her aunt. In a region where good cooking was the standard, her Tante Marie's talents placed her in a class all her own. Having had no children and widowed at the age of thirty-eight, she had readily taken on the task of helping her younger brother raise his infant daughter. And Savannah loved her with the same fierceness with which she loved her father.

For those times Tante Marie was busy catering ritzy functions for the wealthy and tourist parties at local plantations, her godmother, Nenaine Sherleen, gave her the same loving attention and lots of good, fattening foods, a definite threat to her waistline. Pudgy all through childhood, Savannah's going away to college had meant a change in her eating habits. Working out regularly had become a habit after law school, especially when she was able to afford a really nice health club. Taking another bite of catfish, she made a silent vow to search the phonebook for one nearby.

"Poppy was telling me about the fight over the plant." Savannah was helping her aunt wash dishes after dinner. They had finally seen off the last of her welcoming committee.

"That Trosclair ain't nuthin' to play with, no. He low down. I don't put nuthin' past him." Tante Marie shook her head as she scrubbed plates vigorously.

"But what do you think?" Savannah knew that her aunt was sharp.

"They right about one thing: every plant been put up in the last twenty years or so been in or near poor folks' neighborhoods. And usually without a whisper being raised. Ain't no coincidence, cher."

"But black people owned a lot of the land in Easy Town."

"Old Claude is slick. He paid them more money than anybody else would have and made sure they knew it. Then he hired some of the men to work. Some of them hadn't been workin' for months.''

"And jobs are scarce here," Savannah said.

"What with prices down on crawfish and shrimp . . . and then the oil refinery laid off almost fifty people."

"I worry about Poppy, Tante Marie. He looks so tired. I hope he knows what he's doing. He can be so stubborn sometimes."

"How you two doin', sha?" Tante Marie paused in her cleaning up to regard her steadily.

"So far, okay. It's just, he tries to keep me a little girl." Savannah traced an invisible line on the table top with her finger.

"He jus' love you so much. Kinda hard for him, lettin' you go. You his pride and joy. Oughta hear him talk 'bout his baby girl. An' you look so like Therese. When she died like that, so young, almost killed him, too. I still can see him, sittin' in that chair, starin' out the window. For three days, he wouldn't talk to nobody, didn't leave that house. I had took you home with me, ya know. Only thing brought him out of it was seein' you. That's what kept him going. Had to take care of his baby girl."

"But he never really came out of it," Savannah sighed. "No matter how I tried, he never seemed to truly enjoy anything. It was scary, seeing him going through the motions. I don't ever want to love someone that much. Being left behind hurts too much."

"One thing about it, sha, life can be cold and empty without love. Plenty done wakened too late to find they protected theyselves right out of somethin' precious."

"But look at Daddy. Holding on to a memory so hard, you can feel it. Sometimes it's like he's more with Mama than here with us." Savannah turned to stare out the window, hugging herself as if she felt an aching cold.

"There's a lot a ways of grievin'. Antoine just went inside himself."

Savannah pushed away painful thoughts of the mother

she barely remembered. She was only four when Therese had died, but the childish anger at being abandoned was strong. Not only had her mother left her, but in some indefinable sense, so had Antoine, by withdrawing part of himself deep into a place that even she could not reach. Eager to change the subject, she turned back to helping her clean up.

"What's Paul Honore got to do with this plant being opened, anyway?" Savannah tried to sound casual. She didn't look at her aunt, but made it a point to busily dry a stack of plates.

"Yeah, I heard y'all tied in wit each other. He a fine young man, yeah. Here you fightin' wit the man and every other woman in town from eight to eighty tryin' to get on his good side." Tante Marie gave her a knowing look. Seeing her niece refuse to meet her eyes, she smiled.

"That's his problem. If you ask me, he's the type who thinks every woman he meets ought to fall at his feet."

"Plenty young ladies after him, sha. 'Course, he ain't been runnin' with a whole lotta gals. Kinda been pickin' and choosin'."

"I'll bet he has," Savannah sneered.

"You tellin' me you don't think he's good-lookin'?"

"I'm not saying that, I'm just saying he's too full of himself for my taste."

"Seems to me he a serious one. He's some kinda smart, yeah. Doin' some testin' to see if that Big River plant is safe. Got his own business, too." Tante Marie poked her and winked.

"He acts like he's really impressed with himself, for sure."

"Oo-wee. Sparks was flyin', I hear." Tante Marie egged her on.

"I guess they were, at that. I had to set him straight, that's all." Savannah smiled with satisfaction.

"Well, watch out."

"For what?"

"Them kinda sparks can lead to red-hot flames, if you ain't careful. I had three husbands, so I oughta know." Tante Marie walked off chuckling to herself.

Embarrassed that her aunt had so easily seen through her and detected her attraction to Paul, Savannah rushed to protest. "I don't think so—" She tried a snappy comeback, but her aunt's retreating back made her lose steam.

The next three weeks were a pleasant but exhausting whirlwind of visiting or being visited by a host of relatives and friends. Savannah was surprised to learn that almost half her high school classmates still lived in Beau Chene. To her delight, hearing a familiar voice call and turning to see the smiling face of an old pal was an almost daily occurrence. Especially her best friend Charice. They were inseparable from first day of third grade at Belle Rose Elementary. Now the divorced mother of two active little girls, Charice taught sixth grade at their alma mater. She had changed little since then, still all sass. Short, with the kind of plumpness the boys never seemed to mind, she now wore her thick reddish brown hair in long braids. Even after a two-year separation, it took her and Savannah no time to reestablish their closeness. Since high school, meeting for lunch on Saturdays had been a ritual. Now they settled back into the old custom with ease. Charice would send the children home with her mother and meet Savannah at the Fish Net, a local favorite that served the best seafood in town.

"So it took awhile, but we finally decided that continuing the same fights we'd been having all the time we were together was stupid." Charice finally wound down after a spirited account of the beginning, middle, and end of her seven-year marriage. "Girl, I gotta admit, you were right not to get married young."

"And I've got to admit, I was a little jealous you got married to one of the handsomest guys at Xavier U. After being in three weddings that year, my bragging about being 'young, single, and free to mingle' began to sound like a lame excuse for not being asked, even to me."

"Yeah, well, none of those marriages lasted. Honey, Imelda just separated from Carlton." Charice lowered her voice after looking around to see if anyone they knew was close by.

"No!" Savannah gasped, leaning across the table. "Not Miss 'Can't-nobody-take-my-man' Imelda."

"I remember how we could always tell when she was on the prowl looking to take somebody's boyfriend for the thrill of it. Had more than one fine boy crying when she dumped him for somebody else."

"Sure did. She could wrap men up like that." Savannah snapped her fingers.

"And Carlton had it worse than any of them, too. But come to find out homeboy been tipping on her with some woman at his job for two years. I felt so bad for her." Charice shook her head.

"Happens to the best of us. Poor thing." They looked at each other for a few seconds before bursting into a giggling fit at their hypocrisy.

"Good afternoon, ladies," Paul Honore called to them as he stood at the counter, paying for a takeout order.

"Speaking of fine, Lord have mercy," Charice whispered, then waved. "What's up, Paul?"

Much to Savannah's dismay, Paul strolled over to their table after paying for his food. As Charice chatted with him, flirting shamelessly, Savannah feigned mild interest.

"So, how is your work going? I think it's great you're in the business of preventing waste contamination. That's something that's become so important, particularly around here, with all these refineries and chemical plants." Charice leaned toward him.

"Not just that, we're working on several ways to safely clean up contamination from the soil. We can't eliminate our need for these products, but we can make sure we don't poison ourselves with them." Paul pulled up a chair to their table and sat down.

"That's so true." Clarice nodded emphatically. She beamed at him as Paul launched into an explanation of a new organism being tested to break down chemical spills.

Savannah's lip curled in disgust at the way her friend was hanging onto his every word. As the minutes passed, her annoyance grew. He seemed to be eating up the attention. Charice was at her most coquettish, inching closer and closer to Paul. Not that it mattered, of course. That was Charice's business, if she wanted to look like a high school sophomore in heat. Savannah fumed. She couldn't help noticing the way his face seemed to light up when he talked about his work. His eyes were the most beautiful shade of brown she'd ever seen in a man. They were perfectly framed by a set of shapely black eyebrows that rose when he was amused. Some witticism Charice had uttered caused him to throw back his head in laughter. This startled her back to paying attention to what they were saying. Savannah drummed her fingers on the table top. When Charice giggled at a corny joke Paul told, it was the last straw.

"So it's no wonder you're supporting this new toxic waste dump in our backyards: you're counting on a fat subcontract to clean up after them." Savannah sat back with her arms folded.

"I'm not supporting anything just yet. My partner and I haven't had a chance to read their reports carefully." Paul's smile froze on his face.

"I doubt we'll be surprised at the results," Savannah said.

"What's that supposed to mean?"

"Well, they *are* paying you."

"The university is paying for our study."

"And the Trosclair family has contributed heavily to that school. They even endowed a chemistry chair," Savannah said.

"Nobody buys my integrity. If I don't think it's a safe site, I'll say so." Paul stood abruptly. Looking down at the top of Savannah's head, he seemed about to say more.

"Don't let us hold you up. I mean, your food'll get cold." Savannah ignored the cutting glance from her friend.

"Goodbye, Charice. At least it was nice seeing you." He strode off without waiting for a reply.

"Now, just what was that ab—oh, I see." Charice smiled to herself.

"See what?" Savannah said evasively.

"Listen, girlfriend, why didn't you just say? I'd never have come on so strong." Charice shrugged.

"Oh, please. Sure, he's good-looking, and he knows it. He's one of those pretty-boy types who like to keep several women dangling at a time."

"Okay, okay, you're not interested. So it won't bother you if we happen to get together, right?"

"No problem. If you don't care that he tries to be a lover boy, well—" Savannah shrugged and picked at her shrimp salad.

"Uh-huh." Charice stared at her friend for several moments.

"I mean it. Don't give that look, now."

"Okay, okay. Hey, I've got a great idea. Remember Sack Daddy's? Honey, they have got a fantastic hump day party every Wednesday evening, starting at six. What say we go?"

"Why? You better not be trying any of your tricks." Savannah shook her finger at Charice. Since junior high, Charice had been a relentless matchmaker. Savannah could reel off the disastrous dates she'd had thanks to her friend.

"What are you talking about, child? I'm just saying we could have ourselves a good time, is all." Charice shrugged, her face the picture of innocence. "Oh, lighten up. Every chance I get, I go on Wednesdays. It's a great way to relax during the week. Come on."

"All right, but—"

"No buts, just pick me up when you finish at the shop,"
Charice said.

Wednesday came and Savannah was beginning to regret
this idea of going to what sounded like a pick-up juke joint.
After a thorough search of her closet, she chose an outfit
she thought was conservative enough to discourage any
unwanted attention at the lounge. The wraparound denim
skirt was mid-calf length, the red knit blouse fitting but
not clingy. Watching Charice bounce down the front steps
of her cottage-style house, she shook her head.

"Try not to be too shy." Savannah looked up and down
at her friend's outfit.

"I may be a little, let's just say, full-figured, but I'm in
shape." Charice spun around to display all profiles. The
white knit tank top was revealing, with a deep V neck. This
combined with white shorts to make her look anything but
dumpy.

"You look great." Savannah laughed and put the car in
gear.

"You look like you're on your way to the church picnic."
Charice plucked at the hem of Savannah's skirt.

"Don't start with me."

Thus started the familiar sisterly bickering about how
Savannah should loosen up, with Savannah fighting it all
the way. Walking into the lounge, they took a seat at a
table far from the bar.

"Nobody can see us way over here, girl," Charice com-
plained.

"Will you sit down, please? Look at the men perched
on the bar stools. Do I want them within easy reach?"

"Hey, those are some pretty nice guys. All right, so they
are—okay. All right, all right, they're so-so." Charice
responded to Savannah's scowling looks of skepticism with
each comment. They both began to laugh.

The waitress took their orders. Soon she returned with their drinks. Setting the frosted mugs on the table, she poured out a light beer for Charice. Then she served up a dark brown liquid from an old-fashioned soft drink bottle for Savannah.

"Savannah, root beer?" Charice crowed.

"I'm the designated driver, remember?"

To their delight, a four-man zydeco band had set up and now began to play blues, sung in Creole French. Savannah tapped her feet to the music, while Charice swayed back and forth, snapping her fingers. It wasn't long before Charice was on the dance floor with a neatly dressed man who had been sitting with a group of friends at a nearby table. Savannah's attempt to remain unnoticed failed. She had turned down two requests to dance before the song ended.

"Whew, he's pretty good. Why you sitting here like Lady Madonna, your hands in your lap? Get up and move to the groove, sugar." Charice fanned herself with the cocktail napkin.

"I'm enjoying myself just fine, thank you. Oh no," Savannah sneered. As the crowded dance floor cleared, she could see Paul across the room, laughing with a group of people. A gorgeous woman dressed in a revealing sundress jockeyed to get close to him whenever possible. It was obvious she wanted his undivided attention.

"Honey, you can hang it up if Kay gets her claws in him."

"Who cares? She's welcome to him." Savannah took a swig of her root beer, setting the mug down very hard.

"Uh-huh."

"The way you carried on the other day, you ought to be upset. Thought you were interested," Savannah snapped.

"I was admiring him, sure. But the way electricity was crackling between you two, that's something different from a little flirting."

"What you saw was him getting on my last nerve, that's the only crackling noise you heard."

"Uh-huh." Charice signaled to the waitress.

"Now, why did you wave to that lizard?" Savannah spoke through clenched teeth. Paul, having spotted them, responded to the gesture instead of the waitress.

"I was trying to order another beer, honest," Charice protested, even though the look on Savannah's face said she didn't believe her.

"So, we meet again. How are you ladies this evening?" Paul sat down.

"Hello." Savannah looked elsewhere, her voice cool.

"Fancy meeting you here." Charice smiled as if surprised to see him.

"You see me here most Wednesdays since I came to town, you know that," Paul blurted out, before he noticed her signal a warning.

"Oh, really." Savannah cut her eyes at Charice, who refused to look at her.

"Can't sit still to this tune, my favorite." With that, Charice jumped up. Moving to the fast beat, she grabbed her recent partner's hand, pulling him with her onto the dance floor.

Several moments of strained silence stretched between them as Savannah feigned interest in the couples stepping so gracefully to the band's lively tune.

"You wouldn't want to dance." Paul's statement indicated he already knew the answer.

"No, thanks." Savannah began to feel a bit guilty at being so cool.

"So, Charice tells me you're a lawyer. What area?"

"It was corporate law, but nothing right now."

"The law firm you left is very big. It has some of the biggest clients in this state. You must have graduated at the top of your class."

"I did okay. When did you learn all this?" Savannah looked at him, his full lips glistened from the drink he had just taken. She forced her attention away from them.

"Charice ran into me at the grocery store the other day."

"And the conversation turned to me somehow," Savannah interrupted.

"Wait a minute, we were just making small talk. Charice was telling me about how long you two had been friends; one thing led to another."

"I see."

"How y'all getting along?" Charice surprised them as she plopped down in a chair.

"Wonderful. Paul was telling me how you filled him in on my life story." Savannah raised an eyebrow at her.

"Oh, you mean, the other day." Charice took a drink, oblivious to her friend's disapproving tone, her attention still on the man she'd been dancing with. "I'm trying to recruit him to come to my class to talk about being a black engineer. I told him I was going to ask you about coming, too. Give the girls a sense that they could become a lawyer, like you." Almost before she finished speaking, she was back on the floor with him.

"Oh." Savannah gave Paul a mildly apologetic smile.

"I was surprised to find that Charice has started a mentor program. She's got at least six troubled kids hooked up with African-American professionals. Too bad I won't be here long enough to take part."

"She's always been like that, can't stand to see others in need without doing something about it. Why don't you want to at least try it for a while?"

"Those kids deserve a commitment. You do more harm by not being in it for the long haul. They've had enough experience with broken relationships. No, I may be gone in another three weeks. Besides, between helping Mama with Pop since he suffered a stroke and coaching peewee football back home . . . I wouldn't even be able to make the one-hour drive over here once a week to visit."

"How awful. I hope he's okay." Savannah softened even

more at the thought of Paul dividing his time between a business, giving to children who needed him, and his parents.

"Actually, he's doing pretty well. Since being sick keeps him from working much now, he's been coming out to watch me coach. His doctor says it's good therapy. And those boys need all the positive attention they can get from men."

As they talked about the needs of African-American children for role models, Savannah found herself drawn to this handsome man with a social conscience. She couldn't help but respect his sincerity. It was no act that he really cared about children. His eyes lit up as he described some of the boys he'd come to know as a volunteer coach for inner city kids in Lafayette. Once again, she noticed the strong jawline. His skin, the color of milk chocolate, was smooth. She wondered if it felt as good as it looked. Watching his mouth as he talked, she felt her suspicions of him begin to melt away.

Paul might have been talking about social issues, but he did not fail to appreciate the shape of her full mouth, made even more luscious by the deep red lipstick she wore. It matched her knit blouse. Rewarded with a radiant smile as he told the first story of his working with the boys in the football league, he kept the anecdotes coming. Captivated by her, he listened intently as she spoke with fervor about saving children from the dangers of the street. His heart skipped at seeing a stray lock of her hair fall forward, the way her lovely hands smoothed it back in place. The split in her wrap-around skirt had parted to reveal a shapely brown thigh. He was more than slightly disappointed when she noticed and pulled it closed again.

"Say, y'all been sitting here all this time without dancing once. Come on." Charice took each of them by the hand, dragging them onto the dance floor. Savannah tried to resist, but Charice made such a scene that the crowd began to egg her on.

"I think it'd be better just to give in." Paul had not been

unwilling. In fact, Charice had let go of his arm when she'd realized he'd gotten up eagerly.

Savannah, seeing there was no way out, tried to convince herself that some part of her did not feel anticipation at the chance to be close to him. As if to further test her ability to withstand his magnetism, the band launched into a slow, sentimental ballad about the sweet agony of forbidden love. Savannah fought to steady her breathing as she felt his muscular arms enfold her. Turning her head in an effort to resist burying her face in the triangle of flesh revealed by the open collar of his shirt, instead she was further tempted by the smell of his cologne. She surrendered, closing her eyes, allowing him to tighten his hold. His warm embrace caused a wonderful mix of excitement and contentment to flow through her body. They seemed to hover on a beautiful cloud all alone where all her dreams of a strong, tender lover would come true. Being so near to him conjured up visions of his lips on hers, his powerful yet tender hands caressing her body. Savannah felt a tiny shudder. At the closing strains of the baritone lead singer, she longed for an encore. While those around them applauded, they remained as if frozen in time, arms around each other. With a start, Savannah stepped back. Looking around in embarrassment, she was relieved the other couples seemed not to have noticed them lingering in each other's embrace. But naturally, none of this escaped Charice.

"Nothing like the old songs to put you in the right mood," she whispered in Savannah's ear, a naughty smile on her face.

"Oh, shut up!" Savannah hissed, as she passed her on the way back to their seats.

Unable to shake the feeling that she had indeed made a spectacle of herself, she refused to dance again.

Paul, sensing the return of her reserve toward him, made an effort to recapture the mood that had held them only moments before.

"Ooh-wee, it's almost eleven. I told Mama I'd pick up the kids at ten o'clock." Charice threw enough change down to pay for the last beer that had sat growing warm while she'd enjoyed dancing with the good-looking man at the next table.

"Yes, we'd better get going. You have class tomorrow." Savannah was relieved.

"Listen, Rodney can take me home. You stay, have a good time. We'll talk." Charice started to leave, but she gasped sharply as Savannah jerked her back.

"Charice, you only just met the man. You shouldn't ride with strangers; didn't your mother teach you that?" Savannah spoke through clenched teeth. Now that the music was over, her defenses came back up. She had no intention of being left alone with Paul.

"I've known Rodney for a while, he manages that new big hardware store on—right, we'd better get going." Charice, reading the expression on Savannah's face, knew what she was supposed to do.

"See you soon for sure—next Wednesday, at least?" Paul spoke directly to Savannah, watching her expression closely.

"Sure—I mean, maybe so. Bye." Savannah read the invitation in his eyes, a now well-known cool tingle spreading over her.

"Wow, he left old Kay flat for you. She might as well have been the invisible woman. Go, girl."

"Charice, you'll pay for this."

Thus the evening ended much as it had begun. Though their voices were loud, there was never any real anger. Charice insisted Savannah admit she'd succumbed to Paul's allure. Savannah insisted no such thing. They stopped only when they were at Charice's mother's house to pick up the girls. Savannah helped her carry the two sleeping children inside. Already in their pajamas, they were taken straight to bed.

"Well, goodnight." Savannah yawned.

"See you later. Savannah, don't fight so hard to be alone." Charice dropped the teasing tone to be serious. "Take it from me, it's no fun."

Savannah responded with a quick hug before leaving. That night, as she dressed for bed, the ballad she'd danced to with Paul still played inside her head. She cursed softly, chiding herself for being so easily caught up in what was sure to be a heartbreak. Yet the music played on, lulling her to sleep after a time.

Paul stood outside the expensive suite of offices, his heart pounding. He thought he'd prepared himself for this moment, but now he knew differently. What would his grandmother say, if she were living?

Marguerite had been a proud woman who'd faced difficulty with a determination not to be defeated. She had supported herself and Paul's father with a variety of back-breaking jobs. When she'd married Henry Honore, Paul's father, Charles, had been two years old. Henry had raised Charles with the same love and strict discipline he'd given to the six children they'd had—so much so that Paul was shocked to learn that Henry was not his natural grandfather.

"Hello, I'm here for a meeting with Mr. Singleton. Paul Honore." He stood nervously while the blond receptionist called to tell Singleton's secretary that he was waiting.

"Have a seat, Mr. Honore. He'll be with you shortly."

Paul sat down in a comfortable leather chair. He stared at the prints on the wall and tried not to get any more jumpy than he was already by the nerve-wracking wait. Although it had been only fifteen minutes by his watch, it had seemed longer. Finally, an older and more conservatively dressed woman came to the reception area.

"Mr. Honore? Come this way. Mr. Singleton is sorry for the delay. A long-distance conference call took longer than he'd anticipated." She ushered him into a conference

room with a large oval-shaped oak conference table. He
sat down and began taking out his notebook.

"Good to see you, Honore. Have some coffee. Rose,
you forgot to bring in the coffee." He barked in irritation
at his secretary, but to Paul, Kyle Singleton was as ingratiating in his manner as he'd been at their two previous
meetings. His dark brown hair was badly cut, his expensive suit was a little too tight around his portly frame.

"No thanks, I'm fine." Paul nodded a greeting at a
second, younger man already seated in the conference
room.

"Well, you just make yourself to home, then. Oh, where
are my manners? This is my vice president of operations—
ah, here you are." Singleton looked over Paul's shoulder.

The second man walked into the room with the air of
one who felt he belonged no matter where he was. Tall
and distinguished, he stood erect despite his years. Paul
guessed he had to be at least seventy-nine, yet he had a
thick head of silver gray hair. His suit was just as expensive
as Singleton's, but the fit was perfect.

"Claude, this is the young man who'll conduct what I'm
sure will be an objective and unbiased assessment of the site
for our new treatment facility." Singleton's toothy smirk
implied that he wanted anything but that. "Paul Honore,
Claude Trosclair."

"How do you do?" Claude held out his hand.

"Oh yes, this is his grandson Quentin, our senior vice
president." Singleton grinned.

With that simple greeting, Paul reached out and shook
hands with his grandfather and cousin.

Chapter 3

Savannah stood gazing out the shop window. The leaves on the pin oak and sycamore trees had begun to turn lovely shades of dark red and yellow. Mixed in with some of the still green vegetation, the colors were a beautiful blend of nature's best early fall redecoration. Bright sunshine spilled over the lovely landscaped little downtown of Beau Chene. Typical for southern Louisiana, late September had begun to foreshadow the splendor of the change of seasons, not just from the change in the leaves, but by the cooler nights. The temperature dropped only by as little as five or ten degrees, but drop it did.

Just as she'd done as a little girl when deep in thought or troubled, Savannah absentmindedly twisted a thick lock of her hair. Her return home had gone much more smoothly than she'd expected, but she felt restless and uneasy. The conflict over the Big River plant loomed on the horizon like dark storm clouds. She knew there was no easy way it could be settled, no compromise available. No matter the outcome, there were sure to be bitter feelings. If it was proved that the plant would harm the people living nearby, it could be forced to close. That would please some, but those losing jobs would not forgive neighbors, even relatives, who'd helped make it happen. Paul's report on Big River was going to be critical to the outcome. As she thought of the handsome engineer, his face seemed to float in the plate glass window for a split second. She blinked rapidly. Her thoughts were of his hands touching her shoulders, then cupping her face as he lowered his lips to hers. No matter how she tried, she couldn't think of him without having such fantasies. Never had she reacted so strongly to a man. True, she had found others attractive, even been infatuated, but this silly adolescent obsession was getting out of hand. She should be spending time worrying about her father and how she could help keep him out of trouble.

Across the street and still several blocks away, Savannah noticed a vaguely familiar figure walking toward the shop. A thick black braid hung down the woman's back. She wore a simple cotton dress that served to emphasize her figure and reveal bare shapely legs. She crossed the street and headed straight toward Savannah. Recognition dawned slowly as the woman reached to open the door.

"Hello, Savannah. Heard you were home. Welcome back." LaShaun leaned across the counter and brushed her cheek against Savannah's. Her slightly almond-shaped dark brown gaze swept the shop. "I only been in here once before, and that was, goodness, over six years ago. Nice stuff. So, what's up with you?"

LaShaun Rousselle had changed from an awkward, brooding little girl into a sultry young woman. She regarded Savannah with a look of cool appraisal, letting her know nothing had changed. LaShaun wore a look of disdain. It was clear she would make sure Savannah knew of her enmity. The animosity LaShaun's mother had felt for Therese and Antoine seemed a caustic legacy left to be carried on by her daughter.

"Not much." Savannah's smile was strained. LaShaun

seemed crafty to Savannah, and she reminded herself to watch her back.

"You giving up your job in Shreveport to run your daddy's shop? Seems strange—you had such a big-time law career, so they say. Making a lot of money, so they say." She paused in her examination of a small female figure carved from a piece of oak.

"Sometimes that type of success is just not enough. Besides, with my father getting on in age, he could use some help around here with his business interests."

"I guess. 'Course, Mr. Antoine is in good shape, from what I can see. What I mean is, you don't have to worry about him getting senile anytime soon." LaShaun faced her briefly, then turned quickly to examine a shelf of spices.

"That's not what I meant at all. He could just use help with this plant dispute getting so intense." Savannah was immediately sorry she'd mentioned it.

"Oh yes. Claude Trosclair wants to make even more money than he has already. And your daddy, bless him, is getting in his way. Always was a bold man, your daddy. Least, my mama always said so." LaShaun faced her, a sly smile spread across her face.

Savannah clenched her teeth to keep from rising to the bait and instead forced a smile. "He believes in what's right. And he won't let people walk over him, or make a fool of him, either."

"Oh, he's good at getting out of things, for sure. 'Course, Claude Trosclair is good at getting what he wants. Hope he knows what he's doing, crossing him." She walked over and leaned against the counter.

"He does." Savannah did not want to talk about her father anymore, especially not with LaShaun.

"Well, guess I'd better get going. I'm working at the museum."

"I didn't know we had one here."

"It's kinda small. But we've got a real interesting set of exhibits on local history, artifacts and such."

"Sounds nice." Savannah made a show of moving things around on the counter near the cash register. She hoped LaShaun would take the hint.

"Oh yes, we've been written up in some tour magazines. Come over sometime." LaShaun started to leave. She paused with her hand on the doorknob.

"Maybe I will."

"The most popular section is the one I set up myself. The tourists just find it fascinating. I think you would, too. On voodoo."

Savannah looked up sharply. LaShaun was still smiling. Her eyes had narrowed, making her face take on the look of a cat stalking prey. Savannah's hands shook, causing her to drop several pens she was trying to place in the round container along with other small souvenirs.

"Bye now." LaShaun gave a low, throaty chuckle as she went through the door.

The lingering aroma of Tante Marie's famous cooking drifted through the warm evening air. Savannah and Charice sat on the large front porch, watching Charice's kids play in the front yard. Antoine sat at the other end, puffing his pipe. Stuffed on chicken and sausage jambalaya, mustard greens, and hush puppies, it was all they could do to lift a hand to wave the straw fans to cool themselves. Despite her protests, all had pitched in to clean up the kitchen. Tante Marie finally came outside. She plumped up a large flowered cushion, then sat down heavily in a cane chair.

"Ah, that breeze feels good, yeah." Tante Marie mopped her face with a patterned handkerchief.

"Nothing like a quiet Sunday afternoon after a good home-cooked dinner. Tante Marie, that was some kind of delicious meal you cooked. Umph!" Charice patted her stomach.

"Yes, indeed. That was the one thing I never got over after I left home, missing your food. I don't think I could move if I wanted to, which I don't. Look at those two, where do they get the energy? Hey, Crystal and Nikki, don't you want to take a nap, or at least slow down?'' Savannah called out to the girls, who just giggled and kept playing.

"Forget it, honey. They stopped taking naps long ago, unfortunately. Were we ever that bouncy?"

"Yes, Lord. 'Member the time y'all was always having slumber parties or king cake parties or somethin'? House full of little noisy gals.'' Tante Marie shook her head with a laugh.

"Speaking of king cake, we used to really have a ball at Mardi Gras. Especially in high school. And can we ever forget who was queen of the Krewe of Noir Mystique carnival ball in her junior year? That gown you wore knocked 'em dead. Strapless, with a wide hoop skirt.'' Charice gave Savannah a playful pat on the arm.

"Oh, please. I've still got scars from that dress. Those pretty green sequins and beads made sitting down a pain, literally. And standing up was worse. That thing must have weighed a ton.''

"Back then, we didn't care about being in agony if it meant being beautiful. You were so busy strutting your stuff for Andre LaMotte, you didn't even notice.''

"Don't remind me. And what about you? Dewayne did this, Dewayne said that.'' Savannah spoke in a high-pitched little voice.

"Hmm, I haven't thought about him in years. Last I heard, he was living in Houston. Andre still lives here.''

"So far, I haven't seen him, which is okay by me,'' she added, to ward off Charice's matchmaking plans.

"He was always a little wild, but he got downright crazy in our senior year. When you broke up with him, that was something. LaShaun spent the next six months bragging that she took him from you.''

"She came in the shop the other day.'' Savannah spoke quietly, all amusement gone from her voice.

"What did the devil's daughter want with you?" Charice grimaced.

"To tell me about the museum."

Charice shuddered. "She still gives me the creeps. Living in that big old house with crazy old Mama Odette."

"All them Rousselles is sly, from Odette's mom on back. She's crazy like a fox, old Odette is. She made herself plenty of good money in her time. Even had some property down in New Orleans," Tante Marie said.

"They say all three of her sons came to a bad end. And Francine, LaShaun's mama—"

Antoine got up abruptly and went in the house. The women exchanged glances. Shortly they heard the bang of the back screen door, the signal that he was going for a walk.

"Sorry, I should keep my big mouth shut." Charice sighed.

"No, cher. Don't worry 'bout that. It happened years ago."

"What happened, Tante Marie?" Savannah asked. "Every time there was trouble between LaShaun and me, Poppy would get this strange look. And every time somebody mentioned LaShaun's mama, somebody else would cut off the conversation if we kids were close around." Savannah gripped the chain that held the swing attached to the roof. Planting her feet on the floor, she stopped the swaying bench.

"It's best left alone." Tante Marie folded her arms and stared straight ahead.

"But if it was so long ago, then we ought to be able to talk about it now. I'm not a child anymore, Tante Marie. So stop treating me like one. There were whispers about voodoo or hoodoo. And it had something to do with my mama, LaShaun's mama, and Poppy—" Savannah leaned forward with a look of intensity, as if willing her aunt to reveal more.

"Leave that alone, I said." Tante Marie spoke in such

a loud sharp voice, the two girls playing several yards away stopped abruptly to stare at the adults sitting on the porch. Tante Marie stood slowly with a grunt. "I'm goin' inside now. My show comin' on."

Moments later they heard the sound of the television. Savannah was deeply shaken. Not by Tante Marie's harsh rebuke, but by the thought of the secret that had caused it. Remnants of the dark fears of her childhood began to crowd around the edges of her mind. The breeze across her arms now sent a chill that raised goosebumps. She hugged herself, swaying slowly in the old cane rocker.

"Don't worry about it," Charice said, after a long silence between them.

"Not knowing is worse than anything they could tell me. I remember overhearing Miss Julie telling Tante Marie that Poppy should have listened to her and put something in the front yard to protect Mama from Francine. I used to have nightmares about some witch grabbing my mama and then coming after me."

"Miss Julie always was a little weird. You don't believe in that voodoo junk and you know it," Charice said.

"What I believe is that something happened between them that a lot of people think led to Mama dying young."

"That's crazy. You said yourself an aneurysm was the cause of her death."

"But it doesn't matter, don't you see? They think Francine caused it. Just as Odette blames Poppy for Francine dying. And why LaShaun grew up hating me. Odette taught her that. Since we were little kids in nursery school, LaShaun has never missed an opportunity to pick a fight or try to hurt me. It all goes back to Mama and Francine, how they died."

"Maybe they didn't get along, maybe it had something to do with your father, but that was over twenty years ago. It had nothing to do with your mama's death. It's in the past."

"Seeing LaShaun after all these years, it was the same

as when we were kids. No, whatever happened is not in the past for her, or for me.''

"You may not meet the standards as a recycling site, at least, not with the equipment and disposal processes you have now." Paul stopped abruptly, aware that he was sounding less than objective.

This was the third meeting with Trosclair and Singleton. He had done an extensive review of their plans, even to the point of visiting the site with their construction people to walk through how and where all facilities would be placed. Though he knew of his reputation, he had been surprised at the interest Trosclair had shown in the actual operation of the plant. The questions he asked showed that he was not just a member of the idle rich, but that he possessed a keen intellect. Trosclair listened carefully to Paul's explanations of his findings. Even from their first meeting, he and Trosclair seemed to communicate easily. Paul was impatient with Singleton's clumsy, obvious attempts to charm him. But Trosclair made no such attempts. He seemed to be sincerely interested in seeing that the plant operators made every effort to safely deal with the dangerous substances that would be handled at the site. Grudgingly, Paul had come to respect him. Even more disturbing, he had begun to feel a growing urge to tell Claude who he really was.

Two things held him back. One was his promise to his father. Charles had shocked Paul at his violent reaction to the possibility of any contact with the Trosclair family. The other was Quentin Trosclair. He was everything his grandfather and father appeared not to be. Quentin had their looks, the long, thin nose. He was tall and wore expensive clothes well. He would have had his grandfather's smile, were it not for the way his mouth curled into almost a sneer. Before he opened his mouth, his expression said he thought a lot of himself. From their first meeting, he let Paul know in words and actions that he thought of Paul as little more than a servant.

"I don't see why this delay is necessary, frankly. I've been looking into it and I don't think we have to follow the standards for a waste disposal site. With this new process for making road construction materials, we are a recycling site, which means the more strict standards don't apply. I say we go with what we've got. They can't stop us." Quentin, as usual, didn't even look at Paul or acknowledge his presence.

"You might be able to get by with it, but in the case of Bayou Processors, they eventually paid heavy fines," Paul said.

"But they are still operating, which sets precedent. Really, Grandfather, do we have to go over this again? I think it's clear we've got the upper hand. We've gotten the permits we need, and Mike has assured me—" Quentin waved his hand in Paul's direction in dismissal.

"Of course, but we also want to be able to assure the public that we are sensitive to their concerns." Claude cut off his grandson smoothly, addressing Paul directly.

"He's done his report. And from reading the conclusions, there is nothing there that would make the DEQ change the type of permits we need. Especially since most of the research shows the high feasibility of using slag for roadbeds and even house foundations. Even at high temperatures, the chemicals do not break down and leach into the environment. We don't need anything else from him." Quentin sat back in his chair.

"This process is new." Paul spoke in a measured tone, pointedly ignoring Quentin. "Continuing to monitor the possible long-term environmental impact is essential."

"There is no conclusive evidence that our product is unsafe," Quentin snapped.

"That may be true, but Paul's right," Claude responded. "We should be cautious. We might even conduct our own research in this area and anticipate any problems. Your reports have been very thorough. I have learned quite a bit these last two weeks." Claude turned to Paul, smiling.

"Thank you, Mr. Trosclair." Paul gathered up his papers, tucking them into his leather portfolio.

"I hope you will continue to work with Kyle and Quentin. We'll discuss terms, of course."

"But we have our own staff. I still fail to see why we need him." Quentin leaned forward, speaking in a rapid undertone. "Grandfather, I think we should discuss this later—"

"Kyle and I have discussed it, Quentin." Claude spoke in a tone that dismissed his objection. He turned to Paul. "We'll be in touch."

Paul shook hands with Claude. As Singleton led him out, he chattered away about discussing the details over lunch. Paul nodded but only half listened to him. Looking past Singleton's ingratiating grin, Paul saw Quentin staring at him, his face a dark mask of contempt.

As he drove away, Paul wondered not for the first time how they could have developed a kind of sibling rivalry when Quentin didn't know they were cousins. The enmity that radiated from Quentin was unmistakable, and Paul had to admit he did not like him, either. Where Claude was gracious, even charming, in the face of opposition, his grandson was caustic, condescending, and tactless. Quentin made it easy for others to despise him.

Paul had been in Beau Chene for only two months. Seeing and speaking to his grandfather only served to deepen his need to know the whole story. He longed to know the Trosclair family history, now part of his own family history. Without it, he felt somehow incomplete. His father's side of the family had been gracious in receiving him. Welcomed to dine with them on several occasions, he found them to be warm, hard-working people. Lively talk, jokes, and singing filled their homes. But the one time he'd mentioned his dealings with the Trosclairs, the atmosphere had changed suddenly. Joe and George, cousins of his father's age, shifted nervously before switching to another subject abruptly. And his only living great-uncle grew quiet for the rest of the evening. He had not mentioned the Trosclairs again. He had visited the gravesite of his great-grandparents, even the site on which had once stood the home where his grandmother had spent her childhood. His work might be finished soon, but he was not ready to leave.

In addition to this unfinished family business, there was another attraction holding him to this small river town. More and more, he looked for the beautiful woman whose temper was as hot as Creole gumbo. If he was in town for any reason, each corner he turned made him conscious of how far he was from Antoine's shop. The memory of her face, those brown eyes flashing as she tossed her verbal grenades, caused him to smile in spite of her direct hits on his ego. It bothered him that she saw him as an enemy. He needed her to know he was not. In a way he had never experienced before, he cared what she thought of him. There had to be a way in which they could at least be friends.

His work might be finished soon, but he was far from ready to leave.

The small city hall was jam-packed with people. They spilled out into the hallway. They had come from the surrounding small towns that would be affected by the plant. Outside, cameras from a station in Lafayette panned across the crowd while a few reporters conducted interviews. A sizable crowd was there representing both those who were opposed and those who were in favor of the new plant. Not a few were holding spirited arguments.

Savannah and her father made their way slowly through the crowd. She looked around anxiously as the supporters of the plant appeared to close in on all sides after spotting Antoine. A female reporter turned from a man she'd been interviewing before a camera and stepped in their path.

"Mr. St. Julien, a prominent local citizen, has just arrived for the hearing. Several officials from the Department of Environmental Safety will listen to testimony regarding how the people of Acadia Parish feel about the new plant that has opened. Mr. St. Julien, what exactly will you have to say?"

"What I've been saying all along: this is the last thing we need here. We're already surrounded by chemical plants and such. They still haven't cleaned up the old Stower site. And down in Morgan City, where Singleton put up another one of these things, they children dying of some rare form of leukemia."

"Do you still maintain that this is a form of environmental racism?"

"Look at where most of the new plants are being located—near small black communities. They don't think we can or will fight. But we tired of all this pollution."

"We need jobs. This plant gonna bring almost one hundred new jobs and construction jobs, too!" a man standing nearby shouted angrily.

"We don't want to die for no job, man. You wanna poison your children's water for a job? It's time we start looking at other ways to put our people to work," Antoine answered, to applause and shouts of approval from some in the crowd as he pushed his way into the city hall. He linked arms with Savannah so they would not get separated.

With help from friends who had gathered early, Savannah and Antoine were able to find standing room along the wall near the microphone set up for members of the public to speak. At the front of the hearing room, three large tables formed a semicircle of sorts where the twelve members of the local police jury sat. Two men wearing white shirts and ties were seated with them.

Savannah glanced around the room and saw him. She waved a return greeting to a group of their neighbors who were directly across from where she stood. Paul smiled and nodded. He spoke briefly to the man seated to his left before heading toward her. Savannah watched his progress, admiring the way he moved in spite of herself. He wore khaki slacks, a white shirt, and a navy jacket. The jacket was open, revealing a wine-colored leather belt around his narrow waist. He stood taller than most of the other men in the room. Several women ogled him as he passed. When he turned his head to return their greetings, she noticed the way hair curled ever so slightly over his collar. His dark brown skin against the white shirt made a striking and very appealing contrast.

"Ms. St. Julien. Hello again." He smiled, a bit tentatively. "Uh, how have you been?"

"Fine. And you?" Savannah shifted from one foot to the other, a little suspicious of this new low-key approach of his.

"You look very nice today." He admired the cornflower blue summer dress. The scoop neck was not revealing, but the gentle rise and fall of her breathing was suggestive of a hidden bounty. A strong urge to touch the soft mound struck him so forcefully he blinked. Sure his thoughts could be read on his face, he pried his gaze away from her. Paul willed himself to tame such lustful ruminations.

"Thanks." She looked away, embarrassed that he had caught her staring. "Are you scheduled to testify?"

"Yeah, my report is almost finished. Just need a few finishing touches, but the work is done." He paused and stuck his hands in his pockets. Looking back at her, he found she was still gazing straight ahead at a blank wall. "I don't guess we'll be here but maybe two hours at most."

"Oh, they limit speakers to about five minutes each. Except experts. I suppose that includes you." She looked down at her dress and smoothed wrinkles that weren't there.

"I'm going for something to eat after. Would you—"

The sound of loud tapping on a microphone cut him off. Paul tried to finish but was drowned out. Seeing his partner beckoning to him impatiently, he started back to his seat.

"I'll talk to you later, okay?" Her answer was just a smile and nod. "Okay, all right. Sorry, excuse me." He bumped into several people, not surprising, since he was walking backward, unable to look away from that smile. That smile was for him, only for him. Without remembering how he'd gotten there, he was back in his seat.

"Testing. It's working, suh." A city hall employee passed the microphone to a portly balding man to his right.

"Thank you, Leland. Evenin', everybody. I'm Shelby Leblanc, Police Jury president. Most of y'all know me." He bobbed his head to the crowd. "Ladies and gentlemen, this will be an informal hearing for public comment on the new facility operated by Batton Chemical Corporation. We have Jim Garrett and Frank Mouton from the Department of Environmental Quality. Thank you for coming. We will have a presentation from Mr. Kyle Singleton, president of Batton Chemical. But first, Mr. Garrett will say a few words."

"Thank you, Mr. Leblanc. The Department of Environmental Quality, as part of its procedures to issue licenses to businesses that receive and handle toxic substances, takes many factors into consideration. Of course, we consider environmental impact. We have standards that any proposed facility must meet and those standards are based on the type of substances the facility will be dealing with. We also consider the impact on the surrounding community. We at DEQ are very concerned that you have a say in any decision that will affect your town, your neighborhoods. But we must consider economic impact as well. If we do not, we could very well ignore a very real need for jobs in this state and a strong economic base of industry." He was interrupted briefly by scattered applause.

"Thank you, Mr. Garrett. After the presentation by Batton Chemical, we have time set aside for comments from members in the audience who have registered to state their positions. Each speaker will have five minutes. Mr. Singleton, if you're ready."

"Thank you. Just let me begin by saying we at Batton Chemical are very concerned about safety. We have the welfare of the community in mind, not to mention our employees. You have before you a copy of our own report and the independent report from Mr. Paul Honore of Eco Systems Consultants. I will briefly summarize our plant operations. I will then review the findings of both reports. It will then be quite clear—crystal clear, gentlemen—that we meet or exceed industry standards of safety as a recycling facility." With assistance from a Batton Chemical engineer, Singleton launched into a technical explanation.

"Look like they impressed with all them big words and fancy charts." A man standing close to Antoine spoke loud enough for only a few to hear.

"All the high an' mighty talk in the world ain't gone change nuthin'. These people gone have a lot to say 'bout all them chemicals they wanna bring here." Antoine tried to sound confident. He frowned in concentration trying to follow Singleton's jargon.

"Poppy, did you get anybody who understands all this to do a report for our side?" Savannah knew some environmental law. She also knew that without a track record of violations to attack, the opponents would have an uphill battle.

"Mencer says they scheduled the hearin' so fast, we didn't have time. But I don't think that matter nohow. The law say they got to listen to how we feel 'bout this here."

"But you need at least *some* research as ammunition."

"We got how many people got cancer, how many times we get sick from that old dump site that nobody done nothin' about. That oughta count for somethin'."

"But—"

"Thank you, Mr. Singleton. Mr. Garrett, Mr. Mouton, do you have any more questions? Then we'll take comments from the audience."

A string of outraged citizens vented their opposition to

the proposed plant. Like Antoine, they spoke about the toll cancer had taken on their families and friends. More than one expressed frustration that state officials seemed more inclined to listen to the plant owners. They expressed skepticism at the insistence that no proved connection had been made between certain diseases and the tons of waste discharged by the oil and chemical industry.

"Why, for the last thirty years, have all these plants been in poor black areas like Kentwood, Evangeline, and Bayou Rouge? They passed up River Bend, forty miles down the river road from Iberia. Put that plant smack in poor folks' backyards." Miss Lucille, a statuesque woman the color of dark chocolate, shook her finger at the white men as if scolding children caught being bad, a habit acquired from forty years of teaching.

"Yes, ma'am," the president of the Police Jury said. The other men nodded respectfully. "Miss Lucille, your time is almost up."

"I know that, Mr. Shelby Leblanc, I've been keeping time. You hold on a minute. Antoine, come up here. We need you to talk." She shooed away several others who had gotten up to speak. They sat back down obediently.

"Wait, now. They done had they chance to talk. Not everybody tryin' to buck this thing. Ain't some of us gonna get a chance?" Encouraged by a few voices of assent, a wiry man with limp brown hair stood. From his weather-beaten skin, it was clear he had spent much time in the hot Louisiana sun.

"We want to hear everybody's side to this, Manny. Go head." The Police Jury president nodded for him to go on.

"One thing ain't been said: that is, we need jobs down here. Every one of them what's spoke up against this here plant, they ain't been out of work for months. Now, this man done said can't nothin' show what y'all been sayin' about it's being, how you say, unsafe for the environment. Now, if y'all can't prove what you sayin', and we need jobs, then I say, let 'em build it. It's plenty us that's barely makin' it."

"That's right!" a short man shouted from the back.

"I got a family to feed," another man yelled.

"And I tell you this, it's a lot more than me that feel this way." There were shouts and applause to support Manny's assertion.

"We need jobs bad—real bad. Nobody said we didn't." Antoine spoke from where he stood, his voice ringing clear even without the microphone. "But they play on that so we don't ask too many questions. They figure we gone be so grateful that we take anything and too ignorant to know enough to think past gettin' a job to what that job gone do to our health."

"Who you callin' ignorant?" Manny spun around to face Antoine.

"Don't take that stuff offa him, man," a gruff male voice spoke over Antoine's shoulder.

At the same time someone shoved Antoine toward Manny, who swung wildly at him. Antoine received a glancing blow that caused his head to snap back. A woman swung her large handbag to hit Manny. She missed him but smacked one of his defenders full in the face. Suddenly, a wild free-for-all with shouting, shoving, and a few punches landing broke out. Savannah tried frantically to push through the press of scuffling bodies to her father. Paul tried wading through to her, shouting that she should get back. As he reached for her, a stocky man rose from nowhere to deliver a right jab to his jaw. Savannah somehow managed to get behind the attacker and gave him a sharp kick to the back of both knees. He went down like a sack of potatoes, falling against another man who slammed him in the midsection. Savannah stepped on his back to reach Paul's side. Grabbing her arm, he pulled her away from the crowd. He pushed her behind the table, where the two state officials stood looking desperately for a safe way out.

"Stay here," he shouted over the din, and went back

into the fracas. Paul found Antoine quickly enough, but he had to fight several men to get him free. They joined Savannah at the front of the auditorium just as several sheriff's deputies arrived.

"Galee, if dis ain't a mess!" Sheriff Triche paused to look around in amazement. "What y'all waitin' on? Get on in dere an' break dis up," he shouted to his men, even as he grabbed two sweating combatants and pried them apart.

Paul tried to lead Savannah and her father out by a side door but was blocked by a deputy.

"Don't nobody leave here 'til we sort out who done what to who." Sheriff Triche took a large striped handkerchief from his pocket to wipe the sweat dripping from his chin. His plump face was red from exertion.

"I tell you right now, he the one started it." Manny, his shirt torn open with all the buttons gone, pointed at Antoine. "I'm filin' charges on him, Sheriff."

Loud voices on both sides of the fight competed to be heard. The sheriff shouted several times before restoring order.

"Manny, number one, much as I done picked you up offa the floor after you done started a fight you couldn't finish, if somebody hit you, then they probably had a reason." Low grumbling could be heard. Manny scowled but didn't speak. "Number two, when I come in, Antoine wasn't nowhere near you. But I saw you punchin' on Floyd. Fact, I'm gonna issue a whole bunch of disturbin' the peace citations before I let anybody go on home."

"That ain't right, no. I wanna file charges on him! You s'pose to enforce the law," Manny barked.

"Enforce the law, huh? Okay, since you ain't done paid the last fine for brawlin' over at the Gator Bar and Grill, since you was released without paying no bond for public drunkenness last month, I b'lieve we gone start enforcin' the law with you." Sheriff Triche stared at him hard while Manny squirmed.

"You ain't worth the trouble, old man," Manny snarled, not daring to look at the sheriff.

For the next hour, the deputies issued citations. Paul insisted he follow them home, in case Manny and his friends decided to pursue them and continue the fight. Later Paul, Antoine, and Savannah were seated around the kitchen table at Antoine's house. As they drank strong coffee, Tante Marie pumped them for details.

"Lord, a wonder somebody didn't get killed. But I'm thankful nobody got hurt bad. Bet Miss Lucille left her mark on a few behinds, though." Tante Marie chuckled.

"I swear, that old lady cleared a path. Last time I saw her, she was walking out of there without a scratch not long after the fight started." Paul smiled.

"Well, I just hope we got enough said to them DEQ people for them not to renew that permit. That Claude Trosclair got more up his sleeve than a magician, yeah. Got a permit to recycle so he don't have to follow all them strict regulations for handling that, how you call, toxic waste." Antoine frowned into his coffee cup.

"But how did he get by with that? I mean, Big River is taking in waste from other plants, construction sites that can't be disposed of, like other waste materials. Seems as though the state should be concerned about how that waste is being disposed of once they get it. I looked over the research on this slag. It's conflicting. Some of the studies show it's potentially dangerous, others say not," Savannah said.

"Singleton claims that the high heat used in the kilns for burning that stuff makes it into a safe material that can be used. As you say, we can show 'em what some of the studies indicate. But he can turn around and show just as many that say different. I just don't know how it's gone come out." Antoine took a deep breath and rubbed his eyes.

"Are you sure you're not hurt?" Savannah got up to examine his head for bruises or swelling.

"Quit fussin', now. I done told you I'm okay. The day I can't take a punch from scraggly-butt Manny Langlois is the day you can put me out to pasture."

"Go on to bed, Poppy. Get some rest." Savannah hugged him, then planted a kiss on his forehead.

"Ooh," Tante Marie yawned loudly. Catching Antoine's eye, she jerked her head toward the door. "No wonder my eyes gettin' so heavy. It's almost midnight. I'm goin' to bed myself." She gave a Antoine another cue by cupping his elbow as she got up.

"Hum, oh yeah. Gotta get up early to—well, got things to do. Goodnight." He patted Paul on the arm even as Tante Marie none too gently propelled him out of the kitchen.

"Real subtle exit, huh?" Savannah gave a small nervous laugh. She began busily picking up the dishes. "I wanted to thank you for what you did; you sort of rescued us." She spoke over her shoulder as she stood with her back to him, rinsing out the cups in the sink. Suddenly, he was standing close to her. She could smell him, a warm musky scent that enveloped her.

"You were doing pretty well, though. That one guy you kicked will be limping for a while." He began drying the dishes.

"Did you see the look on that guy's face after that lady's purse connected with his nose?" Savannah widened her eyes and wobbled her head in imitation.

They both started laughing so hard they almost dropped the dishes they were putting away. She turned to shush him, pointing toward the bedrooms. They tiptoed out to the front porch, smothering their laughter as best they could. After several minutes, an awkward silent descended. Savannah sat next to him on the porch swing. A little voice warned her not to let him get too close. Before either side had a chance to prevail, he slid right up to her, their arms touching.

"Savannah, would you like to go out sometime? For dinner or something?"

"All right. I mean, that would be nice—" She turned to find his face only inches from hers.

His warm breath brushed her cheek. Without thinking, she pressed against his body, gently rubbing her lips over his. She wanted to savor this closeness, to taste the sweetness a little at a time. His arms formed a circle around her waist. He moaned softly and took full possession of her lips, her mouth, and in that moment, her heart. Savannah could feel the heat from his body mixed with her own. Burying his hands in her hair, he began softly kissing her face. His lips etched a hot trail over her nose to her chin, finally urgently caressing her neck. With her head thrown back, Savannah's mind was filled with him. All of her senses seemed heightened. The warm fragrance of the night flooded over them both. The sound of crickets seemed beautiful music composed just for this night. Arching her back, she trembled all over as his hands lightly touched her breast. The feel of his hands rubbing the fabric of her dress was a tantalizing prelude to having them touched without the barrier. The loud bang of a door slamming deep inside the house caused them to pull apart quickly. Remembering her aunt and father were only within a few yards brought Savannah reluctantly back from that wonderful place he had taken her. She took a deep breath to steady herself.

"I'd better go in now, I need to get an early start in the morning." Savannah moved even further away from him, flustered by her lack of control. This man had brought out something in her that was as frightening as it was wonderful, something she had been determined not to feel for anyone. In her agitation, she grew short with him.

"Of course, it is pretty late." He stood uncertainly, trying to think of something to say. "Savannah, I really want to see you again." He reached for her hand.

"Yes, well, I'll let you know." She folded her arms to avoid his touch, fearing what it would do to her reserve. She had to find some way to withstand the onslaught of his effect on her senses.

"Goodnight." He made no move to go for several minutes. Finally accepting that the magical moment that had drawn her to him had passed, he went to his Jeep. With a tentative wave, he drove away.

Paul could still feel the glow of Savannah's touch. Still unnerved by the power of his longing for her, he could not get to sleep. Not once in all the times he'd dated other women had his passion stirred so deeply. The combination of beauty, courage, and sensuality in this one woman packed a mighty punch that knocked his defenses flat. Staring into the night, he determined to make her want him just as much.

The next morning dawned brightly. As usual for Louisiana, the late September weather remained balmy. But for Savannah, everything seemed to go wrong. She was tired and irritable from a restless night of trying to clear her mind of Paul. The blouse she wanted to wear had a ripped seam. The skirt she put on missed a button at the waist. Fuming, she dug through the bottom of her closet for the sandals she planned to wear, but they seemed to be playing hide and seek. Finally dressed, she avoided her aunt, not wanting to answer questions about last night. She left as if in a big hurry, calling out that she would just get a donut on the way to the shop. A huge knowing grin stretched across Tante Marie's face as she stood at the window watching her leave. Savannah felt even more annoyed.

At the shop, the figures she tried to double-check kept dancing around, refusing to add up. Every time she punched them into the calculator, a different total flashed annoyingly on the screen. About an hour after she'd arrived, her father came in. She gave him a distracted

"Good morning" and continued to mutter under her breath at the way everything was going wrong.

"Cher, I been watchin' you for a while. You got your mind elsewhere. Sure thing not on what you doin'."

"There is nothing on my mind. These invoices are illegible and not in any order. Why you haven't fired that bookkeeper I definitely do not know." She looked at the calculator display hopefully, then groaned at the result. Flinging several pieces of paper to the floor, she covered her face with her hands.

"Cher, every time you try to total up the supplies I bought for making my statues, you pick up a different set of invoices," her father argued. "This one, for instance, is for souvenirs I got at market. This pile is sales receipts for Marie's gumbo filé mix and stuff, this pile—"

"Okay, okay. I'll start over." Savannah restacked the papers without looking her father in the eye.

At the sound of the bell, she started up to herd the early shoppers away until they opened in another hour.

"Poppy, you left the front door unlocked again. You've got to be more careful. This isn't the same small town it was twenty-five years ago."

"Hold on, now. You're safe, it's only a harmless engineer." Paul held out both arms as if to show he was unarmed.

"Mornin', T-Paul. How you feelin' today, man?" Antoine slapped him on the back. His grin was wide as he glanced at Paul and then at Savannah significantly.

"Pretty good, shaping up to be a beautiful day."

"Sure enough, sure enough." Antoine took a deep breath. His grin began to fade when he noticed that Savannah was not sharing in their good humor. "Well. I got some . . . stuff to take care of, in the stockroom. I'll be in the back, out there . . ." His voiced trailed off as he did his best to fade into the background.

"You okay?" Paul frowned. As he reached out to touch Savannah's shoulder, he could feel her stiffen.

"Sure, fine." She stared straight ahead.

"Did I do something to upset you last night? I thought, I mean, we seemed to connect."

"Yeah, well, maybe that's the problem. We connected too hard and too fast."

"Listen, I don't want you to think I'm pushing you. But with you so near, so damn fine, I just reacted." He tried to put his arms around her, but she moved away.

"I'm not looking for any kind of relationship right now, understand? There are a lot of other things I want to concentrate on, like my career, or what's left of it. My experience working for a big law firm left a bad taste in my mouth, but I haven't given up on practicing law yet." Savannah could feel her resistance slipping as she stared into those remarkable eyes. She wanted to erase the concern in them.

"I do understand. I've got a few life issues to resolve myself. We can take it as slow as you want. Hey, since we got off to a bad start, let's take it from the beginning. Hi, my name is Paul. What's yours?" He reached out his hand. Refusing to be ignored, he grabbed hers and pumped it comically.

"Savannah, all right? Savannah." She laughed in spite of herself. "Just don't break it. I need those, you know."

"That's much better. I meant what I said about taking it slow. This thing is too important to rush." Paul folded her hand in both of his as he stared into her eyes.

Her gaze traced the strong curve of his jaw and lingered on his sensuous lips. A surge of heat began at the base of her spine, the same heat that been so easily kindled last night. Searching his face, a calmness spread over her that no other man had inspired. She couldn't deny that being with Paul made her feel she'd finally found her place, a place she'd not even known she was missing. This made finding it even more marvelous.

As they began to exchange small talk, continuing the game of a first meeting, Antoine peeked at them. Since he didn't hear any shouting or loud thumps, he figured Paul must be safe. He went back to sit at his desk and began straightening up the invoices. He whistled a sprightly zydeco tune as he worked.

"I'll come by later at around twelve-thirty—how does lunch at Lafayette Park sound?"

"Great. I'll pick up the sandwiches from Snooky Boo's." Snooky Boo's was little more than a one-room shack that served up the best old-fashioned homemade sandwiches for a song. It was at the edge of the small business district, situated perfectly for truck drivers and blue-collar workers on road crews.

"You got it." He waved happily as he walked off with a new bounce in his step.

"Bye." Watching him move away, Savannah stood on the sidewalk for several minutes enjoying the view. She sighed deeply at the sight.

As she turned to go back into the shop, something made her look to her left. A block away, standing at the end of the street that led to the museum, was LaShaun. Even at that distance, Savannah could feel her malice curling out like a water moccasin. LaShaun traced something in the air. The smile on her face was anything but friendly. Unable to look away, Savannah felt her sense of calm drain away with each movement of LaShaun's hands to be replaced by a sense of chilly dread. She wanted to back away, to run, but something held her rooted to that spot. LaShaun nodded as if to acknowledge her effect on Savannah, then left. Savannah stood at the door, gazing after her, rubbing the raised flesh on her arms. Breathing shakily, she went inside.

Chapter 4

For the next three weeks, Paul was so cheerful his partner Sam was getting really annoyed. Sam hated small towns, having grown up in one on the wrong side of the tracks, so to speak. He visited only a few times, preferring to attend to the contracts in the larger cities. "Man, if you start whistling some corny song, I swear I'm going to throw up. There can only be one reason for this kind of irrational behavior—a woman." Sam cocked one bushy eyebrow at Paul's knowing laugh. "Just what I thought."

"What are you so grumpy about, anyway? Business is great, we've been having sunny weather, and you don't have to stay here overnight if you don't want to because most of my testing is done." Paul stretched gracefully and sank a perfect shot with a ball of paper in the wastebasket next to Sam's chair.

"That last part is truly cause for rejoicing. How you stood it for six weeks is beyond me. But don't change the subject. Who is she?" Sam hooked one long denim-covered leg over the chair arm. They had been reviewing test result figures for over three hours, and he was more than ready for a break. The spacious living room of the mobile home Paul had rented doubled as his office.

"Savannah St. Julien," Paul said, savoring each syllable.

"That name sounds familiar. Hey, wait a minute—I heard that on television. Some reporter was interviewing a St. Julien about the plant. No, you wouldn't be that dumb."

"What are you talking about?" Paul handed him a soft drink before taking a seat on the sofa across from him.

"You are the opposition, buddy boy. You are working for the enemy. These little numbers are going to get us in good with a major industry and your name is going to be mud." Sam picked up some of the reports and shook them to emphasize his point.

"We did an independent assessment that showed the aggregate will not harm the soil if it's processed correctly," Paul insisted. "The soil mixture around the plant would not easily allow contamination of groundwater if a large spill should accidentally occur—"

"Save it for your honey, man. When this baby hits the fan, you'd better be wearing a flak jacket, is all I can say." Sam waved part of the partially finished report.

"I'm not working for the enemy, either." Paul scowled into his glass. "Singleton is taking all necessary precautions. What's more, Claude Trosclair even got him to follow some of my suggestions to change some of their operations."

"Does she know about your relationship to the Trosclair family?" Sam squinted at him.

"Of course not. There's no need for her to know." Paul shifted uneasily, his voice defensive.

"Uh-oh." Sam pursed his lips.

"Don't give me that look." Paul's irritation came from knowing what Sam was thinking. Exactly the nagging worry he tried to suppress.

"Let's hope it doesn't come out." Sam leaned back.

"Nobody knows who I am, and this happened years ago. There's no way it could."

"Not tempted to tell cousin Quentin who you are and rock his little privileged world?"

"It would almost be worth it to see the look on his face, but no. I remember the look on my father's face when I read Monmon Marguerite's diary to him. He was trembling. The last thing he wants is for this to be known. Papa's health isn't good, and getting him upset could send him back to the hospital."

"Yeah, and what about grandpa? He exploited your grandmother and went on his merry way." Sam seemed as angry as Paul should have been.

"That's the way I felt, too. But we're talking over fifty years ago in a small southern town. Mixed couples didn't march down the aisle, man. She just fell in love with the wrong guy at the wrong time, in the wrong place."

"This is incredible. Listen to yourself, making excuses for him."

"Okay, so he didn't have the guts to buck generations of convention or risk his social standing, not to mention his inheritance. How many would? Could *you*?"

"If I truly loved her, yeah, you damn right I could."

"Real easy to say. We don't know what it's like to be in their skin, raised a certain way. It would mean giving up everything you have, including your family." Paul crossed the room and began arranging the files on his desk.

"He's got you fooled, man. Claude Trosclair is one those southern aristocrats that sees having a black mistress as his right."

"You haven't met him. Besides, the way my grandmother's diary reads, they had a real love affair going—poetry, flowers, the whole nine yards. And she knew only too well that it would have to stay that way for both their sakes."

"If you say so. I just hope you know what you're doing here. Things are getting real complicated."

"What is that supposed to mean?" Paul asked.

"We get this contract, and you tell me your family secret." Sam ticked off fingers, counting.

"You're my best friend and partner. I felt you had a right to know."

"Then you date and dump, of all people, Marie Leveau."

"Her name is LaShaun Rousselle, she works at the museum, which happens to have a voodoo exhibit, and our parting was cordial."

"Uh-huh, just don't eat anything with red gravy from her. Then you fall hard for Ms. Greenpeace. When I was teasing you about how you needed to lighten up and get a life, I didn't mean all in one day, my brother."

"It's cool. Don't worry about it, all right?" Paul rubbed his face with both hands.

"If you say so. I gotta get going." Sam raised his eyebrows and shook his head. He paused and turned back. "Call me if you need anything." He extended his hand.

"You bet." Paul gripped his hand hard for several seconds before letting go.

After Sam left, Paul was more subdued. So lost in joy that he and Savannah were moving toward one another, Paul had not allowed himself to think about the complications—complications that could spell disaster. Paul could still see Savannah's lovely face smiling with pleasure. Closing his eyes, he could almost smell the lovely warm scent of her skin. Her effect on him was not to be denied. Opening his eyes again, he faced the growing fear that he could lose this woman who had become so precious to him.

Now the days were much shorter, and temperature became frosty several times as cold fronts moved through. But in typical subtropical fashion, it could be forty degrees in the morning and seventy degrees by noon as the south Louisiana sunshine spread across the countryside. The next five weeks were a whirlwind of activity for Savannah. She was busy helping her father get ready for the Christmas season. In the weeks just before Thanksgiving, business at the gift shop really began to pick up. Keeping merchandise

in stock was important. Strangely, she had not missed prac
ticing law or even given thought to reviving the career fo
which she'd worked so hard. Managing the shop had com
easily to her. She'd made changes that had increased th
profit margin. With her customary zeal to do anything sh
did right, she had studied everything she could find abou
how to operate a retail business or gift shop. At her sugges
tion, they were now doing gift baskets. Stuffed with Tant
Marie's famous pralines and handmade crafts, they becam
an instant hit.

When not in the shop helping customers or taking car
of business details, she was with Paul. Her attempts to kee
him at arm's length had failed in a big way. She found i
impossible not to respond to him after that night on he
front porch. Her skin tingled deliciously at the memor
of his kiss, so sweet and hot. Thinking about being in hi
arms filled her with a delicious warmth that streamed ove
her. Savannah blushed at the memory of how he so easil
evoked such burning desire with the lightest touch. Ye
this strong physical attraction was only part of it. *I love h
mind, too.* Savannah giggled to herself. Without thinking
she had gradually accepted him into her life. It was as i
he had always belonged there. Her father, not an eas
man to please when it came to men dating his little gir
expressed his approval by the absence of a scowl wheneve
his name was mentioned. Yet he did have reservations.

"This was a pretty good day, cher. Them carvings o
deer and nutria are sellin' fast. I'm gone have to take
couple of days to work on some more. Maybe I'll get
Leon to work a few extra days helping you in the shop.'
Antoine held up the list of the few remaining wood carving
left on the shelf.

"Sure, Poppy. That would be fine." Savannah had hire
the high school student through a program that helpe
troubled and low-income teens find part-time work. Just
little attention from Antoine had worked wonders on

Leon's attitude. Once sulky and resistant, he now seemed eager to come to work.

The phone rang.

"Hi, Paul. Sure, here she is." Antoine handed her the receiver. Continuing to work, he listened as they made plans to meet later.

"Y'all goin' out again tonight?"

"Just to the Fish Net. Paul rented a couple of movies we've both been wanting to see." She smiled to herself.

"Be careful, sugar. Remember, you just met him."

"I thought you liked Paul. You and Tante Marie practically pushed us together."

"Paul is a fine young man, but you don't know much about him." Antoine fidgeted with a pencil.

"What do you mean? Have you heard something?" Savannah looked up sharply. She could feel her stomach muscles tighten.

"No, no. Nothing, but—well, he's working for Trosclair on that plant, you know." Antoine spoke quickly.

"No, he's not, Poppy. He's an independent consultant who is being paid by a third party to assess the site and the possible environmental impact." Savannah knew she sounded a bit too defensive. It was probably because she still had doubts about his relationship with Trosclair.

"I just don't want you to get hurt again, baby. Like with that Devin fella."

"I can take care of myself, thank you." She softened her tone. She planted a playful kiss on his forehead before sitting down to continue her work. "You just concentrate on how you're going to spend all this money you've been making lately."

"Poo, I don't need much. Maybe I'll get me some new fishin' gear."

Savannah's mind was only half on the papers in front of her. Was it her imagination, or had her father seemed to hold something back? She went over their short conversation several times. No, he was just being a dutiful father. She pushed her misgivings away as she remembered the way Paul's handsome face became beautiful when he smiled at her, the strong outline of his jaw, the way he tenderly touched her face while they kissed. She repeated the defense of Paul that she had given to her father to herself. Reassured, she was finally able to focus the task in front of her.

"Whew! You wore me out." Paul slumped onto the couch fanning himself with exaggerated motions.

"Get off it. A big strong man like you ought to be able to hang. Come on now, get up, get down. Oo-wee." Savannah swayed rhythmically while pulling him to her.

"Woman, you wanna give me a heart attack? Rest, I need rest."

"Pitiful." Laughing, she turned off the seventies disco music. She sat next to him on the couch.

"Whose idea was this, anyway?" He groaned.

"Yours, that's whose. Watching those old black exploitation movies went to your head. Only a few minutes ago you were yelling, 'Let's get funky!' Remember?" She slapped his thigh playfully.

"I had definitely lost my head." He pulled her to him. "Ahh, I feel better already." He gave her a passionate kiss.

"Ummm—what happened to can't catch your breath and needing rest?" she murmured between kisses.

"Your giving me mouth-to-mouth is just the medicine I need."

Savannah's giggle was soon smothered by his tender assault. As he took her mouth completely, she felt the hammering of his heart against her breasts. Or maybe it was hers; lost in him, she couldn't tell the difference. But it didn't matter. All that mattered was what they had right here, right now. She squirmed deliciously, helping his hands roam in places that ached for his touch. His tongue caressed hers, then darted across her lips. With one last simultaneous shudder, they parted.

"Wow." He shook his head, trying to regain his equilibrium. Paul marveled at the power of one kiss from this sensuous woman.

"And how." Savannah pulled her blouse straight. Wiping her face with a paper napkin, she sat back against the couch, away from him.

"Take it slow, right?" His eyes were bright with passion. The question burned between them.

Savannah gazed at him searchingly. They talked for hours about all kinds of subjects. Paul's commitment to giving of himself to the community, his fervor about working with young people, impressed her. This intellectual admiration fanned the flames of desire, deepening each time they were together. A powerful desire that tugged against her inner voice cautioning her to be wary.

"Yes." She sighed. "Sometimes I feel as if I have always known you. Other times, you seem so, I don't know, remote."

"Hey, no fair. I was anything but remote a minute ago." He inched toward her, leering.

"Be serious. We've been seeing each other for almost two months now, and I don't think we've ever really talked."

"Sure we have. You know all about me. Where I'm from, where I went to school. You have my whole life history. How about something cold to drink?" He got up suddenly.

"No, thanks." Savannah fell silent. She stared straight ahead, a small frown on her face.

"What about another movie? Let's see, we got one more great action-packed thriller that is sure to satisfy your craving for cliff-hanging excitement." He waved the cassette in the air. When there was no response, he sat next to her heavily. Putting his arm around her shoulder, he tried to pull her to him.

"Think I'll go on home." Savannah looked at him, not moving.

"Sure, if that's what you want." He drew away abruptly. Reaching for his car keys and jacket, he spoke over his shoulder. "It is kind of late, and I told Sam I'd finish up some last surveys from another job so we could start that report."

The drive to Savannah's house was a tense one. She sat as near to the window as possible, staring out into the darkness at the almost invisible scenery. Paul stole glances at her, trying to think of something to say.

"I'll be returning to Lafayette for Thanksgiving. But I'll be back that night." Paul waited, but got no answer. "Maybe we can see each other?" The car slowed to a stop in front of her house.

"When you want to share, is that it? Only when you feel comfortable being close. Well, the holidays are a time for being with those you feel close to, Paul. Right now, I don't think that includes us."

"Baby, come on, now. What do you want from me?" Paul reached out to her, but she opened the door and got out.

"More than you're willing to give, obviously." Slamming the door, she hurried across the yard into the house before he could respond.

"Hey, man. Open up. Paul, you in there?"

Groaning, he rolled over and went deeper under the covers. He tried to block out the pounding that seemed to be in his head. Muttering curse words, he finally got up. He eyes, red and scratchy, blinked painfully in the weak winter morning light. As he stumbled toward the bedroom door, his little toe slammed against the leg of the chair.

"Damn! What do you want?" Paul yanked the door to the trailer open. "Oh, you." Paul waved in his partner.

"Zow-wee, you look like hell. You either had a real good time or a real bad one, ha!" Sam laughed loud at his own joke, ignoring his friend's dark look.

"What do you want at this hour?" Paul flopped down on the couch, stretching out.

"Just passing through on my way to Metairie. I've been in Baton Rouge. Thought you might want to hear the latest on this permit thing."

"Yeah?" Paul sat up, suddenly wide awake.

"Word is, Batton Chemical has got some heavy hitters on their side. Keeping the permit is a done deal."

"Nothing in our report indicates they should do anything else. That site is as safe as any could be."

"You know and I know how hard it is to correlate rates of illness, or even mortality rates, to the impact of industrial by-products. When they throw in lifestyles, lunar phases, whatever, it muddies the water so nothing definitive can be put in those reports."

"So what's the answer? I can't say the site is unsuitable based on my data or comparisons to other similar sites with plants."

"And more good news. Your report helped them back up what they were going to do anyway." Sam munched on a large apple. "The news will hit the papers tomorrow. Too late for it to get into today's editions."

"Damn, just what I need."

"Since it can't be my news that has you looking so dogged out, must be trouble in loveland."

"Three nights ago we had the 'we've-never-really-talked' conversation. We haven't spoken since then." Paul started a pot of coffee.

"And?" Sam scratched his chin.

"And nothing." Paul shrugged.

"You been in here since then, drowning in misery? No wonder you look so bad."

"Of course not. I've been working. A lot," Paul shot back. He pointed to several stacks of papers.

"Bad news, man. Maybe it's for the best. Time to start packing up."

"I guess." Paul stared out the kitchen window.

He couldn't accept defeat so easily. Paul wanted Savannah in a way and with a depth he'd never experienced before. And he was sure that she wanted him just as much. The heat of her kiss had left a brand on his heart.

"Listen, did you ever consider that she's trying to pump you for the inside scoop on your report for Batton Chemicals?"

"Wait a minute. Savannah has never tried—" Paul blinked as if Sam had struck him.

"Really? Don't tell me you haven't discussed it at all." Sam went on despite Paul's attempts at protest. "You did, admit it."

"Naturally, we did. It's all anybody in town has been talking about. But—"

"Shown a great deal of interest in your work, too, I bet. Look, her dad is the unofficial leader of the opposition. Seems she got real cozy a little fast after dumping on you at first. Don't forget, the lady's a lawyer. They are masters at hiding their true strategy."

"You are wrong, man. Very wrong." Paul shook his head, reaching over to plug in the coffeemaker.

"If you say so, but her need to get inside your life even more tells me something different."

"They all want to do that, it's a woman thing. Not some devious plot. You're still paranoid after Sheila." Paul went into the bedroom to get dressed.

"Hey, I had faith in her, just like you have in Ms. St. Julien. A word to the wise, my brother."

"I did not even hear that. Let's go. I want to finish up so I can go see Savannah. I want her to hear the news from me first."

"What if he's just into the same old hit-and-run routine? What if he was getting close to me so he could find out about Daddy's next move to oppose Trosclair?" Savannah paced the length of the living room in front of Charice.

"So he's been asking a lot of questions?" Charice watched Savannah go back and forth.

"Well, no," Savannah admitted. "But he could be biding his time. You know, buttering me up so he can."

"Sit down, please. I'm getting queasy trying to follow you. You're making no sense, girl. Everybody in this little town knows exactly what your daddy plans to do. Paul would have to be pretty stupid not to figure it out without pumping you for information. And stupid he ain't." Charice took another sip of diet cola.

"Maybe so, but something is going on with him. He talks, but when we get too much into his family, he starts changing the subject."

"Let's see, his parents live in Crowley, he's got two brothers and two sisters. Sounds like he's been saying quite a lot to me."

"But something is missing. You know, it's more to it than that. I can feel it. I should have followed my first mind. He came on like a jerk the first time I met him." Savannah sat down with a thud. "The fact that he hasn't called shows he's got something up with him. Good riddance." Savannah punched the throw pillow.

"Yeah, you look relieved to me, all right. And he's finished his survey and report, so he may be leaving soon. That ought to make you feel even better." Charice eyed her friend closely.

"That's another thing, that report. It was a cop-out. He didn't even address the issue of alternative sites."

"They hired him to assess that site. Stop all that noise, you two," Charice shouted into the next room at her daughters, who were fighting over the television. "Let me get them home before they kill each other. I say, give him a break. In fact, you ought to give him a call."

"Bye, girls. Be good and try not to drive your mama too

crazy." Savannah helped Charice get the two girls into their jackets.

"Too late, honey. Bye now. Come on here. No, I don't want to hear what she called you. Lord, give me strength."

As Charice herded her still bickering children to her car, Paul pulled up. They exchanged brief greetings, the girls thrilled at the fuss he made over their matching jackets. Savannah stood in the door waiting. Charice gave her a thumbs-up sign as Paul turned to walk away from them.

"Hi. Can I come in?" Paul didn't advance past the top step.

"Sure." She opened the door wide.

"How've you been? Wait a minute, I don't want to make stupid small talk." Paul had hardly made it into the living room when he turned to her. His face mirrored his torment as he took a deep breath, his voice raspy with emotion. "I've missed you a lot."

"After my big talk about rushing things, maybe I'm the one who's been traveling too fast." Savannah took a step closer to him. Seeing his eyes bright with pain only increased the clenching urge to rush into his arms. She gave in when he opened them to her.

"No, I was too touchy. It's just not easy for me to open up." Paul put his arms around her. "Old habits die hard."

"I've been a little defensive, too. Tell you what, let's just take it as it comes," she murmured softly, weak with relief to have him with her. Savannah couldn't even remember what her reservations had been, not with him this close. She helped him out of his coat. "Come into the kitchen for some café au lait, my specialty."

"Sam, my partner, came by this morning to discuss some other jobs we have. He found out from some contacts that Batton Chemical will get to keep the permit." When she turned from the stove, Paul watched her face intently.

"I should have known. Trosclair has lots of low friends in high places."

"Well, there's nothing that rules out that site for development."

"But that's just it . . . why that site? Why not thirty miles south? Why not the other side of the river? I'll tell you why. Trosclair wouldn't dare contaminate the estates of his rich pals, or his own, for that matter. But Poppy is right. Look at the toxic waste sites along the river for sixty miles. Almost all are located in poor minority communities."

"All that land is accessible to the river, which makes it desirable." Paul took a deep breath. "That's a powerful argument in their favor. That, and the jobs the plant will bring. Economic impact is a big consideration, especially in a parish with ten percent unemployment."

"It's past time for me to get back into being an attorney. First thing in the morning, I'm going to start doing some research."

"Hold on. Working at the shop and being a lawyer—when will I ever get to see you?"

"Oh, don't worry, I'll be sure to pencil you into my schedule."

"Thank you so much. Let's go over to my house to finish those old movies." He kissed her neck.

"Can't. Promised Tante Marie we'd visit my cousins in Scott tonight." She snuggled closer. "Of course, it's not like they won't be there another time."

"Hey, now," Tante Marie called from the living room.

"Evening, ma'am." Paul jumped back. Grabbing a napkin, he hastily wiped his lips.

"You cut your mouth, son? Heh, heh. Didn't move fast 'nough, cher. And yeah, you gone visit your Tante Rita tonight. She done asked me three times when you gone come see her. Might as well get it over with. You know how she gets. Now, get ready. Bye, Paul. Nice seein' ya." She flounced out without waiting for an answer.

With a shrug, Savannah blew him a kiss before seeing him off.

"Knock, knock."

"Who's there?" Paul played along.

"Didn't get to," Savannah sang out.

"Didn't get to what?" Paul's silhouette towered over her, his broad chest rose and fell rapidly beneath the tank undershirt.

"Didn't get to finish making up." Savannah climbed the steps slowly to him.

Boldly, she placed her hands on his narrow waist. With one hand he closed the door behind her, with the other, he drew her further into the room.

"Paul, I—"

"No. Every time we talk at a time like this we end up arguing. Not this time, baby, not this time." He covered her mouth with his.

Savannah wrapped herself around him. All her doubts and suspicions seemed groundless in the face of his sweet attack on her senses. Feeling his tongue gently exploring, she gave up to him, opening her lips wider. His fingers gently raked her hair, then traced down her back in ever-widening circles until they rested on her hips.

"Wait. Didn't we just talk about moving too fast?" Gently she extricated herself from his embrace. Dazed, she sat heavily on the seat.

"I want you." He sat close without touching her. Waves of desire made his voice unsteady. His body ached to press tightly to hers. Though it was excruciating not to clutch her, he sensed Savannah's need to wait.

"It's just, not yet. Let's take our time." Savannah sighed shakily.

"Listen, I won't tell you that I'm a virgin. But I've been careful in selecting my partners, and I used condoms."

"I've been careful, too. It's not that, though that's important. I just think we should spend more time getting close emotionally."

"I'm not him, Savannah." Paul spoke in a gentle voice.

"Being with you is what I want, but . . ." Savannah's voice broke as a tear escaped and rolled down her cheek.

"I want to be with you, Savannah. Sexual attraction is only part of what I feel for you, not even the biggest part." He held her close, his hands locked at her waist.

"Two hurts back-to-back would be too much." Savannah's eyes brimmed with tears. Fighting not to cry, she stared at her hands folded in her lap. "Before giving myself to anyone, I want to be sure I really know who he is—not who I want him to be. Can you understand?"

"Yes, baby. Let's start right now," Paul said, his lips close to her ear.

They talked for hours about family, high school, his work. Finally, she told him why she'd returned to Beau Chene.

"I trusted Devin. I mean, when I came on board, he took me under his wing. He pretended to, anyway."

"Are you sure he's not still important to you?" Paul pulled back and searched her face.

"Positive." She kissed him long and hard.

"I'm sorry about what happened in Shreveport, but I'm glad you came back when you did." Paul breathed in the smell of her hair.

"I'd better get going," Savannah spoke faintly against his chest. Despite her words, she shut her eyes and snuggled closer.

"Stay a little while longer, babe," he spoke into her hair.

"My God, it's three o'clock. No telling what Tante Marie or Poppy think." Savannah giggled as she slipped her shoes on and straightened her sweater. Giving him one last hug, she started to go.

"They think what I think, that you're a fabulous lady with respect for herself."

Chapter 5

The house looked exactly as Paul had imagined, large and elegant. It not only spoke of money, lots of it, but of old money. Set back from the highway at the end of a long, winding drive, a large veranda on both floors stretched the length of the house. Huge white columns, four, in fact, were spaced equally along the front. Without a trace of envy, Paul admired the beautiful oak and magnolia trees flanking the drive. They spread out over the acres surrounding the Trosclair big house. As he parked his Jeep, Paul wondered, not for the first time, the purpose of his being summoned here. He could not help but think of Savannah and what she would make of this visit. As much as he hated keeping secrets from her, he had more than just himself to consider. Catching himself straightening his collar for the third time, he felt foolish. Resisting the impulse to check his appearance in the rearview mirror once more, he mounted the wide steps to the door.

"My Lord." The stout black woman who opened half of the double front doors stood for a moment, her eyes wide. "I mean, uh, how do, suh?" She stepped back and motioned him to come in.

"I'm here to see Mr. Trosclair." Paul fidgeted under her stare. "Something wrong, ma'am?"

"Humm, oh no, child. Just gettin' to be old and slow. I'm Louise. Come on in here. Mr. Claude's in the library." She grabbed his arm, then seemed to think better of it and let go. "Right in here." Smiling, she looked at him from head to toe.

Paul would have continued puzzling over her strange reaction to him had not the room he had been ushered into overwhelmed him. He gazed at the floor-to-ceiling bookcases lined with both leatherbound classics and contemporary works. His eyes traveled from the ceiling to the beautiful Persian carpet that covered most of the floor. Spaced about the room were leather armchairs and tapestry settees. Arranged around the fireplace were three large antique sofas upholstered in different patterns but with the same emerald greens, ruby reds, warm beiges, and muted yellows of the carpet and other pieces in the room. Fine artwork, including a number of Audubon prints, hung along the walls. The late-afternoon sunlight shone brightly through the full-length windows framed by rich dark green draperies held back with ornate sashes.

"Glad you could come, young man." Standing near a large mantel, Claude had allowed Paul time to take in the room. "Here, have a seat."

"Thank you, yes." Paul recovered enough to realize he still stood in the door.

"I'm gonna be right back to y'all with some coffee," Louise said.

Paul started at the voice that came over his shoulder. Turning around, he was again favored with a wide, affectionate smile. Nodding encouragingly for him to make himself at home, she then bustled off humming a tune.

"Thank you, Louise. Been working for us for over forty years now. She was only fifteen when she started taking care of us. You haven't lived until you've tasted her pecan pie. Just like a member of the family."

"Oh, really?" Paul wondered how Louise felt about that.

"Your family live near here, Mr. Honore?" Claude sat opposite Paul.

"In Crowley." Paul had prepared himself for this kind of question. Watching Claude's expression, he was reassured that this was only polite conversation. "My mother and father live there."

"Nice little town. Ah, here we go. Louise is just as famous for making a wonderful cup of coffee." Claude savored the first sip. "Umm, perfect, as usual."

"Claude, there is a strange vehicle in our driveway. Oh, hello."

Mrs. Trosclair came into the room looking over her shoulder, but upon turning to find a stranger in her home, stopped abruptly. She wore a dark blue dress and had a lacy shawl draped around her shoulders. The tiny pear-shaped pearl earrings she wore accented her delicate features. Her dark hair, mixed with gray, was done in a single French braid and pinned back. She was not a beauty, but she was a handsome woman who appeared to be at least ten years younger than her husband.

"Mr. Honore, this is my wife."

"Pleased to meet you, ma'am." Paul rose to greet her.

"Mr. Honore is here on business, dear," Claude said.

"Really? I so seldom get to meet my husband's business associates. What business are you in, Mr. Honore?" Mrs. Trosclair motioned for Paul to sit down. With practiced grace, she sank down onto a settee, careful to arrange her skirt. It was all done with the fluid motion of a southern belle, a veteran of countless teas and Junior League meetings.

"I'm an environmental engineer."

"My, that sounds very interesting. Are you from Beau Chene?" Mrs. Trosclair inquired. Her delicate voice had the silky southern drawl so common to female members of the old families.

"No, ma'am, Crowley. I'm just in town to complete a survey on the Big River plant your husband's corporation is operating."

"My, my, Claude and Kyle sure stirred up some folks with that one. Is it true the materials they handle there are dangerous? Why, I heard on the news the other day—"

"Annadine, we have important matters to take care of now. Will you excuse us?" Claude gave her a chilly smile, then glanced away at some distant object.

"Why, of course. Yes, you go right ahead. I'm sorry, Claude." Annadine stood wringing her hands in quick, jerky movements. She wore an anxious frown.

"Go on, now." Claude got up and guided her out of the room. "I'm sure you're wondering why I asked you to meet me without Singleton or Quentin."

"Yes, I am, frankly," Paul said.

"The work you did was excellent. You didn't take sides. Your report is thorough and objective. Very impressive."

"Thank you."

"From my sources in Baton Rouge, I think it's fair to say that the plant will be built. And when it is completed, Batton Chemical will continue to need your expertise. In fact, we have several sites around the state and in Texas that would benefit from an analysis of their procedures in protecting the environment surrounding them." Claude paused to take another sip from his cup.

"I don't know what to say. It's quite a compliment. But there are larger operations than ours with a track record of handling big corporate clients. Why me?"

"Big isn't necessarily better, and I like your work. My family has lived in this area for over a hundred years. We have always tried to help this community and the people working for us. We look after our own. Besides, I think knowing that you will be working with us to monitor the plant's operations will do much to reassure those with concerns."

"Is that so?" Paul put down his cup.

"You have credibility with our opponents. I want them to trust that we will make safety a priority."

"I see."

"Of course, I don't expect an answer today. I understand that you will want to discuss this with your partner."

"Yes, certainly. It would definitely be a big step for us. In many ways." Paul instantly thought of Savannah.

"It certainly would, not to mention the possibility of work for other companies in this area. With all the pressure from the public and government, many of our business associates would almost certainly be interested in having you do some work for them."

"What is going on here? You are offering him a contract without consulting me or Kyle?" Quentin came into the room and stood before his father with his back to Paul.

"I mentioned it to Kyle last week. He agrees that it would—"

"I see. When did you plan to mention it to me? Apparently it slipped your mind that I happen to be vice president of operations."

"You've been tied up with other things. We were going to discuss it with you Thursday." Growing very still, Claude spoke with an even voice, his face blank of expression.

"No, we weren't going to discuss it. You were going to tell me what you decided to do behind my back!" Quentin shouted.

"This is a business move that's to our advantage for many reasons. This isn't the first time a decision has been made without you being in on it from the start. Kyle and I—"

"Yes, that's right. Kyle and you—but mostly you. I'm the vice president of operations; this should be my decision. And I think we should go with a larger company with more experience dealing with large businesses like ours."

"Quentin, using a small contractor with no ties to the

big names with credibility with environmentalists is what we need. If you stopped throwing this childish temper tantrum for a few minutes, you might see that." Claude stood up and faced his grandson.

"Listen, this is a big step that I would have had to talk over with my partner anyway. Since it's obvious you need to kick it around some, I'll be on my way." Paul started for the door.

"I apologize for my grandson's behavior. He seems to think good manners are unnecessary in business discussions."

"I wouldn't have even been part of this discussion if I hadn't happened to get in from Dallas early. Honore, you may have my grandfather dazzled, but not me. This blatant attempt to cash in on our success won't work." Quentin's voice barked angrily as he first glared at Claude, then turned his ire to Paul. The muscles in his jaw were tight knots showing his barely contained fury.

"We were doing just fine before we got this bid, and we'll survive when this job is over. I started my company without help from my daddy to make me vice president. Who the hell are you to accuse me of trying to hitch a ride on somebody else's coattails?" Paul gave a harsh, contemptuous laugh.

"Let's see how well you do after I spread the word. You won't be able to work for free." Quentin came toward them, but Claude shoved him back into the library with surprising force, considering his age.

"Get real. You have no contacts. You've already been trying to bad-mouth us. It just happens that we have a solid reputation. Yeah, I know about your little campaign. It hasn't worked. And if I ever hear you've been spreading negative comments about my work, you'll have a lawsuit on your hands." Paul came back to the door to the library.

"Is this how you prove to me that you can make major decisions? What next? Are you going to hold your breath until I do what you want?'' Claude whirled around to face his grandson. Though his voice never rose, his tone was withering.

"Grandfather, I—" Quentin stammered, his anger melting under Claude's glare.

"That is quite enough for now. Go put up your things. We'll talk about this later." Claude dismissed him as though he were a naughty little boy.

Quentin flushed deeply. As he left, he shot Paul a fiery look of hatred. Without another word, he raced up the large staircase.

"I apologize again for that ugly scene. Quentin is a bit high-strung. My wife has tended to spoil him, I'm afraid, ever since my son and daughter-in-law died in a car accident when he was only six. He'll come around, though. His feelings are hurt that I didn't ask him first, that's all."

"Sounds like there's more to it than that." Paul shook his head.

"Believe me, that's all it is. Now, talk to your partner and get back to us. No rush, really. We can work out the details later." Claude walked him to the front door.

"We'll consider your offer carefully. But we have as much work as we can handle right now. Besides, your vice president of operations objects. That could be a big problem to any kind of working relationship." Paul walked to his car.

"I'll handle Quentin. Let me know soon." Claude shook hands with Paul and clapped his shoulder.

Paul nodded and was about to get into his car when a movement from a second-story window caught his eye. Quentin stood staring down at him, a stony look on his face. Claude stood on the large veranda, smiling and waving goodbye to him. As he drove away, Paul could sense both sets of eyes following his exit.

*　*　*

"So, what did he want?" Savannah fidgeted with the objects on Paul's desk. She tried to make it sound like a casual question. They had been walking a tightrope, avoiding his connection to the Trosclairs and Batton Chemical. This was the subject they both feared to discuss at any great length. But she couldn't help it. When news of Paul's visit spread, which was inevitable in tiny Beau Chene, all her suspicions came rushing back.

"He wants to throw more business my way. He was pleased with my report," Paul answered, without looking at her. After arranging the silverware on the small dining table, he went back and served their plates straight from the wok. He put down the plate of steaming vegetables. "Dinner is served, madam." He made a little bow.

"How much business?" Savannah still did not look at him, but she showed an intense concentration in arranging the napkin in her lap.

"You know, do some follow-up reviews on the new plant. Take a look at some of their other plants. Here you go. Add just a dash of soy sauce to make my wonder dish perfect."

"Thanks. Sounds like more than a little business to me. Sounds like a major deal that can get you into some serious cash flow." Savannah pushed the vegetables around on her plate.

"As I said, he likes my work." Paul's tone took on an edge.

"I guess so. You supported his claim that the site is just fine for his big toxic producing business that is going to make him even richer."

"My report is based on facts. The fact is, the site he chose is not unsuitable. The heat process to be used is within current regulations. And there is no evidence that the product that comes will not be handled safely or be safe to use."

"No, they just want to put it in our community, not

theirs. Look around, Paul. The dumps, the chemical plants, the refineries surround us. Why don't they crowd the rich white folks? Why didn't you look at other sites? Trosclair's backyard, for example." Savannah stabbed angrily at a large piece of broccoli.

"I was asked to evaluate that site, that's all. That's what I did. It wasn't my job to make judgments or locate an alternative."

"But you could have. You still can." Savannah leaned forward.

"Drop it, will you? I don't want to be caught in the middle of this battle. I did what I was paid to do. Fighting the permit is up to your father and his group."

"Oh, right. You don't want to jeopardize your fat deal. All that money would take wings and fly if you did the right thing."

"Why am I always defending myself to you when it comes to this?" Paul threw down his fork.

"Because you are helping these creeps poison this town, that's why!"

"If you had bothered to read my entire report, you would know they made all the changes in their emission-control systems I suggested even before my report was issued. The last recommendation made was to look at a location further from here so as not to saturate this area."

"Thrown in at the last minute just to appease the opposition. How does it go? Oh yeah, 'It may be advisable to look further down the river, since two other major plants are fairly close to this site.'"

"One reason I started my business was to find a way to help plants operate safely so our people can have jobs without sacrificing their health. I resent like hell that you accuse me of not caring," Paul said, his voice taut with outrage.

"Trosclair got this plant the same way he's gotten everything else in life—by political pull. Doesn't it bother you that he didn't follow the rules, rules that are in place to protect the public? Those blinders you're wearing need to come off," Savannah shot back.

"That may be, but at this point it doesn't matter anymore. There will always be men using influence to get what they want. I happen to think being part of the process can make a difference. We can make them that much more accountable."

"So far, nothing you've said makes me think anything but that Trosclair has you for show. He's so good even you are convinced. Meeting with him about making changes. Ha! As if he's interested in what you think." Savannah gave a short laugh empty of mirth.

"So it finally comes out. Formed an opinion based on what I've told you so far, huh? Maybe Sam was right, you've just been looking for some ammunition to use against Batton Chemical." Paul left the table.

"What? Are you saying—" Savannah bolted from her chair to follow him.

"Yeah, you got real cozy with me right after you found out about my work on the Batton project. All the questions about my work, about the report." Paul paced in front of the couch.

"Who do you think you are, anyway? Get serious. You're an unknown black engineer with a tiny business going nowhere until by some miracle you get this huge contract from a corporation that does international business."

"We got this job by being the best and lowest bidder!" Paul sputtered.

"Right. It was a set-up from the beginning. You went through the motions with that report so you could earn your thirty pieces of silver. It's so transparent you might as well have printed the thing on glass. Where's my coat?" Savannah whirled around and stomped down the hall to the bedroom. "I'm getting the hell out of here."

"There's the door, use it," Paul shouted.

"Don't worry, baby, I will. But get this: it won't work, so get your money and run. We'll shut Big River, count on it." Savannah slammed the door so hard as she left, the whole trailer shook.

Paul's fist clenched and unclenched in frustrated anger. How *dare* she call him a sell-out? Couldn't she see how critical it was, being on the inside of an industry poised to do as much good as harm for the community?

The week of Thanksgiving was beautiful, the weather sunny, yet with a crispness in the air. Beautiful red and yellow leaves hung from the trees and covered front yards. Savannah hardly noticed. Despite all of Tante Marie's attempts to get her into the holiday spirit, Savannah moved around as if in a daze. The week since her confrontation with Paul had been bleak. Even the slightest task seemed to drain her. Though she hated herself for it, she held her breath at the ring of the phone or the tinkling of the shop bell over the door. But he never called, he never came. This was what she had dreaded, why she had never given herself completely to any man: this agony of loving. In silent misery, she followed the same routine every day.

"Cher, did you order those little crawfish lapel pins? I'm gone put some in these gift baskets Mr. Rodrigue ordered for his clients." Tante Marie was helping out during the rush.

"Yeah, and that paint I use for the animals," Antoine yelled from the back.

"By the way, we almost out of Spanish moss. Did you send T-Leon to get some more?" Tante Marie's hands moved quickly to complete another basket.

"Yes, I think I ordered—oh no! I forgot to call. I'll call now." Savannah pulled the phone toward her.

"Use the office line, girl. We gettin' orders on that one. Now we gone hafta pay an express shippin' charge to get that stuff here," Antoine muttered.

"I'm sorry, okay? Can't I make one mistake without getting jumped on? It's not like there aren't a million things to do around here.'' Savannah snatched up the papers with the order information and stomped out.

"What's wrong with that girl? She been either mopin' around with her face hanging down or snappin' folks' heads off.'' Antoine scratched his head.

"You ain't noticed Paul ain't been callin' or been 'round here lately? They had a big fight an' now they ain't speakin'.'' Tante Marie shook her head at her brother-in-law's ignorance.

"Lord, I can't keep up with them kissin' one minute, fussin' the next. They'll be lovey-dovey, next thing you know.'' Antoine chuckled.

"I don't know. This was 'bout him goin' over to Trosclair's house. Got offered a job. Savannah says he's lettin' himself get bought off to help them open more plants and get permits. You know that was a touchy thing with them anyhow. Been more than two weeks now, they still ain't talkin'.''

"Went to Trosclair's house, eh? Does sound bad. But still, I can't hardly see him doing somethin' wrong like that. He just don't seem to be that kind,'' Antoine said.

"Stop talking behind my back. Yeah, he's a real standup guy.'' Savannah marched back into the shop.

"Well, what you think the man gone do? They ask him to evaluate if the site is safe, not if it oughta be in a black neighborhood.''

"Poppy, I can't believe you're defending him.''

"Look here, he told me what he was gonna have in that report long before it come out. He didn't have to do that. And he put in some recommendations he didn't have to, neither.''

"Are you serious?'' Savannah looked up sharply.

"If I'm lyin', I'm flyin'. That boy coulda got himself in some kinda trouble, yeah. Trosclair got a long memory, he could see to it Paul don't get no more business. But he told me he wanted me to know what to expect.''

"Oh.'' Savannah sat staring out the window. She cringed,

remembering the harsh accusations she'd flung at him. She felt ashamed at her behavior, now that she knew how earnestly Paul had tried to help the people of Easy Town. She reached for the phone after several minutes.

"He visitin' his mama and daddy for Thanksgiving. But he gonna be back Sunday." Antoine grinned at her.

"And how do you know I was about to call him?" Savannah blushed.

" 'Cause you been itchin' to call him even before you knowed you was wrong." Antoine gave her a peck on her forehead before going back to his combination storeroom and workshop.

"Cher, don't be so quick to jump on the poor man. I been married, well, never mind how many time, but I know men. And I tell you, he's a good-hearted person." Tante Marie gave her a pat and went back to packing gift baskets.

For Paul, returning home seemed strange now. He saw everything about his family in a whole new context. He longed to talk to his father, but he knew that was out of the question.

The day he announced his big contract with Batton Chemical at the traditional family Sunday dinner, everyone was excited. His oldest sister, Adele, grilled him for details as only she could. In typical big brother fashion, Robert slapped him on the back and began giving him unwanted advice on how to handle himself with the big boys. And his father sat beaming with pride. Always a quiet man, the family gauged his frame of mind by noticing his body language. Charles said little but nodded his approval as he watched his large, boisterous brood. Then, with lightning speed, his mood became dour.

"Don't worry, Robert. When I meet with Claude Trosclair, I'll remember to stand up straight." Paul laughed, but the sound died quickly at the sight of his father's face. Gradually everyone realized the subject was no longer one that pleased Charles. They endured several edgy moments of silence before Robert eased the strain with a funny story from his job. For the next two weeks, Paul tried to think of what had displeased his father. Finally, he went to his mother.

"He won't say anything to me, Mama—just keeps brushing it off." Paul and his mother sat on the front porch of his parents' home.

"You know how he is. Sometimes he got things on his mind." Reba was being evasive, something uncharacteristic of her.

"Mama, come on. His mood changed too quick. Papa was feeling fine, then something happened that Sunday. I want to know what's going on. And I'm not going to let this drop until I do." Paul folded his arms to wait, making it clear he wouldn't leave until he got a satisfactory answer.

Paul could not simply dismiss his father's change of attitude. They had only in the past few years eased their strained relationship. As the youngest and most rebellious son, Paul had always wanted to go his own way. Clashing with his father had become inevitable. Since his graduation from college, Paul had matured and Charles had mellowed. Slowly, they'd made an uneasy peace as Paul had begun to accept his father's wisdom in some things. Charles, in turn, had begun to accept that Paul was not the impetuous, irresponsible young man he had feared.

"I know, son." Reba sighed and patted his leg. "Last thing I wanna see is you and your papa havin' bad feelin's again."

"This is a big break for me. But for some reason, Papa disapproves. There's no pleasing him. No matter how I try." Paul turned to her, his face etched with sadness and frustration.

"It ain't you, baby. It's . . ." Reba groped for a way to explain.

"Of course it's me. It's always me." Paul shook his head.

"Now, that ain't true." Reba's expression changed from

one of uncertainty to one of decision. "Guess you got to know sometime." She got up and went into the house. Several minutes passed before she emerged carrying a bundle of small notebooks tied with a faded blue ribbon. "Take these with you. Read 'em, but don't tell nobody else yet. Your papa would be very angry with me if he knew. But I'd rather you find out the truth than have this come between y'all." Reba pressed the notebooks into his hands.

When he was alone, Paul began reading his grandmother's diaries. Monmon Marguerite had faithfully recorded her thoughts even until the last months. The simple, straightforward manner in which the young Marguerite talked about her family and acquaintances and her wry sense of humor about human nature were a delight to him. More than once the narrative brought her world so alive to him and he became so deeply engrossed that he felt caught in a time warp. It was as though Marguerite was near, watching his expressions, eager to tell him even more than the words on the pages. He marveled at the difference between this lively creature and the subdued, even melancholy, grandmother he knew.

From the date on the first book, it appeared she'd begun keeping her diaries at fourteen. It was in the sixth volume that Marguerite began to speak of her growing affection for a "young gentleman," as she called him. Paul read with amusement the flowery language, some of it in the form of mediocre poetry, singing the praises of this most wonderful man. It was after thirty pages or so that Marguerite wrote of the agony she felt that they could never expect to court like other lovers.

"I truly love Claude. It is painful that I must hide my feelings, as he must hide his. So sweet to be near him, to know that he is just on the other side of the hall as I dust the parlor or sweep the gallery. There are times I let myself imagine that this is our home, that we are man and wife. But always there is a cruel reminder of who I am, a nobody colored girl who is paid to clean up after others.

Guarding my expressions, I find more and more that I must turn my face away from others rather than have my true heart known."

Then, a later entry: "The taste of his lips still lingers. There is warmth where they touched mine, a warmth that covers me completely. It is worth the heartache to be with him."

As he read, Paul had a growing sense of where this affair was heading. Despite feeling like an invader prying into an intimate part of her life, he could not tear himself away.

"May God forgive us. We were lost in each other; no one and nothing else mattered. We became one, forgetting everything."

Inevitably, there were the frightened entries of a girl "in trouble."

"Papa will not look at me, he is so ashamed. He shouted that I had disgraced our family, that I am no better than the whores on the streets of New Orleans. His words stung much more than the sharp slap across my face. Monmon says I must go away to live with Tante Clovis in Grosse Tete. With all this, I long for Claude, yet I know he can never come to me."

The hardships, taunts, and sacrifices she endured were there in writing, described without a hint of self-pity. She spoke of being resigned to it all, just payment for the sin of lust. She later wrote of her realization that she was a passing fancy for Claude, that she'd been no different from other girls in her position who'd deluded themselves that they had inspired true love in the young master. Finally, she had put her son above all else.

"All fanciful dreams must be discarded. This little one needs a strong monmon who can take care of him, no stars in her eyes. I must make a way for us; there's no time, no use for silly whims. This life is hard for me, but I must shield him from this trouble I have brought him into. No matter what Monmon and Papa or Tante Clo say, he will stay with me. No one will take mon petite bébé."

Weeks passed before he had the courage to approach his father. He'd prepared himself for a strong reaction, but the force of it rocked him all the same. Charles had made it all too clear that this was not to be revealed to anyone. Not only did he not want to know more; he insisted the diaries be burned. Luckily, Paul's mother had been able to reason with him on this last, but only because Paul had turned the diaries over to them for safekeeping.

Now, a year later, this secret hung heavy between them. For a long time his father was distant in his presence, unable to meet his eyes. Gradually, with his mother as a bridge, they moved toward each other until Paul felt the gap was almost closed. This Thanksgiving was like so many before, noisy and cheerful. Everyone gathered at his parents' simple wood frame house. His sisters and female cousins kept up a constant chatter above the clamor of their offspring. His two brothers and brothers-in-law talked about hunting, fishing, and football. They also took pleasure in teasing him about his enviable bachelor state. He endured it all good-naturedly, delivering a few jabs back at them. But he was more distracted this time. Seeing his father alone, he joined him in the large den that had been added when they were teenagers.

"You doing okay, Papa?"

"Fine. Just takin' a break from all that racket. Them little ones can keep up enough noise to rattle the walls." He chuckled.

"Yeah, sure can." Paul fidgeted for several minutes, watching the television screen without really seeing it.

"You been doin' good, I hear. Got yourself a new girl, so your mama say." Charles rocked gently in the recliner that was his favorite chair.

"Yes sir, she's something special. I met her in Beau Chene. Where I'm working on that Big River contract."

The smile faded from his father's face as he continued. "That plant Mr. Trosclair opened has stirred up some bad feelings. But he really is trying to make it safe. I met with him several times. He seems reasonable."

"Paul, you know how I feel about this. And I ain't askin' you to hurt your business, neither. Go on with your contract. As for him, what he is or ain't don't mean nothin' to me."

"But he's your—"

"I didn't have but one papa, his name was Henry," Charles snapped back, his voice hoarse with emotion.

"But aren't you curious? I mean, when I read Monmon Marguerite's journal, I felt as though I had never really known her. The girl who wrote those words was so passionate and funny. What I remember is her being real quiet and solemn when I was a little boy. And I couldn't help but wonder what changed her and what the Trosclairs were like."

"Hardship changed her. Having a baby and no husband was a shameful thing for a Catholic girl in those days."

Paul stared at his father until Charles began to fidget. Not for the first time since he'd arrived, he noted the strange mixture of features. Charles had the stocky build of the Ricards, resembling his grandmother's father, whose picture was on the wall near the stairway. But he had the nose and mouth of Claude Trosclair. His hair, thick but cut close to his head, was curly. There the resemblance ended, as he displayed the mannerisms of Henry Honore. The way he held his head or sat back with his arms folded when he was thinking deeply about something reminded Paul of Pawpaw Honore. Charles was fiercely loyal to the memory of the man he considered to be his one, his only true, father.

"Isn't there anything you want to know about them? About him?"

"Look, it don't matter to me. I got my family. What the Trosclairs do, what they like, is nothin' to me. They live in their world, we live in ours. When you try to bring them together, somebody gets hurt. Let it stay buried, Paul."

Charles got up abruptly and went into the living room to join the rest of the family.

Paul sighed. Maybe he was right. What did it matter after almost fifty years? They could never be "family" in the true sense of the word. His curiosity was not enough of a reason to hurt his father or cause his family the kind of notoriety such information could bring. Better to let secrets stay secret.

"Everything all right, sweetie?" Paul's mother took his hand as she sat next to him. "Why you not in here with us? Your brother is tellin' some of them silly jokes. Got us cryin' from laughin' so."

"Yeah, Robert always could tell jokes."

"One thing, he ain't even brought the first smile to his papa's face." Reba looked at her son, waiting for an answer.

"It's all right, Mama. Really."

"Your papa wants this kept among us three. You know how he felt 'bout his mama. Took years for her to live it down. Charles heard the whispers when he was a little boy. It was only 'cause folks had so much respect—some a fear of Mr. Henry—that the talk was never more than that. Please let it go. And be careful. The Trosclairs might turn nasty if you bring this up."

"Don't worry, Mama. I just wanted to learn a little more about them, to understand what it was like for Monmon back then. The Trosclairs have nothing I want. No one knows, and I'll be sure it stays that way."

Paul rushed into the house, frantic to get to the ringing phone. Throwing his bag down, he snatched up the receiver just in time to hear the dial tone.

"Damn!"

He held the phone for several minutes, first dialing, then pressing the button to hang up. The sharp ring while he still held the button caused him to jump.

"Hello." He spoke softly into the mouthpiece. He thought of Savannah's full lips curving into a smile.

"Hello to you, too, big boy." Sam laughed. "Save your bedroom voice, man. It's a little too deep for my taste."

"Very funny. Is there a reason for this call, and if so, can we get to it?" Paul spoke sharply.

"Hey, I call to say I hope you had a nice Thanksgiving, and *this* is what I get."

"Happy turkey day to you, too. Sorry about that."

"No problem. Been there, my brother. The other thing I wanted to tell you is, it looks like all the publicity has turned up the heat on the politicians. Seems your lady friend and her group will get their day in court."

"What do you mean?" Paul asked sharply.

"The Environmental Protection Agency has filed a suit saying the Big River plant is burning hazardous waste without a permit. Seems they don't buy it that they are recyclers turning toxic waste into a safe aggregate."

"Wow. Talk about things getting heated. This town is already divided." Paul frowned. He rubbed his chin deep in reflection at the possible consequences of this latest turn of events.

"Just thought you'd like to know. My pal at DEQ says it should be announced Thursday."

"Umm-hum."

"Say, man, you just about through there. You planning to ever come back to Lafayette?" After several moments of silence, "Anybody home?"

"Yeah, I mean, sure," Paul answered after a pause. "Just a few more loose ends."

"Guess I know what that's about. No problem. Bye now. Oh, and tell Ms. St. Julien 'hello' for me." With another laugh, Sam hung up before Paul could say anything.

Twenty minutes later, he stood on the wide front porch feeling very conspicuous. The late-afternoon sun was bright, but it provided little warmth from the chill wind that blew red and brown leaves across the lawn.

"Happy Thanksgiving." He watched her expression anxiously.

"Happy Thanksgiving." Savannah opened the door wide and stepped back.

Without hesitating, before saying anything else, he pulled her to him.

The old woman carefully lowered herself into the large overstuffed chair in front of the brick fireplace. With a low grunt of satisfaction, she arranged a large woolen shawl around her shoulders.

"Come on, gal. Bring me my coffee." Her voice was still strong despite her physical weakness.

"Sit still, Monmon. You in such a hurry all the time," LaShaun barked back from the old-fashioned kitchen. With a rattle of cups and spoons, she came into the room balancing a large tray.

"Ah, just right." Monmon Odette smacked her lips after sipping the hot coffee cautiously. She cradled the cup with hands gnarled by arthritis. After another sip, she sat back in the chair and studied her granddaughter. "What you been up to, eh, gal?"

"What you mean, Monmon?" LaShaun stirred her coffee with languid motions.

"Heh, heh. Know you been up to somethin' for sho when you answer me a question with a question. Therese's chile is home. Lookin' jest like her monmon, too. Pretty thing." Monmon Odette eyed LaShaun. "You been to see her." The last was a statement.

"I dropped by to welcome her back. Jumpy little thing, though." LaShaun grinned into her cup.

"Humm, big job didn't last up there. Now she here."

"Yes, she's here. Strutting around like she owns the

place. Just like always." LaShaun's grin faded into a grimace.

"St. Julien taught her well." Monmon Odette spat into the fireplace, a grimace of contempt twisting her face. "Every time I turn, look like dem in the way of me or mine."

"No, Monmon. She won't stand in the way of what I want. I know just what to do about her."

"I want Antoine to pay for what he done to Francine. Drunk herself to death, grievin' over dat man. Therese's death didn't change nuthin', neither. Don't know what conjuh she put on him, but Therese had hold even from the grave."

"Well, I'm not like Momma. Savannah won't take from me, and no man will ever be anything but a way to get what I want."

"Savannah not her monmon, either; best to watch her close. And come to dat, keep your eye on that man friend you got. More than one trained animal done turned on him what thought he was the master."

"I know what I'm doing, Monmon. He's mine as long as I say he's mine. And Savannah is about to start feeling sorry she set foot back in Beau Chene."

"Mais, yeah. Here somethin' you might wanna use." Monmon Odette gave a low chuckle as she dug deep into a large covered basket she kept near her chair on the floor. She pressed an object into LaShaun's hand.

"Oh yes. This will do, for a start. This will do fine. Merci, Monmon." LaShaun fingered the object and stared into the fire.

Chapter 6

Savannah sipped the hot coffee in her mug. Smiling, she read the bold green letters bordered with holly in the corner of the first page of Beau Chene's modest weekly paper.

"Twenty-four shopping days 'til Christmas," she whispered to herself. Gazing ahead, she didn't hear her aunt come into the kitchen.

"Penny." Tante Marie had leaned near her ear from behind.

"What?" Savannah blinked rapidly, startled from her reverie.

"For your thoughts."

"Just thinking how this is my favorite holiday."

"When you were little, every holiday was your favorite when it arrived. You loved to make a big fuss with decorations and such."

"Remember the time when I was—oh, eight, I guess, and I insisted we leave oats for Santa's reindeer? Poppy talked for days trying to convince me that they had too many stops to make, so Santa would feed them well before they left the North Pole." Savannah laughed.

"Coo, but didn't you carry on 'bout them poor hungry reindeer. Then there was the year you just had to decorate every room with a tiny Christmas tree."

"I tried real hard to celebrate, especially at Christmas. For Poppy."

"So much burden on a baby, tryin' to comfort your daddy."

"Every Christmas of my childhood I remember watching him miss Mama. Pain was written on his face each time he heard a song she used to sing or when we hung the ornaments she'd made on the tree. I could never make him smile, not for very long."

"Cher, you made your daddy so happy, don't you think no different. But the love he missed was something you couldn't give—the love of a woman for a man."

"I always felt that I had failed him somehow." Savannah felt tears pushing to spill forward. She pressed her lips together.

"Mon Dieu, non. You are his heart. His sadness was a natural grief, not your fault. Not your fault, cher." Tante Marie wrapped her soft, chubby arms around her.

"Thank you. You always say just what I need to hear." Savannah dried her eyes. "But there's something between us that hasn't been discussed."

Tante Marie began searching through the cupboards, gathering ingredients to bake more cookies for the children at her church.

"Now, where I put that bakin' soda? You been rummagin' through my cabinets, I can tell. I always put it in the same place, an' it ain't here."

"Tante Marie, about Mama's death . . . I need to know, please." Savannah placed her hand gently on her aunt's arm to stop her from moving away.

"Oh, cher. Your daddy would have a fit if I was to—"

"I'm twenty-six years old, not a child to be sheltered from the truth anymore. My mother was taken from me so early. Poppy and I mourned her, but he, at least, had more of an explanation of why or how than I did. All I had was an emptiness, and all the whispered rumors. Don't you think I deserve more than that?''

"But that was thirty years ago; it ain't no use to bring that up again. Start the trouble all over again's all it'll do.'' Tante Marie rubbed her hands together as she talked.

"It seems that the trouble, whatever you mean by that, has never gone away. Since we were kids, LaShaun has made it clear how she feels. But why? Tante Marie, please.'' Savannah took her aunt's hands, separated them, and held them in her own as she guided her to a chair.

"That gal is no good. She don't look just like her mama for nothin'. Hateful, downright mean to get what she wants.'' Tante Marie stared out the window, her face a grim mask. It was as if she could see the two women.

"Francine, LaShaun's mama. I heard she was pretty.'' Savannah spoke softly, encouraging her aunt to remember out loud.

"Mais, yeah. LaShaun got them same eyes. Folks say they got them eyes 'cause Francine's daddy was a roogaroo, a demon.'' Tante Marie shook herself as though feeling a sudden chill. Her voice dropped low and became somber with the telling of a dark tale whispered through the years. "I used to hear my memere say how old Odette's first husband left her. Said he swore up and down she would go out to the bayou at night an' stay gone 'til daybreak. Come back looking all wild, clothes half off her. Sho, they is pretty in their way, but everythin' they touch moodee, cursed, no good.'' Tante Marie's voice took on a grim intensity.

"Cursed how?'' Savannah leaned forward, already lost in the past with her aunt.

"Now, you can't tell it to look at her now, but Odette was fine lookin' herself in her young days. She could get them men. But one by one they was gone. A couple just up and disappeared. Some say they buried out in them woods behind that house with the others. Some say they saw somethin' what scared 'em so bad, they left town and didn't tell nobody where they was goin' so Odette couldn't find 'em.

"Then all her chirren come to a bad end, one by one. That oldest boy got drunk and ran his car off the road into the bayou. Three days later, they found him in there, drowned. The youngest boy, Jules, went down to New Orleans, got into a fight. Some man stabbed him to death. She got plenty property from them two husband she buried. She done seen her share of misery, buried 'em all on that property, too."

"A cemetery is near their house?" Savannah shivered despite the warmth of the kitchen.

"Family plot, yes indeed. Odette's monmon, papa, two husbands, and three chirren. Back a ways in the woods, but there all the same." Tante Marie accepted the cup of black coffee put in front of her.

"How did Francine die?"

"In a fire. She was always gettin' drunk and runnin' off with some man. Wasn't nothin' for her to stay gone a week. She was laid up in some old raggedy roomin' house over the other side of Bayou Lafourche, whorehouse is what it was. Anyway, they say she fell asleep smokin'. Heard that old place went up like a matchbook."

"What a horrible way to die. But what does that have to do with Mama? With me?" Savannah said.

"Odette says your daddy was the reason she died." Tante Marie stopped. She seemed to falter in the telling of the tale for the first time since she had begun.

"Tante Marie, why would she say such a thing?" Savannah placed her hand on her aunt's arm to prompt her to continue.

"Francine was crazy for Antoine, had been since they was little. They all grew up together, Antoine, Francine, and your maman, though Therese was younger. Trouble started when they got to be teenagers, I guess. Francine was pretty enough, but wild, with a mean streak. At first,

Antoine found her exciting. They were sneakin' round to the juke joints. You see, back then, we wasn't allowed to go out on dates alone at that age, just a boy and girl. Lord, how Francine used to hang onto Antoine. Anyway, Therese had always been a pretty child, too, but when she turned fifteen, she just seemed to blossom overnight. Beautiful, she was. Had pretty dark brown skin so clear, she looked like one of them movie stars, 'cept she didn't have no powder on her face. Big, dark eyes with long black lashes. She was kinda shy, real sensitive. A good-hearted person. Antoine started payin' more and more attention to her and less and less to Francine. True enough, he had a time pullin' away from Francine. But it got to be clear Therese was the one for him. Francine got frantic, doin' all kinda things. Started runnin' with all kinds of men, tryin' to make Antoine jealous. But that didn't do nothin' but make him know she was too wild for his taste. Fact is, he was hard in love with Therese by that time. Told me once he'd always loved her, just hadn't realized it.

" 'Course your maman loved him, too, but she thought he was so gone over Francine that she didn't have no chance. They was somethin' to see. Walkin' around in a daze, so wrapped up in each other it was like wasn't nobody else on this earth. Antoine only laughed when folks told him 'bout the mess with Francine. He used to say she was just bein' herself, that she liked havin' attention from all them men. But I knew better. So did Therese. She tried to talk to Francine, tell her she understood that she was hurtin'. Francine spat in her face like an alley cat ready to strike.

"It was when Antoine and Therese got engaged that things got out of hand. Francine went crazy. Late at night, she'd show up outside our house, screamin' threats. When Antoine went out to talk to her, she'd start wailin' so, it sounded like a lost soul. That went on for months. It got quiet after the wedding. 'Cept that was worse in a way.'' Tante Marie wiped her eyes with a shaky hand.

"Therese started having nightmares. She started bein' so jumpy, she couldn't hardly stand bein' in the house alone. She swore Francine was watchin' her day and night, that Francine was burnin' candles on her. Got so bad, Antoine decided to take a temporary job in Morgan City, as much to get her away as for the money. They lived there for almost a year and Therese seemed to get stronger every day. They even come back to visit a few times. One day Francine showed up at our cousin's house. She spoke to everybody, then stared hard at Therese. Your maman stared right back. Before we knew what was happenin', Therese walked right up to Francine without battin' an eye. Real calm, without raisin' her voice, Therese told her that she was not scared no more, that she had a spirit workin' for her that was stronger than anything Francine had fooled herself she could do. Francine grinned real evil-like, made some kinda sign, then walked away without lookin' back.

"When they moved back six months later, Therese was pregnant with you. For the first time since they'd gotten married, Therese was happy. She wasn't nervy, like before. She went through being pregnant with no problem. Folks was whisperin' that Francine was gonna do somethin' to her and the baby. But when you was born, normal, healthy, just as pretty as your monmon, folks said old Odette must've lost her power. But then, Therese started to fret every time you coughed. When you had the colic so bad, she was beside herself, thinkin' you was on death's door. She took to gettin' up all through the night, checkin' on you. There was times she woke Antoine up screamin' that you wasn't breathin'.

"Antoine and the doctor finally got her to settle down some, but she went back to bein' on edge just the same. It was two years later that your monmon started gettin' sick. Therese started havin' pains in her joints. She was tired all the time; some days she could hardly get outta bed. She'd get headaches and fevers for no reason. Then she started forgettin' things, like where stuff was in the cabinets, or the way to church. She just went down, cher. Broke my heart to see her waste away. Antoine took her to the doctor. He started treatin' her for anemia, then gave her nerve pills. Doctor Patin ended up givin' her medicine for high blood pressure, too. A year later she was dead. That's when the whispers started. Folks said Odette had worked a powerful gris-gris on Therese." Tante Marie took a deep breath, then made the sign of the cross.

"It can't be true. I won't believe that. It's all just old superstition," Savannah said, her voice unsteady. She gripped her hands together.

"Superstition can affect folks in a powerful way, cher."

"You believe it, then, that they killed Mama?"

"I'm a Christian, baby. I believe in spirits, good and bad."

With the announcement that the Department of Environmental Protection would bring suit against Batton Chemical and the Big River plant, the level of tension in Beau Chene rose. People who had been friends and neighbors all their lives quit speaking to each other. Antoine became the focus of hostility from those who were in favor of the plant. There were men who confronted him about trying to take their jobs. Savannah was getting very worried for him for the first time.

"Hey, what's with the frown, baby?" Paul tugged at Savannah's chin playfully. They sat together over dinner.

"Nothing. I just hope this Christmas isn't spoiled by everything going on." Savannah stirred the untouched bowl of corn-and-shrimp soup in front of her.

"It's going to be a fantastic Christmas. We'll be together. I'm really looking forward to getting you under some of that mistletoe." Paul's caress changed from playful to loving. His eyes shone bright with yearning for her.

"I'm looking forward to spending the holidays with you, too." The frown was smoothed away as she returned his gaze.

Once again, a touch of his hand transformed her. No other man could arouse such a craving, could soothe away all apprehension with so little effort. Savannah felt a thrill, knowing that this marvelous man cared for her. And that she no longer doubted. Each time he looked at her, it was written in his eyes.

"I know you're preparing that report, and maybe I've said some mean things about that." Savannah grasped his hand firmly.

"Savannah, you don't have to apologize. Really, honey. Your commitment to see that your community is safe is one of the things that drew me to you." Paul raised her hand to his lips. "I understood where you were coming from. Even when you took a few well-aimed licks at me." He grinned at her.

"Hope it didn't do too much damage. You don't seem to be bruised still." Savannah grinned back.

"Well, there's one wound left. But it's one that hurts so good." His lips curved into a smile that was warm with passion.

"What wound is that?" Savannah held her breath. The grip of his hand caused a physical, aching hunger to ripple through her.

"The wound on my heart. Feel." He raised her hand to his chest. "I don't care if it doesn't heal. This is one injury I'm more than willing to live with."

Paul was filled with joy to see the sparkle in Savannah's eyes. For too long, he'd convinced himself that falling in love was the last thing he needed. Now, he was astonished and delighted to find himself rushing headlong into the very thing he'd made efforts for so long to avoid. Savannah ignited his passion in a way that had taken complete hold over him. He wanted to meld his life with hers, to wipe away any barrier to having her with him.

"I don't want Big River or Batton Chemical to come between us," Savannah said, her voice trembling.

"We won't let it." Paul spoke with more conviction than

he felt. More than ever, the secret of his relationship to Claude hung heavy on him. Seeing the trust and affection in her face, he felt a twinge of guilt. "Nothing will come between us," he said firmly. Pulling her to him, he sat with his arms about her in the booth.

Back at the shop, Savannah breezed through inventory, a task she normally grumbled about. Still feeling the elation of Paul's words, she no longer felt the tension surrounding the Big River plant that existed between the town's residents. But threats scrawled on the door waited for her when she left the shop that evening. She was glad her father had gone out of town on business. With help from Leon, she saw that the ugly words were quickly scrubbed away.

"Was you gone tell me 'bout that graffiti on the shop?" Antoine gave her an admonishing look at home that night. He stood in the door to the den.

"I didn't want you to worry, Poppy."

"In case you done forgot, I'm grown. I been handlin' hard times a lot longer than you, little girl."

"That was just some juvenile delinquent with too much time on his hands. Forget it, Poppy."

"I hope so, cher. I surely do hope so."

The next day they arrived at the shop to find one of the large windows shattered.

"Merry Christmas from the Big River fan club, eh?" Savannah looked around in dismay.

"Could have been worse." Antoine headed for the phone to get the glass replaced.

Savannah sighed deeply, then set about cleaning up the mess. Moments later, she was grateful to see Paul coming through the door. He grabbed a broom and started sweeping up glass.

"Did you file a report with the sheriff?" Paul picked up a basket that had been smashed.

"Yeah. Won't do much good, though. There are no

witnesses, no physical evidence left behind to identify who did it.''

"Don't let it get you down. This coward won't dare stand up to you in the daylight.''

"One thing, I'd better get used to it. By the time that trial starts in February, this town might be split so that it will never be the same.'' Savannah began rearranging the window display as best she could with what was left, replacing items from the shelves.

"There's got to be some sort of compromise, a way we can have industry that is safe *and* good-paying jobs.''

"Maybe so, but compromise means both sides give something up. Obviously Trosclair doesn't see that as an attractive option.'' Savannah pointed to the large shards of glass in the wastebasket.

"You don't believe Trosclair did this? That's really stretching it.''

"He may not have broken the glass, but that doesn't mean this wasn't his handiwork. He has some real scum working for him. Remember good old Manny? And he's not the only one.''

"Oh, come on. The man is wealthy, cultured, and from what I've seen since meeting with him, concerned about how Big River affects the community. This sort of thing doesn't seem to be his style at all.'' Paul sounded defensive.

"Claude Trosclair is concerned about one thing, his own interests. He can be vicious when someone gets in his way. And you better remember that.''

"What do you mean?''

"How's he going to react when he finds out you're getting friendly with the enemy?''

"Number one, I really don't think he's the person you say he is, and number two, who I get friendly with is my business. It has nothing to do with the work Batton Chemical pays me to do. Which, by the way, is pretty much completed.'' Setting the broom aside, he came up behind her and hugged her around the waist.

"Yeah, but he wants you to do even more work for him."
Savannah turned to face him.

"And if I do, it will be business only. Now, give me a
smile." He brushed his lips up and down the side of her
face.

"I can give you a little more than that. How about some
sugar, sugar?" Savannah forgot her anxiety, all her doubts
swept away by the intoxicating touch, smell, and feel of
him.

A horn blew and someone let out a long whistle. Realiz-
ing that they were on display just as much as her father's
merchandise, they separated.

"Lady, you had me so wrapped up, I forgot where we
were for a minute." Paul laughed, then became serious.
Gazing into her dark brown eyes, he felt it hit him full
force how much she meant to him. Never had he known
such sweetness and strength in one woman. A strong need
to protect her always surged through him. He twisted a
thick, dark lock of her hair through two fingers, savoring
its velvety texture. "You mean a lot to me," he murmured.

Savannah stared at him for a long moment before brushing her hand lightly along his jawline. All that had gone
on between them, the fights and the loving moments, came
together in one magical instant, forcing her to acknowledge the sweet surrender of her heart to this marvelous
man. A man whose strength, caring, and tenderness had
won her completely.

"Hey, y'all ain't no help, standin' around starin' soulfully
into each other's eyes. Get to work," Antoine rumbled a
good-natured scolding.

For the next three hours they laughed, exchanged jokes
on one another, and worked to restore order to the shop.
Savannah felt as though she really was home now, a home
she'd missed all her life without even knowing it.

The crisp, sunny days added to the general mood of
happy anticipation of Christmas Day. All around Beau
Chene, homes and businesses were decked with traditional

decorations. Few doors did not sport a large green wreath wrapped gaily in red or gold ribbon. Mistletoe, gathered from oak trees in the woods surrounding the town, hung in restaurants, shops, and even the gas station, gleefully used as an excuse to get a quick kiss when the unwary stood beneath it. Laughter and good food were plentiful. Adults and children alike eagerly awaited the arrival of Papa Noël.

The division over the Big River plant put a strain on the festive mood, and especially the usually jovial community meeting to plan the town's annual celebration, which would include a traditional bonfire on the levee on Christmas Eve. After a bumpy start, old Mr. Melancon blurted out, "Aw, come on, y'all, it's Christmas, after all. Let's put all dat aside and make dis a Joyeux Noël." After that, there was a more relaxed attitude. Men who'd argued with each other worked side by side. All hands were needed to construct the elaborate creations that would be set ablaze so spectacularly. With each passing day the logs, large and small, gradually took shape. It wasn't long before a viking ship, a grand mansion, a fire truck, even a large rocking horse were among the temporary landmarks that took shape high above River Road.

Paul threw himself into the preparations as though he had been a part of them all his life. He marveled at the inventiveness that went into the building of each figure. He pitched in to help erect the booths that would sell barbecue, sausage, chicken, and beef. Large cast-iron pots that would be used to fry hog skin cracklins, not used since the last festival, were brought out of storage. His mouth watered as he listened to the men and women who'd cook describe the jambalaya, gumbo, pralines, and sweet potato pies they'd make for the occasion.

Savannah was kept very busy by the growing number of visitors in town. Last-minute gifts, some to be shipped as far away as Canada, claimed her attention for most of the day. She was grateful that Leon was out of school for the

holidays. His extra pair of hands were much needed with
Antoine and Tante Marie setting up a booth for the Christmas Bonfire Festival. Yet she and Paul found time to be
together, happily planning Christmas Day. At Antoine's
suggestion, Savannah had invited Paul's family to town.

"They'll love it, cher. Since you so nervous, maybe you'll
feel better meetin' 'em the first time on your stompin'
grounds. Besides, who don't wanna come to see the bonfire, eh?"

"Poppy, besides being handsome, you're a genius."
Savannah planted a big kiss on his beaming face.

"Now, are you certain your mother will like this cameo
pin? I want to be sure," Savannah questioned Paul. "And
your father, you did say he could use this key chain with
the little tools attached? And the cakes and cookies for
everybody else?" Savannah was critically evaluating the still
unwrapped gifts under the large Christmas tree in her
living room.

"Babe, I told you, they'll love it all. Especially your Tante
Marie's cookies and cakes. And you." Paul, seated on the
couch, patted the cushion next to him.

"I just want us to get off on the right foot." Savannah
sat next to him, moving comfortably into the crook of his
arm.

"It isn't about material things with them, they're good
people. They'll see you for the beautiful person you are
and make you feel at home. Trust me."

"If you say so." Savannah sighed.

Looking around, it seemed to Savannah that combining
the two families was an unqualified success. Mrs. Honore
and Tante Marie took to each other instantly. They chattered away in French about everything from cooking to
what it had been like in the old days. There were games,

eating, and story-telling in every room. Paul was like the Pied Piper with his nieces and nephews. Watching him play with them, getting them sweets, wiping their little faces clean, Savannah felt a longing to put her arms around him. His red sweater did not conceal his muscular build. The memory of how it felt to be pressed against that hard warmth caused a stirring deep within her. As he gave a tiny kiss to one of the youngest of his nieces, Savannah remembered the touch of his full lips on hers. Suddenly, Paul looked up into her eyes. His smile seemed to say he knew exactly what was on her mind and that he felt the same way. The noise faded, everyone else disappeared. A voice to her left forced her to leave that magical place. She sighed shakily, hoping what she was feeling wasn't written all over her face.

"An attorney, very impressive." Paul's oldest sister, Adele, stood almost as tall as he did. Her hair was cut in a short pageboy style. When she blinked, her bangs moved.

"Takes brains." Bridget nodded. "You a criminal lawyer? You know, defending the innocent? Getting at the truth so that justice can be served?"

"Well, not exactly." Savannah shifted uneasily. She was beginning to think they were being sarcastic. But when she looked into Bridget's large brown eyes, she saw nothing but a guileless twenty-two-year-old.

"Excuse my little sister. She loves to watch Perry Mason reruns."

"Unfortunately, it was dry old corporate law." Savannah couldn't help but laugh at Bridget's obvious disappointment.

"It's wonderful all the same. Mergers and such can be just as cutthroat," Bridget declared brightly. "Tisha, get down from there!" She rushed off to pluck her two-year-old from the top of the piano.

"That child can climb anything." Adele turned her attention back to Savannah. "Thanks for inviting us. I haven't seen Paul this happy since the day his business got its first contract. In fact, he can't do anything but smile whenever he talks about you.''

"Well, I—'' Savannah blushed.

"We're all thrilled. He's the last one, you know. The rest of us are married.'' Adele leaning forward, stared at her, blinking rapidly.

"Uh, yeah. We haven't quite gotten that far yet.'' Savannah ran her fingers through her hair. She cleared her throat and looked around the room.

"Sorry, didn't mean to embarrass you. It's just that Paul has always been the intense, quiet one, like Daddy. The rest of us are rowdy.'' She waved her hand toward her siblings. Laughing and talking boisterously, they seemed immediately to connect with Savannah's relatives.

"Robert, as usual, has got somebody in stitches with one of his jokes. Then there's Sheldon. He's in heaven whenever he can find somebody willing to talk about gulf fishing. And Bridget, she could make friends with the devil, given half the chance. Seriously, though, I hope you'll come visit us often.''

"Thank you, I will.'' Savannah felt like she now had an older sister, too. She became a little misty eyed when Adele took her hand and gave it a gentle squeeze before letting go.

"Don't you believe anything she says about me.'' Paul, who'd been watching, was pleased at the way his sisters had obviously warmed up to Savannah.

"She hasn't said anything about you. Why? There must be a lot to tell.'' Savannah winked at Adele.

"Girlfriend, can we talk? Since he brought it up, there was that ugly incident when he was in the tenth grade.'' Adele quickly bought into the game.

"Oh, I was framed! Greg put that pig embryo in the jar of formaldehyde in Miss Trill's bookbag,'' Paul protested with a wide grin.

"Hey, y'all, it's gettin' dark. Let's head out for big fun,'' Robert called out.

It took another ten minutes to get everyone dressed warmly and to line up the caravan of cars so that they could all arrive at the same time. Savannah and Paul rode together in his Jeep. Sitting next to him, feeling his hard thigh pressed to hers, was so right. She placed her hand there, wondering how long she could resist him. Doubts and fears of the strong emotion he stirred in her held her back. But now, being here with him, that emotion was steadily chipping away at them, until they seemed small and unfounded. This was a season of joy and hope. Surrounded by family and being with Paul filled her with both.

It was Christmas Eve and excitement was in the air. The downtown historic area was decorated with tinsel and ribbons. But it was the thousands of twinkling Christmas lights that brought the most "oohs" and "aahs" from the thousands who strolled the small main street. The citizens of Beau Chene had spent weeks stringing them from every rooftop, in every tree and shrub of the entire six-block area.

There were five-foot-high wooden toy soldiers, teddy bears, and other figures carved by locals. The antique shop's front porch was set up as a replica of a traditional nineteenth-century Acadian home at Christmastime, complete with carols being sung in Cajun French by a family dressed in period costume.

"I have to say, this is the best one yet." Paul's mother turned around. She and her grandchildren darted from one display to the next, squealing with delight at each.

"Now, for a little time alone." Paul seized Savannah's hand and quickly pulled her away from the others.

"What are you doing?" she gasped, looking back at the crowd they were leaving. Adele and Bridget were merrily waving goodbye, giggling at the surprise on her face.

"They'll understand. Let's get a good spot for the bonfires."

Most of the crowd was still wandering the streets below. There were relatively few people on the levee since the bonfires would not be lit for another hour or so. They followed the soft dirt path along the top of the levee, gazing at the imaginative structures that would shortly light the way for Papa Noël to find his way down the river.

"Here, over here." Paul, smiling mysteriously, led her down the slope of the levee to a small wooden lean-to with a bench. He swung his arms wide with a flourish. "For you, Mademoiselle. A gift from your humble servant."

"Merci beaucoup." She sat down, making a great show of daintily arranging the folds of invisible full skirts.

They rested against each other, embracing, kissing with increasing passion.

"This is a very special Christmas for me. You're the reason." Paul ran his hand lightly across her back, pleased at the responding shiver of delight.

"Very special." That was all she could manage to say, feeling that strange painful, yet pleasurable, hunger between her thighs. She brushed her lips along his neck, aching to unbutton his shirt.

"Savannah." Paul spoke her name, his voice made even deeper with desire.

"Yes," Savannah whispered huskily before pulling away.

They were forced to gather their wits again at the approach of more and more people.

"Look, here they are!" one of Paul's nephews called gaily to the others.

Soon they were again swept along in the general mood of revelry. They began to dance as a band started to play zydeco. Moving together, they two-stepped to a love song sung in Creole French.

"Well, well. Y'all having a good time, I see. Hi, Paul. Nice to see you again." LaShaun appeared out of the darkness, a handsome man at her side.

"Hello, LaShaun. How you doing?" Paul smiled at her and nodded.

Savannah looked from her to him. Suddenly, the magic of the night was gone. What did LaShaun mean, "again"?

A familiar sinking sensation grew in the pit of Savannah's stomach. In a flash, Savannah remembered Devin's deception and that Paul had been in Beau Chene for several weeks before she returned home. And Tante Marie told her how he had his pick of women. *LaShaun?* Savannah fumed. Staring at him, she wanted to slap that goofy grin from his face.

"You two know each other?" Savannah was stone faced.

"Oh yes. I showed Paul around some when he first got to town." LaShaun smiled as if she could say more, but wouldn't.

"I see." Savannah pulled away from Paul and folded her arms.

"Let's go, girl." LaShaun's companion tugged at her elbow.

"Hold on, Andre." LaShaun flashed him a warning look that caused him to let go. "See you later. Let me know if you need to do any more research." She looked directly into Paul's eyes. "Bye now." She flounced off, Andre in tow.

"You failed to mention your—acquaintance—with that one." Savannah sat heavily on the bench.

"Sure, she was nice to me when I first got here and didn't know anybody. She helped me do some background research on how the land was used for the last twenty years or so—flood patterns, stuff like that."

"How nice for you to have found a friend so quickly." Savannah looked ahead into the darkness.

"What? Say, you're jealous!" Paul was clearly delighted.

"Get real. Just disgusted at your taste in pals," Savannah snapped.

"Look at me. Come on." Paul cupped her face with his hands, gently turning her to look into his eyes. "There never was anything between me and LaShaun. Never."

Savannah searched his face and eyes for any sign of deception. All she saw was an earnest plea for her to believe in him. As if in slow motion, she watched him lower his head to her. His full, warm lips enveloped hers; his hands caressed her shoulders, then traveled to her waist. He held her tenderly, kissing her eyes, her nose, whispering her name.

Shouts of glee went up as one by one the wooden structures caught flame, lighting the night sky. They sat watching, the pop and crackle of the fires all around them. As the band played "Silent Night," hundreds of voices rose into the star-filled darkness as the flames began to die. Paul and Savannah linked hands with family.

"It was just beautiful, being here with y'all. Me and Charles want you to come to Crowley now, here?" Paul's mother and father stood next to their station wagon. Each gave her a hug. While her husband got into the car to start the engine and get the heater going, Reba lingered.

"Thank y'all for coming, too." Savannah already felt close to her.

"Paul really likes you, and I'm glad he found somebody special." Reba smiled broadly, her plump face alight with cheer. She tugged on her wool coat and pressed a knit hat down over her tightly curled hair. "He's a good man, and I ain't just sayin' dat 'cause he mine," Reba chuckled.

"I know," Savannah replied.

Then, with a serious expression, she put both hands on Savannah's shoulders. "Hold on to each other, don't let nothin' come between you." Reba hugged her again before joining her husband. She waved as they drove off.

Savannah pondered Reba's last statement. What did she think could come between them? Reba had spoken as if there were something in particular that would cause a rift, something Savannah needed to be warned about. She started to question Paul, but the feeling was vague; she didn't really know what to ask. The tiny troubling thoughts were interrupted by the rush and crush of goodbyes to her family. Shouts of "Merry Christmas" or "Joyeux Noël" echoed as loved ones left for home.

"I don't know 'bout nobody else, but I'm beat down to

my socks. Ain't gone give Papa Noël no excuse not to leave my presents. Goodnight." Tante Marie yawned widely.

"I'm right behind you. Let these young folk stay up all night. Night, cher. Night, son." Antoine kissed Savannah and shook Paul's hand.

They watched the taillights of her father's car fade into the night. In the distance they heard the music of a band.

"Wanna go to Sack Daddy's?" Paul grabbed her and began to sway to the music.

"No. I promised Charice I'd help her wrap the toys tonight. You know kids, she'll have to wait until they're totally exhausted and sound asleep before she can risk bringing them out of hiding."

"Then you could use an extra set of hands. Let's go."

"I thought you were going to spend the night with your parents." Laughing, she followed him to his truck.

"Hey, it's barely eleven. It'll only take me an hour to get there. Let's go. Santa has other stops, you know." He winked.

They spent the next several hours wrestling with complicated instructions and struggling to fit big batteries in tiny spaces. When they were through, it was almost three o'clock in the morning.

"Whew, thanks for the help. Next time I'll pay more attention to the words 'Some assembly required.'" Charice sank onto the sofa.

"No problem, it was kind of fun." Savannah poked Paul in the ribs. She howled when he responded by tickling her mercilessly.

"Quiet, you two," Charice shushed them playfully. "I want to get at least two hours of sleep before those little gremlins pop out of bed at the crack of dawn."

After draining their last cup of café au lait, they left for home. Holding hands with Paul during the ride, Savannah wished this night could last forever. She sighed softly when they arrived at her front door.

"Merry Christmas, ma chérie." Paul held her tightly, his mouth covering hers.

Savannah parted her lips to admit his soft explorations. The small gasps she made were not from the force of his embrace, but from the force of her need for him, a need that swept her away into a soft, velvety rush of longing. When at last they separated, Savannah walked the short distance to her front door on wobbly legs. Before she drifted off to sleep, she began to plan a very special New Year's Eve.

For the next week the whole town seemed content to spend these few days taking life easy before ringing in the new year. Yet business at the shop remained brisk, making the time fly. At last the final day of the old year arrived. And Savannah was more than ready for the evening.

"Damn, some party." Paul looked around the packed dance floor.

Dozens of couples danced to the unique sound of zydeco. The combination of American blues, Caribbean, African, and Acadian rhythms perfectly represented the lineage of Creoles. Sack Daddy's was the most popular place to be anytime, but New Year's Eve seemed to have brought out everyone within a fifty-mile radius who was looking for a good time. Savannah simply sparkled dressed in a daring form-fitting red dress. She had modeled it for Charice two days earlier.

"What do you think?" Savannah watched her best friend's face anxiously. She obeyed her gesture to turn around and take a few steps.

"Girl, that dress has got 'brazen hussy' written all over it. In other words, it's perfect."

Judging by the way Paul's eyes had traveled the length of her body when he'd first seen her, he more than approved. Though it had a modest neckline in front and three-quarter-length sleeves and came just below the knee, it was plunged in the back in a way that drew appreciative stares from men as she walked by. Her thick black hair was swept up in a loose pile of curls at the top of her head, long corkscrew tendrils trailing down her neck. By the way he kept watching her hips and whistling as she walked ahead of him, Paul seemed to enjoy the view from behind as well. Together, they marveled at how easily they matched each other's cadence, as if they'd been dance partners for years. Savannah smiled mysteriously at him.

"You seem mighty pleased with yourself, as if you know something I don't." Paul rubbed his nose against hers playfully.

"Why, I don't know what you mean." She batted her lashes at him, the picture of wide-eyed innocence.

"Come on, tell me." He gripped her tighter. Feeling the soft mound of her full breast against his chest sent a flood of lust through his pelvis.

"Nothing." She breathed hard against his neck, trying to maintain a casual tone in her voice. She wanted this to be a surprise. "It's eleven. I'd rather not be surrounded by a crowd at midnight."

"Oh? What do you suggest?" He pulled away to stare at her, wearing a puzzled frown.

"Let's go to your place, okay? We can get there in ten minutes."

"Okay." Paul cleared his throat. "Remember, we're supposed to be taking it slow," he mumbled under his breath.

Feeling safe in the crowd, he wasn't at all sure he could maintain his cool alone with her, especially seeing her in that dress. The wonderful fragrance she wore added fuel to the fire.

Once they arrived, Savannah took charge, first producing a bottle of chilled champagne from the back of the truck.

"Where did you get this?" Paul laughed.

"I bought it at the lounge. Remember the third time I went to the ladies' room? You teased me about drinking too much ginger ale."

As he poured them each a glass, Savannah switched on

the compact disc player. One of her favorite female blues singers began a husky torch song, made even more provocative by the alto sax that served as a rich background. Savannah began a slow, graceful dance in front of the speakers, her body gyrating. Approaching her, Paul concentrated on keeping his hands steady. Taking a glass from him, she lifted it.

"To a happy and prosperous New Year." She took one small sip, her eyes never leaving his as he took a sip also. Then she took his glass and hers setting both down on the end table nearest them.

Wrapping both arms around his neck, she moved to him and began rocking gently in time to the music.

"Savannah, much as I enjoy this, I can't think clearly with you this close in that dress. I'm not sure how long I can resist the urge to—" Paul moaned softly into the rich mound of curls as Savannah pressed even closer against his growing erection.

"Then don't, cher," Savannah whispered huskily. This strong, wonderful man would be hers tonight. No doubts nagged at her now as she watched his face change from one of uncertainty, surprise, then lust. Everything about making love to Paul felt right. Never before had the power of unparalleled physical desire and admiration of character for one man been combined, effectively shaking away all her carefully forged defenses. Gazing into his arresting almond brown eyes, she felt awed by her hunger for him.

Unable to believe his ears, he lifted her face away from his shoulder to gaze into her eyes. The passion he found there sent a hot blaze through him. He closed his eyes and his mouth found hers. He found her more than willing to admit his probing tongue. In a soft, smoky haze of desire, they moved together in a circle. They came closer and closer to the bedroom. Still kissing her, Paul slowly pulled the dress from her shoulders until her firm, round breasts were exposed. As he cupped both in his hands, his lips traced a fiery path down her neck. Savannah gasped, arching her back to him, aching to feel his lips on her rigid nipples. Teasingly he stopped at the top of the cleavage and with deliberation eased the dress down around her thighs. With a one quick motion, Savannah pushed it down to her ankles and kicked it away. She removed his sweater, then began hurriedly to unbutton his shirt. In rapid succession, the rest of their clothes flew off. Her red silk panties were thrown beside her dress, near the foot of the bed; his pants and underwear landed in a heap beneath the window. Both groaned with desire as flesh met flesh. Filled with the warm, manly smell of him, she lowered him gently to the bed beneath her. Paul surrendered to her tender assault. His hands lightly stroked her buttocks. Savannah reached to the nightstand for the square of foil. Paul started to take it from her.

"Let me."

Savannah tore open the package. With a delicate touch, she covered his hard manhood with the latex condom. Paul jerked her hand away, fearful he would explode. Savannah, feeling the hot wetness between her legs, could wait no longer. She straddled him, holding his hands in hers as she settled down. With a low moan, she took every inch of him into her. Time seemed to slow as they matched each other stroke for stroke, setting their own sensuous cadence. She cried out his name over and over as Paul lifted his hips to her, his hands gripping her thighs.

"Savannah, look at me," he called to her. A grimace of lust made his face seem to be in pain, yet filled with pleasure, too.

"Yes, yes." Fighting not to close her eyes, she stared in hot fascination at the way they rode the wave of sexual desire as one. There was only this sweet oneness, this agony of wanting more. With increasing urgency brought on by the sight of his muscular chest and arms covered with a sheen of sweat, rippling as he moved with her, she whipped her body wildly up and down. Unintelligible sounds started at the back of her throat and burst forth. His groaning matched hers as his shaft became even more rigid. Her screams seemed to be outside herself as she felt the moment of ecstasy. Trembling, she felt a hot splash as he, too, reached a climax, setting off new waves of hunger deep within. With a shuddering sigh, she came again. They finally collapsed together, drifting off into a velvety blackness.

"Listen," she murmured against his chest. The faint pop of firecrackers came from all directions.

"It's almost one o'clock." Paul glanced at the clock radio on the nightstand. "Happy New Year, love."

"Happy New Year." Savannah ran her tongue across his nipples, giggling at his reaction.

"If we keep this up, I won't live long into 1996." Paul came fully awake, caressing her into life again.

Chapter 7

"Honey, there were so many people at Sack Daddy's I couldn't get to y'all. But one thing, I saw how y'all couldn't keep your hands off each other. So, what happened?" Charice leaned forward, eager to hear every detail.

"We had a lovely time." Savannah smiled. She twirled the straw in the tall glass of iced tea.

"Come on, now. It's been two weeks since we've talked. The last time I saw you, you were struttin' out of Sack Daddy's with Paul grinning from ear to ear. Did you two have your own fireworks at the *stroke* of midnight?" Charice winked at her.

"Let's just say, it was a very special night."

"Oo-wee, I bet it was. For me, too."

"So, you and Rodney—?" It was Savannah's turn to dig out spicy details.

"No, not yet. We're still getting to know one another. These days, it pays to take your time and be cautious. But he's so sweet, and kind of shy. We held hands in front of the fireplace."

"The holidays were great," Savannah said. They both sighed, already nostalgic.

"And in no time, it's back to the old grind. It's taken me until now to get my class into the routine. These breaks are murder."

"Speaking of which, I've been thinking that it's time I got back to being a lawyer. That research I did for Poppy and the Citizens for a Clean Environment reminded me how much I enjoyed it. Environmental law is getting to be very important."

Savannah had spent hours in the library flipping through pages of legal reference books searching for precedents in cases similar to theirs. Pages upon pages told the story of a growing public willingness to challenge the power of huge corporations to protect themselves from the devastating effects of hazardous substances. Following a hunch, Savannah had decided to investigate exactly how the Big River plant had gotten into operation so quickly.

"That was brilliant, the way you found out how Batton Chemical avoided having public hearings. I didn't realize there were so many different types of permits," Charice said.

"Sure, by the time the people who lived near the plant found out about what they were doing, it was too late. Because they claimed to be a recycling center, they avoided public hearings and additional costs companies that dispose of hazardous wastes have to pay."

"When is the trial going to start?"

"The end of this month. On the twenty-seventh at ten o'clock in U.S. District Court, New Orleans, Judge Henry Duplessis presiding." Savannah did her imitation of a court bailiff.

"Bad blood is going to be stirred up again over this for sure. By the way, does Paul know you helped supply the ammunition that got the feds gunning for his most important client?" Charice raised her eyebrows.

"We haven't been talking about that lately, no. But Paul wasn't hired to defend the process or assess just whether or not the site is suitable. Besides, he's finished that job."

"Yeah, but that offer you told me Trosclair made is mighty tempting. He could take on more work for them."

"Paul says the work he'll be doing will be strictly as safety consultant. It won't be a problem." Savannah didn't feel as sure as she tried to sound.

"Hope you're right, girlfriend. Well, hello there, handsome." Charice looked over Savannah's shoulder.

"Hi. How's it going?" Paul winked at Charice before leaning over to plant a light kiss on Savannah's cheek. He pulled an extra chair to the small table and sat down.

"Hi." Savannah moved over to make room for him.

"We were just talking about what a great time we had during the holidays." Charice gave them both a knowing smirk.

"Oh, yes. Best I've ever had." Paul smiled at Savannah, placing his hand on hers.

"Uh-umm, yeah. And the trial, we were talking about that." Savannah was eager to get on to another subject. In the corner of her eye, she could see her friend enjoying her discomfort. Charice would be teasing her for days about this.

"Let's hope some of that holiday goodwill lasts when it starts," Paul said.

"Don't count on it, honey. It's only because nothing has been in the newspapers or on television lately. But when that trial starts, people will be back on opposite sides. Some are already grumbling about it." Charice propped both elbows on the table.

"You're probably right. Jobs are tight, especially here. I think the oil and gas industry will rebound, but with technology, fewer workers are needed," Savannah said.

"Sure, but there are other industries that can be brought in. It would take time, but we can have a more diverse economic base and even cleaner plants that deal with toxic waste." Paul tapped the table with his index finger as he spoke.

"Yeah, but that isn't what men like Bo or Manny want

to hear. They need jobs now, not sometime in the future," Charice said.

"Sounds like you think Citizens for a Clean Environment may be wrong in what they're trying to do." Savannah was surprised at her friend's view.

"No, not really. All I'm saying is they have a point about them being the ones who end up on the unemployment line when the dust settles."

"But it doesn't always have to be a choice between a clean environment or jobs. I think these large corporations are beginning to see that reducing the waste products they release into the air, ground, and water is good business. There are new techniques and products that can clean up some of the most toxic substances. Not to mention the state-of-the-art technology being developed to make a lot of industrial processes more efficient and produce fewer toxic by-products."

"But not all of them want to spend the money. Like the Trosclairs. From what I've read about the three other plants they put up in the last ten years, they have definitely not gone in for expensive waste-control systems. You would do better working with environmental conservation groups, Paul. Not that I'm being critical," Savannah added quickly.

"Maybe you're right. But I still think it's worth a try. Man, I'd better be on my way or I'll be late. Call you later." He gave Savannah a kiss and hurried out.

As he waited to meet with Claude Trosclair and Singleton, he could not help but think about Savannah. He had asked for and received her trust. How was he going to explain accepting Trosclair's offer?

"Good to have you aboard, Honore. That ought to silence the damn environmentalists." Kyle Singleton slapped Paul on the shoulder. His back turned, he was oblivious to the effect of his words.

"Really?" Paul frowned.

"Yeah. You're black, and even better, you've got kind of a reputation for being a liberal. I mean, that work you did with that earth conservancy group a couple of years back. To be honest, I was skeptical when Claude first told me. But he was right, as usual." Singleton poured coffee into a black mug with the company name printed in gold letters.

"So, hiring me is for window dressing." Paul started to rise. A restraining hand on his shoulder guided him back into the leather conference chair.

"As usual, Kyle proves that he has more skills as president of a company than as a diplomat. Relax, I was honest when I said your credibility with environmentalists would be an asset. But as we have already shown, any recommendations you make will be given serious consideration. Look at how we implemented several here at Big River." Claude sat beside him.

"Now, wait a minute. I didn't mean to imply that we hired you for show. But let's face it, image is critical in business. Hell, we got a couple of black guys in our commercials," Singleton blustered.

"Kyle, be quiet." Claude spoke in the same controlled voice he had used with his wife. "What he's trying to convey, quite ineptly, is that we are sensitive to the issues the African-American community has raised. Of course, Batton Chemical is committed to being in the forefront of the trend toward working with environmentalists. We want to have a diverse team to make sure all views are considered. Safety is good business."

"Nice save. My mama didn't raise no fools, Mr. Trosclair. I know I'm useful to you. I'll be just as honest and say I have every intention of making sure you live up to those words, whether you mean them or not."

Laughing, Claude put his arm around Paul's shoulders. "Young man, we are going to make a great team."

Paul left the office, copies of the contract in his leather portfolio. He was concentrating on the questions he would ask his attorney and the answers he would have for Savannah when he saw Quentin emerge from the adjoining office suite.

"You don't have what it takes to deal with an operation as big as this one, Honore. And it won't take long for that to be obvious." Quentin stood several feet away, his arms folded.

"Wrong again, Einstein. I've been handling big jobs since I was in college."

"I'm going to be watching every move you make. One mistake, and I'll be all over you. Forget trying to sabotage us to help your little lawyer girlfriend and her old man."

"Anything I do will be done well and honestly. Seems your grandfather thinks so, or else I don't think he'd have hired us." Opening the door to his truck, Paul threw the portfolio on the passenger side of the seat.

"My grandfather is an old fool. He won't be in charge much longer, so don't get too comfortable with that contract."

"You think so? He looks pretty healthy to me. Besides, isn't Singleton next in line when it comes to running things?" Paul raised a mocking eyebrow.

"You just wait and see who'll be giving orders. Don't kid yourself it could ever be you."

"Hmm, I hadn't thought of that, but now that you mention it, your grandfather does seem to be a man who promotes on ability. If you're my competition, I've got it made." Paul smiled, baring his teeth.

"What does that mean?" Quentin flushed a deep red.

"It means he knows what I can do. What have you done lately?" In anger, Paul had taken a random poke at a possible weak spot. He struck a raw nerve.

"I'll see you in hell first, you black bastard. Before I'm through, you and that piece of brown sugar of yours won't own a pot to piss in, much less a business." Quentin jabbed a finger in Paul's chest.

For several seconds, Paul looked at the finger. With

one quick motion, he slammed his fist into Quentin's jaw, knocking him down. Paul stood over him, waiting for him to get up. Quentin pushed himself to one knee. Cursing, he started to rise, but hesitated when he looked into Paul's eyes.

"Don't ever touch me again, and she's Ms. St. Julien to you." Paul spoke through clenched teeth, every muscle straining at the effort to keep from punching him again.

Quentin backed away from him holding his face. Singleton and another male employee came outside. Singleton tried to help Quentin to his feet, but was brushed away.

"This isn't over! You hear me, you're going to pay for this! You're going to be nothing when I finish with you, nothing!"

"Don't be an even bigger idiot than you already have been. Now, get up," Claude snarled. Stepping around Singleton, he threw his grandson a look of disgust.

"He attacked me for no reason. I'm going to press charges." Quentin spoke in a whining voice.

"Knowing you, there was probably sufficient provocation. Now, stop your whimpering and go back inside."

Paul climbed behind the wheel. Glancing back just before he drove away, he saw an obviously angry Quentin trying to speak to Claude. His grandfather walked past him into the building without a word or a look in Quentin's direction.

Claude sat in the library listening to Chopin, a glass of brandy at his elbow. His head tilted back, eyes closed, he was lost in the music. As the last strains of the lovely melody died away, he raised the glass to his lips. He looked up to find Quentin standing in the doorway. Sighing deeply, he crossed the room to the antique bar for a refill. Quentin came into the room, a tall glass already in his hand.

"I see you don't need a drink." Claude still had his back turned.

"No, indeed. I'm doing very well, thank you." Quentin took a long swallow of the amber liquid.

"Humph." Claude went back to his chair.

Quentin paced restlessly for several minutes, fingering his grandfather's collection of antique glass paperweights arranged on a nineteenth-century lady's writing desk that had belonged to Claude's great-grandmother. He crossed to the window to stare out into the darkness, then began another circuit of the room. When the music stopped, Claude got up to change the record on the old-fashioned phonograph.

"Why do you bother with that old thing? Compact discs have a much better sound," Quentin said. He was slumped on one of the small sofas.

"This old thing, as you call it, is a fine example of quality workmanship. I enjoy operating it, watching the precision movement as it operates so smoothly after so many years. Besides, part of the pleasure in having this wonderful collection is choosing which selection I'll listen to next."

"Something you can do just as well with a compact disc player. Really, doing the same things you've done for years isn't always the damn virtue you make it out to be. Tradition? Just another way of saying you can't adjust to change." Quentin gulped more of the drink.

"I don't think we're talking about my phonograph anymore, are we?" Claude crossed his legs. Leaning back in his favorite chair, he was relaxed.

"Why are we poking along with this new plant? The process of creating slag for use in roadbeds and building foundations is brand new. Which means that there is no track record that says it's unsafe. We've got customers lined up because we can provide the product they need at one third the cost."

"True. It may take another ten years or longer for the health effects to really be known. But it may not be completely safe."

"The tests have shown no leaching under test conditions."

"So it doesn't bother you that over time it could be hazardous?" Claude gazed at his grandson wearing a slight smile.

"No, and you don't care either. Before this Paul Honore showed up you were willing to do whatever it took to get this plant fully operational. His report is nothing new and you know it. And why are you lapping up every word he says. I'm sick of him. We don't know enough about him. I wouldn't be surprised if he's been feeding information to those damn protesters." Quentin's jaw tightened. Noticing that his glass was empty, he went to the bar. He searched for several seconds before finally settling on Scotch.

"You're right. I don't give a damn about all this whining over the environment. Those people do more to pollute this planet than most industries. But Paul Honore is no fool. I've investigated his background thoroughly, both his professional life and his private life. I know quite a lot about him." Claude paused to stare ahead thoughtfully before continuing.

"And?" Quentin growled, impatient for him to go on.

"And he's right that the politicians have begun to take note of how many voters blame big business for dirty air and water. Caution will not cost us as much in the long run. Besides, he can be very useful. A really sharp young man."

"As usual, you don't think my advice is worth much. Some two-bit engineer with a degree from one of those underfunded colleges shows up and you hang on his every word. I don't think you feel comfortable with the new ways of doing business," Quentin snapped.

"Oh, I see."

"We need to move aggressively, fast. While you hold hands with Honore, trying to please every local crackpot with a gripe, most of whom can barely read, some other company could move ahead. Now, I would take the reports we have and move up our timetables. Make the plant fully operational, and profitable, and the objections would get drowned out.''

"I'm a bit too slow, am I?''

"The way you've always done things isn't relevant any-more. This is a new market that's wide open. With all the publicity, some other company will see the opportunity and seize it while you're still sipping tea with Honore.'' Quentin failed to notice the steely look in his grandfather's eyes. He spoke as though he were alone. "Batton Chemical could soon be as much of a relic as the dinosaurs if some-thing isn't done to bring it out of the Stone Age.''

"And you are the man to do it, I suppose?''

"If you'd stop making me feel like some incompetent kid you have to watch every minute. Yes, I have plenty of ideas that could get us on the right track.''

"How interesting that you should mention my having to watch you every minute. There was the time I sent you to Dallas, remember? You insulted some of the best staff and slept with the wife of one of my most valued executives, who promptly jumped ship, taking valuable information with him to our chief competitor. Production fell by ten percent when you decided you could step into his shoes. Then there was the fiasco in Atlanta, when you decided that Williams, one of the top contract negotiators working for me, was moving too slowly. You met with the Argentini-ans without him, and they walked away with a wonderful deal at *our* expense—a deal we couldn't get out of without losing our shirts.'' As Claude spoke, his voice took on the sharp edge of a scalpel. With each word, he carved his grandson down inch by inch until Quentin seemed physi-cally to shrink under the onslaught.

"There were already staff problems in Dallas, I told you. I was making headway before you stopped me. Sharpton's wife had slept with half the office, anyway. Atlanta wasn't my fault. I tried to work with Williams, but he—'' Quentin's voice became strained.

"You'd be unemployed if I held you to the same standards I set for my other employees. Now, let's get this straight: you're vice president of 'Do as you're told,' do you understand? When I want your opinion, I'll tell you what it is. I've been cleaning up your messes since you were fourteen, and sadly, you haven't learned anything from your numerous mistakes. At least your father had the guts to try to make it on his own." Claude snorted in disgust, not even looking at Quentin.

"My father would be alive if you hadn't tried to run his life. You might as well have put a gun to his head."

Claude whirled around, grabbing the front of Quentin's shirt with both hands, pulling him close. Claude spoke with such intensity his whole body shook.

"Don't ever speak to me like that again or I'll beat you to a pulp, then throw you out on the street without a penny."

"Claude, let him go. Please, he's your grandson." Annadine stood in the doorway, wringing her hands.

"Get out of my sight," Claude said through clenched teeth, releasing him.

Quentin backed toward his grandmother, rubbing his neck. His breath came in ragged gasps, lips trembling with the effort not to cry. He opened his mouth several times, but seeing the look on Claude's face, said nothing. Annadine put her arms around his shoulders. Quentin faced her.

"Let go of me." He shook free of her hold and ran down the hall. After a few minutes, the door slammed and the roar of an engine could be heard.

"At least he didn't snivel to you this time. That's some small improvement." Claude sat down. Smoothing his hair in place, he reached for his glass.

"How can you say such horrible things? He's always been a sensitive boy. Losing his parents so young had a devastating effect on the poor child. You should be more sympathetic to him."

"His mother was a spoiled, selfish brat who taught him

nothing but how to whine for whatever he wanted. His father was a silly dreamer who spent time digging in dirt for centuries-old garbage. But then, I always thought he went on those long trips as much to escape her constant complaining as to discover some new civilization. At least for that I can't blame him."

"Vivian was used to the finer things in life and came from such an old, wealthy family. And Louis had a brilliant career ahead of him in archeology, his professor said so."

"Spare me the fiction, my dear. The only career either one of them worked at was drinking expensive liquor until they were too drunk to see straight and partying all night with their equally fatuous friends."

"Louis wanted your approval so much. If only you could have been more understanding."

"As usual, you make excuses. I tried to teach them to be men and you babied them. Encouraging Louis with that archaeology nonsense!"

"But it was what he wanted."

"He was young; he didn't know anything about what he wanted. You encouraged every silly notion that came into his head. Just as you've done with Quentin. Every time he's done something, no matter how reprehensible, you've blamed everyone else. I'd have thought you'd have learned something over the years."

"Claude, please don't say that. I've done the very best I could."

"Yes, a pity isn't it?" Claude put on another recording. Turning the music up, he sat down and closed his eyes.

With a strangled sob, Annadine stumbled from the room. Slowly, she climbed the stairs to her bedroom, a separate room on the other end of the long hall, opposite her husband's.

LaShaun wandered around the large living room, pausing occasionally to admire a piece of furniture or work of art. Most of these things she had selected. Going to the window, she gazed at the scenery below. From the fourth-floor apartment, the view of the French Quarter was quite lovely. The best in Spanish architecture could be seen in the buildings with ornate ironwork gracing the balconies, enclosed courtyards concealing well-kept gardens with water fountains. She tightened the sash on the expensive satin robe she wore. Alive with lush tropical flowers in vibrant yellow, blue, and purple, it was a gift—one more indulgence she had insisted on as proof that her control was complete. She heard rustling in the bedroom, then the sound of running water. Sighing, she went into the kitchen to pour two cups of coffee from the pot.

"Morning," Quentin mumbled, as he took the offered mug from her.

"Sorry, baby. It's afternoon now, one o'clock, to be exact." She stretched out on the large sofa.

"Whew, some party." Quentin blinked painfully in the bright light coming through the large windows. The elegant drapes had been pulled back.

"You could say that. If I hadn't gotten you away from there, somebody was going to kick your tail." LaShaun smiled at him, her eyes seemed to say she might have enjoyed that. Following his eyes, she looked down. The robe had parted to reveal her naked body.

"I can take care of myself, thank you." He put the cup down on the long, low table in front of the sofa and sat at her feet. Slowly, he began to rub her thighs.

"Shouldn't you call home? I'm sure your grandparents must be worried that you've been gone all night."

"They're used to it by now. The old man doesn't care, as long as I don't cause too much of a scandal to the good old family name." He began to pluck at the knotted sash.

"I don't think it's a good idea to get him too pissed off, Quentin." LaShaun slipped away from him nimbly. She went into the kitchen to refill her cup. "He still holds the purse strings, you know."

"No need to worry. Whatever else he may be, grandfather has a strong sense of family. He may threaten to throw me out, but since he has no other heirs to carry on the family name and fortune, he'd never cut me out of the Trosclair estate."

"But he can always slow the money to a small trickle."

"Grandmother wouldn't let that happen." Quentin put his head in her lap as she sat down on the sofa again.

"Get up," LaShaun barked.

"What's the problem?" Rising sharply, Quentin's voice had the tone of a wounded little boy.

"How can you be such a dumbbell? Claude is not going to let your grandmother rule him in anything. Everybody in Beau Chene knows she has been worshipping at his feet from the moment they met. Now, you get this through that thick fog in your head: all my—our—plans depend on you not getting Claude suspicious or too angry." Scowling, LaShaun sat across from him in one of the large chairs that matched the sofa.

"By the time he realizes what's happening, I'll be in control of the company. Grandmother will see to it. With her shares, and Singleton's help in getting shares from two other old goats, the board will make me CEO. They'll have little choice."

"If you don't tip your hand before that happens. Tread carefully. Stop arguing with him and criticizing his style of doing business. He might begin to wonder if you plan to do something about it."

"Grandfather thinks I'm an empty-headed moron with nothing on my mind but liquor and women. This is one time his low opinion of me will work to my advantage." Quentin gave a short, bitter laugh.

"The smartest thing is not to take anything for granted." LaShaun tapped a long fingernail against the side of the coffee mug.

"Angel, relax. The old man doesn't know anything about

us. Didn't I fix it so your grandmother's land was paid for at top dollar? I'm going to take care of you. Those stocks you bought have tripled in value, like I said they would. Batton Chemical may be buying another company soon. Come back over here. Come on." Quentin patted the sofa cushion next to him.

"Yes, lover. You've certainly come through for me. Just keep your eye on Claude. He's not stupid." She sank down next to him, leaning with her back against his chest.

"He may not be, but he can't be everywhere at once. This opposition to the plant has been keeping him distracted, lucky for us."

"That's another thing. Savannah and her father are really making a lot of noise." LaShaun spoke in a low growl, like an angry alley cat.

"Yes, they're a nuisance with their self-righteous speeches," Quentin said with a voice dripping with disdain. He began to languidly stroke the curve of her jawline. "But from your reaction at the mere mention of Savannah, your dislike must go deeper than just their environmental activism." Quentin nuzzled her earlobe.

"Savannah and her father think they're better than me. Since we were kids she's pranced around like she thinks she's Miss It," LaShaun hissed.

"Well, they can make all the noise they want. That plant is not going to be shut down—not with the connections we have." Quentin's fingers moved across the fabric covering one of her breasts.

"I'm going to show her. When I'm through, she's going to leave town so fast, she'll be moving at the speed of light." LaShaun spoke with relish, her eyes gleaming at the thought of vengeance.

"My, my, she really has gotten to you. What is the feud between the Rousselle and St. Julien clans?" His hand became still as he paused to study her.

"Never mind about that, you concentrate on making

sure Claude doesn't think too hard about how you spend your days at the office. Like I said, he's no fool," she warned.

"He can be gotten around. That bastard Honore sure has the wool pulled over his eyes. Grandfather is eating out of his hand for some damn reason." A slight frown creased his forehead. He shifted his attention back to her and resumed caressing the soft mound of flesh. "But they'll both be in for a big surprise."

"Paul is no fool, either. He doesn't miss much," LaShaun said. She darted a sly side glance at him.

"Paul, eh? How do you know him?" Quentin gripped her arm.

"I met him when he first came to town. He stopped at the museum. Quite charming, very handsome." LaShaun smiled as she felt his hand close even tighter.

"Is that all? Tell me." Quentin breathed heavily, speaking low, with his lips at her ear.

"What do you want to know, lover? Should I describe it in detail? Is that what you want?" She wriggled closer, allowing his hands to go farther under the hem of the robe.

"He's one of the others, isn't he? The ones you won't tell me about."

"Of course, one of the dozens under my spell." She threw back her head, laughing.

"You know, if I thought for one minute that was true, I'd break your lovely brown neck. Now, say it." His voice was hoarse with lust as he urged her once again to play the game.

"I have another lover . . ." LaShaun slipped the robe from her shoulders. Bending her face low, she kneaded the flesh on his thighs. As her hands moved in circles, higher, she whispered a description of what she and her other lover did in bed. "Is that what you want me to do?" Her tongue left a wet trail on his skin.

"Oh, yes." With a groan, Quentin lay back on the cushion. With his eyes closed, he gave himself up to her.

In the weeks leading up to the trial, wherever Savannah happened to be, LaShaun frequently appeared, although always at a distance. At the local grocery store, suddenly LaShaun would be at the end of the aisle, smiling at her. Stopping at the dry cleaners, Savannah would look up to find LaShaun standing at the end of the block, waving as though they were best chums. Leaving the law library at the university in Baton Rouge late one night, Savannah had the uneasy feeling that she was being watched. Seeing no one, she chided herself for being paranoid. As she was backing out of her parking space, a shadowy figure appeared in her rearview mirror. She slammed on her brakes and jumped out of the car only to find that she was alone in the parking lot. Low but distinctive mocking laughter faded as if carried away by the wind.

After two weeks of this, Savannah began to dread having to step outside. Her sleep was troubled nightly by strange dreams, vivid and menacing. She jumped at any sudden sound. Though she tried to put it to working long hours, Tante Marie still wasn't convinced.

"Cher, you got a look that's more than tired. Somethin' else wrong with you."

"Honest, Tante Marie. I'm just bushed from putting in too many hours at the library after working at the shop all day. But I'm about finished with my research. Then I'll be okay."

"Uh-huh." Tante Marie obviously wasn't convinced, but she said nothing more.

The winter days were short, so that by five o'clock it was completely dark. This only fueled Savannah's growing uneasiness about running errands after leaving the shop. Between keeping up with her father's business and working on learning everything she could about state environmental regulations, she rarely got home before seven o'clock. One evening she was locking up the shop when she saw a familiar figure standing two stores away. Anger overcame fear. Savannah headed straight for her, the sound of her steps an angry staccato on the pavement.

"What's the deal, LaShaun? What is this appearing, then disappearing, act?" Savannah stood within three feet of her.

"Why, I don't know what you're talking about." LaShaun's expression was impassive.

"You seem to have a problem with me, or something."

"You have the problem, not me. I'm just out running errands and minding my own business." LaShaun turned back to the trendy clothes artfully displayed in the women's boutique.

"There is something, some bad feeling that has been between us since we were kids. I've never understood why. What have I ever done to you?" Savannah took a step closer. "Tell me."

LaShaun's body still faced **the** shop window, but her head turned slowly in Savan**nah's** direction. In the light from the window, Savannah **could** see her lips part slightly. A soft hissing came from them. All other sound seemed to become muted. Eyes glittering with hatred, LaShaun smiled as she spoke.

"Sins of the father. My mother died before her time because promises your papa made weren't kept. He used her, then tossed her away like she was yesterday's garbage. You will not take from me."

Savannah backed away slowly, her breath coming in short gasps, her chest tight. The hissing increased, swelling around her. She turned quickly to find herself in front of the flower shop two blocks from her car. Grateful for the bright, cheerful lights that winked from the festive display for Valentine's Day, she leaned against the front door and fought to slow her breathing. After a time, she looked back down the street. LaShaun was gone.

"Excuse me, ma'am." A man and little boy had cautiously pulled open the door to come outside. "You all right?" They both peered at her with concern.

"Yeah, I'm okay. Just running around trying to get too much done at once, I guess." Savannah smiled weakly.

"You want us walk you to your car? Tony, pick up the lady's bag she dropped."

"Thank you, no." Savannah began to feel better under their kindly attentions. The little boy's plump brown face, turned up to her, tugged at her heart. "I'm fine now, really. Thank you, Tony." She tucked the small bags into a larger one.

After Savannah once again reassured them her car was close by, they left. Eager to leave, she threw the packages onto the back seat and got in behind the wheel. As she reached to adjust the rearview mirror, she screamed. A tiny doll swung slowly from a string inches from her face. Its arms were tied behind its back. A black veil covered the head.

Chapter 8

Her eyes felt as if fine grains of sand had been rubbed across them. Savannah blinked into the mirror of the ladies' room for the third time. Taking a deep breath, she straightened the crisp white blouse she wore beneath the charcoal gray jacket of her suit. "I told you, you look great. Why do you keep staring at your eyes like that?" Charice pulled her away from the mirror.

"Just checking to make sure my eyes aren't bloodshot. How you look in court is as important as how you perform, believe me." Savannah tried to turn back to see her reflection again.

"Listen to me, you look okay—"

"Okay? A minute ago you said great. Be honest with me."

"Savannah, you are tripping. Steady yourself, girl-friend."

"I'm all right, just jumpy because it's been awhile since I was in a court. Most of my corporate work involved contracts, not trials."

"Now, you be honest. I've seen you face down alligators without breaking a sweat. What's up with you?" Charice stood between her and the door, a sign that they were not leaving until she had an answer that sounded like the truth.

"Nightmares. I have been having them for two weeks. Some nights I dream I'm out deep in the bayou, fishing with Poppy. Suddenly he turns into a large black snake with a mouth the size of a football field closing in on me. In another one, I'm in a huge old house and all of a sudden I hear footsteps. I know some horrible creature is coming after me, but I can't find a door." Savannah jerked a paper towel from the dispenser on the wall. Wetting it in the sink, she dabbed her face with it.

"Damn!"

"I haven't been getting much sleep lately. Some nights I'm actually afraid to close my eyes. There's this one dream where I look down and blood is all over me—" Savannah took a shuddering breath.

"Listen to me, this is not real. Just tell yourself LaShaun and Monmon Odette have no power. It's all smoke and mirrors."

"I know that in the light of day. But at night, in my dreams, it's a different story." Savannah smiled weakly at her friend.

"Is there anything I can do?" Charice put her arm around Savannah's shoulder.

"Yeah, get me a garlic necklace. That should ward off any evil." Savannah gave a short, forced laugh.

"And anybody else. Seriously, girl, what can I do?"

"Charice, this is a boogeyman from childhood that I have to face alone."

"No, you don't." Charice stared off as if seeing something written on the dingy green wall.

"Yes, I do. I have to come to terms with this somehow, but you stay out of it. Especially stay away from LaShaun. One of us getting hexed is enough." Savannah didn't like that look in her eye and nudged Charice in the ribs in an effort to joke.

"Hmm, oh sure. Now, how are you feeling?"

"Better. No, it's true. This is the first time I've talked about the dreams to anyone. I'm feeling steady now."

"Well, you do look less jittery. Come on, you know you've done your homework. Go, girl."

"That's true. One thing about not being able to sleep, I got plenty of work done putting together information for Simmons."

For the past few weeks, Savannah and a local attorney had teamed up to build the government's case. Savannah and Gralin Mencer did extensive research to show how Batton Chemical had violated clean water and air statutes. Savannah picked up her leather portfolio and took one last look at herself in the mirror.

"I shouldn't have to tell you this, but you know you can call me to talk anytime." Charice stared at Savannah's reflection.

"Sure thing, Pork Chop."

"Shh, don't call me that. Somebody might hear you." Charice glared at her.

"I think it's cute, Pork Ch—"

"Yeah, almost as cute as Miss Burpee." Charice smirked.

"Hey, that's low."

"Uh-huh, big line in the third grade annual school play, and you let loose. I told you not to drink that carbonated cold drink before the curtain went up. 'Today we pay tribute to our founding fathers—*urpp!*'" Charice laughed as Savannah pushed her out the door into the hallway.

"One youthful mistake and they never let you forget."

"You started it."

They teased each other about embarrassing moments from childhood until the demons of the night were completely dispelled. Entering the crowded courtroom, both women instantly became serious. Seeing her father wave to her, Savannah led the way to the seats he had saved for them. Savannah and Charice sat down two rows from the front. The hard wood benches were behind a low wooden gate that separated the attorneys from the audience. Savannah was encouraged to see Gralin Mencer, a local attorney who had been active with the citizens' group, already sitting at the one of the long tables on the other side of the gate. With his head bent towards Jason Simmons, the attorney from the U.S. Department of Environmental Protection, he wore an intense expression as he spoke.

"Where is the opposing lawyer, I wonder?" Antoine nodded toward the second empty table to their left.

"I figure they'll make an impressive entrance soon. I expect some heavy-hitting hired gun to show. Batton Chemical has too much on the line," Savannah said.

"Yeah, but we got the feds on our team." Charice winked at her.

"The feds have been beaten in court many times, so don't think the verdict in our favor is in the bag."

"Still, I feel between them and us, we've got a good shot."

"I hope you're right, cher." Antoine patted Charice on the back of her hand.

"Man, I'm glad I took off to be here at least on the first day. Maybe I'll bring the class here as a field trip. Look at everybody that showed up." Charice waved at several acquaintances as she turned around to scan the crowd.

"Will you sit still? You just saw all those people at Sack Daddy's the other night. Quit squirming." Savannah poked her in the side.

"Look, there's Rodney. Hey, Rodney." Charice half rose from her seat.

"I bet your students behave better than you when they come. Good gracious." Savannah shook her head.

"Hello! Look at this fabulous ebony prince that just walked in. Girl, look. Oo-wee," Charice whispered loudly.

"Quit pulling on me. What is it—" Savannah's eyes went wide with shock.

"He's looking over here. Thank you, Lord, he's coming this way. Quick, is my hair all right?" Charice could barely contain her excitement.

"Savannah, fancy meeting you here." Devin, as impeccable as ever in a tailored navy suit with red paisley tie, gave her a dazzling smile as he extended his hand. His other hand held a fine leather briefcase.

"Hello." Savannah stared at his hand for several seconds before taking it.

"Friends of yours?" Devin stood, obviously waiting for an introduction.

"This is my father, Antoine St. Julien, and my friend Charice Collins. Poppy, Charice, this is Devin Martin." Savannah spoke shortly.

"It's a pleasure to meet you, Mr. St. Julien. Savannah has spoken of you often. And it's very nice to meet you, Ms. Collins."

"Yeah." Antoine gave him a long look up and down.

"What are you doing here?" Savannah already had a good idea. She had only just finished saying Batton Chemical would bring in big guns. And in Louisiana, they did not come any bigger than Clayton, Briggs, and Schuster.

"Batton Chemical's been a client of the firm for over twelve years. Mr. Clayton had handled much of their work personally, but in this instance, he felt I could be more effective. Truth is, he hasn't been in a courtroom for some time." Devin lowered his voice for the last sentence and leaned down close to Savannah's ear.

"I see."

As contemptible as it might be, Savannah had to appreciate the tactic. Not only was Devin a skilled litigator, but he was African-American. His presence would do much to diffuse the charge of environmental racism.

"And you? Of course, you are a member of the Citizens for a Clean Environment. Well, seems it's about to start. I hope we get a chance to have lunch while I'm in town, Savannah. Ms. Collins, Mr. St. Julien."

Seeing Judge Duplessis enter, Devin went to the counsel table opposite the government attorney. One of the young law clerks trailed behind him carrying several large brown envelopes. Placing his briefcase on the table, Devin opened it and began organizing papers in preparation.

"That's Devin? Low-down, no-good Devin? Man, of all the rotten luck. Why do all the worst ones have to be so fine?" Charice puffed in dismay.

"Believe me, you don't want to pay the price of having that weasel crawl into your life." Savannah folded her arms and sat back.

"Is he good?" Charice gave Devin an appraising look.

"One of the best young legal sharks in the country." Savannah tried to keep the growing sense of doubt about their chances from showing.

"No, I meant is he *good . . . you* know." Charice nudged her and winked.

"Girl, please! Is that all you can think about? The man is scum, toxic radioactive scum." Savannah closed her eyes in exasperation.

"I agree, I agree. I hope he gets his for the way he body-slammed you when you weren't looking. But I'm just wondering, you know. Come on, you can tell me." Charice grinned impishly.

"I am not having this conversation with you, Charice. I am not."

The bailiff ordered all to stand as the judge took the bench.

Watching Devin go through his opening statement, Savannah was almost hypnotized by his smooth delivery. Every motion, every facial expression seemed to say that Batton Chemical was being wrongly accused.

"Despite anything Mr. Simmons has said, we are sure Batton Chemical will be vindicated. We will present evidence that the state and federal environmental agencies gave conflicting orders as to the regulations under which the Big River plant is required to operate. The permits were obtained and the standards were followed in a good faith effort to fully comply with accepted state and federal laws. Further, we will demonstrate the extraordinary steps my client has taken not only to assure safety, but to address any legitimate concerns of the surrounding community."

"Damn, I see what you mean. He ain't no slob at this," Charice whispered.

"Wait until he really gets into it." Savannah stared ahead grimly. At the first available break, she planned to pull Gralin and Simmons aside to coach them on what to expect from Devin in the way of tactics.

"You look worried, which is makin' me worried, cher."

"Don't expect the worst, Poppy. He's good, but he's not invincible. We've got a strong case." Savannah squeezed his arm.

For the next two hours Devin called preliminary witnesses. It was obvious from the way Simmons cross-examined them that they were not crucial to the case. Devin was simply attempting to lay the groundwork for proving that Big River was like any other business that could benefit the community. A parade of engineers and industry experts took turns talking about the plant's safety features and back-up plans and the kiln process that produced the aggregate for use in construction. Under cross-examination, Simmons got several to admit that the process was so new that the safety procedures had never been truly tested. He even got one of scientists to admit that it could take several years before the effects on people who come into close contact with the aggregate could really be evaluated.

"That Simmons is doin' some job up against Mr. Big Time." Antoine smiled, encouraged that his side seemed to be holding its own.

"Redirect, Your Honor." Devin rose a few seconds before Simmons sat down again.

"Go ahead, Mr. Martin." Judge Duplessis nodded without looking up from the notes he was taking.

"Mr. Bankston, you just stated under cross-examination that it could take years to evaluate the safety of the aggregate."

"That is correct." The small balding scientist adjusted his heavy-framed spectacles.

"Isn't it also true that tests show that even extreme heat conditions, exposure to large amounts of water, and other elements that might be encountered in the environment have shown no leaching of dangerous chemicals?"

"That is also correct."

"And isn't it also true that the extreme conditions would not be expected to occur in the natural environment?"

"Most definitely. We tested at temperature 200 degrees Fahrenheit, just as one example."

"So, what would you conclude from this?"

"That under normal weather conditions, the aggregate should pose no threat whatsoever."

"Thank you. No more questions, Your Honor." Devin strolled back to his seat.

"As it is now noon, this court will adjourn until ten tomorrow morning." Judge Duplessis dismissed court with a sharp rap of his gavel.

Outside the courtroom, groups on both sides compared notes and opinions. Antoine was still upbeat, despite the obvious score Devin had made at the end.

"It's the first day, Simmons got time to put on our witnesses. That Devin won't be so smart faced then," Antoine reassured several committee members.

"Sorry I didn't get here for the first day. How did it go?" Paul had finally been able to make his way through the milling crowd to find them.

"I'd say it was about what and what. We holdin' our own." Antoine clapped him on the back before moving off with his friends to pick up sandwiches and root beer at Snooky Boo's.

"Sounds like Mr. Antoine is encouraged." Paul walked between the two women as they headed for the exit and lunch at the Fish Net.

"Well, this is just the beginning." Wearing a distracted expression, Savannah bumped into several people.

"I kind of agree with Mr. Antoine. Seems like we've got a fighting chance," Charice said.

"Hey, earth to Savannah." Paul laughed as he gently steered her from yet another collision course. "Snap out of it."

"Savannah, Savannah."

Devin caused heads to turn as he came toward them. The crowd parted around him. Some were hostile, but quite a few were impressed at the tall, handsome figure he cut.

"I meant what I said earlier. I will be pretty busy while I'm here, but I'd like to have dinner sometime." Devin spoke without acknowledging Paul or Charice.

"I don't know if that's a good idea, Devin."

"Why not? You may be opposed to the plant, but we certainly have more to discuss than this case."

"Oh, really?" Paul looked from Savannah to Devin.

"Devin, this is Paul Honore. Paul, Devin Martin. We were . . . associates at the same law firm."

"How are you?" Devin gave Paul a curt nod before turning his attention back to Savannah. "So what do you say?"

"I think she said no." Paul moved close to Savannah, putting his hand on her waist.

"Did she?" Looking up from Paul's hand on Savannah's waist to Paul, Devin studied him longer this time.

"Sure did." Paul's stance suggested that he was ready to go on the defensive.

"Back off, Paul. I can speak for myself," Savannah snapped, as she pushed his hand away.

"Why don't I give you a call? By the way, are you the Paul Honore who wrote the site report?"

"Yes."

"Excellent. Your testimony, the objective assessment of an African-American engineering consultant, will go far in helping my client. I'll be contacting you, Mr. Honore. About the case, of course. Well, I have to be going. Mr.

Trosclair has invited me to lunch at some fancy restaurant. Savoie's, I think is the name. Savannah, in case I haven't mentioned it already, you look fabulous, as always. I'll be in touch about getting together. Ms. Collins.'' He brushed his lips against Savannah's cheek before striding away.

"What was that about you two getting together?'' Paul whirled on her.

"He wants to have dinner. Probably to brag about himself. And you made a real scene with your 'she is my woman' act.''

"Oh, well, excuse me. I thought he came on too strong. Didn't you say he was no good and not to be trusted?''

"Yes, but I don't need any help handling him.''

"Oh, sure. You were definitely handling him when you told him you didn't think dinner was a good idea. Yeah, that sure set him straight about where you were coming from.''

"Wait a minute. Are you saying you don't trust me?''

"For someone who claimed not to be interested, you seemed to warm up to him pretty fast.''

"Hey, hey, kids. Cool it, we're drawing a crowd here. Let's go outside.'' Charice stepped between them. Grabbing an arm from each, she led them onto the courthouse steps.

"I'm sorry. Guess I just lost it when he started acting so cozy toward you.'' Paul spoke without looking at Savannah.

"Yeah, well.'' Savannah hesitated. The expression on her face had not yet softened.

"I jumped too fast.''

"True,'' Savannah retorted, but the frown was gone.

"He's up to something, but you're right. You can deal with him.''

"Thank you.'' Savannah turned to him, hand on one hip.

"Oh, come on. The man has apologized up and down. Cut him some slack.'' Charice shook Savannah's shoulders.

"Okay, okay. Under the circumstances, I can understand

your first reaction. But believe me, any contact I have with Devin is not for pleasure or by my choice. He probably thinks he can finesse me into revealing something he might find useful. What he doesn't realize is that I'm not the naive little law school graduate he met five years ago."

"Damn right, babe. Set him straight," Paul said.

"Will you please kiss and make up? I'm starving!" Charice clutched her stomach.

"You heard her." With a swift sweeping motion, Paul pulled Savannah to him and planted a solid kiss on her lips, leaving her breathless. "Now, let's go, before we have to fight our way into that restaurant."

"I didn't want to get Poppy down about our chances, but Devin is good. Clayton didn't send him just for window dressing, you can count on that." Savannah sat with her arms folded watching the still long line waiting to get in the Fish Net.

As Paul had predicted, the lunch crowd was heavy. After a twenty-minute wait, they were finally able to get a table. Ordering the lunch special, the salad bar and a bowl of gumbo, had at least meant that they wouldn't have to wait long for their meal to arrive.

"Listen, don't think this is some classic case of bad guys versus good guys. Trosclair isn't stupid. Any accidents at Big River and he'll have more trouble than profit. He knows that these days, being green is good business," Paul said.

"Get real, Paul. Trosclair will go through the motions, but he's not cutting into his bottom line," Savannah retorted with a sneer.

"He hasn't said no to anything I've suggested yet. And a few of those changes cost him some big bucks."

"I gotta agree with Savannah on this one, babe. We know the Trosclairs. Old Claude may be smooth, but he has a reputation of going for the throat when he gets pissed off," Charice said.

"The spotlight is shining on everything they do right

now. But as soon as things were to quiet down, it would be back to business as usual." Savannah leaned forward, tapping the table with her finger for emphasis.

"I just don't see it that way." Paul shook his head.

"I know you think you can influence him to do the right thing. Maybe you can, for a while. I doubt that it will last, though."

"Well, I hate to see the hard feelings this thing is causing here in town. If the plant does stay open, we need to have some common ground to get people back together. A way both sides can come together. Safety measures and jobs. I think it can be done, that's all I'm saying."

"Yeah, but if it closes—" Charice looked around her, watching the faces. Like them, many of the diners were discussing the case.

"If it closes, there'll be bitter feelings for a long time. Losing jobs and the money pumped into a depressed local economy won't be easily or soon forgotten." Paul finished the thought that came to all of them.

Savannah felt as though the weight of the whole world was on her shoulders. She was tired all the time, her sleep still disturbed by frightening dreams. After so many weeks, she didn't jump when she found gris-gris at home, in the shop, or on her car. She threw it all away with grim resignation. She was determined not to let it get the best of her, but the strain was wearing her down. One afternoon, Tante Marie found some of the gris-gris stuffed down in the trashcan. In her weakened state, it took only seconds for Savannah to confess all when her aunt demanded an explanation.

"Uh-huh, that's what I thought. I knowed something was goin' on." Tante Marie picked up the telephone receiver. "Shirleen, we got some work to do."

Tante Marie and Nenaine Shirleen sprang into action. Over her objections, Nenaine Shirleen collected the gris-

gris. She would perform some ritual to counteract the curses, then burn them.

"Tante Marie, will you talk to Nenaine, please? What she's doing is silly. What's more, it's unnecessary." Savannah stood watching Nenaine Shirleen sprinkling dust of some sort on the sidewalk in front of the shop.

"She believes what she believes. Can't hurt, I say, cher. Some of them gris-gris is powerful." Tante Marie moved around the shop, examining things.

"What are you looking for?"

"See if that wench done left anything lately."

"She hasn't, I checked. Oh great, look at this."

Savannah watched as several tourists stopped to observe Nenaine Shirleen. With an audience, her gestures began to take on a dramatic tone as she took an old straw broom and swept the bricks while she began a colorful explanation of what she was doing. It was clear that the tourists thought this was a performance for their benefit alone. After having her pose for pictures, they applauded before moving on.

"Nenaine, I wish you wouldn't do stuff like that." Savannah took the broom from her hand and took it to the back storeroom.

"You got to fight fire with fire, darlin'. A woman, I can't tell y'all who, 'cause she don't want it known generally, is advisin' me just what to do. Ain't nothin' gonna happen to you if I can help it."

"But nothing will happen anyway. This voodoo stuff is all psychological. If I let it get to me, then she wins. You spreading goofer dust, or whatever that is, is just making me more nervous."

"That ain't goofer dust, it's brick dust to protect you. And Marie say you can't sleep at night, so it *is* gettin' to you."

Looking at the determined expression both women wore, Savannah gave up. It was apparent that they would never be convinced that these measures were useless. As much as she could, she ignored Nenaine Shirleen's activities.

Savannah also felt the tension brought on by the fight against Big River. No matter where she went these days, she found herself defending the actions of her father and the others who opposed the plant. Even being with Paul became an exercise in walking on eggshells. They avoided talking about the case or about Devin, which meant there were no arguments, but they both knew how close they were to the edge. Savannah felt stretched to the limit. She hoped that things would at least get better between them once Paul testified.

"Then at least we might be able to relax around each other." Savannah's only relief these days was confiding in Charice.

"I'm not so sure about that. You may not like what he says." Charice pushed a stuffed rabbit out of her easy chair so she could sit down. The girls had left their toys everywhere in the tiny den next to her kitchen.

"I already know that. But then we could discuss it. Now he can't. Besides, it isn't as bad as I thought, anyway. He's just going to say that they are taking precautions and following industry safety standards."

"What about Devin? Have you been out with him yet? That's another unexploded bombshell you're playing with, if you ask me."

"Paul understands now that I have no feelings for Devin. If we did see each other it would only be to scope him out, about the case, that is."

"Uh-huh." Charice puckered her lips.

"He does!"

"Sure he does. Let me ask you this, have you told him that you are definitely going to have a date with dashing Devin?"

"No, but—"

"Have you discussed it since that first day at court?"

"No, but see—"

"So as far as you know, Paul may be assuming that since it hasn't happened yet, it won't. I mean, that was almost two weeks ago."

"Not necessarily. I think we just haven't discussed it because it's not an issue." Savannah picked up the rabbit and began playing with its floppy pink ears.

"Hey, this is me you're talking to, girlfriend. You haven't discussed it because you know what would happen. Boom!"

"So what do you think I should do?"

"Honey, don't ask me. The last time I was caught between two gorgeous men that wanted to see me was, let me think—oh, never," Charice said.

"Some help you are."

For several days Savannah had a reprieve from being forced to make a decision about Devin. Every time the phone rang, the bell jangled over the shop door, or there was a knock on the front door at home, she jumped. She was beginning to think he had changed his mind when her father tapped her shoulder one day as she sat engrossed in completing sales tax papers at his desk in the shop.

"That fella is out front for you." Antoine jerked his head toward the open office door.

"Devin." Savannah knew from the scowl on his face who he was talking about. Taking a shaky breath, she went out to greet him.

"Hi, Devin. How's it going?"

"Not too bad, sweet. I would ask how you are, but I can see for myself. You are fine." The same line from anyone else would have sounded phony, even ridiculous. But Devin, with his famous gentle smile and modulated baritone voice, could carry off even the most wornout come-on lines.

"Uh-huh. The trial is keeping you busy, I guess." Savannah was now immune to his charms.

"You guess correctly. Simmons has done his homework,

but then, so have I." With practiced smoothness, Devin switched gears to follow her lead.

"So you're not worried about the case? I mean, the issue of whether or not Big River can legitimately claim to be a recycling site is serious enough to jeopardize its future, but then there's the question of the plant operating in violation of its permit."

"Got my work cut out for me, that's for sure. However, as you well know, for every point there is an equally effective counterpoint. Now, what have you got planned for dinner this evening?" Devin performed another lightning-fast subject switch. This one caught her before she could prepare for it.

"Well, I'm not sure."

"I tried to get in touch with Honore to go over his testimony coming up day after tomorrow, but his partner said he was on-site doing some work in Breaux Bridge. He won't be back until late tonight. So I'm free." He gave her that smile again.

Savannah agreed. At least she would not be tense, worrying Paul would show up. At her suggestion, they went to a small restaurant in the tiny town of Lebeau that was renowned for its steak and seafood. Yet the reputation and atmosphere of Petite Maison were not the reasons she'd chosen it.

"Nice place. Quiet and out of the way, even further into the country." Devin wore an amused grin.

"It's packed on Fridays and Saturdays." Savannah settled in the chair across from him. She pretended not to pick up on what he was implying.

"It's obvious Tuesday is a slow night. Not many working people would drive here from Beau Chene to get dinner," Devin pressed.

"I guess." Savannah pushed down the urge to wipe that conceited smirk off his face with an insult. Instead, she changed the subject. "So, how are things at the firm?"

"Never better. We hired a new associate to replace you about two weeks after you left. Not as sharp as you, but a hard worker. We needed the help, what with taking on two major new clients. We've been working like crazy. By the way, Clayton sends his regards."

"I have a lot of respect for that man. He's not only a smart lawyer, he's got integrity," Savannah said.

"Not like me?" Devin raised an eyebrow at her.

"I was talking about Clayton, not making any implications by omission."

"But if the shoe fits, eh? I can understand if you think of me as a no-good snake."

"How is Karen, by the way?" Savannah bared her teeth in an imitation smile.

"Sadly, not too well. Lately her performance has been less than brilliant, to say the least. The lady has had some unfortunate setbacks."

"Oh, how terrible for her."

"Now, now. It's unworthy of you to be unkind. Still, she did fumble some important assignments for several of our biggest clients. Seems she just can't handle the work."

"Aw, too bad. And after all the trouble she went through to stab me in the back to get those assignments." Savannah wore the first genuine smile since they'd been together.

"Listen, I swear to you I had no idea she'd pull something like that."

"Come on, the only way she could've known about my work and the file names in my computer is if you told her," Savannah snapped.

"Sure, we talked about work, but I didn't tell her anything about your file names. She's a computer whiz. It never occurred to me that she was using working late with me as an opportunity to dig into your files."

"Then why didn't you tell Clayton the truth when I was on the hot seat? No, you let me take the fall because you were protecting her."

"I didn't find out until after you'd resigned. When you

made that accusation, it got me to thinking. You remember how wrapped up I was in Smith vs. Walton et al.? Karen was helping me with the research. I'd never do anything intentionally to hurt you, sweet. You know that." Devin leaned across the table. As he reached for her hands, she drew away, placing them in her lap.

Savannah wanted to believe him. She did recall how immersed he was in a big suit the firm was handling. Devin had been a good friend to her for so long at a time when she'd really needed one. Maybe she had jumped to conclusions.

"That still doesn't explain why you didn't bust her little scam with Clayton."

"I had no proof, just a suspicion. Please believe me, I would never have let her pull that stunt if I had known." Devin stared at her with an earnest, anxious expression.

"Well, you know what they say about blessings in disguise. I needed to come home. I was thinking of establishing my own practice, anyway. In fact, I have gotten very interested in consumer and environmental law," Savannah said.

"Not much money in crusades for the underdog."

"Fighting for environmental safety isn't a lost cause anymore, Devin. There have been more and more judgments against big business when they were caught polluting. Communities aren't willing to take whatever gets handed to them. Even poor people have stopped being intimidated by the notion of going up against large corporations. And government officials and politicians are listening to them."

"Sure, but don't count out the influence of the Batton Chemicals of this world. Right now the federal and state regulations are a mish-mash in certain areas. They can be contradictory or enforced inconsistently."

"Is that what you're going to argue? Batton Chemical complied in good faith, so it's not their fault that the feds and state bureaucrats haven't gotten their acts together? Come on."

"What I'm saying is this self-righteous act coming from Simmons won't wash."

"The people who have to live near these plants are scared, and judging from the environmental nightmares that we are waking up to every day, they have a right to be. Thousands of barrels of toxic chemicals dumped in empty fields or dumped into rivers. Tons of waste released into the air. The big companies will get away with whatever they can to avoid giving up their huge profit margins."

"Listen, I didn't ask you out so we could debate environmental issues or talk about this case. Let's just say you believe in your cause and I have a responsibility to defend my client. Now, tell me, how are you doing, really? I've missed you." Devin leaned across the table, his voice a husky whisper.

"Devin, you were a good friend to me at a rough time in my life. Maybe we could have become more once, but now—"

"But now you've decided to punish me for Karen. It was no heavy love affair. Just one of those things that can happen when a man and a woman spend lots of time alone working together."

"You don't owe me an explanation. We didn't have anything romantic between us, and we sure didn't have any understanding that we wouldn't see other people."

"After you left, I realized that you meant much more to me than a friend. Let's give it a try, sweet. We were so good together as friends. Think of what we could have as lovers." As he spoke, Devin moved to the chair next to her. He began to stroke her arm lightly.

"No, Devin. It's too late for that." Savannah moved away from him as far as she could without changing chairs. She didn't want to draw any more attention to them.

"Honore. That was fast. Even in Shreveport you didn't want to get serious. He must be one smooth operator to puncture your armor."

"He isn't a so-called smooth operator."

"Really? He works for Batton Chemical. He's going to testify that the company you want to put out of business isn't so bad after all. All that, and he gets next to you? He's got something special."

"Yes, he does. He's got integrity and heart." Savannah stared down at the plate of food she hadn't touched. Suddenly, she felt all wrong. In the wrong place, with the wrong man.

"Well, judging from the dreamy look you get in your pretty brown eyes at the mention of his name, it's official." Devin moved back to the chair across from her.

At that moment the waitress came to clear the table and give them the check. Savannah tried to pay for her half of the dinner, but Devin insisted on paying for everything. Savannah observed him closely. Was it her imagination, or was there a fleeting look of anger on his face that he'd quickly disguised right at the instant that he'd moved away from her, minutes before? Maybe it was her imagination because he was smiling and chatting about mundane things as easily as though they were the best of friends.

As they turned down her street, he slowed the rental car. Devin turned down the radio that was playing jazz. The music had been a backdrop to the casual conversation Savannah had labored to keep up during the agonizingly long twenty-minute trip back to Beau Chene.

"I want you to know that the old cliché holds true for us: we can still be friends. I mean that. My only concern is that he makes you happy." He put the car in park behind a dark vehicle in front of Savannah's house.

"I'm glad, Devin. Thank you for understanding. I didn't want to have this hostility between us."

"For what it's worth, if you ever need me, I'll be there." Devin gave her a firm hug.

As Savannah got out of the car, her heart thumped when a tall masculine figure emerged from her house. The porch light switched on and she breathed a sigh of relief. It was her father, not Paul.

"Poppy, you scared the life out of me. Is anything wrong? Whose car?" Savannah pointed to the minivan that resembled Paul's until the light from the porch revealed it to be a different make and color.

"Gralin. He stopped by to get some of your research. I'm sure glad you showed up finally. He's in the den with all your stuff, trying to find something on some case in your files, and I ain't much help." Antoine swung the door wide for her to enter.

"Let me put my jacket up and I'll be there."

"Sure, baby. Uh, so you went out with that lawyer?" Antoine followed her into her bedroom instead of returning to the den.

"Yeah. He didn't say much of use to us, though. He's too slick. Guess I should've known. But he did hint at one strategy he might be taking. I want to discuss it with Gralin and Simmons."

"Uh-huh. Paul, he don't mind this?" It was clear that Antoine's question was not about the case.

"Mind how?"

"Ain't you two courtin' kinda heavy? I mean, you out with some other guy, he gone be real mad."

"Poppy, I can't believe this. That is so outdated to think that I have to check with Paul. He knows Devin and I were friends. He also knows that there's nothing wrong with my having dinner or lunch with an old *friend.*" Savannah's throat felt tight as she uttered those words.

"If you say so, cher." Antoine went down the hall.

"Who you think you foolin', li'l gal?" Tante Marie stood in the door, her arms folded across her bosom.

"Now, Tante Marie, don't *you* start in on me. I already went through this with Charice and now Poppy." Savannah had forgotten the down side of being in a small town. Your relatives and friends were close enough not only to know all of your business, but to stick their noses into it, too.

"That man gonna be fired up when he find out. Goin'

out with a good-lookin' lawyer. Yessir, things gone heat up round here.''

Savannah was about to defend herself when the twinkle in Tante Marie's eye brought her up short.

''You're something, you know that? You're getting the biggest kick out of this. Well, I hate to disappoint you, but Paul is cool with me seeing Devin.'' Savannah lifted her chin as she passed her aunt to go to the den.

''Sure, Miss Priss. That's why you jumped two feet when your papa stepped out the front door before I turned on the light.'' Tante Marie chuckled as she followed her.

''He startled me because I wasn't expecting him to appear so suddenly.''

''Yes, Lord.''

Savannah was about to continue her defense when Gralin rose to meet her carrying a long sheet of computer printout. They quickly got into reviewing particular precedent-setting decisions that he hoped would aid Simmons. To her chagrin, Tante Marie and Poppy left the room whispering together and throwing backward glances in her direction.

''What's that about? They're not worried about the case, I hope. I really think it's going to be close. With a little hard work, it could easily tip in our favor.'' Gralin peered over his glasses as he pulled a large law book to him.

''No, unfortunately they're meddling in my personal life right now.''

''It's good they have a distraction.'' Gralin, engrossed in his reading, did not notice Savannah's mouth fly open in amused amazement.

Before long they were both shuffling papers and pausing to discuss complex legal questions. Checking her watch, Savannah was surprised to find that two hours had passed. It was clear that Gralin would spend the night combing through every book, every bit of paper. She yawned loudly several times as a cue, but he didn't even look up. The direct approach was going to be necessary.

"Gralin, it's late. Let's finish this some other time." Savannah said.

"Hum? Oh, right. I'm sorry. I got so wrapped up that I didn't think that I might be imposing." He smiled sheepishly. Packing his briefcase with some of the papers, he prepared to leave.

"It's okay. This is something that could affect our lives in a big way. It's no wonder you are working so hard." Savannah got his coat out of the hall closet.

"It means more to me than that. I lost my mother and my oldest sister to cancer. You know what they call this area? Cancer Alley. Six months ago my wife found a lump in her breast. Thank God they were able to remove it and it didn't show up in her lymph glands. I'm not willing to lose anyone else dear to me. I just can't accept that it's some fluke the cancer rates are so high around here."

"I know." Savannah could think of nothing else to say. She had been speaking about the effects from the viewpoint of a distant observer. She had forgotten that many had been touched tragically.

"Anyway, things are going to slow down with Mardi Gras coming up. Probably Judge Duplessis will call a recess at least until the Monday after Ash Wednesday."

"That's right. He's the king of the Krewe of Aurora. Every year during Mardi Gras, he stops any case he's presiding over." Savannah laughed. This wasn't unusual, since most people in Acadia felt the same way. Few things were so important that indulging yourself before Lent did not come first.

"Thank you for putting up with me for so long. I'll get in touch with you if I need anything else." With a wave, Gralin hopped into his van and drove off.

Savannah was lost in thought as she checked the doors and turned off the lights before retiring. The sound of movement in the kitchen drew her there.

"I figured you was gonna have to throw Gralin out. He is some kind of intense when he gets going." Poppy sat at the table, a glass of milk and a slice of Tante Marie's sweet potato pecan pie in front of him.

"He's a good man who has a solid reason to be so intense about this case in particular."

"I know." Antoine paused and nodded, a far-off look on his face for a few seconds.

"Look at you, raiding the pie pan late at night. How you keep your boyish figure is a mystery." Savannah kidded him out of his blue mood.

"Yeah, I just know how to pace myself. Which, by the way, is something you oughta do with that Devin fella, cher." Antoine wiped a few crumbs from his mouth.

"We talked it out, Poppy. Devin is ambitious, he can be devious, but I really think he got taken in by Karen. Besides, I learned my lesson. I intend to keep my eyes open to that one."

"And LaShaun, you can handle her, too, I suppose?" Antoine rinsed the saucer and glass in the sink.

"Tante Marie shouldn't have worried you with that silliness. It's nothing. LaShaun's been pulling mean tricks on me for years and I've survived."

"Your Tante Marie didn't have to tell me, I found a few of them gris-gris that you didn't even see. I got a good mind to go see Monmon Odette myself." Antoine threw the dish towel down onto the counter in anger.

"No, Poppy. That's just what they want, to see us get upset. Let's carry on as though nothing is happening. Promise me you won't go near them." Savannah hugged him tight, panic rising that he would become stubborn and insist on facing the Rousselles. Despite her words, the thought of them turning to threaten her father as well sent chills through her.

"All right, cher. You calm yourself down, now. I was just blowin' off steam. You right about ignorin' them. That's the one thing they can't stand."

That night Savannah found it hard to sleep. Finally accepting that much-needed rest would elude her at least for a while yet, she went into the den. Picking up her canvas bag containing pens, pencils, and extra notebooks, she reached in to get some of her supplies. She could at least get a little work done to help the case. A sharp object pricked her fingertips. Drawing her hand back, she rubbed away two tiny drops of blood from puncture wounds. Swearing softly, she dumped the contents of the bag onto the couch. A dark item stuck with nine pins fell to the floor. Touching it with her toe, Savannah gave a cry of disgust. It was a cow's tongue, powerful gris-gris used to bring down a foe. With the broom from the kitchen closet, she swept it into a paper bag and hurled it into the garbage can that sat outside the back door. She scrubbed her hands with hot soapy water until they were red. Breathing raggedly, she climbed into bed. Shivers shook her despite the heavy patchwork quilt pulled up to her chin. Now every sound, every shape in the darkness, seemed to signal some menace moving toward her. Drawing her body into a ball, she cried herself into a restless slumber.

Chapter 9

Purple, green, and gold were everywhere. Streamers were hung from the replica nineteenth-century lampposts downtown. Grocery stores, drugstores, even the dry-cleaning store put up window displays of Mardi Gras masks. The town's only bakery was buzzing day and night to supply king cakes for parties. Local companies were sending them all over the country to clients. Bosses served them at staff meetings. The society pages of Beau Chene's small newspaper were filled with pictures of elaborately costumed kings and queens presiding over the fancy balls of their krewes. Savannah and Charice were thrilled to revive a girlhood tradition, king cake parties. Beginning the month before, a circle of their childhood playmates began to host the Saturday night parties. A huge king cake was the most important item on the menu. Whoever got the baby, a tiny plastic doll concealed somewhere inside the cake, had to host the next party. But no one minded, since the whole point of Mardi Gras was to find as many opportunities as possible to party. Now that they were all grown up, they had decided to include males. Because Imelda had gotten the baby at Charice's house the week before, she was the host for the party they were attending the Saturday before Fat Tuesday. Savannah and Charice watched with amusement as she went around trying hard to convince everyone that Carlton had only turned to another woman because she had rejected him. "I guess he had to settle for something since I lost interest. Child, she is welcome to his tired butt. He wasn't exactly the most exiting man in the boudoir, if you know what I mean," Imelda told one more bored listener for the hundredth time that night.

"That is pitiful. Everybody knows he found something he wanted more than her." Charice, standing nearby, tittered.

"Yeah, and I can understand why. I dated her for two months. The only time she stopped talking about herself was to ask me to buy her something, take her someplace expensive, or tell her how good she looked." Terrel, another old acquaintance from high school, stood to her left. He shook his head before walking away.

"And she wonders why she has no man." Charice gave a snort.

"Stop being so catty. I think it's sad that she has to put on such an act." Savannah gave Charice a look of admonishment.

"I suppose so. But she makes it hard to be sympathetic."

Savannah reluctantly had to agree as she watched Imelda behave condescendingly toward two old classmates who had never been a part of the accepted cliques in high school.

Soon, though, her attention was drawn back to Paul. He had seemed moody and preoccupied all evening. His conversation and laughter had a forced quality. More than once, she'd glanced at him and found a grave, thoughtful expression on his handsome features and a distant look in his eyes. Savannah, aware of how fast small-town gossip could spread, was afraid to ask what was wrong. She felt guilty about having had dinner with Devin, yet angry with herself because she had done nothing to betray his trust. So why couldn't she tell him?

"Here you go, honey. Say, Paul, y'all ready for the next few days of parades?" Rodney, Charice's date, came back with a refill of punch for her.

"Yeah, man. We'll pick you up at about noon. We should get there in time for the first big parade in Metairie." Paul continued to hold the same full glass of punch.

A blast of music came from Imelda's elaborate compact disc system. On hearing the words "When you go to New Orleans, you oughta go to the Mardi Gras," one of the traditional Mardi Gras anthems, the whole room began to sing along and dance wildly. Savannah laughed at the antics of her friends. Paul smiled only briefly.

"You are certainly quiet tonight," Savannah ventured cautiously.

"Not much company. Sorry."

"This is the time to put all your troubles aside. Come on,. let's dance." Savannah took the glass from him.

"Maybe later."

"Have we had an argument that I don't know about?"

"What? Oh, no. I'm really sorry for acting like a zombie tonight. It's just that I'm not looking forward to testifying. I was hoping to get it over with before the holiday. Now I have more time to dread being put on the spot." Paul picked up the glass, taking a long sip of the powerful punch.

"Oh, right. That's the way trials go. Legal wrangling over rules of evidence, making motions about evidence being entered, can cause these kinds of delays." Savannah was able to relax for the first time since their arrival.

"God, I wish it were over."

"You'll do fine. Just stick to your report. Don't hesitate to refer to notes, if you have to. They won't expect you to have it memorized. And only answer the question you've been asked."

"I know. I'm not nervous about being on the stand. It's how I feel about being on the opposite side of you and your dad in this thing."

"Paul, we understand. You're an independent consultant hired to do a job. Why, even most of the committee understands your position. It's Trosclair and Singleton we don't trust. They pulled some pretty dubious stunts in business over the years."

"You are something else. Here I am, standing around with a gloomy look, won't dance, and keeping you from having a good time. I wouldn't blame you if you poured this punch over my head. Instead, you coach me on how to testify against your side and try to make me feel better about doing it." Paul drew her close to rub his cheek against hers.

As the tempo of the music wound down, he led her to a small clearing. Wrapping her in his arms, they moved to the slow pulsating rhythm of a love song. For the next hour they danced together. Savannah wanted so much to tell Paul about Devin, but something held her back. For the first time in weeks they were totally at ease with each other. The fabled enchantment of Mardi Gras seemed to have torn away all barriers between them. She did not want to lose this feeling, though it might only last for another three days.

"Hey, it's almost midnight." Paul spoke into her ear so that she could hear him over the music and laughter.

"Yeah. This party is winding down." Savannah glanced around at the dwindling crowd. Across the room Charice waved goodbye, then gave an exaggerated wink.

"Maybe we should be heading home, too." Paul followed her gaze in time to see Charice and Rodney, holding each other close, leave through the front door.

"Maybe you're right."

Back at Paul's trailer, he wasted no time. With a wink, he turned on his compact disc player.

"Let's have a little mood music. I bought this one just for you."

"Oh my, you know what that song does to me." Savannah threw her head back, allowing the clear, rich strains of Dorothy Moore singing "Misty Blue" to wash over her.

"Yes, indeed. Why do you think I put it on first?" Paul began to kiss her neck.

Soon they were locked together in a tight embrace that hurt so good. The sweetness of his kiss sent a warm flush down her throat to her breasts, then her pelvis. Feeling his hands push her hips against his, she moved with him in a soft rocking motion in time to a music of their own making. Without breaking contact with their lips, they went down onto the large stuffed pillows on the floor. They took their time undressing each other, pausing to caress, nuzzle, and lovingly appreciate each stage. Paul moaned low as he covered her breasts with both hands.

"So good," he breathed huskily against her skin.

Rising to meet him, her whole being quivered deliciously as he filled her. The next few moments were an eternity spent in a glorious rapture as they moved in harmony, responding to their desires. His whispered words of love guided her to touch him in ways and places she would not have thought she could.

Later, at home, she sank into her bed exhausted, but wonderfully so. Savannah hugged her shoulders remembering the red-hot touch that had left her weak only moments before. No, she would not allow Devin to spoil such a precious time. Without one thought for LaShaun or nightmares, she drifted off into a deep sleep.

Music, laughter, garish colors came from all sides to delight the senses. People from around the country thronged the streets with drinks in hand. The calculated surrender to chaos liberated the most conservative visitors. As usual, Mardi Gras New Orleans strutted and swayed with the brazenness and exuberance of a lady of the evening—one who, despite her age, can still entice all those foolish, or lucky, enough to touch her. Astonished tourists gawked at the fantastic sights and sounds of revelers cavorting in a wild abandonment that would make Bacchus himself blush. Men dressed in scanty women's lingerie, women not dressed at all, costumed characters from mythology, cartoons, became the norm, even mundane.

Savannah and Paul stood on the balcony, waving to the mass of humanity below.

"My Lord, look at that!" Paul pointed to a line of naked people running joyously through the crowd, oblivious to the cool, windy weather.

"That has got to be the least of the outrageous sights to see, Paul." Savannah was having a great time watching Paul take in the antics of the crowd.

"Maybe, but that second lady works as the office manager for one of my biggest clients."

"You mean you were actually looking at faces?" Savannah howled with glee as she leaned over the railing to get a better look.

"Man, this is the party to end all parties. An entire city has lost its mind." Rodney came out with a tray of drinks.

"Paul, this apartment is fabulous. Not only luxurious, but right on the parade route with a balcony." Charice followed him with another tray of food.

"Thanks. Brandon is a friend of Sam's. He hates being in New Orleans during Mardi Gras, so for the past four years he's let us use it. I've only been a couple of times. Sam comes almost every year."

"I heard my name." Sam strolled in holding the hand of a statuesque woman with auburn hair that set off her golden brown skin perfectly.

"Say, man." Paul shook hands with his friend.

"Everybody, this is my homey, Sam." Paul introduced everyone around.

"Nice meeting you, especially you, Savannah. You're the gorgeous lady who has got my man walking on clouds." Sam kissed her cheek.

"Thank you." Savannah blushed.

"This ebony princess is Danielle." Sam beamed at his date.

"Hello." Danielle flashed a dazzling smile at the men and gave the women a cool appraising glance.

"Put on some music, guys, let's party!" Charice raised her glass.

For the next several hours they danced, sang, and caught trinkets thrown from the huge ornate floats gliding by. Lost in the giddy atmosphere, Savannah felt free for the first time in weeks. Filled with happiness, Savannah was thoroughly enjoying herself despite her misgivings about the crowd and the danger of rowdy New Orleans when it pulls out all the stops.

"I have to say I'm surprised you got Miss 'Small-town parades are good enough for me' to come, Paul. Hey y'all, catch!" Charice yelled, as she threw plastic bead necklaces provided by Sam to someone below.

"And I can't believe old workhorse Honore showed this year. What could it be?" With a comical shrug, Sam looked at Charice.

As if on cue, both pointed to their foreheads in mock contemplation.

"Hum-mmm?" They said in unison.

"Okay, Laurel and Hardy." Paul grinned in spite of himself.

"It's true, though. If last year anybody had told me I'd be here, I'd have said don't count on it." Speaking softly into his ear while the others were preoccupied watching a fanciful float with a huge mechanical belly dancer, Savannah leaned against Paul's chest.

"Guess it depends on who you share it with, huh?" Paul wrapped his arms around her.

"Hey, come on, it's time to join the fun. We said we would go down to street level."

Rodney's suggestion was greeted with enthusiastic yells from the others. Strapping on small packs with cash and other necessities, they descended through the locked lobby and merged with the crowd. They were immediately engulfed in a sea of humanity from all walks of life speaking in different languages and accents. Stopping in front of a bar, all three couples danced to the New Orleans ragtime blaring through its open doors. They found themselves surrounded by others. They were skipping and dancing with everyone around them. Savannah giggled uncontrollably when a large man dressed as a sumo wrestler started to do the twist in front of her. She began to laugh so hard not only couldn't she dance, she could hardly catch her breath.

"Some friends you are. Why didn't you get me out of there?" Savannah fanned herself with a menu.

"But you made such a lovely couple," Charice quipped. She pranced around, gyrating in imitation of Savannah's portly partner.

It had taken them all quite some time to regain control after that sight. They stumbled, still laughing, into a tiny restaurant about four blocks away to grab lunch and wait for the next parade.

Until dusk they alternated between frolicking with the mad masses and collapsing in the nearest bar or restaurant. Holding hands, Paul and Savannah were the picture of a happy couple. As darkness fell, the area began to glow with Technicolor brilliance from the lights of huge floats that were part of the fabulous Rex parade. With the knowledge that it would all end in just four hours, the partying took on a kind of frenzied pace.

Standing close to the curb, Savannah shouted in triumph as she caught a long, gaudy purple-and-gold necklace with a large medallion attached. Turning to show the others, she found herself separated from them. She scanned the crowd, but could not see them. Making a full circle, she stood on tiptoe for a better view. A smirking white mask, a large red-lipped smile painted on it with bright red spots on its cheeks, bobbed in the crowd. Savannah found something disturbingly familiar about it. The wearer waved at her jauntily before melting back into the crowd. For reasons she could not explain, an icy stab of fear crept up her spine. Now, being separated from her friends in the crowd made her feel vulnerable. As she pushed against the press of bodies, her search for them took on a frantic urgency. Suddenly, something slammed her from behind, shoving her into the path of the parade. The next few seconds were a flash of bright hues that blinded her temporarily. Screams pierced the air as several people close by saw the gigantic wheels of a float bearing down on her. Savannah opened her mouth wide in a desperate attempt to call out for help. Her vocal cords refused to work as the monstrous shape moved to crush her. The fabric of her blue jeans ripped as numerous hands reached out, dragging her over the pavement and away from danger.

"Damn, that lady almost bought it!" a male voice cried.

Savannah wavered on knees of rubber, clinging to strong arms. She fell forward and tears flowed as she recognized the strong, reassuring scent of Paul's cologne.

"You're okay, baby. Sssh, now—it's all right." Paul held her tightly to him, crooning soothingly.

"My God, is she hurt bad?" Charice appeared, a frightened frown twisting her features. She examined Savannah for injuries.

"A few scrapes and scratches is all, I think," Sam said.

"Ma'am, we'd better let the paramedics check you out to be sure." A uniformed policeman took control, leading them to a first-aid station.

The female paramedic gave Savannah a pat on the arm after gazing at her pupils with a tiny flashlight. "She's fine, but she's pretty shook up. Y'all need to watch her for signs of disorientation for the next four or five hours. If she exhibits them, she'll need to see a doctor, okay?"

"Man, these people can be real animals when they're trying to get those beads," Rodney said.

They were back at the apartment. Savannah was curled

up on the loveseat, staring into space. Paul only took his eye from her for seconds at a time.

"With that mob and all the pushing, accidents happen. You have to be extra careful. Sam, I'm ready to go." Danielle, examining her lipstick in a compact for smudges, sat across from Sam with her long legs crossed. Closing it with a snap, she smiled at him alluringly.

"That was no accident. Somebody pushed me deliberately," Savannah spoke softly.

"Trying to beat you to the beads, sure." Danielle stared at her and shrugged.

"No, she was trying to hurt me." Savannah rubbed her forehead wearily.

"She? She who?" Paul folded her into his arms.

"LaShaun Rousselle."

"LaShaun!" Charice yelled, staring wide-eyed at Savannah.

"Told you Marie Leveau was bad news, brother," Sam said in an undertone to Paul.

"Savannah, that's crazy. Maybe we'd better get you to an emergency room." Paul took her face in both hands to study her closely.

"There is nothing wrong with me. I tell you, it was her. I saw her. She was dressed in red, wearing a large mask. A harlequin, I think, or was it a clown?" Savannah shook her head.

"Come on, you're scaring me. That medic said disorientation is a sign that you could have a serious concussion as a result of your head hitting the concrete." Paul tried to get her to stand up.

"No, damn it. I'm not going to any hospital. I tell you, she was *there!*" Savannah jerked her arm back.

"That other junk was bad enough, but the bitch has gone too far now." Charice paced the room glaring.

"You hit your head, too? And what other 'junk' are you talking about?" Sam said.

"Charice, shut up. You're right, Paul, I guess I'm more

rattled than I thought. Let's go home. I'll be okay after I get some rest." Savannah tried to smile and failed.

"I want to know what you and Charice are talking about, Savannah. Why do you think LaShaun tried to get you killed? Well?"

"LaShaun believes in voodoo, and she hates Savannah because her mama hated Savannah's mama because—"

"Say what? Voodoo? I'm out of here." Danielle jumped to her feet. "Sam, take me home, now," she said in a strained voice.

"Wait a minute, I want to hear this." Sam did not budge from his seat.

"You either take me home now, or don't bother to call me again."

"I will in a few. Chill," Sam tried to appease her.

"I'm leaving with or without you. If I leave without you, forget you ever knew me." Danielle stood by the door.

"Okay, okay. I'll take you home. Fill me in on everything when I get back," Sam whispered to Charice, as he passed her. "This ultimatum stuff is getting old, I hope you know that," he grumbled as he opened the door.

"I'm waiting." Paul turned back to Savannah.

"LaShaun hates me the way her mother hated my mother. Not because of anything I've done to her, but because that's what her mother taught her." Savannah spoke in a strangled voice as she sat twisting her hands. "I remember once when I was about seven years old, she and her mother were in the dime store, shopping at the same time Tante Marie had taken me to get school supplies. LaShaun's mama stared at us, then whispered something to LaShaun. LaShaun shook her fist at me. Tante Marie pulled me away and wouldn't answer when I tried to question her. It got worse after LaShaun's mama died in that fire." Savannah paused and breathed deeply. She looked at Paul with haunted eyes. "Monmon Odette has always blamed my father."

"But all that happened a long time ago. And even if she

is the one who's been leaving voodoo dolls to scare you, that's a long way from attempted murder.'' Paul shook his head.

"She hates me that much. You should see the look in her eyes when we meet.'' Savannah bit her lip.

"Listen, baby, you've been putting in long hours at the shop and at the library. You're stressed out, not to mention exhausted.'' Putting a protective arm around her shoulders, Paul spoke in a soothing tone. "Combine that with these attempts to intimidate you, it's natural that you would be jumpy and imagine all sorts of things.''

"I'm not imagining things, Paul.'' Savannah gripped his hand. Her eyes begged him to believe her.

"If Savannah says she saw her, then it's LaShaun. You don't know her, Paul. She can be hell on wheels,'' Charice said.

"This is unbelievable. What are we talking about? It was an accident. It had to be.'' Brows drawn down, Paul rubbed his chin.

"Savannah, you've got to watch your back. I'm telling you, this witch is serious about taking you out.'' Charice sat down hard.

"Um-hum. Maybe we'd better get going, Charice.'' Rodney, who had been sitting quietly through their exchange, startled them. They had almost forgotten he was present.

"Sam's not back yet.'' Charice handed Savannah a glass of water.

"So what? Look, it's late, I'm tired. Let's go. Hope you feel better, Savannah.''

"But we were going to follow them back home.'' Charice argued with him as they went through the door. With a resigned wave, she followed him out.

"Why didn't you tell me about what's been going on?'' Paul glared at Savannah, his voice harsh with reproach.

"Because it's *my* problem. There wasn't anything you could do, anyway.''

"Maybe not, but if you're in trouble, I want to face it

with you. Promise me if anything else happens, you'll tell me, okay?"

"Promise. Now, let's see if we can give you a happy face." Savannah put her arms around his neck and kissed his forehead.

"I mean it, tell me if anything else happens." Paul tried to sound stern, but her lips brushing his face softly melted any attempts to sound tough.

"You've got it. I feel revived knowing you're in my corner, you big, strong man." Savannah hammed it up with a high-pitched simper.

"Joke if you want, but—" He found her mouth more inviting than trying to finish his sentence.

"You know, I'm not so much scared now as I am angry. I don't care if it's LaShaun or whoever, I am not going to let them get to me. I'm going to help the people get their concerns about the plant heard, and I am going to go on with my life in Beau Chene. To hell with them."

"Hey, now. Break it up, 'cause I'm back. Where's Charice?" Sam banged in, unzipping his black leather jacket.

"She left. With her *date*, Rodney. You remember Rodney?" Savannah needled him.

"Right. The guy who wore that sucking-on-a-lemon expression every time she tried to have a good time."

"I think they make a real handsome couple. So does Paul. Wasn't that what you said earlier, Paul? How good Charice and Rodney look together?" Savannah poked him in the ribs.

"Will you cut it out?" Paul mumbled.

"Whatever, if that's what she wants. Ain't my concern." Sam spread his hands as if dismissing the subject. He lifted his eyebrows in disdain. "I've got several honeys to occupy my attention. You two going to stay here, or what?" Sam stood at the door.

"We're heading home." Paul looked at Savannah as she rose to stand beside him. His arm still encircled her as if to ward off harm.

"Goodbye, Sam. I feel like we've been buddies for a long time, even though we just met." Savannah pecked his cheek.

"Take care of yourself. See you, my brother." Sam grabbed Paul's hand.

The ride to Beau Chene was silent, but it was an easy silence. Savannah sat close to Paul, her hand on his thigh. Music from the radio combined with the glow from the dashboard lights to make the car a cozy romantic world with only the two of them. Words were not necessary. Content with this new intimacy, Savannah rested her head on Paul's shoulder.

"Say, Sleeping Beauty, we're home," Paul whispered.

"Humm. Already? Goodness, I didn't think I was tired."

"You forget, we've been up and going since six this morning."

"This is my house." Savannah wore a disappointed expression.

"I thought you might want to go straight to bed."

"I do." Pressing herself to him, she used her tongue to part his lips.

Without any more discussion, Paul put the car in gear and headed for his trailer.

After the hoopla that surrounded the beginning of the trial, the public quickly lost interest in the long technical explanations and dry legal wrangling, most of which they did not understand. In the third week of the trial, the audience had dwindled by two-thirds. Even the few reporters left were obviously bored stiff by most of what they heard.

"It's funny, but everything going on now is the meat of what will persuade the jury the fate of the plant, jobs, and even the environment around here. But hardly anybody shows up to hear what's being said." Gralin Mencer looked around the courtroom over the top of his glasses. The heavy black frames made him look more like a school principal dissatisfied with his pupils than an attorney.

"Don't be fooled, Gralin. Miss Lucille has been here every day. She is interpreting all this for most of the folks in Easy Town. They know exactly what's being said and why." Without looking up from the stack of organized and neatly typed notes in front of her, Savannah jerked a thumb toward the benches behind them.

Gralin turned to find Miss Lucille smiling at him like she knew exactly what they were saying. She waved as if to confirm what Savannah had just told him.

"I should have known. Nothing important affecting black folks in this parish has happened in the last fifty years that Miss Lucille hasn't been a part of in a big way," Gralin said, as he returned her greeting with a respectful nod.

"And you can bet that if she wasn't happy with the way this case was being handled, you'd have heard about it."

"Good morning." Simmons opened his briefcase with a loud snap after twirling the combination locks. Without comment, the tall red-haired attorney from the Dallas office of the Department of Environmental Protection got right to work.

"Good morning." Gralin began passing him sheets of paper.

Savannah smiled at the way the northerner skipped the southern custom of exchanging niceties before business.

"I think we'll be wrapping up the first phase soon. We've got three witnesses left to call. I saved the most powerful, in terms of the impact I think his testimony will have, for the end of this part. We will need it to counteract their star witness . . . Paul Honore." Simmons read his name from a notepad in front of him.

"Do you really think his testimony is that critical?" Savannah shifted a little uncomfortably in the hardwood chair next to Gralin.

"He's done a pretty thorough assessment, he's got great

credentials and a lot of experience, and he's African-American. What do you think?"

"Gentlemen, Ms. St. Julien." Devin strolled in, the picture of relaxed confidence. His smile for Savannah seemed to hint at a special intimacy between them. He turned to follow her gaze.

"Hi," Savannah answered curtly, acutely aware that Paul had entered the courtroom and was headed their way.

"I hope we can get together *again* before I leave. The other night was like old times. Oh, hello, Honore. Let me just review a few points with you for clarification." Devin drew him aside.

Savannah tried to focus on the conversation between Gralin and Simmons. Finally, she gave in to the irresistible urge to look over her shoulder. Paul was listening to Devin, even answering his questions, yet his eyes were on her. From the set of his jaw, she had no doubt that he had heard Devin's well-timed comment. When he didn't return the small wave she gave him, a tiny flutter of anxiety started in the pit of her stomach.

As the judge entered, Savannah and Gralin moved to sit directly behind Simmons in the spectator section. Watching him from the corner of her eye, Savannah tried to convince herself that the grim expression Paul wore was nervousness about his testimony. For three hours or more, Devin led defense witnesses through a meticulous description of the procedures used by the plant to assure that all hazardous wastes and the aggregate meet regulations. A chemist employed by Batton Chemical began to wind up his explanation of the production procedures that occurred before the aggregate left the plant.

"So, Mr. Fielding, this material is put through *five* separate tests?" Devin, one hand resting on the wooden rail surrounding the jury box, scanned their faces before turning back to the chemist.

"Yes, including certification from an independent laboratory," Fielding said.

"Thank you, sir. No more questions for this witness. I would like to call Mr. Paul Honore to the stand, Your Honor." Devin went back to consult his notes while Paul was being sworn in by the bailiff.

Devin had Paul describe his qualifications, educational background, and experience to establish him as an expert witness.

"Now, Mr. Honore, what were your findings?"

"I found the procedures being used to be in compliance with industry standards. All state and federal guidelines have been met."

"Did you identify any areas that needed improvement?"

"Yes. Mr. Singleton and Mr. Trosclair followed each of my recommendations for improvements." Paul gestured past Devin.

Savannah was surprised to find that both were seated across the aisle from her. For the first time in years, she was seeing Claude Trosclair up close. He was the same, immaculately dressed and composed. He favored her with a gracious smile, as if to say there was no reason they could not be cordial, even if they were opponents. Not to be outdone, Savannah returned his greeting.

"What has hampered their attempts to meet all these regulations?"

"Some of the state regs conflict with the federal regs. At one point the state officials with the Department of Environmental Quality disagreed with the feds on the permit procedures."

"Thank you, Mr. Honore, please sum up your conclusions for the court." Devin stopped halfway to his seat to face Paul again.

"Mr. Trosclair and Mr. Singleton have worked closely with their staff to ensure that the aggregate is treated correctly. The findings in other sites where it has been used suggest that the product that results is safe for certain uses."

"Thank you very much." Devin sat down with a self-satisfied grin.

Simmons handled his redirection skillfully, forcing Paul to admit that no long-term studies on environmental impact had been done, therefore the full effects of the aggregate were not known. Still, Paul's testimony had been effective. He appeared calm and confident in his findings.

Savannah fidgeted for the next hour, impatient for court to be adjourned for the day. Simmons called the first of his witnesses, a metallurgical engineer. Anyone observing her would have sworn she was intent upon the technical detail being provided by the witness. But Savannah's thoughts were across the aisle. Glancing sideways several times, she noted how chummy Paul seemed to be with Trosclair.

"Your gentleman friend seems to genuinely believe that Trosclair has the community welfare in mind. I was watching the faces of the jurors, especially the black jurors. He made some good points." Gralin leaned close to whisper softly.

Savannah nodded, still looking ahead. She had to admit he was right. What she couldn't understand was why. *Why* was he so intent on painting a picture of Trosclair as concerned citizen?

"We can only hope the folks who have lived in these parts for a while remember some of the misdeeds he's committed over the years." Gralin sat back.

Leaving the courtroom, Savannah started toward Paul, then hesitated when she realized he was standing between Trosclair and Singleton. They began walking out together. Savannah moved quickly to catch them.

"Excuse me, hello." Savannah gave a curt greeting to the other two men. "Paul, may I speak to you a moment?" she said in a low, tight voice. Savannah tried to will him away from the others. If only they had time to talk . . .

"Ms. St. Julien, isn't it? How nice to meet you finally. My, but I haven't seen you since you were a little girl. Now you're a respected attorney, I understand." Claude, suave as ever, intercepted her attempt to move Paul away from them.

"Yes, thank you. Paul, please—it will only take a second." Savannah's voice was desperate. Out of the corner of her eye she could see Devin striding in their direction. Stubbornly, Paul made not the slightest move to follow her.

"Ah, Martin. Doing a fantastic job. No disrespect, Miss." Singleton gave Devin a bone-shaking slap on the back.

"Yes." Devin gave him a tiny condescending smile. "I didn't do it alone, though. Honore here was a very effective witness today. Why, hello, Savannah." Devin stepped close to her.

"Paul and I—" Savannah put a hand on Paul's arm. Dread for the inevitable scene filled her. She had to have time alone to explain.

"And your statements about how Mr. Trosclair has personally involved himself in making sure all standards are met, well, it was priceless." Devin beamed at Paul.

"Thank you." Paul stared at some distant point just over Devin's shoulder.

"How've you been, sweet? Let's have dinner later. Mr. Trosclair told me about this wonderful restaurant in Lafayette, right on Bayou Vermillion. It's called Le Maison des Amis. Pick you up around six?" Devin gave the impression that they had all but planned to see each other regularly while he was in town.

"No, Devin. Paul and I were going to—" Savannah shot an anxious glance at Paul. She shrank back at the bitter glint in his eyes as he turned on her.

"No, we didn't." Paul cut her off. "You're free to do whatever you like."

"Could I speak to you privately, please? Excuse us." Savannah fought to control her temper. He followed outside. They stood away from the crowd behind one of the large white columns that stood so imposingly at the court-house entrance.

"What is it?" Paul would not look at her.

"Look, Devin and I had dinner once. Hard as I tried, I couldn't get him to talk about the case very much. He made some lame excuses for the way he treated me at the firm, then took me home."

"Your place or his?"

"Mine, damn it. What *is* your problem?" Savannah forced him to look at her.

"My problem? You went behind my back while I was out of town, that's my problem. If there was nothing to it, why then? And why go to some out-of-the-way place?"

"I only wanted to get a hint at his strategy, that's all there was to it." Savannah looked away. She searched for a way to justify not telling him about having dinner with Devin.

"Uh-hum, I notice you didn't answer my questions. Just to get information, huh? Real cool little number, switching your attention whenever it suits your purpose. Okay, so maybe you were only trying to milk him for information. Maybe that's what you've been doing with me, too." Paul's voice was hoarse with emotion.

"Just who the hell do you think you are, talking to me like this?" Savannah faced him, her feet planted apart. Her anger returned full force. His accusation cut her like a knife. How could he say such a thing to her? First his fawning, self-serving testimony to help Trosclair, and now implying she had prostituted herself to get information from him. Once again, someone she'd let get too close had turned on her. The image of a warm, caring man she wanted to have in her life vanished. In its place, Savannah saw a calculating man thwarted in his attempts to enrich himself at the expense of others.

"The way you were coaching me on how to testify. Did

you go back and tell Simmons which weak spot to go for, once I got on the stand? I can't believe I fell for it."

"Well, excuse me for not being a Batton Chemical fan, like you. Of course, I don't have a lucrative contract hanging in the balance."

"I am sick of you insulting my integrity. Especially considering the stunt you pulled with Devin. At least you've always known where I stood." Paul gripped her forearm.

"Sure, we all knew. Sell out the poor black folks, sure, let them die of toxic poison. What do you care? You'll get your money and move on. Take your hands off me." Savannah snatched her arm free.

"Let me tell you something—" Paul hissed and his voice shook with outrage.

"No, let me tell you something. You can go to hell!" Savannah stepped away from him. "If I never see your sorry ass again, it will be too soon!"

Chapter 10

Savannah stood at the front counter, staring out at the beautiful late March morning. Sunshine cast a lovely yellow wash over the scene. Tiny sparrows flitted in and out of tree branches, their air ballet provided with a perfect backdrop by the blue sky with its fluffy white clouds. This was the kind of day that could usually bring her out of her darkest mood. But for the last two hours the natural beauty before her had had no effect. It had been three weeks since that awful fight with Paul. They had spoken only once, two days later. There was still a bitter metallic taste in her mouth from the cold words they had exchanged.

"I think we've said all we should say to each other." Savannah had cut off his hello on the phone before he could finish his sentence.

"I was only calling to say I left some of your things at your house. Your aunt was home," Paul had said in a clipped tone.

"Fine." Savannah replaced the receiver with a firm bang.

Those words had been in her head since then. Though she had constantly told herself that she was right, that thought did nothing to make her feel better.

"Maybe some music will help." Savannah switched to a classical music station. She was taking no chances on hearing a mournful love song to plunge her more deeply into depression.

The soft strains of a Tchaikovsky piano concerto lulled her as she moved around the shop. A sudden swell of violins made her pause. Savannah became lost in the music, full and passionate. Closing her eyes, she could smell Paul's skin fresh with soap just from a hot shower. She could hear the rich, deep, dulcet tones of his laugh and see him tilt his handsome head to one side. She could feel the heat of his flesh press hard against hers, the steady thrumming of her heart as its pace quickened with their lovemaking. At the sound of the bell over the shop door, her eyes flew open. With extreme effort she composed herself before making her way to the front again. Hastily she wiped a light sheen of perspiration from her brow. Could it be? No, it wasn't.

She tried to arrange her face so that he could not see the deep disappointment she felt, a disappointment that stabbed through her body like jagged glass. With great effort, she forced her lips to stretch into a tight smile.

"Oh, hi, Gralin," Savannah said. The meager attempt faded all too quickly.

"Hello. I know you've been busy here at the shop, so I just dropped by to let you know that the trial is going well for us."

"That's good," Savannah said.

"Simmons has done a fine job lining up witnesses. I think we have a shot at winning. And to tell you the truth, I had my doubts when we started."

"That really is nice."

"That's great, believe me. I even hear that the Justice Department is going to conduct a national survey of chemical plants and waste sites to see if there is something to the charge of environmental racism. They want to see if there's a pattern of how sites in minority communities are selected."

"I see."

"You do know we're in to the second phase of the trial now?"

"No. No, I didn't." Savannah was finding it hard to focus on his words. Her gaze kept drifting away from his face and out the window.

"Yeah, closing statements could come as soon as tomorrow afternoon. And from what Simmons has shared with me so far, his should pack a wallop."

"That's real nice."

"Are you feeling okay?" For the first time, Gralin noticed her far away expression.

"Fine, I'm fine."

"Look, I know . . . I mean, try not to let it get you down." Gralin, in his typical shy way, said just enough.

"Thanks, Gralin. Listen, I really am glad you took the trouble to come over here. And don't worry—I really am okay." Savannah turned off the radio on the shelf behind the counter.

Several days after the jury retired to deliberate the case against Batton Chemical, Savannah was home, taking a day off from the shop at Antoine's insistence. Since T-Leon was now going to school half a day and working in the shop half a day twice a week, he told her to get some rest. Sure that Antoine would have plenty of help, she reluctantly agreed. It was almost noon and Savannah still sat on the couch in the den, flipping through catalogues and magazines. Tante Marie had been puttering around the house all morning. Savannah eyed her curiously. Strangely and quite uncharacteristically for her, Tante Marie had not brought up the subject of her breakup with Paul. Savannah was beginning to think maybe she had escaped when finally Tante Marie cleared her throat loudly.

"Hump! I told your papa you was askin' for trouble,

encouragin' that Durwin." Tante Marie slapped her dust-cloth on the bookshelves.

"I did not encourage *Devin* in anything."

"Then you stand up out in front of everybody and say bad things to Paul, and you in the wrong." Tante Marie placed a hand on one hip.

"Hey, you should be on my side. I thought blood was thicker than mud. How come I'm the one who's wrong?" Savannah stood up to face her.

"Well, you got a point."

"Thank you." Savannah sat down again.

"Both y'all was wrong." Tante Marie ambled out of the room mumbling to herself. She didn't react to Savannah's loud groan.

Later that night, Savannah sat in front of the television, switching from channel to channel. The only sound was the soft babble of voices as one program changed after another within seconds of appearing on the screen. The loud thud of the back door told her that her father was home from the shop.

"What you doin' still up, cher? It's almost midnight." Antoine had stopped in his bedroom only long enough to put on his house slippers.

"Watching television." Savannah sat there listlessly.

"That's true enough. You watching television, not seeing any of them shows, the way you whippin' through them stations like that." Antoine reached out to take the remote control from her.

"Get whatever you want, Poppy." Savannah pulled the collar of the robe to her nose.

"Come out of there, 'tite tortue. I could always tell when you was feelin' real low down and sad—you'd cover up your little face just like a turtle. Then, when I'd come ask what was wrong, all I could see were your eyebrows. And I'd hear sniffles." As he spoke, Antoine pulled her to him. Feeling her tremble as she sobbed silently, he rocked her gently.

"I feel like such a fool, Poppy," Savannah said, hiccupping. Fumbling in her large pocket, she pulled out a wad of tissue to dab her eyes, then her nose.

"Now, why you say that, cher? Tell Poppy."

"First thing I do is fall for some sweet-talking, no-good *man*," Savannah spat out the word as if naming a vile thing. "Oh, no offense, Poppy," she added quickly, between sniffles.

"None taken, cher," Antoine said, as he continued to pat her back.

"And he sells out to big business without any regard for what that damn company is trying to do to us. Then he gets an attitude just because I have dinner with an old friend, even though I told him it was possible and there was nothing to it. And he accused me of being deceitful, of using people." Savannah's tearfulness was giving way to anger.

"It can go hard when a man and woman are trying to work through to get to each other. There's gone be up and down."

"There won't be another time for us to be up, Poppy. He never completely trusted me. Finding out about my dinner with Devin just brought it out into the open."

"So that's it, then? Maybe if you try to talk about it?"

"No, Poppy. It's over." Savannah sat back from her father. "And I plan to forget about him. Life's too short." Savannah picked up the remote control from between the sofa cushions where it had fallen. She switched to a shopping channel, where they were advertising cookware.

"You sure you gone be all right, cher? You know it hurts me to see you so torn up." Antoine brushed her hair away from her face.

"Getting one of your special hugs has done the trick, sweet Poppy. You wait and see. I'm going to be better than ever." Using both arms, Savannah squeezed him tightly.

"Well, I guess I'll go to bed." Despite his words, Antoine paused in the doorway.

"Goodnight. Oooh my," Savannah said, yawning widely, "I'll probably be going to sleep soon, too." She sank back in a relaxed pose.

Savannah waited until she heard the slight sound of her father closing the door to his bedroom. Tiptoeing to the hall, she saw the thin line of light at the bottom of the door go out. Wide awake, she returned to watch the large-screen television. Her face showed none of the optimism she'd expressed to Antoine.

Though the jury had been deliberating for the fourth day now, Savannah took little interest. She threw herself into the shop, decorating, attending a huge retailer's market in Lafayette, doing everything she could to keep her mind occupied. Perched on a high stool with her back to the front door, Savannah carefully unpacked a box of ceramics shipped from a craftswoman in Mamou. In an instant the air grew still and seemed to thicken. The hair on Savannah's arms stood up. Every muscle in her body tensed at the sound of a familiar voice.

"Well, why you not hanging out down at the courthouse?" LaShaun was inside the shop, yet Savannah had not heard the bell.

Forcing herself to turn slowly, Savannah tried not to appear rattled. "Business has to be carried on." She began putting the new merchandise on the shelves near the picture window.

"Lord, thought a legal eagle like you would be all caught up in the case. Haven't you been helping that white lawyer, Simmons?" LaShaun strolled over to where Savannah stood.

"Some. Gralin is mostly doing the work." Savannah moved away from her quickly.

"But I hear you've been gathering all kinds of helpful information. Got just stacks of research done. Burning the candle at both ends, so I hear. Better slow down. You need your sleep." LaShaun followed her closely around the shop.

"My sleep is fine, if it's any of your damn business." Savannah's voice began to rise.

Turning around shakily to face LaShaun, she gripped a corner of the glass counter to steady herself. Savannah found herself alone in the shop. With a start, she saw LaShaun outside walking away casually. Not breaking her stride, LaShaun waved over her shoulder as though she knew the instant Savannah would see her. Savannah closed her eyes to whisper a short prayer. Shaking herself, she got busy again.

An hour later, Leon came to work, all raw adolescent energy and raring to go.

"Hey, Miss Savannah—did those new ceramics come in? Did Mr. Antoine tell you she's my fourth cousin on my mama's side? Man, I bet these things gonna move like crazy. Mr. Antoine says I can have a percentage of the sales, sort of a commission. We gonna have a booth at the festival. That was my idea, too."

"Yes, T-Leon." Savannah had to chuckle as he spoke in a rapid fire of words, hardly noticing she'd barely had a chance to answer.

"Savannah, Gralin just called. The jury done reached a verdict." Antoine rushed in with Tante Marie close behind, struggling to keep up.

"Y'all go on. Me and T-Leon can look after things here." Tante Marie gave T-Leon a peck on the cheek.

"Come on, cher. We don't wanna miss this." Antoine stood at the door, impatient to leave.

Savannah had indeed hesitated, unsure that she wanted to return to the last place of her painful exchange with Paul. Yet she could think of no ready excuse to avoid it. As she hurried the four blocks to the courthouse, another thought panicked her. Almost as if conjured by her, Paul appeared at the top of the steps heading inside ahead of them with the Trosclairs and Singleton. Naturally he would be there. If he could face it, then so could she.

Antoine and Savannah could feel the crowd growing behind them as word spread through town that a verdict had been reached. Because they had been only a few blocks away, they were able to get into the courtroom. They squeezed their way into space left at the end of a bench about midway up the aisle. Not long after that they heard the sheriff's deputy announce that the courtroom had reached maximum capacity.

"Frank Junior, you let me in there," Miss Lucille barked at the burly black deputy blocking her entrance.

"Now, Miss Lucille, I got to follow the fire marshal's orders. It's not safe letting too many folks crowd in here." Frank's voice pleaded with her for understanding.

"Fire marshal, huh? You see him in here?"

"Miss Lucille, please—"

"You think he's standing outside, counting to make sure you not one over? Stop talking foolishness." Miss Lucille came in the door. A young man gave her his seat.

"Et bien! He should have known better." Antoine laughed, along with everyone nearby.

Savannah did not hear them or her father. Her eyes scanned the crowd to locate Paul. Without thinking, she rose slightly from her seat. Devin, seated at his counsel table with the Trosclairs and Singleton, was the picture of confidence. Turning to speak to Claude, he saw Savannah. Seeing her above the crowd, Devin gave her a dashing smile and wink. Savannah looked away without returning his greeting and found Paul's eyes moving from Devin to her. Savannah plopped down in her seat in an attempt to escape the accusation she read there.

The judge gave a succinct summary of the issues the jury had to consider before asking if they had reached a verdict.

"We have, Your Honor. On the question of whether the facility is a legitimate recycler of hazardous waste, we find in favor of the plaintiff." The short stout forewoman sat down as the crowd reacted with rumblings that grew louder.

"Does that mean we won?" Antoine spoke into Savannah's ear so she could hear him above the noise around them.

"It does. Now the judge will decide if Batton Chemical violated any laws. And they still have another hearing on alleged hazardous waste storage violations and air emissions violations."

"What does that mean?" Antoine almost had to shout.

"Batton Chemical could be fined over a billion dollars if found guilty on all three thousand counts, plus the five years of operating in violation of the Clean Air Act."

Judge Duplessis banged his gavel insistently to silence the audience. The loud shouts were a strange mixture of celebration and angry protests. The deputy had removed several men whose anger at the verdict was so great they would not sit down and shut up when ordered. Once the noise subsided, the judge began the business of setting dates for the penalty phase.

Outside, Savannah stood with her father, waiting for Gralin and Simmons to emerge. The crowd, aided by the deputies, had quickly dispersed.

"I thought there was going to be a riot," Savannah said, glancing around them uneasily.

"You got what you wanted. Now we prob'ly gonna lose them jobs." Manny, surrounded by a group of equally scruffy-looking characters, glared at them as a deputy urged them to move along. Seeing Sheriff Triche's patrol car pull up, they hastened away, yelling insults as they left.

"That's good, boys. Clear this area up fast so's we won't have no trouble out here. Lord, I knowed no matter what the verdict, somebody was gone be mighty mad."

"They'll calm down some. He ain't closed the plant yet." Antoine nodded to the sheriff.

"I hate to be pessimistic, but dis here is going to be boilin' for a good long time. Let's hope it don't boil over into nothin' too bad." Sheriff Triche tipped his hat to Savannah before moving away to talk to a group of his men.

Savannah and Antoine were soon joined by members of Citizens for a Clean Environment. Savannah tried to feel their elation with the verdict but could not. The memory of her caustic encounter with Paul over a week ago in front of the courthouse after his testimony cast a dark cloud over her, a bleak shadow that blocked sunshine. She could still see the bitter dislike in his eyes. Nodding mindlessly to something that was being said to her by one of their neighbors, she saw the Trosclairs emerge from the court-house. Claude appeared to be giving instructions to Devin and Singleton. By the grim expression on his face, Savan-nah could tell he was not at all happy with the responses Devin was giving him. Paul trailed behind them at a small distance. Claude turned and motioned for him to come closer. As Paul approached, Claude began an earnest dis-cussion with him, Devin, and Singleton. Quentin Trosclair stood behind his grandfather looking strangely left out, a scowl twisting his face.

"Yeah, they steady plottin'. Already plannin' what to do next." A woman spoke with scorn, misunderstanding the look of concern on Savannah's face as she watched the men.

"Yeah, but they gone hafta do up some schemin' to get outta this one." Mr. Gaston, another member of the committee, gave a sharp laugh.

"Didn't get a chance to say nothin' to him," Antoine said, as they walked back to the shop.

"Just as well."

While Savannah went about the shop dusting shelves that did not need it, rearranging already perfectly arranged merchandise, Antoine gave Tante Marie and T-Leon a detailed account of the events at the courthouse. Savannah finally went into the office.

"We plannin' a celebration, child. Miss Lou done already called us before y'all even made it back here, gettin' the menu lined up." Tante Marie sat heavily in the chair across the desk from her.

"That's nice." Savannah began to shuffle papers in front of her.

"You can't enjoy 'cause of breakin' up with Paul. An' quit rattlin' them papers. You didn't come in here to do no work."

"Look, it's over between me and Paul. I was angry—"

"And hurt, too," Tante Marie broke in.

"Well, he did say some things that hurt my feelings, but I'll get over it. Life goes on."

"Maybe instead of tryin' to pretend you gone get over him, you oughta try to meet him halfway and work it out. I watched y'all, there was something powerful between you. Reminded me of Antoine and Therese."

"No! We were nothing like that," Savannah said, her voice raspy with emotion.

"Cher, you listen to me—"

"No, Tante Marie. I have no plans to spend my time feeling bad about some man who doesn't care enough about me to trust me. Now, let's not waste any more time talking about it."

"All right, Miss Know-It-All. I guess you know what you're doing." Tante Marie gave a short snort before leaving.

"As a matter of fact, I do." Savannah jerked a large accounts book to her and plunged into the figures.

Savannah was still sitting at the desk several hours later when the jingling of the bell brought her out into the shop. Devin stood smiling as he leaned against the counter.

"I wanted to—" Devin began.

"Gloat? Those little scenes you acted out in front of Paul

at the courthouse were worthy of an Oscar nomination." Savannah gave him a fierce stare.

"Act? I didn't have to pretend, sweet. We did have dinner. It isn't my fault you got caught." Devin, wearing a smug grin, shrugged.

"I didn't get *caught* because I wasn't doing anything wrong," Savannah said, in a voice taut with fury.

"Then why didn't you tell him we were going out to dinner?" Devin gave her an amused look.

"I did mention we might—" Savannah faltered, acutely aware of her own complicity in giving Devin ammunition. "That's none of your business. You deliberately behaved as though there was something between us," Savannah snapped.

"Isn't there?" Devin looked her up and down with a leer. "There was a time—"

"Yes, was, past tense. There was a time I thought you were someone I could care for and trust. You even came close to convincing me that sabotaging my work was all Karen's idea. Seeing you in action now, you know what I think? I think you used us both so you could be the only senior associate left when Clayton and the other senior members decide on a new partner." Savannah glowered at him. She was convinced Karen's troubles at the firm had resulted from Devin's machinations.

"Seems losing your engineer has made you not only bitter, but paranoid as well. I guess dinner before I leave for Shreveport is out?" Devin cocked his head to the side as he regarded her. Seeing her wrathful expression, he gave a theatrical sigh. "I suppose not. Well, it's goodbye, then." He turned to leave.

"Goodbye. And Devin," Savannah called, causing him to hesitate at the door, "with any luck, the Trosclairs won't take it out on your career because you were their lawyer when they lost a big case that could cost them a billion dollars. Oh, maybe not. Maybe at his age, Claude Trosclair's famous long memory is failing. So long." She smiled maliciously. He was blinking rapidly, and his smug look faltered as anxiety took hold.

Her glee at shaking his composure was short-lived. Once again she thought of Paul. Somehow, she had to take hold of her emotions and go on without him in her life. She forced images of his face from her mind. Frightened that stronger memories would plunge her into a paralyzing sadness, Savannah went back to her work with grim determination to think only of the tasks.

"Girl, what are we going to do? That devil woman is bad news. Now, my Auntie Mae has got some really good potions." Charice ignored the large half-eaten po-boy that lay ignored on her plate for once as they had lunch one Saturday.

Since the end of the trial several weeks before, there had been a few more acts of vandalism directed against members of the committee. But even more unsettling, Savannah had begun to be a particular target. Her tires had been slashed, a dead black cat had been left hanging on her bedroom window, and there had been more gris-gris.

"That's a joke, right? Besides, we don't know it's LaShaun. Plenty of people are mad at us for helping put the future of Big River on the line." Savannah nervously tossed her salad.

"This has got that witch's name written all over it. And no, this is no joke. You gotta fight fire with fire."

"You're starting to talk like Nenaine and Tante Marie. Hoodoo, voodoo, and hocus-pocus?" Savannah stabbed her fork in the air for emphasis.

"Oh yeah, well, there must be something to this stuff."

"What do you mean?"

"Look at you."

"At me? There's nothing the matter with how I look."

"So sorry, but as your loving friend, I have to say you look like death on a soda cracker. You've lost weight, you're jumpy as hell, and you have that 'I-got-the-low-down-my-baby-done-left-me-blues' daze on your face. Girl, you ain't been taking care of yourself!" Charice shook her arm.

"Thank you for that little pep talk."

"You claim it's not because of Paul, but who do you think you're fooling? I bet Morticia put the hex on that, too."

"Will you get up off that kind of talk? Paul and I were never solid, especially when it came to his working for Trosclair. I'm telling you, it wouldn't have lasted, anyway."

"Y'all looked pretty solid to me for a while there. But I have to agree, being on opposite sides of that fight didn't make for smooth sailing in the tunnel of love. So maybe it was inevitable." Charice shrugged.

"Well, at least you've finally agreed with me on that."

"Yeah, especially seeing as how you were always provoking him on the subject."

"Say what?" Savannah sat up straight in her chair for the first time in weeks.

"Lord knows, maybe I could have helped, had I gotten to you two wonderful kids in time. And now, seems like I'm going to have save you from the voodoo queen."

"Why, you—"

"Now, now. No need to say how thankful you are. Hey, I'm here for you."

"Gratitude wasn't what I was about to express, you can believe that. And you, save me? You still jump three feet when I come up behind you and yell 'Boo!' every year on Halloween night. Damn, won't you ever catch on? It's me, fool!" Savannah gave her a swat with her large napkin, laughing.

"Shoot, you keep catching me off guard." Charice howled with glee.

For the next several minutes, they fought to regain control. After reliving more silly memories they were able to speak without sputtering incoherently in mid-sentence.

"Thanks for that, girlfriend. You could always say the right thing, no matter how foolish—" Savannah made a face.

"Wait, now. You started out okay."

"You know what I'm saying." Savannah put an arm around her friend's shoulders. They didn't need to say any more.

"Seriously, though, you and Paul are finished?" Charice stared straight into her eyes, as if she read the truth there, rather than in her words.

"I'm afraid so. We said some things I don't think we can take back."

Charice took a deep breath. "With everything else you've got to deal with now, I hate to bring it up, but . . ."

"Well?" Savannah prodded her, after a few seconds of silence.

"LaShaun. That woman has got to be dealt with head-on."

"I think that would play right into her hands, Charice. This business she is trying to put on me won't work if I ignore it." Savannah began twisting her hair.

"You are still having serious questions about what happened between your momma and her momma. You telling me that deep inside you don't believe something evil went down?"

"People can commit evil without voodoo being the cause. Tante Marie told me some of what happened, but Poppy could tell the whole story—I'm sure of it."

"Yeah, but do you really want to know?"

"What are you talking about? I've been wanting to know more all my life."

"You say that, but remember that old curse—be careful asking for what you want; you just might get it."

"I need to know the truth, all of it. No matter how bad it is, it's worse not knowing."

The next day Savannah rose early to attend mass with Antoine and Tante Marie. The church was filled with friends and neighbors. She was delighted with the changes the new young priest had made in the service since he'd come six years before. The choir was filled with young people whose voices were robust and rich. Drums, a guitar, and an electric piano had been added to the old organ as accompaniment. Along with traditional hymns, the church was filled with the sounds of hand-clapping, foot-tapping gospel songs.

"Hey, Miss Savannah, hey, Mr. Antoine," Crystal and Nikki chimed sweetly in unison. Crystal wore a pink jumper, Nikki a pale blue one. Each wore a crisp white blouse underneath with lace around the collars and the cuffs.

"Hey, sugar dumplings. Don't y'all look pretty this mornin'?" Antoine bent down to speak to them.

"Hello, you cute things. You sure do." Savannah smiled at them.

"Thank you." The girls stood holding hands.

"Don't let 'em fool you, they haven't been the little angels they're pretending to be now." Charice shook her head in affectionate exasperation.

"I like high-spirited girls, they the sweetest kind." Antoine tickled them both and was rewarded with the bright tinkle of little-girl laughter.

"Good morning, everyone. My, what charming kids." LaShaun appeared suddenly from the crowd. The old woman holding onto her arm glowered at Antoine, but said nothing.

"Good morning, LaShaun. How are you, Monmon Odette?" Antoine faced them.

"You ain't been in dis church too regular, Antoine. I know 'cause I be here most Sundays even wid all my ailments." Monmon Odette's voice was surprisingly strong, her heavy Creole accent an indication that she felt more comfortable speaking the patois. Her frail body seemed shrunken from old age and arthritis, yet her eyes were bright and alert to her surroundings.

"No. Been comin' more since my daughter come home. How's your health?" Antoine spoke in a respectful tone.

"Well as can be expected at my age. You lookin' spry yourself. Now, this girl of yours, she kinda pale, like she ain't too well. What's wrong wid you, child?"

"I'm just fine, ma'am." Savannah returned her stare boldly.

"Look like your monmon. She was a good-lookin' child, too. A little nervy, though. You get to feelin' too poorly, you come see Monmon Odette. She's got some old herbs that'll fix you right up." The old woman cackled as she patted Savannah's hand.

"Yes, come by to visit," LaShaun grinned. "I don't think you've ever been to our house."

"Mornin', Monmon Odette, LaShaun."

Tante Marie joined them, along with Nenaine Shirleen. Nenaine Shirleen said nothing, but her sour expression spoke volumes.

"Marie, how you doin'?" Mama Odette squinted her eyes at the two older women, her expression losing its humor.

"We all doin' good. In fact, we doin' even better since old Trosclair been put in his place." Tante Marie drew up her shoulders with pride.

"Better be careful who you cross. Mr. Claude, he don't like nobody messin' up his business. Then too, plenty folks got somethin' to lose if that plant got to shut down." Monmon Odette cocked her head to one side.

"I 'spect you right." Tante Marie raised an eyebrow at her. "Got to be real careful 'bout who you cross."

"Yeah, well . . . best we get on home, girl."

Monmon Odette nodded curtly to them before turning to leave. LaShaun sneered unpleasantly at them all. They slowly made their way to a large dark blue Cadillac Seville. They heard the beep of the car alarm being shut off. With much care, LaShaun got her grandmother settled in the front seat.

"Will you look at their car? That thing is loaded." Charice's eyes were wide with admiration.

"They get a new one every two years or so. Monmon Odette got money. How she got it—well, I'd rather not say in front of the church." Nenaine Shirleen grunted in disapproval.

"You ought not to repeat old nasty gossip nowhere. Monmon Odette ain't nothin' but an old woman got left well off by her husband—" Antoine spoke sharply.

"More than one." Nenaine Shirleen was undaunted by his scolding.

"And you should feel sorry for her. She never did get over Francine dyin' like that. Losin' somebody you love sudden like that is hard." Antoine left them, his shoulders hunched as if he walked against a strong wind.

"Why is Mr. Antoine being so generous about that old— Crystal, Nikki, y'all go say bye to Father Trahan." Charice stopped short at seeing her two young ones were all ears.

"He's a good-hearted man," Nenaine Shirleen said, after the children had left.

"Antoine been feelin' bad 'bout them Rousselle women for years. He kinda feels like a lot of what happened was his fault. Odette losing a daughter, LaShaun her mother." Tante Marie watched the figure of her brother moving away down the sidewalk toward town.

"Maybe I should go after him." Savannah had been watching him, too.

"No, he gone walk off his sadness. He needs to be alone for a while. Let's go."

Later that afternoon, the house was quiet. Tante Marie nodded off while sitting on the porch. The April weather was cool, the sunshine added just the right amount of warmth, and the humidity was low. Birds chirped happily as they flitted from branch to branch.

Savannah had wandered restlessly upon leaving Charice and the girls. They had taken them for a ride in the country, ending up at Old River. After buying cream sodas and sandwiches at a little café, they'd sat on the boat landing, watching the covered pontoons take tourists on a tour of the bayous. But Savannah's light-hearted mood had gradually dissipated once she was out of their company. After riding around for another hour, she went home.

Walking into her bedroom, she picked up the large picture of her and her mother. Therese certainly was as beautiful as everyone said. Her thick dark brown hair cascaded to her shoulders. Her eyes were a light brown, and her full lips curved into a wide smile. She was wearing a white sundress with lavender flowers, and her shapely brown legs could be seen even beneath the demure hemline. Savannah, only a year old, was propped on her mother's hip, waving at the camera. Without even thinking about it, Savannah went outside on the back porch to climb the ladder to the small room they used for storage. She did not know how long she had been sitting on the low stool, pictures and mementos from her mother's early life strewn around her, when she realized her father was there.

"Your monmon was always shy 'bout gettin' her picture taken. Reason we got that many is 'cause of me worryin' her so. 'Specially after you was born. She used to say you couldn't move an inch without me grabbing my camera to snap a picture." Antoine pulled up an old cane-bottomed chair and sat next to her.

"I'm glad you did. Looking at these always seemed to help me feel close to her." Savannah allowed her father to take an old black-and-white picture of Therese as a young girl from her hands.

"Lord, but she was something to see. Not vain, either. That made her even prettier."

"Poppy, tell me the story. I mean the whole story."

Antoine's chest rose and fell as he breathed deeply, his eyes never leaving the photograph. He knew exactly which story she meant. In a low voice he began to speak.

Chapter 11

"We was kids together—'course, you know that." Antoine sat back in the chair. Still he held the picture of Therese in front of him almost as if he was speaking to her, too.

"Tante Marie did tell me a little." Savannah drew her knees up, wrapping her arms around them.

"Your monmon was 'bout four years younger than me. Four years means different things at different times. When I was twelve and she was eight, we let her come around some with the other little kids. Of course, we thought we was grown. Me, George, Willie, Lulu, Eva, Francine, Clancy—oh, a whole gang of us within one or two years the same age hung around together. We sneaked our first smoke together and went swimmin' down to the river when we wasn't supposed to. Tell you the truth, I didn't much notice your monmon back then. Like I said, to me she was a just a baby. We had some good times, especially in the summer. There was always something to get into, something excitin' goin' on. Don't know why, but all I remember of those days growin' up was sunshine, wildflowers everywhere, the river nice and cool when you stuck your feet in. Happy memories, ya know?'' Smiling fondly, Antoine looked at Savannah.

Savannah nodded. She, too, smiled to picture the image of a group of children roaming the countryside, seeking adventure. Savannah felt strangely as though she were one of them. Antoine picked up other pictures from the shoeboxes at their feet.

Antoine sighed, shaking his head. The smile began to disappear. ''We got older. Francine and me got to be sweet on each other, I guess as young as twelve or thirteen. I know what folks been sayin' 'bout her, but they forget how she was smart as a whip. And quick, man. Couldn't nobody say nothin' that she didn't have an answer for. She was full of spice and kept us laughin'. Most of the adults said she was too full of sass, that her monmon let her run wild. Fact is, they wasn't too crazy 'bout us playin' with her. See, folks was sayin' things 'bout Monmon Odette ever since she was a teenager. Some say her monmon, Estelle, was a voodoo woman. That they family been into voodoo since way back when Odette's great-grandpapa came from Haiti to New Orleans some fifty years before the Civil War.

''We didn't care 'bout that. Truth is, it just made us want to be around her that much more. What they didn't see was how she hurt over the things they said about her and her people. She didn't act no different from the other kids, so our monmons didn't make no fuss. My monmon did get real upset when she heard talk about me and Francine. Seems she thought maybe Monmon Odette put some kinda spell on me to like Francine. But Papa laughed and told her not to worry 'bout all that hoodoo talk. Said it was plain old-woman foolishness.

''Like I said, we got older. When we was 'bout sixteen, me and Francine was dating full out. Goin' to the old Dixie Drive-in, dances the church used to sponsor, even sneaking to a juke joint over in Breaux Bridge that wasn't particular 'bout how old we was. I ain't proud of some of the things I did, Savannah. But like most young folks, we thought none of them 'old' people knew anything. Crazy, how each new crop of kids thinks they done invented everything. Or if they didn't invent it, it was somehow all theirs. We drank, stayed out later than we should have, sometimes. Francine was always more bold than most of us. She used to say we needed to whoop it up, to breathe some life into this dead old country town. Yep, we was tearin' it up back then.'' Antoine paused, staring at the wall as if seeing the past reflected there like an old movie.

"I remember the exact day I stopped thinking of Therese like she was a baby. It was that summer I turned nineteen. My monmon made my papa lay down the law. 'Course, he did it with a sorta wink, you know, between us men. But Monmon was determine to get me back on the right track. She made me spend a lot more time at the church helpin' old Father Vavasseur by workin' around the rectory. Somehow, I convinced Francine to come to a church dance one Friday night. She decided it would be good for a laugh. Monmon was not too pleased when I showed up with her, but she didn't say nothin' to me.

"We'd been there for a while when Francine spotted Therese sittin' all alone. We went over to sit with her, keep her company. The next song that played, Francine told me to dance with Therese. You see, to her it was a joke, makin' me dance with a scrawny little kid. She hooted and made faces about Therese's dress, the way she danced, everything. But I didn't notice none of that. What I saw was something different.

"Therese was wearing a simple cotton dress that had a big bow at the waist. Her hair was tied back with a large white ribbon. I remember lookin' down into them beautiful eyes. They was like the color of cedar wood, with long black lashes. And when she put her little hand in mine, her skin was silky smooth and smellin' of gardenia-scented perfume.

"From that night on I found every excuse to be where

I thought Therese would be. I was seein' very little of Francine after a while. Lyin' became the easy way out. I fooled myself into thinkin' I was bein' kind. Naturally, with everybody talkin', it wasn't long 'fore she knowed. Even when she finally made me tell her the truth, she turned all her anger against Therese. Francine said some nasty things 'bout Therese, then I said some pretty hateful things about Francine. We parted with a lot of bitterness between us.

"Two years later, Therese and I got married. Lord, not even Francine could spoil those first few years we was together. I don't think we ever stopped honeymoonin'. Therese got more beautiful every day. I'm shamed to say I didn't give Francine much thought. Oh, I heard the gossip 'bout how she was with lots of different men, drinkin', even dope. But Therese was my whole world.

"Then when we found out she was pregnant. It was wonderful to see the happiness in her face. That miscarriage almost killed her—in more ways than one."

"A boy." Savannah bit her lip, remembering the lonely pangs of a little girl for a brother she would never know.

"Therese got desperate to get pregnant again when the doctor said there was no reason she shouldn't do fine the next time. Folks was sayin' Francine and Monmon Odette was burnin' candles on Therese. Therese got pale, couldn't sleep, and cried all the time. When she did get pregnant with you, I was worried she was gettin' too weak. But she had you without too much trouble. At first, I thought things would be okay. Then you turned out to be a sickly baby— colic, high fevers. We was up all night with you cryin' night after night. Therese was beside herself. No matter how old Doctor Butler tried to tell her you was gone be all right, she got to sayin' it was her fault. Sayin' that Monmon Odette had taken her first child, now she was gone take this one, too. Her health began to fail. She got to where she wouldn't leave you alone for a second. She stayed up all night watchin' you, even though your crib was in our room. This went on right up until she died." Antoine rubbed his face with both hands as he moaned softly once.

"Poppy." Savannah leaned against his knees, hugging them as she had all those years ago when she had been too young to understand completely. "What killed her?" She felt a cold fear work its icy fingers up her spine.

"Aneurysm on the brain, Doc Butler said."

"But folks say it was voodoo. Mama was slowly driven insane, then killed by Francine in revenge." Savannah's voice trembled.

"Now, you listen to me, the autopsy showed your monmon had lupus. Doc Butler said it attacks the body like that. He said most likely the disease weakened her arteries." Antoine pulled her away to look her straight in the eye. "Your monmon was sick for a long time and we didn't know it. That was probably why she lost the first baby."

"But the gossip—" Savannah was stunned by this explanation, which she had never heard before.

"Was nothin' but old foolish superstition."

"But why didn't you tell me this long ago? Why didn't Tante Marie say something?"

"It was my fault she didn't see a doctor, maybe even check into a hospital for tests. I knew wasn't no voodoo makin' her get sick. There were times . . ." Antoine's voice broke momentarily. "There were times I fussed at her. Told her she was bein' silly, lettin' Francine and Monmon Odette make her believe that nonsense. Maybe if I'd been a little more patient. I closed up. Whenever I tried to talk about it to you, to anybody, the words would stick in my throat."

"You couldn't have known." Savannah put her arms around his neck. As she pressed her cheek to his, their tears blended.

"I tried to tell them all, including Marie, but back then, folks didn't really understand somethin' like lupus. Voodoo they could understand. That Monmon Odette made Therese take sick and die—that they understood. Didn't matter what name the doctor give it. Me, I was out of my mind over losin' Therese. I didn't have the strength or the will to argue, to do much of anything. I just crawled into some dark corner of my soul. It was all I could do not to scream out loud at the thought of livin' without her every day for the rest of my life."

"Monmon's disease would have progressed no matter what you did because there's no cure for lupus. And you fell in love like any young man. From what I've heard about Francine, she was already using too much alcohol and had emotional problems long before that." Savannah cupped his face in her hands.

"A lot of the things Francine done was outta hurt. She wanted somebody to care 'bout her. I coulda treated her better. And I shoulda helped your monmon more. I let 'em both down." Antoine hung his head.

"No, Poppy. You couldn't have done any more. It wasn't your fault Francine or Mama died." Savannah cradled him in her arms.

"Oh, cher. I still miss her so."

"It's time for both of us to let ourselves heal."

For another hour they held each other, talking about the past, and beginning to mend.

"What are our options?" Claude sat in the executive leather chair, elbows on the vast conference table, his long fingers forming a steeple in front of his face. He looked at the men seated around him.

Claude had summoned Devin, Singleton, Quentin, and Paul to Batton Chemical to plot their next move.

"At this point, try to convince the judge that you acted in good faith so he won't impose the maximum fines," Devin said.

"Why don't we appeal?" Quentin slapped the table.

"Because the trial isn't over yet. We're into the penalty phase, where he considers how long you were operating without the proper permits, what kinds of emissions occurred—"

"This is outrageous. He was supposed to be advising us on this." Quentin pointed an accusing finger at Paul.

"As you so eloquently stated, you didn't need me. You were taking advice from your own chemical engineer. Besides, I was not hired by Batton Chemical, and certainly not to give you advice." Paul spoke in a low cool tone. He sat opposite Claude at the end of the table, away from the others.

"Be quiet, Quentin. How bad is it, Mr. Martin?" Claude said, his voice tight with irritation. He continued to stare ahead.

"If he finds that the plant has been operating without the proper permits since it opened, the fines could be enormous. As high as one-point-five billion dollars." Devin consulted the figures in front of him.

"Sweet Jesus." Singleton turned as pale as a sheet and began mopping his brow with a white handkerchief.

"Is that a real possibility?" Claude still sat as before. He wore the steely look of a general considering which battle plan to follow. Clearly he had no intention of surrendering.

"I think Judge Duplessis will take into account the jobs involved, and again, we could make a case for confusing regulations, play up the feud that went on between state DEQ officials and the feds over the permits. But you still could be looking at millions."

"Then let's begin to prepare for either outcome." Pressing a button on the phone at his elbow, he barked into the intercom, "Elizabeth? Get our accounting firm on the line. Then put in a call to Clayton in Shreveport. No offense, young man, but I want everything that hugely expensive law firm has to offer."

"By all means. In fact, he should be expecting your call, since I talked to him this morning." Devin nodded crisply. He began gathering other notes and typed documents to be reviewed in preparation for questions from his boss.

"The accountants? Why are you calling them?" Quentin blinked rapidly.

"Because, my dear boy, if hefty fines are going to be assessed against Batton Chemical, we need to know where that money is coming from and how to minimize the financial impact on the rest of our interests." Dismissing him, Claude turned his attention to Singleton. "I'll expect you to work closely with them to get a full accounting of every penny."

"But we don't know yet that we'll even have any fines. We might even appeal and win, get an injunction to stop the fines." Quentin's voice rose stridently. "I don't think—"

"No, you generally don't. I have neither the time nor the patience to argue something that is obviously the best course for us to take, now that we are in this position," Claude said, his tone that of a parent speaking to a trying child.

"But what about putting up a fight? If word gets out we're doing that, it could start a panic with the stockholders; key staff could start jumping ship. I really don't think this is necessary." Quentin's voice cracked.

"Singleton, get in touch with Wilkes in Rio." Claude, already making plans for his next steps, did not bother to answer him.

For twenty minutes, Claude issued orders, discussing legal strategy once Clayton was put through on a conference call that included the other senior partners. He took several overseas calls and gave instructions to the accountants. He even smiled coolly as he plotted to outmaneuver his opponents and use the system to his advantage. With Clayton and the accountants, a plan to restructure Batton Chemical began to take shape. Paul fidgeted and looked for an opening to make his exit. Finally he stood up.

"I'll be going, since it doesn't seem you need me."

"No, wait." Claude waved the others to silence as he saw Paul head for the door. "I need you here. We may have some questions about improving operations. Besides,

I value your opinion enough that I'd like you to be in on more than just that. Please stay.''

Paul was amazed at the way Claude began to marshal his forces. Once again, Claude showed that he was an astute businessman. He was very much in control of the situation, grasping wide-ranging implications immediately. But watching him, something began to bother Paul after a while. With everything moving so fast, phones ringing, rapid fire conversations, a disturbing new picture of Claude began to take shape.

"Get Ed Legarde on the phone. He told us that those permits would hold up under fire. I thought he had taken care of those state inspectors.''

"Remember, Taylor resigned unexpectedly last year as head of the Department of Environmental Quality. The new guy didn't play ball, I mean, appreciate our position fully.'' Singleton glanced at Paul uneasily.

"I thought our friend had that under control.'' Claude frowned, referring to a top state official without naming him even in a small group behind closed doors.

"The new guy's one of those professors. A real maverick,'' Singleton snorted in disgust.

"Damn it, he knows what's at stake here. He should have laid it on the line for this guy early in the game.'' Claude's fist made a loud bang on the desk top.

"I have another appointment. I'm leaving.'' Paul got up abruptly to stride from the room. His body language left no doubt that he'd be leaving this time.

"All right, but listen.'' Claude rose and crossed to him. He stood close to Paul, near the door. "We'll be busy for the next few days. If you're sure you don't want to be here, could you at least come back by my office, maybe Thursday? There are some things we need to discuss. Important things.'' Claude placed a hand on his arm.

"Singleton and I are going to be in New Orleans for

the next day or so with Babin. I don't think—'' Quentin spoke loudly through clenched teeth.

"I know that, Quentin. Well, will you come back?" Claude squeezed Paul's arm slightly.

"Yeah, sure. I, uh, should be free then." Paul felt Claude's grip on his arm relax. A curious tremor started in his chest as he saw the intense look in Claude's eyes.

"Good, good," Claude said. His face eased into a smile.

"Uh-oh, here it comes." Sam watched Paul packing boxes, labeling them, arranging them neatly for moving.

"Now what are you talking about?" Paul's eyes swept the trailer for any items that were still to be put away.

In the two weeks since the verdict, Paul had begun his preparations to leave Beau Chene. Since his lease was only from month to month, arranging to move when it was convenient for him was not a problem.

"The old man is going to offer you big money, a bribe, to keep your mouth shut."

"I don't know anything that would be worth money to him."

"What about that stuff you heard today?"

"Nothing I heard could be used as evidence that they were doing anything illegal. It was bits and pieces, no names, no details." Paul lined up boxes along the wall.

"Yeah, but it might be enough to put a sharp investigative reporter or prosecutor on the trail to finding the evidence they'd need." Sam picked through a basket of fresh fruit, then selected a large orange.

"No, I didn't get the impression that it was anything like that. Besides, if he'd been worried about me hearing too much, he could've let me leave when I wanted to earlier."

"Well, just be real careful you don't let him drag you into his shady deals. Say, you have got this place stripped clean." Sam gestured to the bare walls and table tops.

"Might as well. No reason to stay any longer. I'd have gone back to Lafayette two weeks ago except for some loose ends with that last bit of work for the university." Paul shifted the boxes again.

"Get serious. The only work you were doing for the university was that report on Big River, and it was finished well before the trial," Sam said.

"They asked me to review some of the research Simmons presented at the trial. They want to study this kiln process to evaluate the usefulness of it. In fact, they want to do a longitudinal study of the aggregate and compare it to health statistics in areas where it's currently being used."

"Uh-huh, so your hanging around has nothing to do with hoping Savannah might call?" Sam raised an eyebrow at him skeptically.

"Damn right." The muscles in Paul's neck went rigid. "She made it clear where she was coming from. Too clear."

"Maybe you shouldn't have assumed her seeing Devin meant she still has a thing for him." Sam went to the kitchen sink to wash orange juice from his hands.

"I can't believe this. You were the one who said she was using me. You were the one who said not to trust her."

"So, I didn't know her back then. Look, all I'm saying is, from what I can see, she isn't that type at all. Savannah said she might see the guy to find out anything she could; she told you that."

"She told me, sure. But she knew I wasn't crazy about the idea. Waiting until I was out of town tells me she had something to hide." Paul shoved a couple of boxes so hard there was a loud rattle from inside one of them.

"You didn't bother to ask her for an explanation before you jumped her case about it."

"From the way they were looking at each other in court that day I testified, I could tell there was more between them than she'd led me to believe."

"Now, come on—"

"I should have listened to you back then and gone home.

Just as well that we have a chance to get in on the work being done on the chemical and oil spill in Kuwait with waste-eating microbes. I've wasted enough of my time here."

"You just going to hop on a plane to fly thousands of miles away without at least giving her one more call?"

"You bet. Say, since when did you get so romantic? What happened to 'Man, just move on to the next one'?" Paul crossed his arms on his chest.

"Maybe there are times it's worth the effort. The easy way ain't always the best way." Sam stared down as he rubbed his hands together.

"You're not just talking about me now. What's up?"

"Nah, I'm trying to help you out. I don't want to see you unhappy—"

"Don't even try it. Some sweet honey has turned your head clean around. Danielle? Umm, I don't think . . ." Seeing Sam squirm, Paul blinked once, then slapped his forehead. "Charice? You got a thing going for Charice! Man, I gotta sit down on this one."

"What's wrong with Charice?" Sam squinted angrily.

"Nothing. She's a great person. An attractive woman. A wonderful *mother of two fine children*. You know, what you've always described as little short people who drain bank accounts, tie you down, get in the way?"

Since their days together in college, Sam had been the classic stereotype of a man studiously avoiding romantic commitment. He quickly ditched any woman who showed signs of wanting more than a relaxed dating arrangement. Having grown up in a poor family of twelve children, he swore to never be trapped with such a burden. Paul marveled at his abrupt about-face.

"Okay, so I've been a little wary of taking on responsibility. But this thing snuck up on me, man. Before I knew it, I was dating her and bouncing them on my knee."

"Then that's it, man. If you're playing with the kids and liking it, oo-wee, you are hooked." Paul smirked.

"Why are you enjoying this so much?" Sam demanded.

"Because of all your bragging about how no woman was enough to hold your attention for more than six months. How the only thing a woman with children could do for you is step aside so you good get to the woman without any. Ho, this is too good!"

"All right, have fun. But you never know how lonely you can be until you meet somebody special and then lose her." Sam leaned forward, putting a hand on Paul's shoulder.

"Forget that. She put on a good act, I admit, but she finally showed her true self. And I'm glad to get the hell away from here." Scowling, Paul got up and began lining up his belongings for easy removal. "And if I hadn't told Trosclair that I'd meet him, I'd be on the highway heading home for good right now."

A procession of five cars snaked through the inky night. They drove on an isolated blacktop road that wound its way deep into bayou country, a road so poorly maintained, it forced the cars to move slowly, frequently bouncing over cavernous potholes. Dense vegetation on either side crowded toward the cars. The hot night air was dense with humidity. Crickets and cicadas sang, their chirping as thick as the foliage that hid them. The smell of wet leaves and damp earth was so strong it seemed almost palpable. No sound came from those in the cars as they looked straight ahead solemnly as if seeing their destination. The lead vehicle, a small truck, turned off onto a dirt path that seemed to have been hacked out of the tangle of palmetto, swamp maple, and oak trees. When the small truck stopped at a large clearing, the cars drove around it, forming a circle as they parked. A very tall woman stepped forward and lit a torch. After setting ablaze a pile of wood in the center of the clearing, she proceeded to light tall black candles that were set at the four corners of it. One by one, headlights winked out. A crowd of about twenty-five men and women began to moan softly, some swaying. The light from the fire illuminated dark faces, some with wide eyes, as if they were startled by some fantastic vision before them. Others stood with eyes half closed, but all wore a glazed, glassy stare.

A hole had been dug to one side of the miniature bonfire. With shuffling steps, the group began to spread out just inside the lines drawn in the dirt connecting the candles. Suddenly a hooded figure dressed in a purple satin robe bordered in red with a red sash belt at the waist drifted from the woods. The figure passed among them with outstretched arms.

The purple robe shimmered even in the feeble firelight as a figure began to undulate rhythmically to the moans. At a sharp chopping motion of the arms, all voices fell silent. In the hush that followed, the *slap-slap* of water could be heard nearby. During a whispered chant, twigs were gathered and formed into a broom. A short stout woman brought forward pine straw. During another soft chant, she handed it to the robed figure. A crate was dragged into the clearing. It was pried open and a goat was led forward to the hole; it stood dazedly in the center of the group. The voices began again in a low chant of bizarre syllables. The figure began to chant more loudly than the others, its female voice rising until all others were drowned out. Soon hers was the only voice heard.

"O great one, good mother. I come to you with bowed shoulders and a bruised spirit. My enemies have sorely tried me; have caused pain and suffering to my beloved ones; have taken from me my worldly goods and my gold; have spoken meanly of me, causing friends to lose faith in me; O great one, woman goddess of majestic power, I beg that this I ask for my enemies come to pass:

"That the south wind scorch their bodies and make them wither and not be tempered to them. That the north wind freeze their blood, numb their muscles, and that it not be tempered to them. That the west wind blow away their life's breath and make their bones to crumble. That the east wind make their minds grow dark and their sight fail. Let agony and despair be their constant companion." The voice took on a sing-song quality as it grew louder. Folds of the full robe rippled as the figure began to quiver in agitation.

"I ask that their furtherest generations not intervene for them before the great throne. I pray that their children be feeble of mind and paralyzed of limb. That death and disease forever be with them and that they writhe in agony. That the sun not shine upon them with benevolence, but instead, beat down with burning rays to shrivel their bodies. That the moon not give them peace, but mock them, causing shriveling of their minds. That their friends deceive them and cause them loss of gold and silver. That their enemies prevail and their cries for mercy go unheeded. That all about them be pestilence, destruction, and bloody, torturous death.

"These things I ask of you, great mother, because they have dragged me in the dust, destroyed my peace, broken my heart, and caused me to cry out in pain. Let it be, O great one. So let be written, so let it be done."

Reaching out to grasp its head, the speaker stuffed straw into the nostrils of the goat as it struggled. The gleam of a large steel blade flashed and the animal dropped to its knees, then fell prone, with its mouth open. Slips of paper were thrust into the gushing wound at its throat. The broom was dipped in the blood and the ground swept vigorously the length of the twitching body. The sweeping went on as long as the blood flowed. With a sharp stick, an outline of the sheep was drawn. Being careful not to touch the sheep, pairs of hands holding garden spades began to dig so that the ground under it dropped the body into the growing hole. Nine sheets of paper were laid upon the carcass, then dirt was heaped upon it. A white candle was jabbed into the grave. The twigs of the dying fire popped and crackled as the group straggled back to the waiting cars.

"You know what must be done." The robed figure spoke to two others who nodded their assent.

Chapter 12

Quentin paced up and down in front of the couch where LaShaun sat serenely sipping mint iced tea. For twenty minutes she had attempted to arouse him, to no avail. He was too preoccupied, too overwrought.

"That audit will show money has been diverted from several accounts for payments to nonexistent companies for nonexistent services. Not to mention, showing transfers to nonexistent accounts." Quentin chewed on his fingernails.

"Make up an excuse to delay it."

"I've tried. The old man doesn't listen to me. He acts like I'm not even there. He discusses business details with everyone but me, the old bastard!"

"Well, you have to admit some of the things you do don't exactly inspire trust and confidence in your business decisions." LaShaun shook the glass and watched the ice twirl inside.

"He's never given me a fair chance or the authority to make real decisions. I've been sabotaged at every turn."

"Oh, really, Quentin? You have made a few, shall we say, boo-boos?"

"Shut up!" Quentin pulled her roughly from the couch, shaking her. "You got me into this with your demands, your blackmail." His fingers dug deeply into her arms.

"Calm down, lover." LaShaun spoke soothingly.

"This thing has got me going out of my mind, trying to figure a way out. If the old man finds out I've been using company money to buy drugs, he'll—there's no telling what he'll do." Quentin released her and resumed pacing.

"What do you care, with the money you've made so far? You have what you wanted." LaShaun stood in front of him, causing him to stop pacing. "You have the millions you need to start your own company. You have the contacts to get it going. Let him find out."

"Are you insane? He'd cut me off without a cent from the Trosclair fortune. I could wind up in prison for the things I've done." Quentin raked his shaking hands through his hair.

"No, he won't. Stop and think!" She grabbed his hands, forcing them down to his sides. "For generations your family has been obsessed with the right of direct descendants to the Trosclair fortune. No matter what he says, he won't cut off his only grandson. He hasn't yet, has he? No, Claude Phillip Trosclair is too proud of his bloodline. And he will never see you go to prison, not even charged. Claude will never see the family name disgraced by such a scandal. Sure, he may tie the money up into a trust that gets doled out to you, but so what? You said yourself, Clayton has ambitious associates. You might bribe the attorney into making it vulnerable to attack later on. Think it through."

"I don't know, the old goat can be unpredictable sometimes." Quentin resumed chewing his fingernails.

"Listen to me, all we have to do is examine all the possibilities and have a plan of action for each one." La-Shaun took his hands again. Bringing them to her lips, she began flicking her tongue along his knuckles.

"What about your friend, Savannah St. Julien. I'd like

to see her pay and pay dearly. Her and that father of hers, too.''

"I've already made plans for them both. Dark horrors await the St. Julien clan." LaShaun laughed deep within her throat.

"Such as? Tell me." Quentin's breath quickened.

"The warnings I've been leaving for the uppity bitch will seem like love tokens compared to what comes next. She'll go right over the edge. And take her loving father with her.''

"But we have to do something about my grandfather, damn him. This could all be solved if the old man would just drop dead,'' Quentin murmured. His eyes narrowed as he watched her hands move down his stomach.

"As I said, all possibilities can be explored.''

Stepping back, she allowed her robe to fall open. Her brown body still glistened from the scented oil she had massaged into her skin earlier. Letting it drop to her feet, she used her palms to caress herself.

"You know how I am when I get tensed up like this.'' Quentin gripped her arms tightly, his fingers digging into her.

"Yes.'' Stroking her hips against his, she could feel his excitement.

"And you know what I need.'' Quentin's voice was raspy.

LaShaun, her eyes gleaming, turned without answering and went into the bedroom. Quentin shrugged off his robe before joining her.

Savannah worked feverishly day and night. It was the only way she could keep thoughts of Paul from crowding out everything else. It was the only activity that made being without him somewhat tolerable, or at least, less painful. Not that the feeling of a great yawning hole in the center of her being ever really went away.

But work is like all narcotics; she gradually needed more

to numb the hurt. Because of this, she went to the shop early and stayed late. Now she was thrown mercifully into the frenetic preparation of getting a line of Tante Marie's seasonings, Creole sauces, and recipes onto a national shopping channel. Savannah had gotten the idea during all those long, lonely nights of watching late-night television. Through her tenacious efforts to make contacts, she had finally won an interview with one of the buyers.

"Damn, I'm scared of you. Y'all are going to be million-aires real soon." Charice stopped in one night while Savannah was working late at the shop. She shook her head in wonder at the projected sales figures from the marketing department of the shopping network.

"We did a limited test sale in just a few of their markets. Our products sold out in two hours! This is just the beginning." Savannah began counting the stacks of boxes ready for shipment the next day to the shopping channel's distribution center.

"Savannah—"

"We hired four people down at the pecan shelling plant. Mr. Benoit was nice enough to rent us the space to pack Tante Marie's products. Take that, Mr. Claude Trosclair. We can find other ways to put people back to work." Savannah thumped down a package of red bean seasoning into an open box.

"Savannah, this is all well and good, but . . ." Charice said, putting a hand on her shoulder.

"Don't," Savannah pleaded.

"You're constantly going at top speed, working like crazy. You're pulled as tight as piano wire. I'm afraid you might break under the strain."

"It may seem that way, but working like this is therapy for me. Get that worried look off your face." Savannah pinched her cheek playfully.

"I've just never seen you like this before. I hate to see you hurting!"

"Hey, this isn't going to kill me. Besides, Poppy and I

had a long talk about Mama. He told me things he'd kept pent up inside for years. We're closer than ever. So, while one relationship may have bombed, another one has blossomed in a beautiful new way. I feel like I've got my father back, finally."

"That's great, fantastic. But it's not the same."

"I've made up my mind not to be dragged along by what other people do. I'm going to take control of my life like I started to when I left Clayton, Briggs, and Schuster. No more distractions. I'm working on Project Me."

"Go, girl. Now, come on, it's after seven o'clock. Why don't you call it a night? By the looks of it, you've done the work of three men in here." Charice looked around her at the neatly stacked boxes, typed price lists, and recently organized shop.

"No, I want to finish up a few more things. I won't be too much longer," Savannah said, picking up a ledger. "Besides, when Poppy gets back from market in New Orleans, there will be tons of extra work for us."

"It's late and hardly anybody is around here. With all the stuff that's been happening lately, you shouldn't be in here alone."

"Go on home. I know you have to pick up the dynamic duo and get them ready for bed."

"Ain't that the truth? It's weird, if they don't get to bed by eight-thirty, I catch hell trying to get them to unwind for another two hours at least." Charice shook her head.

"Well, by my watch, your time is running out." Savannah laughed.

"Oh, wow, you're right. Promise not to stay too long?" Charice paused with her hand on the doorknob, a slight frown on her face.

"Go home, please. I'll be in bed before you, at this rate."

Making sure to lock the door behind her, Savannah plunged back into reviewing the figures. She was more than pleased with what she was finding as the whirring of the adding machine produced a printout of the profits.

Satisfied, she began projections on how well Antoine's wooden carvings might do. Savannah had had the idea of offering them as numbered and signed limited-edition pieces on the shopping channel. Two hours passed quickly as she became engrossed in her tasks.

A thump followed by the creaking of wood seemed to echo in the quiet shop. Savannah left the tiny office thinking maybe her father was at the front door. Seeing no one, she decided it was as good a time as any to take one last break before finishing up. She stretched, her muscles stiff from sitting for two hours bent over paperwork. Pushing the last few boxes into the storeroom, she heard a soft rustling sound behind her. She whirled around, her heart beating hard. Cautiously, she took slow, deliberate steps back into the shop. Noticing that the light in the office was out, she began to tremble.

"Don't be stupid. Probably just an old lightbulb went out," Savannah chided herself.

Still, she checked the front door to make sure it was locked. Sighing deeply after finding that it was, she giggled nervously with relief. That relief evaporated when she found that the lightbulb was missing from the desk lamp. The wall switch for the overhead light had been broken for weeks, and T-Leon hadn't gotten a chance to fix it with all the new orders coming in. Fumbling in the dark, Savannah searched a file drawer for the package of extra lightbulbs. Out of the corner of her eye she saw the light behind her blink out. For a few heartbeats she froze in place, too frightened at what she might see if she turned around. All of the nightmare visions that had terrorized her for the past few months flooded back at that moment. Gripping the desk, she fought to steady herself and think clearly. If someone *was* in the shop, her exit that way was cut off. Cautiously, she moved to the back door, feeling her way along in the dark, trying not to make any noise. Suddenly, her knees banged against something hard and she fell forward. Not all of the boxes would fit in the storeroom, so she had stacked them high in the office against the only clear wall. The one with the back door!

With a soft cry, Savannah moved back to the desk. Her hands swept the desk top and in her haste to find it, she knocked the phone to the floor away from her. Now unconcerned about being silent, she moved quickly in the direction of the dial tone sounding from the receiver. As she bent over, frantically searching the darkness, a large hand covered her mouth. She was roughly pulled back into the office. The door leading into the shop slammed shut, cutting off even the faint glimmer from the street light outside the large front window.

"You soul belongs to us now, p'tite fille." The husky whisper close to her ear sent shivers through her.

A strangled laugh sounded to her right and she felt hands roaming her body. Fingers plucked at her clothes in an effort to find a way to open her blouse. Savannah struggled to get free, clawing at the hands over her mouth. She bit down with all her might, tasting sweaty skin. As he let out a high-pitched wail, her captor let go.

"What the—" the other voice shouted in surprise.

"Goddamn wench bit me, man!"

Before they could react, Savannah bolted around them. Groping madly, she found the doorknob and yanked open the door. As she headed toward the faint light of the street lamp outside, she crashed into a wide display case.

"Come on back, honey." A voice came from her left.

"We ain't done with our party. I might forgive you for bitin' me if you were real sweet to me." Another voice came from her right.

"Yeah, be sweet to us." The first voice now came from somewhere in front of her.

Savannah still tried to make it to the front door, but strong hands clutched her. His grip tightened as she struggled to break free.

"Since you like it rough, I'm gonna give you what you

want." Hot, fetid breath brushed her cheek. His hold loosened as his hands squeezed her breast.

Savannah used both arms to push up and out, breaking free. Running blindly, she dashed away only to realize with horror that she was back in the office.

"We back where we started, little girl."

"Yeah, and we gonna have our party right here."

Two dark shapes loomed in the doorway, blocking any means of escape. Savannah backed away from them and bumped into the desk. Suddenly, the six-inch blade she used to open boxes was in her hand.

"Get away from me!" she screamed, as she slashed wildly in the dark.

"Fille de putain!" The curse rang out, followed by a grunt of pain.

Savannah could feel the blade connecting with bodies. She heard fabric ripping as she swung savagely in circles. The enclosed space that had been their means of capturing her now became their torture chamber. With loud banging and shouts, they searched frantically for the door.

"I'm cut, Teedy, man. Oh Lord, get me outta here!"

"This bitch done gone crazy! Yeow!"

With a crash, the door flew open. In a mindless state of fury, Savannah continued her rampage, striking out at any movement near her.

"Freeze! Everybody freeze!" A huge circle of light appeared.

"Savannah? Is my daughter in there?" Antoine yelled, above the clamor.

"Daddy, I'm here," Savannah cried out as the light in the shop came back on.

"Come outta here, come on," Sheriff Triche closed a beefy fist on one man's arm. He motioned a deputy behind him to grab his groaning, bleeding accomplice.

"My poor baby. Oh, cher." Antoine hugged and kissed Savannah.

"Oh, Poppy." Savannah, now spent, went limp against him. She sobbed uncontrollably.

"My little girl. It's all right. They can't hurt you now." Antoine spoke in a soothing voice.

"Hurt her? By the looks of it, dey oughta be glad we got here to save dem. Mon dieu! Look like a buzz saw got hold of dere asses! 'Scuse my language, ma'am."

"Thank God you came." Drying her eyes, Savannah took a shaky deep breath. She was calmer now, but still clung to her father. "But how did you know?"

"Charice called for you. Her and Marie got worried you still wasn't home. 'Bout that time I drove up and we tried callin' the shop. When the operator told me the phone was off the hook, I decided to call Sheriff Triche. With all been goin' on, I didn't wanna take no chance." Antoine kissed her forehead. His tender expression turned hard when the deputy approached, dragging along a scruffy man.

"Sheriff, this is Teedy Wilson. And this is his buddy they call Boo-Man. His real name is Jules Brunet. Real undesirables," the deputy said, glaring at each in turn.

"What is dis here you wearin'? Look like some kinda Halloween outfit." The sheriff plucked at the heavy fabric of the black robes the two still wore, now torn and bloody.

"J'ai rien à dire," Teedy growled. Yet his eyes were wide with fear.

"So, you gonna exercise your right to keep your mouth shut, huh?" the deputy snorted in disgust.

"We ain't done nothin'," Boo-Man muttered, then winced as he tenderly touched a cut to his lip.

" 'Course you ain't. Dis is all a big misunderstandin'. You boys lost your way tryin' to find the all-night liquor store, I guess? Get 'em outta here," Sheriff Triche cut off their howls of protest.

"Do we need to come down to the station?" Antoine said, still holding Savannah close to him.

"Won't take long, I promise."

With his two prisoners tucked away neatly in cells on the second floor of the old stationhouse, Sheriff Triche played the solicitous host, offering them coffee and cracking jokes to help calm Savannah. Antoine had gone back to the shop with one of the deputies to see if anything was missing or if there was more evidence.

"Yeah, we got pretty much all we need tonight," Sheriff Triche said, looking over the two typed statements his deputy had handed him. "Dem two was runnin' dey mouths 'til I tried to find out what dey was really up to. Lots of folks mad wid y'all over protestin' against that plant, yeah."

"You don't think they just broke in to steal?" Savannah signed her statement.

"Teedy and Boo-Man don't break in while nobody 'round. No, what dey do is to wait 'til the place empty. Dey sneak in and clean the place out. Seems like dey knew you was in that shop by yourself."

"You're right. I guess I was hoping . . . and those robes they were wearing." Savannah rubbed her shoulders as if cold.

"Sure somethin' funny 'bout dat, yeah." Sheriff Triche looked at her thoughtfully.

"Yes," Savannah said. Her eyes flashed with anger.

"Those two ain't gone tell who put 'em up to dis. Too scared." Sheriff Triche shook his head.

"But I think I know," Savannah replied.

"Dem Rousselles?"

"How do you know about that?"

"I been livin' in dis town all my life. I been sheriff twenty-two years. Ain't much I don't know 'bout what done happened 'round here."

"As you said, they won't talk. So there's nothing you can do." Savannah rubbed her eyes.

"You let me decide that."

"I have plans to deal with this."

"Now, I can't let you take the law in your own hands.

Don't go do nothin' foolish.'' Sheriff Triche shook a warning finger.

"If you mean break the law, then you don't have to worry, I promise." Savannah stared straight ahead.

"Now, you listen to me—"

"Well, everything all locked up tight. Not too much was damaged." Antoine came through the station door.

"Please, don't mention what we just talked about to my father. Please—" Savannah whispered frantically.

"Shush, cher. I know." Like a kindly old uncle, Sheriff Triche patted her arm in reassurance.

"What y'all sayin'? Ain't nothin' else happened since I left?'' Antoine became anxious seeing the tense expression on Savannah's face.

"Oh no. I was just telling the sheriff thank-you." Savannah smiled.

"You sure you want to do this?" Charice stood well back from the card table set up in Nenaine Shirleen's small storage shed. She did not like to be too close to the items on it.

"Yes, I'm sick of these games being played on me."

"Maybe I should go with you," Charice offered feebly, her voice squeaky with nervousness.

"No, this I have to do by myself."

"Thought you didn't believe in this stuff."

"But *they* do. I think it's time I used the same power of the mind they've been using against me."

Savannah stood outside the large house, her heart pounding. Her resolve wavered, now that she was actually here. The long windows offered no glimpse inside, though they were open. She could see the curtains inside move slightly in the spring breeze. A long porch stretched the length of the house. On it were chairs painted white with gaily colored cushions on them. There were potted plants scattered along the edge of the porch. Standing in the warm sunshine, it was hard for her to imagine there was anything in such a tranquil-looking home that could generate the fear she felt. Seeing no car and no sign of movement within, Savannah got back into her car to leave.

"Come on and sit wid me on the gallery awhile, sha." Monmon Odette came onto the porch, her feet scraping the wooden floor as she took short, careful steps. Choosing the chair nearest the door, she eased down.

"I was just passing this way on some errands—" Savannah got out of the car but stood with the door open.

"You curious 'bout old Monmon Odette, eh? Been wantin' to see where we live, ah know." Monmon Odette nodded to herself. She raised a gnarled hand and beckoned for Savannah to come closer.

"Is LaShaun home?" Savannah asked, as she climbed the steps.

Momon Odette ignored her question. "Sit right here," she said, patting the arm of the chair next to her. She smiled with satisfaction when Savannah sat down. "See on that table, some lemonade. Knowed you was comin, mais yeah."

"No, thanks." Savannah was perched stiffly on the edge of her seat.

"Go on, now." Monmon Odette pointed a crooked finger at the pale liquid.

"No, really." Savannah stared at it with obvious suspicion.

"What? You tink ah put somethin' in dere, sha? Monmon Odette don't pull no trick like dat. No? Suit youself."

"Where is LaShaun?" Savannah resisted the urge to peer through the windows.

"Not here. Off somewhere, runnin' round. She off every other Thursday. Switch turns working on Sundays with Miss Eveline down at dat museum. You didn't come to see her. Knowed already she wasn't here." Monmon Odette shifted so she could get a better look at her. "You is pretty, yes, indeed."

"Thank you." Savannah fidgeted beneath her scrutiny.

"My Francine was pretty, too. Look here." Digging into

the basket next to her chair, Monmon Odette pulled out faded photographs.

"Look, can't see so good dem old picture that done fade, but her hair was coal black. Hung down her back. See? Skin like warm coffee wid just a bit o' cream." Monmon Odette was quiet for several minutes, letting Savannah study the picture. "Know what killed her? Broken heart. Sho, dey say she die in dat fire. She die long 'fore dat."

"And you blame my father." Savannah's back became taut as she sensed confrontation.

"She love him so. Tried to tell her she have anybody she want, but no. Got to have Antoine."

"My father didn't make her do the things she did," Savannah said in a firm voice.

"Oh, here come LaShaun. You gone git to visit wid her, after all."

"So, you've accepted our invitation? Welcome," LaShaun said, a bitter smile twisting her lips.

"I only—" Savannah stood up.

"Wanted to see if we have a huge black cat, burn incense, and have cobwebs hanging from the rafters? Sorry to disappoint you." LaShaun threw a large canvas bag on the floor. Standing on the top step, she blocked an easy exit.

"I don't want a fight with you, either of you. My father feels badly about Francine, has for years. He cared for her and really cared that she suffered so. You must believe that. To carry on a grudge because a young man fell out of love with one girl and in love with another is senseless. They were all children together, but children grow up and infatuations fade away. My father has to learn not to live in the past, as do you." Savannah tried reasoning with her. The lightning change of LaShaun's expression from scorn to wrath warned that she could not hope to succeed.

"You through with your high-toned speechmaking? Let me tell you something, starting with you, everybody in this town has been treating me like trash for years. You, with your sappy-sweet self, got some nerve to come here telling us what we have to do. Your daddy screwed my mama in more ways than one. She wasn't good enough for the almighty St. Juliens. Humph! The St. Juliens are nothing but a group of uppity ex-maids and yardmen sniffing the ground for the white man's scraps. Well, honey, you got some surprises coming to you. Everybody in Beau Chene is going to be falling over each other to get on my good side." LaShaun's eyes blazed as she spit out the words in a rush.

"You're an even bigger fool than you were when we were kids. Nobody looked down on you until you started shooting off your mouth insulting people because of that ten-pound chip on your shoulder." Her resolve and anger back, Savannah brushed past her to stomp down the steps.

"You no-good bitch—" LaShaun growled.

"By the way, those little presents you've been leaving around for me?" Savannah threw them on the porch. All were scorched. "Nice try, but don't get your hopes up. And the next time you send some of your playmates after me, I'll send them back to you in pieces. If I even think you or you," Savannah said looking past her to Monmon Odette, "are trying anything like that on me again, I'll lay something on you so strong you'll be pissing in your pants for days. Oh, one more thing. That little party you had a few nights ago in the woods won't work, either." Savannah's lip curled in a contemptuous smile.

"Who told you—"

Savannah stretched herself to her full height. Taking a deep breath, she spouted the string of patois Nenaine Shirleen had taught her. She spit three times on the ground. To her amazement, a fine gray mist rose from the ground. The sunlight dimmed for a few seconds, then the mist disappeared as quickly as it had formed.

"Mais jamais! Go! Go way from here, gal!" Monmon Odette scuttled back into the house like a crab.

"Contre la force il n'y a pas de résistance. You cannot fight me and win now." Savannah spoke calmly.

LaShaun seemed unable to move, her eyes wide and

unblinking. Laughing, Savannah pointed first at the house, then at the two women. As if in no hurry, she went to her car. Throwing one last disdainful glance their way, Savannah left.

"What does it mean, Nenaine?" Savannah sat in the sunny kitchen of her godmother. She gazed about her in wonder at how different the world looked now.

"You feel what it mean, cher." Nenaine nodded slowly.

"Colors look sharper. Conversations, the way people move, all have messages deeper than what's on the surface. You know what I'm saying?" Savannah shook her head as though dissatisfied with her descriptions.

"You seein' clear now, Savannah."

"Something weird happened at LaShaun's house today. I went over there to psych her out. Then . . ." Savannah groped for words.

"Then a power came out you wasn't expectin', heh? Didn't even believe?" Nenaine set a cup of herbal tea in front of Savannah and eased her wide hips into the wooden chair next to her.

"Superstition and the power of suggestion, that's what I'd have said six months ago. But now—"

"Voodoo been 'round long time, yeah. Come from over in Africa. It's a healin' thing, cher. To bring you in tune with your spirit. Them old ones in Africa, they understand 'bout how le Bon Dieu use nature and spirits to deal with mankind. We what know the true voodoo know it a religion. Healin' religion, cher." Nenaine spoke in a soft, intense way, and her eyes glowed.

"Nothing has ever been said about LaShaun and Monmon Odette using voodoo to heal, but only to hurt others." Savannah frowned as though seeing the two malevolent women before her.

"There's a good and an evil side to everything on this earth. Monmon Odette and her monmon, on back for generations, been using some of the spirits that way, true. Nothin' but evil come of that, cher. They is a high price to pay. Look at the grief they done had.''

"Then why couldn't my mama be healed, Nenaine?'' Savannah said in a small voice. Her lip trembled.

"I don't know, child. Done studied it a long time. Sometime we just ain't gone know the way of God. One thing, Therese' soul at rest. We done the ceremony an' we got the sign. Therese at rest, cher.'' Nenaine covered Savannah's hand with hers.

"Thank you, Nenaine.'' Savannah gripped her hand. Tears flowed down her cheeks, but these were tears of relief. Deep within, she sensed the truth of Nenaine's words and found great comfort knowing that her mother was indeed at peace.

At last Savannah felt free of the cloud of fear that had hovered over her since childhood. Since the confrontation with LaShaun and Monmon Odette, the dark nightmares had ended. So did her dread of unseen forces, of voodoo. Strangely, she felt comfortable knowing that not all things could be neatly defined. She felt connected to these forces in a way she found hard to explain. Tante Marie and Nenaine had been right all along.

And with Teedy and Boo-Man facing stiff sentences, she felt no human threat hanging over her. She could almost be happy now—almost. A longing, a hollow feeling, lingered. Knowing that Paul was still in Beau Chene was even more agonizing. At every turn she expected, wanted, to see him. Yet she dreaded it, too.

"He's packing up to leave,'' Charice said, soon after Savannah answered the phone.

"Who?'' Savannah put on her best flippant tone.

"You know who. You really want to let him go like this?''

"For the hundredth time, it's over! I'm not going to

crawl, or beg his pardon. And how do you know he's leaving?''

"Sam told me last night. He's going back to Crowley, then—''

"Fine. Where he goes is his concern, not mine.''

"Just thought I'd give it one more shot.''

"I know you're trying to help, but it's no good. Hey, wait a minute, what's this about you and Sam being together last night?''

"Well . . .'' Charice stammered.

"Well, nothing. You pretended he wasn't your type, like you didn't even like him. All the time you were moving in on the poor sucker. Bet you reeled him in before he had a chance to put up even a little bit of a struggle.''

"Honey, he thinks it was all his idea! Which is fine by me. I could tell that if I'd shown too much interest, he'd have bolted like a jackrabbit. So I just played it cool. Let him make up his own mind.''

"But you knew he wanted you, girl,'' Savannah teased.

"There it is,'' Charice twittered.

"Seriously, I'm happy for you. He seems like a really good person.''

"He is. And good with the girls, too.''

"That's great. Before you say any more,'' Savannah said in a rush, cutting her off, "I'm going to be just fine, okay? Now, when I see you Saturday, I want all the juicy details; don't hold anything back.''

Savannah went back into the den after saying goodbye. Despite what she'd said to Charice, the reality that Paul was at that moment preparing to leave hit her hard. Once more she turned to work she'd brought home as a way to escape the hurt.

"Can I get you something?'' Claude stood at the handsome bar, mixing himself a drink.

"No, thanks. I'll be driving tonight."

Paul took in the spacious second-floor executive office. It was opulent with rich rosewood tables, dark red leather chairs, and a picture window overlooking a creek behind the office building. He had only been on the first floor and hadn't realized that Claude kept this office for himself. There was another elevator leading to this enormous suite from a covered parking lot behind the building.

"So, you are leaving, then? Singleton had mentioned he thought you might be." Claude sat in the large chair next to him.

"Well, my work is through. No reason to stay, really." Paul stared out the window.

"I see." Claude took a long sip of the amber liquid. "Have you given any thought to the contract? Surely your lawyer has examined it thoroughly enough by now."

"Yes."

"And?"

"The contract provisions are fine. But my partner and I—we've decided we have our hands full already."

"The money would allow you to hire more people to do the extra work. Think of the contacts you'd make." Claude put the drink down on the low table between them.

"We have contacts now. We'll expand, but not now."

"This isn't about being too busy to take on more or not wanting to expand. You've been actively seeking new ventures, new technologies, to make your services attractive to more companies. You'll be leaving for Kuwait soon. And you've been in touch with . . ." Claude went to the desk and opened a brown folder, "a California company called Enviro-Tech, about a new type of sponge for cleaning up oil spills."

"That information isn't in the company materials we provided to you or the university." Paul's brows drew together. "Where did you get it?"

"We did some checking on our own, naturally, since we

wanted more—detail. The point is, this contract fits right in with where you want to go. So what's the real reason for your refusal?" Claude turned.

After a long pause, Paul looked up at him with a stern set to his jaw. "The way you do business."

"The way we do business is no different from that of any other large, successful business in this state, or this country, for that matter." Claude waved a hand, dismissing his objection.

"Not all of them, and not mine, for sure. Back-door deals with politicians and public officials who are willing to sacrifice the health of their constituents is definitely nothing I want to be part of," Paul said, a hard edge in his voice.

"Don't be naive or too hasty to pass judgment. Those politicians and public officials are smart enough to know that we are their constituents, as well." Claude sat back down, smiling at him indulgently. He was the picture of calm, secure in his position in the social order. "Our interests are as valid as a whining group of malcontents who can't possibly contribute to the economy what we can. They'd starve without us."

"Those malcontents, as you call them, pay taxes, have jobs, and contribute to the economy as much or more. But even if they didn't, they have a right to expect that businesses have some control over what they can do in the name of profit," Paul said, distaste evident in his tone.

"Those profits go to salaries, expansions, community projects, and scholarships to help those same people who are screaming into the reporters' microphones. They resent us for being who we are and what we are. Yes, we live well. Sure, why shouldn't we? We're the brains, drive, and guts that make things happen." Claude jabbed a finger in the air between them.

"And what about safety, the environment?" Paul asked.

"Big business has pioneered industrial safety, including

protecting the environment. But things have gone too far with this radical environmentalism. Besides, great strides mean taking risks.''

"Yeah, as long as the risks are taken by someone else. I must have been crazy to think you were genuinely interested in ways to reduce toxic emissions or prevent spills. What you really want is to find ways to fool the public into thinking you are doing more than you are, to find ways to cut corners so your profit margin won't be affected.'' Paul stared out the window again. The hard look on his face made it plain that he would not accept Claude's words.

"Paul, this is senseless.'' Claude spread his arms wide to him in a plea for understanding. "I'm not the evil industrial robber baron you make me out to be. You are more like me than you care to admit. Certainly profit is important. You didn't get where you are by not keeping your eye on the bottom line. You're smart; your father knew your potential. He saw to it that you got the best education possible by doing extra jobs as a paint contractor. You've got both his backbone and your grandmother's brains. Don't waste them by throwing away this opportunity.''

"What did you just say?'' Paul's head jerked up.

"This is the opportunity of a lifetime. Don't—''

"No, about my father and grandmother. What do you know about my family?''

"Everything.''

"You investigated my family as well.'' Paul's eyes narrowed as he looked at the thick folder. Striding to the desk, he leaned forward and yanked the file to him. Scanning a few pages, he looked up. "I guess I shouldn't be surprised.'' He slapped it back down in front of Claude.

"Did she ever mention me?'' Claude said softly.

"No. Never.'' Paul was curt, not caring about his feelings. "Only in a diary. When you didn't try to find her, she realized she'd been used.''

"That wasn't true. Things were . . . difficult." Claude placed a hand on the folder.

"Don't bother to explain. She was the maid; you sowed some wild oats; it happened a lot back then, I hear." Paul sneered. He turned away to leave.

"You listen to me, young man," Claude shouted, standing up, "I cared for Marguerite. She was fine and beautiful. She saw the reality of our situation. We both did. Maybe I could have shown more backbone, but I did the only thing I could for those times. But, well, there was too much at stake. We were both so young. My future—"

"Yes, your future as the heir apparent. After all, what did she have to lose, compared to you?" Paul turned back to face him.

"Believe me, there have been long nights when I couldn't sleep because of missing her." Claude rubbed his eyes. He looked tired and older.

"Yeah, just not enough to give up the family name or a little of the family money to keep her from starving."

"My father wouldn't allow it when she refused the money for an abortion. I had no money of my own to give." Claude shook his head.

"You make me sick. You had money from your grandmother. Oh yes, I know more than you think. You could have done more, and I'm sure you knew where she was all along, didn't you?"

"Paul, I—"

"That's what I thought." Paul turned from him in repulsion.

"I don't want us to part in anger. Maybe I was foolish to think that we could be close. I even thought maybe I could talk to your father," Claude said.

"Stay away from him. He doesn't want anything to do with you." Paul became anxious, imagining the effect of such a meeting on Charles. "You're fifty years too late."

"You're right. But that doesn't mean we can't continue

our business relationship. Batton Chemical is your future, son.'' Claude studied him.

"I won't let you put lives in danger. Don't think because all the fuss dies down, those procedures and changes I recommended can be abandoned. I'll be watching. What's more, I'll tell the Citizens for a Clean Environment what to look for, too.'' He returned Claude's steady gaze with one just as unwavering.

"I see.'' Claude's face became hard, as though chiseled of stone.

"Seems we have nothing else to discuss.'' Paul went to the private elevator and jabbed the button.

"Where do you think you've gotten most of your business for the past three years?'' Claude barked. "I made you, and I can break you. Think about it long and hard, boy. Your father is sick, and those medical bills are piling up. You've been able to help them out more than your brothers, who live from paycheck to paycheck—both of whom happen to work at plants operated by ChemCo. The CEO and I go way back, old fraternity brothers, actually. Neither you nor your family can afford for you to . . . make the wrong business decision when it comes to this.''

"You're threatening my family? Why, you—Grandmother didn't know the *half* of what a slimy no-good bastard you are.''

Paul growled. He took a step towards Claude.

The door to the outer hall opened a crack. "Mr. Trosclair, is everything all right? I heard shouting . . .'' The office manager, her eyes wide with fright, peered at them.

"Yes, Beverly. Everything is fine.'' Claude waved her away and waited until she went down the hall. "Don't doubt that I will do whatever I have to to save Batton Chemical and my family's fortune. Think carefully before you cross me.'' He stood between Paul and the elevator.

Paul went to the door leading to the hallway. He paused after opening it. "Maybe you will win. Whatever happens, you're still a loser in a way you'll probably never fully appreciate," Paul said. All the heat and anger was gone from his voice. His face a mixture of sadness and loathing, Paul closed the door quietly.

"Claude, is everything all right? Dear me, you look worn out. I'll get you a cup of tea. Now, I know you like your strong coffee, but really, tea is better on raw nerves." Annadine half rose, but stopped at the cold glance from her husband.

"Haven't we had this same inane discussion for years? I do not like tea." Claude rubbed his temples with his fingertips.

"Certainly, dear. I just thought . . . I know, a vacation. That's what you need."

"Annadine—" Claude spoke in a low voice.

"We could go to that wonderful old hotel in Biloxi where we spent our honeymoon, then visit our cousins in Jackson. Oh, Claude, if only we could be happy, the way we were then. Remember how we drove along the Gulf Coast, laughing and singing? We were so carefree." Annadine smiled.

"No, it's not possible."

"But Claude, it's been years since we took a trip together," Annadine said. Claude sat opposite her without looking at her. "We don't do much of anything together. I wish we could be close, truly close, the way we were when we first got married."

"Not again, please. This is not a good time to get into another discussion about what went wrong with our marriage. I have a lot on my mind."

"We've been married for over thirty six-years, and for more than half that time, you've treated me as though I were some necessary convenience."

"You've had a very good life, as far as I can see. Travel, clothes, all the right society connections—you seemed to be enjoying it."

"I wanted more from you than that. Please, Claude. Let

Kyle and Quentin handle the business for a while. Clayton
has scores of bright lawyers who know exactly what to do.
It isn't too late for us." Annadine's voice trembled as she
sat next to him on the spacious sofa. She tried to embrace
him.

"Quentin? Allowing Quentin to handle anything is guar-
anteed to end in disaster. Now, will you stop this foolishness?" Claude snapped, pushing her arms away.

"Who is it this time? Another one of your young sluts
at the office?" Annadine drew back as if she'd been struck
across the face.

"Stop this."

"You've spent more time in bed with other women than
with your wife." Annadine's voice rose.

"Not another ugly scene, for heaven's sake. I really need
a drink now." Claude went to the bar.

"Your family has meant less to you than the trash you
pick up God knows where. You spent little time with your
son, breaking his heart. You pushed me away. And now
you've set out to ruin your grandson's life with your selfish
cruelty."

"Don't go too far, woman."

"I've given you my life, my son, and you've treated us
as though we were nothing to you. My family helped the
Trosclairs rebuild their fortunes after the war. We—"

"The Mouton family was only a minor player in our
business, believe me. As for you, it took very little time for
me to realize that there was nothing behind that lovely
smile except a frigid, silly woman who was more interested
in position and appearances. And your son was a weak
simpleton who spent all his time making an ass of himself
in every possible way. As for Quentin, well, his record
speaks for itself. It pains me to know he'll inherit what
generations of men better than he built. I've a good mind
to—"

"To what, Claude? Acknowledge the bastard son of that
colored whore? So, after all these years, I finally get your

full attention. Yes, I've always known about Marguerite. You sank low enough to rut with a common nigra housemaid."

"Marguerite was worth ten of you! You, with your anemic pawing in the dark. You have all the passion of a cold, wet blanket against the skin. The only way I could stomach touching you after a while was to think of her. But even that wasn't enough." Claude's face was vicious as he taunted her.

"No, I won't listen," Annadine said, as she rushed for the door.

"The hell you won't." Claude caught her arm, dragging her back. "You started this; now, you'll hear it all. Courting you was expedient," Claude said, his voice a bitter snarl, their faces inches apart. "The Moutons had the assets we needed to expand and social position my parents believed would be suitable for our children. I thought you'd at least be tolerable, but I was wrong. At least I took comfort from the money our alliance helped me make." Claude released her, shoving her to the sofa.

"How can you say such things? You're vile." Annadine curled into a heap, sobbing loudly.

"What I choose to do with *my* fortune, what I and I alone built, is none of your damn business. Quentin will get the Trosclair trust, but I won't see what it's taken me thirty years to build dismantled by his bungling."

"I'll see you dead first! Do you hear? Quentin will not lose what is rightfully his as a Trosclair to a nig—" Annadine bolted up to face him. "No, Claude!" She stumbled back as he loomed over her.

"Don't ever presume to tell me what to do. Now, get out of my sight!" Claude roared, his face contorted with rage.

With a scream, Annadine fled the room. Claude gulped another glass of Scotch, then took a deep breath. He stood staring in the direction his wife had gone, then laughed disdainfully. Picking up the keys to his Cadillac, he left the house.

* * *

"Papa, it's Paul." He sat in an overstuffed chair pulled up next to the bed.

Reaching out to take his father's hand, he noticed how thin he was. The veins stood out like ropes underneath the man's dry skin. The queen-sized bed was neatly made up with a quilt Marguerite had made for his parents as a wedding present. Despite the warm weather, his father was dressed in long-sleeved pajamas.

"Hello, son," Charles said in a soft, hoarse voice. "What time is it? Lyin' in this bed, I can't keep track of time."

"It's one o'clock in the afternoon. How are you feeling?"

"Better, a little better every day. What time did you say it was? Oh, never mind. Don't matter no way. I ain't got nowhere to go."

"Have you been doing what the doctor tells you to? Mama says you been hardheaded here lately. Not wanting to take your medicine," Paul said, scolding him as though he were the parent and Charles the child.

"Dadgum doctors. They gone kill me tryin' to cure me if I let 'em."

"I just might move in here, you know, to help Mama take care of you." Paul frowned.

"Hey, I might be down, but I don't want you leavin' your business on my account."

"With you lying in this bed not wanting to get up, it's going to be tough on her. She could use another pair of hands."

"I ain't gonna be no burden on Reba." His father perked up. With some effort, he sat up in the bed.

"You won't if you do what you're supposed to. Physical therapy three times a week, right?"

"Yeah, right," Charles mumbled.

"Papa, look at me. I won't leave if I think you and Mama need me. Sam could go to Kuwait. We've got more than enough business as it is; this is just something new we wanted to explore.''

"Opening up new things is how you get to be successful. I done told you that all your life. We didn't get rich, but I never overlooked anything to make a living. I started out with nothing but a brush, some buckets of paint, and working my butt off on weekends. But I ended up with two crews working for me, getting all the business I could handle. No, you go do what you have to do. Me and Reba gonna make it just fine.'' Charles picked up his left arm with his right hand. "I'm going to therapy, son. You go to Kuwait. I'll be on my feet in no time.''

"I just bet you will." Paul kissed his forehead.

Paul found his mother sitting in the living room. She patted the cushion on the sofa next to her.

"Thank you, baby." Reba, tears in her eyes, kissed Paul on the cheek. "I heard you in there, gettin' your papa stirred up. He was givin' up. But you put the spark back in him.''

"He was just depressed. He's used to being strong and healthy, being the one everyone else leaned on. I can imagine how hard it is for him to be dependent on others.''

"But the doctor is hopeful that he can recover from the stroke. That therapy can make his left side strong again.''

"Thank God. And don't you forget, Robert and the others will be some kind of mad if y'all don't call on them to help.''

"You know I don't get a chance to call them rascals 'fore they over here fixing on the house, bringing food. Even my grandbabies done learned how to give your papa what-for if he won't take them pills.'' Reba laughed.

"That's what family is for, loving and fussing just when you need it.'' Paul hugged her.

"What about you? You say you doin' okay, but your face say different. I think you goin' on this trip to run away from your feelings.''

"Mama—"

"Now, you hold on. Don't tell me 'bout how you was plannin' this trip anyway. You wasn't in no hurry to leave for almost a year. Them whatever-you-call-'em gone be right there for a while. You oughta go back to Beau Chene to talk this out with Savannah."

"She didn't feel what I thought she felt for me, Mama. There isn't anything to talk out." Paul's face took on a pinched look as he turned his head away from his mother's gaze.

"I learned a long time ago, livin' with pride can't no way take the place of livin' with the one person what's got a hold on your heart. Uh-huh," Reba said, forestalling his protest, "that's all I'm gonna say on the subject. Now, what about Trosclair, now that you through with that job?"

"Nothing more to that, either. I did what I was hired to do. The end."

"Smart man like that with his money, don't seem likely he didn't know where Charles was, or who you were, for that matter." Reba tapped his arm as she spoke.

"You know."

"I didn't go to college or work in no fancy office, but I got sense enough to see that. Charles has such a block in his mind about that part of his monmon's life 'til he didn't want to think that maybe his real daddy been knowin' where he was all this time. But I pray Trosclair don't do nothin' to hurt your papa."

"Don't worry about it, Mama. I warned him to stay away. Besides, he's got his hands full trying to salvage Big River. I doubt he wants any more complications in his life right now, anyway."

"So, you leavin' for sure. All packed?"

"Yes, ma'am. Plane leaves tomorrow, six o'clock."

"Then you got time to have supper with the family. Everybody gone be here at five." Reba patted his hand affectionately.

* * *

The plane leveled off high above fluffy white clouds. Peering through the small window, Paul looked down at the disappearing landscape around the New Orleans International Airport. Sighing, he settled back against the seat. With a grim expression, he recalled his last conversation with Sam as they drove to the airport.

"We can still call this off, you know," Sam said for the fifth time.

"An opportunity like this can move us into international markets. There's no reason to wait any longer."

"Listen, man—"

"No, you listen. I'm going. I don't need anybody else telling me what I should do with my life. Drop it. Just drop it."

Paul closed his eyes. He was tired, yet could not sleep. The words he kept repeating to everyone had left a bitter taste in his mouth. Yes, he wanted to get away. Get away from any chance that he might see Savannah with Devin. Night after night, he imagined them in each other's arms. Though he tried, he couldn't stop remembering her: the touch of her fingers on his body, the sweet, musky way her skin smelled, damp with sweat, after lovemaking. Folding his arms tightly to his chest, he stared back out at the clouds. Paul hoped each mile put between them would cause the dull ache to ease.

Chapter 13

This early spring was like all others in south Louisiana, sunny, hot, and filled with the sounds of wildlife in the lush, verdant landscape. The swamps south of Beau Chene were filled with bateaux and pirogues dotting the waters as fishermen enjoyed the thrill of catching the first run of fish after the long winter. The only sounds heard were the occasional thrumming of an outboard motor as another sportsman arrived to take his place or moved to try his luck in another spot. In silent companionship, they cast their lines, all just as content with the slow, patient quest as with the sporadic catch.

A sudden shout from one of the fishermen cut through the serene atmosphere. Soon others responded, looking to where the two men in a blue bass boat pushed at something bulky in the water near them. Now five boats of various styles circled the object. After a few minutes, a motor revved up at high speed as one of the boats headed back to the landing.

"My Lord, but ain't dis here a mess?" Sheriff Triche heaved a deep sigh as he watched his men help the ambulance attendants unload the bulky body bag from the green sheriff's department boat onto the cypress planks of the boat launch.

Their faces gloomy, their low voices murmuring speculations, men and women stood in a ragged circle, observing the grisly procedures as the coroner moved with deliberation through his routine.

"What you say, Doc Vidrine?" Sheriff Triche wiped his face with a striped handkerchief.

"He's dead, all right." Doc Vidrine stood up with a grunt. His straightforward statement was not meant as a joke.

"How long?"

"Hard to say right off. Looks like he's been in the water for at least six hours, maybe longer. This is going be something else when it gets out."

"Maybe it ain't him. I mean, all bloated up like that."

"Maybe not, but even in his condition, I'm fairly sure who it is. Face it, Joe—you got one hot potato on your hands. If it isn't him, then he's got a twin brother."

"Well, maybe he drowned accidentally." Sheriff Triche was grasping at straws.

"He went fishing in an eight-hundred-dollar suit? If he drowned, it wasn't connected to any accident."

Sheriff Triche sucked air through his teeth. He was annoyed with the doctor for not allowing him at least a momentary delusion that this was no murder.

"You through out here?" Sheriff Triche waved for the men to move the body at Doc Vidrine's affirmative nod.

"I'll head back to get set up for the autopsy. Have the state police crime scene boys get in touch with me." Doc Vidrine marched quickly to his station wagon.

"Clyde, get on the radio and tell Myrtle I'm gone pick her up on the way."

"You all right, ma'am?" Sheriff Triche grew uneasy watching Annadine. She had not reacted at all the way he'd expected. He motioned for the female deputy to come forward.

"Hmm."

"Did you understand me, Miz Trosclair?" Sheriff Triche said.

"Yes, of course. Claude is dead. Rhodes." Annadine's eyes seemed out of focus.

"Pardon me?"

"Rhodes. They've been handling the Trosclair funerals for over a hundred years now. I suppose we should call the proprietor, Mr. Harrison Rhodes. Very nice family, you know."

"Yes, ma'am." Sheriff Triche looked to Myrtle for help.

"Everything has to be done just right. Claude would be furious if it wasn't, you know."

"Why don't we call some of your family first?" Deputy Myrtle Arceneaux spoke softly but with a firm efficiency that was reassuring.

"Where is Mr. Quentin, ma'am?" Sheriff Triche began to examine the room with a sweeping gaze.

"Grandmother, what's going on? There's a sheriff's car in our driveway." Quentin strode in seeming more annoyed at the intrusion than concerned.

"We just had to give your grandmother some bad news, son. Mr. Claude—"

"He's dead, Quentin. They found your grandfather dead. Dead, dead, dead." Annadine's voice started out as a shrill laugh, then ended in a high-pitched wail. The housekeeper, Louise, moved to help Deputy Arceneaux lead her from the room. The wailing continued up the stairs.

"My God, is this true?" Quentin blinked rapidly.

" 'Fraid so."

"I need a drink. Will you—of course not. You're on duty. This is horrendous. There must be some mistake." Quentin carefully prepared his drink.

"Well, he still had his gold credit card in the inside pocket of his coat. 'Course, we do need a family member to come down to confirm the identification. With Miz Trosclair in the state she's in, it would be best if you handled that."

"Is it really necessary? I mean, can't you use dental records, or fingerprints? Such a gruesome task." Quentin sipped at his drink, frowning in distaste.

"It's procedure. And you gone hafta sign some papers."

"Oh, all right. If you're going to insist on following the rules to the letter."

"You ain't asked for no details." Sheriff Triche stood in a relaxed pose, gazing at Quentin thoughtfully.

"Excuse me?"

"You ain't ask me how he died, or where he was. Folks usually ask them questions. Neither one of y'all did."

"I just assumed it was something natural, you know, at his age . . . a heart attack, I suppose?" Quentin set his glass down on the antique bar and poured another drink from the tall pitcher.

"No, most likely he was murdered," Sheriff Triche said.

"What? Well, I repeatedly warned him about being out alone late, but he was stubborn. Naturally, he carried very little cash. But criminals kill for pocket change these days." Quentin took a long drink from the glass. He glanced quickly at the sheriff, who was eyeing him curiously. "I want the scum found, prosecuted, and given the death penalty!" Quentin said forcefully.

"We gone do everything to catch who did it, that's for sure."

"I'm sorry, Sheriff. It's just that this is such a terrible shock to me. My grandfather and I were close. But I must pull myself together and put aside my grief. My grandmother needs me." Quentin squared his shoulders to show his determination.

"You right, she gone need you to lean on. By the way, why didn't y'all report Mr. Trosclair as missin'?"

"Missing?" Quentin blinked rapidly, as though trying to understand.

"From what Doc Vidrine says, he had to been gone all night. We ain't had no call from Miz Trosclair or you." Sheriff Triche raised an eyebrow at him.

"Well, uh, I spent the night with a . . . friend. You understand?" Quentin flashed a half smile that said they were two men of the world.

"But what about your grandmother? She was here."

"They have separate bedrooms, Sheriff. It wasn't unusual for him to come in late and leave early, without her knowing." Quentin became serious again. "Now, I want to be kept informed of your investigation. Leave no stone unturned, as they say."

"That I can guarantee, Mr. Quentin." Sheriff Triche clapped him on the shoulder a little too heartily. "Now, let's go on into town an' get this over with."

News of Claude Trosclair's death sent waves of shock and dread throughout Beau Chene. The town took on a circus atmosphere as hordes of reporters descended on the town. Cameras were pointed at anyone entering the old brick building that housed the sheriff's office. Microphones were thrust into the faces of even those people remote from the investigation. Big River and the controversy surrounding it were referred to, some of the reporters speculating whether animosity generated by it might have led to the murder.

"Sources tell us that you were questioned within days of the body being found. Is that so, Mr. St. Julien?" A newspaper reporter scurried to keep up, his pen poised over a notepad.

"Sure, so was a lot of us what knew the man."

"Some have said that this murder isn't surprising, given the rancor Claude Trosclair caused by opening the plant so close to your community. Were feelings running that high that someone could kill?"

"Big River was only the latest thing he done to get folks upset. Anyways, the court ruled against him and his big company. We was feelin' good 'bout that."

"So, you're saying that he could have been killed for

any number of reasons. You and your group had more than one dispute with him, then?'' The reporter pounced on the implication of long-held hostility.

"I'm sayin' that you gettin' desperate to whip anythin' I say into a big story for your newspaper, since ain't nothin' much new been found out. Now, I'm busy.'' Antoine brushed him aside to enter the shop.

"One more question.'' The reporter started after him into the shop.

"I said, I'm busy.'' Antoine blocked his way. His shoulders relaxed only after the reporter was at a distance.

"Man! This place is crawlin' with reporters, Mr. Antoine. One of them was waiting for me after school, askin' me stuff about you and Miz Savannah.'' T-Leon stood at the window, looking up and down the street. "But I didn't tell him nuthin'.''

"I know, son. If they bother you too much, just tell 'em to get lost.'' Antoine busied himself behind the counter.

"Hi, T-Leon. Poppy.'' Savannah kissed Antoine's cheek. "Now that you've got your license, you can make deliveries, T-Leon. These gift baskets are for the Mackey Insurance Company. You don't mind taking them over in the truck, do you?'' Savannah held the keys up and jingled them enticingly. With the shop doing so well, they had bought a small blue pick-up with sporty red stripes along the sides.

"Hey, I think I can work it into my schedule for today.'' T-Leon grinned as he took the keys. With all the speed of a teenager eager to hit the road, he loaded up the twelve baskets and was on his way.

"How much you wanna bet he gone go the long way until he find some of his friends to see him drivin' that truck?'' Antoine chuckled.

"Yeah, preferably females.'' Savannah's face became serious. "Sheriff Triche asked me to stop over to his office, Poppy. He wants to ask me some questions.''

"He doin' that with a whole lot of folks, cher. Ain't no need to worry.''

"I'm not, but he said something odd. He said he wanted to know more about Paul."

"Why he askin' you 'bout Paul, I wonder?"

"I don't know. I mean, Paul had left town when all this happened. Besides, he was on good terms with Trosclair. Too good."

"Well, tell him that. Look, I guess he tryin' to get as much information as he can. Talk is, he ain't got no solid leads yet," Antoine said.

"They say it wasn't robbery because he was still wearing his expensive watch, a gold wedding ring, and a diamond class ring, and he had a gold credit card in his pocket. So if it wasn't robbery, then somebody killed him out of hatred."

"Cher, that's gone be a long list of folks they hafta question to figure out which one did it," Antoine snorted.

"Good afternoon." Gralin came in.

"How you doin'? Anything new with the case?"

Antoine shook his head.

"Batton Chemical requested a continuance, under the circumstances. Judge Duplessis granted it today. It'll probably be another two or three months before the hearing. A friend of mine says there's a rumor that Trosclair was dead before he went into the water. A blow to the back of his neck killed him."

The bell over the door tinkled, causing all three to turn. Charice put her book bag down on the floor, spilling crayons everywhere.

"Shoot, I've got to get this thing organized. I bet y'all are talking about the murder. Listen, Florrie Tillman's cousin Clyde works down at the jail, and he told her that the old man was stabbed over fifty times." She talked while gathering crayons from corners and underneath displays.

"Wasn't somebody in here yesterday, saying he was strangled?" Savannah turned to her father.

"To tell you the truth, I done heard so many different

tales, I stopped listenin'. Until Sheriff Triche release it to the papers, don't believe nothin' nobody tell you.'' Antoine shook his head.

"And why's he being so secretive? Maybe he's got a suspect and doesn't want him to know how much they know. Wants to lull him into a sense of security," Charice said, her eyes bright with excitement.

"I've got a chance to find out soon. Sheriff Triche is going to question me." Savannah folded her arms.

"When? Can I come? Oh, please?" Charice dropped some of the crayons she still held.

"Be glad he's not going to shine a white light in your face. In fact, you can go in my place, if you want."

"They don't do that anymore. Fine, just tell me everything." Charice pouted.

"I'm supposed to go over there tomorrow myself. Don't let it bother you, Savannah." Gralin tried to be encouraging.

"I'll be glad when this whole thing is over. With the tension over the Big River verdict and now murder, this town won't be the same for a long time. Now everybody's wondering if someone they know is a killer," Savannah said.

"Yep, it's gone be a long, hot summer, by the looks of it." Antoine stared out the shop window.

"Routine, Miz Savannah. Just routine. Have a seat." Sheriff Triche beckoned to a deputy to join them. "Lonnie's gonna take down your statement."

"Hello, ma'am." Lonnie stood near the door, a large notepad in hand.

"Now, then. You knew Claude Trosclair?" Sheriff Triche rocked back in the old swivel chair behind his desk. Papers were piled everywhere.

"Certainly. Who didn't? We weren't exactly in the same

social circles, you know. It'd be more accurate to say that I knew *of* him." Savannah pressed her lips together. She was trying not to sound defensive.

"Where were you on the evenin' of May twelfth?"

"I was at the shop, as usual. Stayed there until about seven, then went home. I was there the rest of the night."

"You with anybody can say the same?"

"My Tante Marie was there. Oh, and Uncle Coy came by at about eight-thirty to bring her some eggs his chickens had laid. Tante Marie bakes a lot, especially now that she sells her cakes and cookies at the shop."

"Sure enough, an' some fine-tastin' food for sure. I done had my share. Shows, don't it?" Sheriff Triche patted his round midsection with a grin. "When did you last see Mr. Trosclair?" He was back to business.

"At court that day, when the verdict came down. Let's see, April twenty-seventh, a Tuesday, I think."

"Not since then?"

"No."

"And Paul Honore, was he there?"

"Yes, of course. He was with Mr. Trosclair and his people." Savannah watched him closely.

"How much do you know 'bout him? Paul Honore, I mean."

"He's from Crowley, but now he lives in Lafayette. That's where he has his business. His family still lives there. Why are you asking me questions about Paul?"

"Some information need clearing up on him. He out of the country, you know. So I'm havin' to ask other folks 'bout him. Y'all was kinda friendly, I hear."

"Yes, Sheriff, we were dating for a while, if that's what you're getting at."

"Uh-huh. Did he ever talk 'bout Claude, Mr. Trosclair, to you? Mention they'd had any disagreements?"

"He didn't talk about him a whole lot, but he never

mentioned that they weren't on good terms. In fact, he was impressed with how sincere he was about making the plant safe. We even had a couple of arguments, because I thought he was being naive."

"Any reason Paul Honore would leave town so sudden, then head outta the country?" Sheriff Triche sat up straight.

"I have no idea," Savannah answered quickly. She looked down at her hands.

"You ain't keepin' somethin' from me, ma'am?"

"No, I'm not. Look, why don't you ask him why he left? I'm sure his partner can tell you how to get in touch with him."

"He didn't have a big fight with somebody, maybe right before he left? Don't seem likely he wouldn't tell you, y'all bein' so close an' all."

"Look, if you must know, we broke up the same day of the verdict. He would hardly have confided in me after that." Savannah's eyes flashed with anger at the memory of Paul's last words to her that day.

"That so? Well, that's all for now. Might need you to come back later." Sheriff Triche stood up smiling.

"What is this all about, these questions about Paul?" Savannah did not move from the green vinyl chair facing his desk.

"Like I said, just a routine part of a murder investigation."

"But you asked me as much about Paul as you did about me. Sounds as though you have reason to think he's important in this somehow."

"Thanks for comin', ma'am." Sheriff Triche came around the desk. When the deputy opened the door, he led her through it.

A few minutes later Savannah stood outside the sheriff's station, squinting as much in troubled thought as because of the dazzling sunlight.

* * *

The cool interior of the hotel lobby was a welcome change from the dry, searing heat that pulsated from every inch of sand out in the oil fields. The stench of burning oil and huge chemical spills permeated even the elegant, filtered air here. Paul headed straight for the elevators and a cool shower, eager to wash away some of the grime that clung to his skin. Having been in Kuwait for two weeks, he had gradually grown accustomed to the heat, but the devastation left behind after the Gulf War still affected him deeply. The economic, environmental, and public health impact of the spills was staggering. Yet he admired the way the international community had responded to the disaster. And the methods being pioneered here would benefit the whole world. New, safer technologies that could clean up some of the most toxic substances or even render them harmless were a common occurrence.

Paul threw himself into his work. He made visiting sites, meeting other engineers, and attending meetings all day every day a rigorous routine. He sought to fill up the time with activity and his mind with business. But even long hours could not totally banish thoughts of Savannah. He kept pushing her away, hoping the memories would sink to the bottom of his mind. Yet she would bob back to the surface, thwarting his efforts to move on, to live without her.

As he had for many nights, he was up late again dividing his attention between the satellite news stories from CNN and technical books. At last he dozed off to the soft hum of the voices coming from the television. He was startled awake by the phone. The clock on the table next to his bed showed it was five in the morning.

"Yes?"

"I have a call for you from the United States. Is that Mr. Paul Honore, yes?" the operator spoke in clipped English.

"Yes, it is." Paul's heart raced, thinking of his father. "Hello? Hello." Static hummed for a few seconds.

"Paul, it's Sam. Don't panic, your father is okay. That's not why I called." Proving once again how well he knew Paul and how sensitive he could be, Sam spoke quickly. His voice boomed louder than necessary.

"You're coming through clearly, so stop shouting. Now, what's up?

"Man, it has hit the fan big-time back here. Are you sitting down? Claude Trosclair's been murdered. Hello! Hello!" Sam began to shout again after long seconds of silence.

"I'm still here. Damn! Damn!" Paul blurted out.

"That's not the worse part. The sheriff and the state police investigators have been asking a lot of questions about you. They even lifted some of your fingerprints from the trailer you rented in Beau Chene."

"You mean I'm a *suspect*?"

"That's what it looks like, man. They say you're wanted only for questioning, but my guess is you're high on the list, maybe even at the top. I think you might do some traveling. Visit Saudi Arabia, Bahrain. Say, I hear Iran is pretty calm now and safe for Americans, especially us brothers."

"Sam, if you're suggesting that I run, the answer is no. Besides making me look guilty as hell, it wouldn't work anyway. Interpol would track me with no problem."

"Staying on the move to further your business interests is what you'd be doing. How could you know they were trying to get in touch with you? Listen, the embassy could be sending someone to bring you a message as we speak. Book the next thing moving out of there, my brother. Maybe they'll find out who did it before you get dragged back here."

"Sam—"

"*Do it*, man. I've got LaMar Zeno looking into it for me.

Give us the time we need to clear you." Sam's voice, strained with the effort to convince his friend, sounded hoarse with emotion.

"LaMar Zeno." Paul could picture the flamboyant black private detective dogging leads behind the state police investigators. "Okay," Paul said, "but only for another week, two at the most."

"Great. Two weeks tops, you got it." Sam blew out a loud sigh of relief. "Keep in touch, call me at home in, say, three days."

"What made you change your mind?" Trent, an engineer with another company, sat next to Paul on the flight to Jordan. He had invited Paul to accompany him on this trip twice and been met with refusal. "I thought you didn't have time for side trips."

"There are a couple of plants and factories of interest to me. Besides, I could make some contacts." Paul stared out the window, deep in thought.

"Well, I'm glad for the company," Trent said.

Paul smiled and nodded at all the right places as Trent rattled off a list of sites they could visit in Jordan. But he could not shake the feeling of being hunted, the urge to look over his shoulder every five minutes. No matter what Sam had said, this was a mistake. He seriously doubted he could stand this for another two days, let alone two weeks. Remembering the anxiety in his friend's voice, he decided to give it a week—but no more. Whatever happened, it would be better to face it sooner rather than later.

Chapter 14

"What did he want?" Savannah met her father at the door.

"Settle down, now. He was askin' me the same questions all over again. When did I last see Claude Trosclair? Where was I that night he got killed? Then he was askin' 'bout Paul." Antoine paused, a puzzled frown on his face. "Didn't you say he done the same with you a coupla days ago?"

"Yeah, and he never said why."

"Fact, he asked more questions 'bout him than he did anythin' else. Now I think of it, seems like he was going through the motions of repeating them other questions to get to the real ones. Well, no tellin' how this thing gone turn out."

Savannah finally worked up the courage to voice her greatest fear. "Poppy, you don't think Sheriff Triche thinks you did it?"

"Nah, cher. Leastways, he ain't actin' like it. I b'lieve he'd have had me in there a lot more if he did." Antoine patted her head the way he had when she was a nervous little girl.

Watching him amble into the kitchen for a snack, Savannah prayed silently that he was right. The animosity between her father and Claude was well known. Antoine's criticism and dislike of the man were even recorded in newspaper stories. He had not been shy about speaking his mind during protests against the Big River plant, much of it criticism of Claude Trosclair. Savannah sat in front of the television, drumming her fingers on the arm of the easy chair.

"Humm, umm. You cookin' up somethin'—I can tell by lookin' at you." Antoine joined her in the den. He sat on the sofa, balancing on one knee a bowl with Tante Marie's peach cobbler and a scoop of vanilla ice cream.

"Not me." Savannah avoided looking at him.

"You stay outta this, yeah."

"I'm not planning to do anything." Savannah put on her best blank face.

"Yeah, now I know you got somethin' in mind, 'cause you didn't even ask me what I was talkin' 'bout."

"I'm thinking about the shop, Poppy. Really." Savannah smiled sweetly, all the while thinking of the best time to visit Sheriff Triche. "T-Leon comes in at about three o'clock tomorrow, right?"

"I certainly hope this isn't going to take long, Kyle." Quentin did not bother to look up at Singleton as he sat in the chair opposite his desk.

"Oh, I don't think so. Took hardly any time to make yourself at home." Kyle waved a hand at the expensive redecorating that had been done in the weeks since Claude's death.

"Change, Kyle: it's a part of life." Quentin sat back in the new forest-green leather executive chair.

"Yes, things certainly have changed. You've taken the reins and made some changes, big changes. Claude must be spinning in his grave." Singleton brushed lint from his expensive pant leg.

"We saw things differently. My grandfather had limited vision, Kyle. He couldn't see the possibilities of taking this company beyond the usual boundaries." Quentin regarded Kyle with a steady gaze, as if measuring him by the same yardstick and finding him to be the same.

"And you do, I suppose." Kyle did not appear the least bit offended by Quentin's condescending tone.

"I do," Quentin said curtly.

"Those plans with Megatron International are a big risk. Claude and I had decided they weren't worth it."

"Megatron is on the cutting edge of a whole new way to process a host of waste products for dozens of uses in industry. The potential for us, if we get in on the ground floor, is enormous. It could well take this company into making billions," Quentin spoke forcefully.

"What about the fines from Big River? The hearing could well result in taking us to the brink of bankruptcy." Kyle's eyebrows went up.

"Clayton and Collins don't think it'll come to that. Besides, Big River is a legally separate division. Batton Holding Corporation could survive relatively intact." Quentin, still as relaxed and confident, shrugged, dismissing the fines.

"Maybe, but back to Megatron: new technology can be costly. Look at how the case against Big River turned out. And the kiln process has more of a track record than some of what Megatron plans to do. I think it's a bad move at this time." Singleton studied his neatly manicured fingertips.

"I realize that you're accustomed to the way Grandfather did things. As I said, Batton Chemical is moving in a new direction. Frankly, I sense that you don't exactly approve of what I'm trying to do here." Quentin stared at him tight lipped for several seconds. "I've had the accountants look over your benefit and pension package; it's very generous.

You could retire at a relatively young age and live quite well." Quentin opened a side drawer. He held up a brown file folder.

"I'm not interested in retiring. Besides, I still have much to contribute to this company." Singleton smiled at him.

"The deal with Megatron will go through. I need a president who is solidly behind me, Kyle. You've been an asset to this company for close to twenty years, but it's time for you to move on. I want our parting to be congenial. Take the offer." Quentin pushed the folder across the desk to him.

"I don't think so, Quentin. I could benefit more by remaining."

"Not if you end up being fired. This way you could leave with dignity, and much more money. Be smart and take it." Quentin's mouth twisted into an anything but friendly smile.

"Oh, I won't be fired. You need me." Singleton pushed the folder back, still smiling at him.

"Hardly." Quentin sneered.

"Yes, you do. After I explain a few things, you'll agree. Remember the last meeting Claude had with Collins and the rest of us after the verdict? He wanted the accountants to do a comprehensive audit of everything, not just Big River plant and its division. Well, I noticed how nervous that made you." Singleton nodded with satisfaction at the effect his words had on him. "Oh, yes. You see, I didn't get this far without keeping my eyes open. It's one of the things Claude especially valued about me. Anyway, I decided to do a little checking on my own. You didn't know that I was considered an accounting whiz in my younger days, did you? Another talent Claude recognized when he decided to hire me. These new computers are amazing. Why, twenty years ago it would've taken me weeks, months even, to discover your—how can I put this delicately, 'creative rearranging' of company finances."

"You can't prove a damn thing!" Quentin sputtered.

"Oh, but I *can*. You left a trail easy enough for any competent bookkeeper to pick up. And our accountants are, I'm sure you'll agree, more than competent." Singleton coolly observed the impotent fury on Quentin's face.

"I put most of it back. The board will want to avoid a scandal." Quentin chewed his lower lip.

"True. But the board will also take the opportunity to give you an offer similar to the one you just tried to give me. Say goodbye to controlling an empire, my boy. But . . ." Singleton held up a forefinger dramatically. "I can save you from all that."

"How?" Quentin grew very still, his voice barely above a whisper.

"By keeping my mouth shut, of course. Naturally, I'll expect a few added perks. My stock options are quite inadequate, for one thing. And I'll be making the decisions from now on. No one has to know this, it can be just between us." Singleton's soft chin quivered as he smiled broadly at Quentin.

"That's it, then, I have no choice." Quentin spoke in a dull tone, his eyes narrowed to slits.

"None whatsoever. But think of it positively. After all, I helped Claude make Batton Chemical an internationally profitable company. You really have everything to gain with me still in the picture."

"And you've told no one this?"

"You have my word. It'll be our little secret. Now, I've made a few notes about my new benefits package. Since Claude left his affairs in such good order, the probate will go smoothly. With your stocks, your grandmother's, and mine, the board will have little choice but to agree to let me step in as CEO, then we can take care of this. Well, that about does it, I think. Good evening, my boy." Singleton strolled out whistling.

Quentin slammed a clenched fist against the arm of his chair.

* * *

"You sure 'bout this, Doc?" Sheriff Triche waved the autopsy report in the air between them.

"With reasonable certainty. He was dead when he went in the water. The cause of death was a powerful blow to the abdomen; organ hemorrhaging did him in. The liver, spleen, and pancreas were crushed. Died within an hour or so. He had other relatively minor bruises that could've come from falling or being hit, can't say for certain."

"Bruises such as?"

"He had scratches on his face and neck. Several yellow bruises on the upper chest." Doc Vidrine shifted his plump body in the uncomfortably small chair.

"But what about the stab wounds?"

"Those were superficial, maybe got 'em during the fight. He had a few shallow cuts on his hands like he mighta grabbed the weapon."

"Lord. This some kinda maniac, maybe?" Sheriff Triche raked stubby fingers through his thinning gray hair.

"Or somebody that plain didn't like him. This is just speculation, understand? But I'd guess he was dyin' while the killer figured out what to do with the body or was carryin' him to where he was dumped. Well, you know where to find me if you need me." Doc Vidrine huffed to his feet.

"Thanks, Doc."

"Is it true you goin' to question Quentin Trosclair again?"

"Yep."

"You sure you wanna get them Trosclairs mad at you? They got a lotta pull, even if old Claude's dead. They gonna figure to get in good with Quentin, since he'll likely take over Batton Chemical."

"Now Doc, you done knowed me long enough to know when I got me a serious matter like this that don't mean diddly-boo to me. Sure, I got some of our leadin' citizens and their relatives out of a few embarrassin' situations over the years. But not with murder involved, no sir. And I don't need to tell you the state police watchin' my every move on this one.''

"Hey, Doc. Sheriff, Miss Rousselle is here." Deputy Lonnie Dupuis stuck his head in the door.

"That oughta be one interestin' interrogation." Doc Vidrine winked at the sheriff and deputy before leaving.

LaShaun wore a long brick red dress belted at the waist with a colorful scarf that hung to one side. The flowing skirt of her dress moved in whirls as she walked with hips swaying.

"Have a seat, Miss Rousselle. How's Monmon Odette feelin' these days?" Sheriff Triche sat on the corner of his cluttered desk.

"Pretty good, thank you." LaShaun cocked her head to one side, her expression one of mild curiosity.

"Glad to hear it. I'm sure you know all about this terrible thing with Claude Trosclair bein' found dead."

"Shocking. What is this world coming to? When even a prominent man like him is attacked for pocket change."

"You heard it was robbery, ma'am?" Sheriff Triche's eyes went to the deputy standing behind her.

"Why what else could it have been? I mean, that's all you hear, on the news these days." LaShaun looked from the sheriff to the deputy and back again.

"He was killed by somebody, but not for money. At least, not what was in his pockets."

"Really?"

"How well did you know Claude, ma'am?" Sheriff Triche moved on without further explanation.

"Just to know who he was on sight, that's all."

"And his grandson?"

"Same thing."

"You haven't spent time with either gentleman? Mr. Claude or Mr. Quentin?"

"Of course not. What are you trying to say?"

"Seems there's been some talk that you been keepin' company with one of them."

"You got me here to ask about some trashy gossip? It's a lie." LaShaun met his gaze boldly.

"So you sayin' it ain't true."

"That's what I just said. I hardly know Quentin Trosclair."

"I only said with one of them, I didn't say which one." Sheriff Triche stared at her hard.

"I meant, uh, it wasn't either one of them. Look, I'm not answering no more questions without knowing what you trying to pin on me!" LaShaun snarled.

"Why you gettin' so upset? Unless you've been goin' with the boy. Fact is, we got word that you been visitin' his apartment in New Orleans quite regular for almost a year or more."

"How did you—"

"Is that so?"

"What if it is? It's got nothing to do with his grandpapa getting killed by some thug."

"Let's start all over, all right? You been sleepin' with Quentin Trosclair. He been givin' you money, too." Sheriff Triche had picked up his notepad and was consulting it.

"Since you know so much, why are you bothering to ask me?" LaShaun glared at him.

"When did Claude find out about you two?" Sheriff Triche spoke sharply, his eyes boring into her.

"What—he didn't know. I mean, uh—"

"I b'lieve he did. You see, he had somebody checkin' his grandson ever' so often, a private security firm. Seems he didn't trust the boy. 'Bout three months ago, they did their regular check, found out he was meetin' up with you in that fancy apartment. They was a little reluctant to tell us, but Lonnie here reminded 'em 'bout the penalty for obstructin' justice." Sheriff Triche let a long silence stretch.

"That doesn't mean a thing." LaShaun wound and unwound the ends of the scarf that rested in her lap.

"Now, I don't think he'd be too concerned 'bout him seein' you; Quentin has had a long list of lady friends in his young life. But the money part is somethin' else. Seems it was more than money. He got the company to give y'all top dollar for some land Monmon Odette owns. And then there's a matter of some investments you made that were very profitable?" Sheriff Triche ran a finger down the notepad.

Another deputy tapped on the glass window that made up half of the front wall of the sheriff's office. Lonnie stepped out and spent several minutes in muted conversation with him. LaShaun twisted around to watch them.

"He's here, Sheriff," Lonnie said, as he came back through the door.

Quentin came in, accompanied by another deputy. Arguing loudly, he resisted attempts to lead him into an office opposite the sheriff's with miniblinds that were closed. Whirling around, he snatched his arm from the deputy.

"How dare you come to my home at this time of the day and interrupt my dinner! Dragging me here as though I were some criminal! Where is Sheriff Triche? I'll see he doesn't get elected street sweeper come next election. Ah, there you—" Quentin stopped dead upon seeing LaShaun with the sheriff.

"Stay right here with Miss Rousselle, Lonnie." Sheriff Triche walked briskly out to Quentin. "Well, now, thanks for comin' in, Mr. Quentin."

"What the hell is the meaning of this?" Quentin's voice had lost some of its intensity. He peered over the sheriff's shoulder to his office and LaShaun.

"Why don't we step in here. Right here." Sheriff Triche pointed to the office. He moved directly in front of him, effectively blocking Quentin's view.

"Why am I here?" Quentin sat on the edge of a metal folding chair.

"Well, sir, we need to corroborate some information we've received." Sheriff Triche sat heavily in a brown vinyl chair next to him.

"Information about what?"

"You know Miss Rousselle, don't you?"

"What lies have you been listening to?"

"We know you do, Mr. Quentin. We know she's been livin' high since she's been . . . seein' you."

"What the hell has any of this got to do with my grandfather's death?"

"Mr. Claude found out what you was up to, givin' her money, stock tips. Putting his business interests second."

"My grandfather couldn't care less about what woman I happened to be sleeping with at the moment. And the money was nothing." Quentin visibly relaxed as his arrogant look returned.

"Is that a fact?" Sheriff Triche's brows drew together in puzzlement at his reaction.

"Where is he? Take me to him. Quentin, where are you?" Annadine's voice rang through the station.

"Miss Annadine, come on, now. Let's go on home," Jim, the gardener who doubled as chauffeur, pleaded with her.

"No. I've got to find out what they've done to him. Sheriff, listen to me: he didn't do anything. She's lying, Quentin wasn't anywhere near Claude's office that night."

"Now, now, Miz Trosclair. You oughten get yourself worked up like this. Why don't you let Jim take you on back home?" Sheriff Triche pulled the office door closed behind him. He spoke in a soothing tone.

"But you are wrong to hold him here. Please, listen to me."

"Miz Trosclair, we got to question everybody. We—"

"I killed him. I killed Claude. I did. He was a vile, mean man. We argued; I picked up a letter opener and stabbed him. He fell dead. It was me." Annadine swayed on her feet.

"Grandmother, don't say any more until I contact our attorneys. She's obviously in an unstable mental state. She doesn't know what she's saying."

"Ain't dis one big mess!" Sheriff Triche said, as he looked around his office.

"Sheriff, can I talk to you a minute?" Lonnie stepped forward.

"Lonnie, I got somethin' on my hands right now. You s'pose to stay with that Rousselle woman." Sheriff Triche shouted over the voices of Quentin, Annadine, and the other deputy.

"You got to see this, Sheriff." Lonnie waved a sheet of paper high in the air.

"Quiet!" Sheriff Triche boomed everyone into silence. "Floyd, you take Miz Trosclair into that office down the hall, and let her call her lawyer. You," he barked to another deputy, "take him back in there. Now, who is with—"

"Myrtle." Lonnie stepped back so that the sheriff could see the female deputy standing in his office.

"What is so damned important that I got to stop hearin' a confession?"

"Look at this report from the private investigator. Seems Mr. Trosclair checked up on several people."

"My, my, my," Sheriff Triche said, as he scanned the first few sentences.

"Paul? Claude Trosclair's grandson?" Savannah leaned against her father for support. "I can't believe this."

"Seems Paul's grandmother and Trosclair had an affair years ago. She got pregnant and left town. It was all hushed up. Her son, and Claude's, is Paul's father," Gralin said. He had come over to the shop after hearing the news from a friend working at the sheriff's office.

"That was nothin' but a rumor," Tante Marie snorted.

"You knew? You actually knew who he was and didn't say anything to me?" Savannah turned on her aunt accusingly.

"Wait now, missy. I didn't know who his grandmother was. Even if I had, I wasn't gone say nothin' like that. How was I to know if that lady and her husband wasn't still alive? And if she wasn't, they got kin people still livin' here."

"I knew." Antoine took a deep breath when Savannah gave him a wounded look. "I felt like Marie, it was just old gossip that I didn't think was right to be repeatin'. Besides, I figured it was his place to tell you."

"I'll be—Sam never said a thing to me." Charice stood open-mouthed, her stunned look matching Savannah's.

"Poppy, it doesn't matter what you thought about it being just gossip. You knew I had suspicions about Paul and his dealings with Claude Trosclair. You should have said something." Savannah shook with emotion. "He lied to me, deceived me, and you helped him."

"You wait until I see Sam tonight. He's going to get the cussin' out of his sleazy life!" Charice placed her hands on her hips.

"Savannah, I was kinda suspicious of Paul when he first come to town. But he was always straightforward with us 'bout what was happenin' at Big River and how he felt. I have a lot of respect for the way he carried himself."

"He's a liar. You don't know what kind of dirty deal he secretly cut with Trosclair, Poppy. Paul was out to get anything he could, probably used his relationship to get that contract."

"Sheriff Triche has issued a warrant for his arrest. Seems the theory is Paul was trying to blackmail, or had blackmailed, Trosclair in some way. They argued; maybe Trosclair refused to his demands for more and Paul killed him." Gralin blinked behind his bifocals.

"That don't make no sense to me. Paul been a successful engineer for five years. I mean, makin' good money, a lot of money, not just gettin' by. No sir, that don't sound like the Paul I know." Antoine slapped the counter top.

"You don't know him, Poppy. None of us did, especially me." Savannah brushed her eyes quickly.

"Then there's the question of why he left the country so suddenly. And they say he had a violent argument with Claude before he left. It looks very bad, Antoine," Gralin said.

"I been on this earth a long time, and I been judgin' people a long time, too. He may have been wrong not to say somethin' to you, cher, but I'd swear that boy ain't no blackmailer. And he ain't no killer, either," Tante Marie pronounced firmly.

"He kept who he was a secret. He put on a good show, and I fell for it. Everything he ever said was a lie, everything he ever did was only an act." Savannah's voice choked as she rushed into the office. Charice followed her.

"Sugar, come on now. It's okay to cry. That dirty dog." Charice hugged Savannah.

"God, Charice. I feel like such a fool. He used me. It was nothing but a damn game to him." Unable to hold back any longer, she let go. Tears coursed down her cheeks.

"I know, babe. I know."

"Pretending every time he touched me." Savannah shook with agony. Now, even the beautiful memories of their nights of passion seemed sordid, empty of real meaning.

Charice patted her back. Seeing Antoine enter the office, she released her hold. Nodding to him over Savannah's bowed head, she pulled back.

"Cher?" Antoine reached for Savannah. When she did not rebuff him, he folded her in his arms against his chest. Her cries were muffled in his shirt front.

"I'm going home now, sugar. Sam is coming over, and I wouldn't want to miss this evening for the world," Charice said, her eyes glittering with outrage. "I'll call you later, okay?"

"O—kay," Savannah hiccupped her reply. She stepped away from her father, wiping her eyes and nose. "I'm all right."

"Go on home, cher. Me and Marie gone be here. Take some time to yourself." Antoine stroked her hair.

"I'd just go nuts thinking. No, keeping busy is what I need. Here, I've got to figure up our taxes, make some journal entries, and look at this filing that's piled up." Savannah busied herself moving papers around.

Antoine kissed her cheek before going back into the shop. Savannah stared at the papers before her until they became blurred by her tears.

Chapter 15

"LaMar, man, tell Charice what you've been telling me."
Sam sounded desperate.

Charice stood, legs apart, fists on her hips. Examining
LaMar from head to toe, her whole expression said she was
not impressed. Dressed in a huge t-shirt, baggy pants worn
low on his hips without a belt, and expensive high-top athletic
shoes, LaMar grinned at her. He wore long dreadlocks.

"Hey, mama. Whuz up?"

"Who is this?" Charice spoke to Sam without taking her
eyes off Lamar.

"My man, LaMar Zeno. Best black private cop in the U.
S. of A." Sam tapped fists with Lamar to punctuate his
statement.

"Thanks, brother." LaMar dipped one shoulder low to
assume a hip stance.

"Excuse us, please." Charice took Sam by the arm, dragging him into her kitchen. "Is this a joke?"

"No, baby. I swear, LaMar is a licensed private investigator. He worked for Pinkerton close to six years before
striking out on his own. He's got some information that
will clear Paul."

"Uh-huh." Charice pressed her lips together.

"Look, when you agreed to see me, you promised to listen. LaMar has sources all over south Louisiana. He really could clear Paul." Sam put a hand on her arm, pleading his case.

"What's going to clear him with Savannah? He lied to her and you lied to me." Charice shook her finger close to his nose.

"Now, baby, I couldn't betray the confidence of my best friend. I told you, his daddy didn't want anybody to know. Paul was just curious about the Trosclairs. Mr. Honore had a series of mild strokes, then a more serious one only a few weeks ago. Mr. Honore was real upset that all kinds of ugly things were going to be said about his mama. He made Paul swear never to let anyone find out. Paul wouldn't do anything to hurt his daddy, and definitely not for money."

"But you got that contract because of Trosclair."

"We didn't know that! Look, look, Trosclair pulled strings because he already knew who Paul was before he even got to town. Now, why would Paul blackmail him? That doesn't make any sense. Paul told me Trosclair had known who he was from the start. LaMar found out the private investigator he'd hired was only updating a thick file. Trosclair had been keeping up with Paul's father and grandmother for years."

"I don't know—"

"Ten minutes, just ten minutes. Come on, Charice."

"Ten minutes, that's all. Can't believe I'm doing this." She walked ahead of him back to the living room.

"Go on, LaMar. Tell her." Sam sat next to Charice on the loveseat.

"Uh-umm, let me see here." LaMar dug deep into a pocket of his oversized pants and brought out a tiny wire-bound notepad. "Claude Trosclair has been using Crescent City Security since the late fifties for various jobs. They do okay, but they kinda weak when it comes to the tricky cases. Anyways, they didn't have much trouble finding Marguerite Ricard and keeping him informed of her situation. Seems the old man kinda flipped out when he found out she was married to Henry Honore, got stinking drunk. Anyways, he had them offer her money. He also wanted to see 'em both. She told 'em hell no, and to stay out of her life. He got messed up again, but he didn't try to contact her after that. Now we fast-forward to four years ago. He started using his contacts to refer clients to you two for business; done very discreetly, of course." He was speaking in a factual tone, and he had only briefly glanced at his notes during his narrative.

"See, now do you believe me?" Sam asked hopefully.

Charice did not answer, but squinted thoughtfully. LaMar put the pad back into his pocket, sat down and crossed his legs.

"Something funny is going on with the business, Big River Company, I mean. Seems grandson Quentin has been making substantial investments," LaMar said.

"So what? He's a rich boy." Charice shrugged.

"But he doesn't have that kind of money to draw from his trust fund or his stocks. He has put up several million with no decrease in his assets." LaMar paused to let that sink in.

"And he didn't get the money from grandpapa." Charice sat forward, now intrigued.

"You got it. Another thing: though I haven't pinned this down for sure, I think this Kyle Singleton knows about Quentin's transactions and is blackmailing him. My sources tell me that suddenly, the guy is calling the shots at Batton Chemical. Why would greedy little Quentin allow that?" LaMar lifted an eyebrow at them.

"But how does this prove that Paul didn't have a reason to kill Trosclair? I mean, the sheriff can say all that has nothing to do with Paul having motive, means, and opportunity." Charice sat back.

"Wait, it gets even more interesting. A reliable source

inside the drug trade says Master Quentin was earning those large amounts of cash moving cocaine. I also think Quentin found out about Paul about a month ago.''

''Wow!'' Charice's eyes opened wide.

''Now, so far we've got two possible scenarios. One, Claude found out about Quentin's embezzling and drug deals; they fight and the old man gets wasted. Two, Quentin finds out Claude has plans to give some of his estate to Paul and his father; they fight; ba-dam! The old man gets it.''

''My Lord.'' Charice let out a long puff.

''There's more, but I need to check out a few additional details,'' LaMar said.

''More?''

''Look, I'm on my way.'' LaMar stood up. ''I got some work to do on another case. I'll be in touch. Later, homeboy.'' With a bouncy walk, he went out to a low-riding electric blue pick-up truck parked in front of Charice's house. The rhythmic thumping of a reggae rap tune blared as he started the engine. Head bobbing to the music, he drove off.

''Savannah should hear this, babe.'' Sam returned to the living room after locking the door behind LaMar.

''She's not going to talk to you. Poor thing is numb. She's trying to pretend she doesn't care, but it's obvious she's still crazy for Paul. Now she's convinced that she didn't mean anything to him but a temporary good time while he got next to the family fortune.''

''She'll listen to you. At least try,'' Sam said.

''I've got to admit, I'm not so sure as I was before hearing all this.'' Charice drummed her fingers rapidly on her knee.

''So, you'll try?'' Sam put an arm around her.

''Okay, but don't get your hopes up. Like I said, Savannah is pretty bitter.''

* * *

"That no-good son of a bitch!" Quentin paced the floor of the apartment.

"Idiot, he's watching us and you bring me here?" LaShaun peered through the drawn drapes at the street below.

"He already knows. I hardly think sneaking around will work at this point," Quentin snapped.

"Singleton didn't mention anything about the drugs?" LaShaun gulped down a swallow of expensive cognac.

"No, but it's only a matter of time. You can bet he's snooping around for more dirt to use so he can sink his hooks in me even deeper." Quentin started to light a joint.

"Put that down, damn it. This is no time to get stoned." LaShaun snatched it from his lips.

"You're having a drink," Quentin protested.

"Unlike you, I don't drink until I pass out. Now, shut up so I can think." LaShaun tapped a long, multicolored fingernail on the side of her glass. "Tell me again exactly what he said."

"He wants me to announce at the next board meeting that I'm stepping aside to let him assume the CEO position. The reason I'm to give is that I need some time off to deal with grandfather's death and to look after my grandmother. Filthy bastard."

"If you'd been more careful, this wouldn't have happened. Do you know how much money I'll lose because of your stupid carelessness?" LaShaun put down the glass with a bang, splashing cognac on the coffee table.

"Why the hell didn't you come up with some brilliant ideas before now, huh? You've been in on this thing from the start, so don't give me that crap!"

"Okay, let's cool it. We won't get anywhere fighting each other. We need to spend our time coming up with a plan to handle this." She stared straight ahead for several minutes. "When's the next board meeting?"

"Not for three and a half weeks."

"Your contact Juan Carlos—when are you supposed to give him an answer about going in on another deal?"

"About two weeks from now. He says he won't know all the details until then. The Colombian government's latest crackdown has been very effective in putting a real kink in his plans. His partners in Bogota are lying low. What's that got to do with this?"

"So he'll have time on his hands. And he won't be happy to know that someone is threatening his operation here as well."

"What are you talking about?" Quentin still paced.

"Singleton, he's your silent partner. He wants more of a cut, or else." LaShaun picked up her drink again, her lips curving in a slow smile.

"Singleton? But you and I—"

"Singleton," LaShaun hissed through clenched teeth, "he wants you out of the deal. He's forced you to give him most of the profit from the last shipment. He's threatened to expose your activities to the police. He's arranged it so that all the evidence points to you and Juan Carlos. He knows all about the operation and can do real damage unless he gets a bigger share."

"How will I get him to believe me? These people aren't stupid. They can check these things. They can access all kinds of computer systems." Quentin frowned in concentration.

"Perfect. It should be easy to arrange it to look as if money has gone into an account for Singleton. To make it seem as if he made those electronic investments with huge amounts of money. Printouts you can give to your friend as proof." LaShaun spoke in a hard, deliberate tone staring at him intently.

"But they'll . . ." A vicious smiled curled his lip up at the thought.

"Yes, they will." LaShaun nodded, her eyes shining with malevolence. "Here's to international trade partners." LaShaun handed him a drink. Their glasses clinked as they came together.

* * *

"Nice to see you again, Ms. Collins. Bad news," LaMar said, tucking designer sunglasses into the pocket of his coat. Today he wore an expensive dove gray suit. His hair was neatly cut and gave him the look of a young accountant on his way to work.

"How bad?" Sam seemed to hold his breath.

After picking her up at home, Sam and Charice met him at a restaurant in Breaux Bridge, afraid that having him visit Beau Chene would attract attention. The late-afternoon sun slanted across the table set out on a wooden patio overlooking Bayou Vermillion.

"One Beverly Mills, office manager at Batton Chemical, has given the sheriff a statement that she overheard Paul fighting with Trosclair the night before they found his body. According to her, they were having it out, shouting at each other." LaMar spoke in a crisp manner.

"Oh shit." Charice bit her lower lip.

"Oh shit is right." Sam's face was grim.

"Yes, we certainly have a difficult task ahead of us. However, there is more damning information about young Quentin. But excuse me while I make a quick phone call." LaMar's beeper had gone off. He gave Charice a proper smile, then left.

"Good thing I wasn't able to get Savannah to come. This would have blown up any chance to convince her that Paul didn't do it," Charice said.

"Now I have good news." LaMar, true to his word, was gone only a few minutes. "Quentin and a—LaShaun Rousselle have been having an affair for some time now. Know her?"

"LaShaun? Have mercy!"

"Seems that they've been using a New Orleans apartment owned by Batton Chemical for their trysts. 'An unconventional relationship' is the most delicate way to describe it." LaMar sniffed as if offended.

"Like what? Freaky stuff?" Sam sat forward eagerly.

"Calm down or I'm going to pour this iced tea in your lap," Charice warned.

"LaShaun's financial status has dramatically improved in the last year, an indication that she has some knowledge of Quentin's business dealings. One other thing, Quentin has no alibi for the hours leading up to his grandfather's body being discovered. According to the housekeeper, Louise, she thinks he was home right before Claude Trosclair left that evening to return to his office."

"Damn. How did you find that out?" Charice stared at him in amazement.

"A cousin's friend's sister-in-law went to school with her daughter," LaMar said offhandedly. "The point is, he had motive, opportunity, and means, too."

"Yes, but between Paul and Quentin Trosclair, who do you think the sheriff is more likely to arrest?" Sam said.

"I know. However, there is encouraging news of a different sort. I think Singleton should be very concerned about his health these days. Word is out that a certain Juan Carlos, not his real name, naturally, is quite upset with him. This man is the most powerful drug distributor between Houston and Biloxi with connections to a Colombian cartel. Not someone you want to have upset with you."

"But what's that got to do with all this?" Sam frowned.

"Maybe nothing. However, it may be in our best interests to assist Mr. Singleton in avoiding any serious injury."

"Huh?" Charice and Sam spoke together, exchanging puzzled looks.

"Leave it to me. I will keep you informed. Nice seeing you again, Ms. Collins. Sam." LaMar dipped his head toward them. He walked purposefully to a white Volvo parked at a curb nearby.

"LaMar's got a plan." Sam grinned widely.

"I'm just as bumfuzzled as can be. How is knowing about Singleton getting some drug king pissed off, LaShaun's strange sex life, and Quentin's finances going to help get Paul out of this?''

"I don't know, but LaMar does.''

They watched him go through a ritual of putting on the sunglasses, snapping on his seat belt, and adjusting his rearview mirror before driving off.

"How the hell did he do that?'' Charice shook her head.

"Do what, babe?''

"Go from rasta homeboy to a member of the black bourgeoisie in three days? And a Volvo for goodness' sakes. I bet he even hired a wife and two kids.''

Chapter 16

Paul was wound up. Despite the long hours of traveling, he wasn't fatigued at all. His mind raced, not with thoughts of the danger of being convicted for a murder he did not commit—but of what Savannah must be thinking now, hearing about his relationship with Trosclair. He closed his eyes as he pictured her reaction to the news. Surely that would push her into Devin's arms. Paul thought of them together, Devin touching her body. He pounded the armrest furiously.

"You all right?" The chubby businessman sitting next to him was startled out of his nap. His watery blue eyes mirrored his alarm.

"I'm sorry. Sure, I'm okay." Paul made a conscious effort to slow his breathing.

"Ladies and gentlemen, we're approaching the New Orleans International Airport. We hope you've enjoyed your flight with us. Please bring your seats to an upright position and fasten your seatbelts." The bland voice of the stewardess droned on with weather information about New Orleans.

"Paul, over here." Sam waved his arms to get his attention.

Wading through the crowds, they grabbed each other in a quick embrace. It was slow going, waiting for the luggage to be unloaded, then watching for it to appear, bumping along with dozens of others on the conveyor. They did not even try to talk about anything. Finally, they were headed for a hotel room Sam had rented in Metairie.

"I figured we needed to buy some time for LaMar to dig up more stuff," Sam answered, when Paul wanted to know why they weren't going to Beau Chene.

"You could get in trouble, man. Just take me to the sheriff so I can turn myself in. I don't want you to take any kind of fall for me."

"Two days . . . that's all we need. Why didn't you wait another week, like I told you anyway?"

"Because I got tired of dodging the Kuwait authorities, then the Saudi authorities. Besides, what difference would it make, anyway? I'm the only suspect."

"They only want you for questioning still. That's probably why the police weren't at the airport to arrest you. But the minute you set foot back in Crowley or Beau Chene, you'll get invited in for a little talk and be charged with murder, I'd bet. Man, don't worry. LaMar has done a helluva job finding out stuff. Such as that your cousin Quentin's been into drug trafficking big-time."

"Unbelievable!"

For the next few hours, Sam gave Paul a full account of everything LaMar had discovered thus far. They were eating take-out Chinese food on the small table in the hotel room as Sam finished his story.

"So that's about it. LaMar has got something else in mind, but he hasn't told me the specifics. Said it would be better if I didn't know."

"Heavy stuff." Paul had only picked at his shrimp with vegetables. "Have you seen Savannah?" He looked down, pushing his food around in circles.

"Uh-uh. Charice has, though. She didn't take it too well, if that's what you want to know."

"Who gives a damn, anyway?" Paul threw the plastic fork down so hard it bounced to the floor. "She's got Devin to console her. He's still in Beau Chene, I bet."

"Yeah, but—"

"Which means she's been with him, too. Don't lie to me, Sam." Paul stood over him.

"Maybe once, but—" Sam finished weakly.

"That's what I thought," Paul said, his voice heavy with bitterness.

"Cool out, man. I'm on your side." Sam held up both hands, palms turned out.

"I'm sorry. I feel like the world is closing in on me. Like I'm trapped in some nightmare and can't wake up."

"It's all right, man. I understand. We're going to make it through this, I swear." Sam squeezed his shoulder.

"I need to visit my parents." Paul turned to him.

"No, Paul. Stay here at least another day. They gotta be watching their house."

"You sure my father doesn't know all this."

"Your mama says he doesn't. I don't know how, but they've kept him away from the news and newspapers. Of course, between his medication and going to the rehab clinic for physical therapy, he stays pretty exhausted."

"What about my sisters and brothers?"

"You kidding? They insisted on splitting the cost of LaMar's fee with me. I told them I could afford it, but, well, you know how family is."

"I know," Paul said, a catch in his voice.

"Get some rest, okay? I'll be back in the morning."

"Sam." Paul grabbed his arm. "Thanks."

They embraced roughly, then Sam left. For three hours, Paul prowled around the room trying to unwind. He tried turning on the television, listening to the radio, reading. Nothing helped. Looking at the clock, he decided he could wait no longer. They had passed a car rental office a block from the hotel. If he hurried, he could just make it before they closed.

* * *

"Your delicacies are a hit on the 'Quality and Bargains' shopping channel, Tante Marie." Savannah held up another order faxed in that morning. "They want more for what they're calling the 'Gourmet Taste' segment."

"That's good." Tante Marie continued making up a gift basket.

"Poppy's carved animals went like hotcakes and they want to feature them in another four months. Getting us on that shopping channel was brilliant, if I do say so myself."

"Um-hum."

"We're posting healthy profits from the shop with the publicity. A couple of tour operators called to tell me that they've even had a few requests to put us on their routes."

"That's nice."

"Well, don't get too excited. You'll get your blood pressure up." Savannah put down her pencil. "Let's have it."

"Have what?" Tante Marie gave her a guileless look.

"You've got something on your mind, I can tell. You've been as quiet as a mouse for the last week. Come on, spit it out."

"You oughta be ashamed, that's all. Charice been your friend since you was a baby and you won't trust her enough to at least do one little thing she ask." Tante Marie shook her finger at Savannah, her reticent demeanor disappearing in seconds.

"Oh boy."

"Don't 'Oh boy' me, missy. You bein' hardheaded as you papa."

"Why is everybody defending him? He lied, it may be he killed his own grandfather because he couldn't extort money from him, and he's a fugitive. But I'm the bad guy. What is wrong with this picture?" Savannah threw up both hands.

"I'll tell you what's wrong. You so set on him being guilty that you don't wanna hear no other side."

"Hey, now." Leon came in. Noticing the tense silence, he put away his backpack. Picking up the list of deliveries, he got the keys from Savannah. "I'm gone."

"You know, I understand how you feel, cher. But I also know you can't sleep good no more. You ain't eatin' hardly nothin' these days, and you can't tell me you happy."

"Okay, I'm miserable. Satisfied? I've been called a jezebel, lied to, called a liar, and dumped on generally. This from the man you want me to believe in. Well, how could I have been so blind? You are absolutely right, I should give him the benefit of the doubt," Savannah snapped.

"Good, cher. I'll call Charice now. She can have that detective fella come by this evening." Tante Marie pretended not to notice the sarcasm. She snatched up the telephone and began punching the numbers.

"Oooh, I could—you—uhh—" Savannah groaned in exasperation. She stomped back into the office.

"Son, you got no business here. Sam said you was to stay away." Reba now wore a worried frown after jubilantly welcoming her son with a shower of kisses.

"I couldn't stay in that hotel room another minute. I had to see how Papa is doing."

"The sheriff been here askin' for you. They probably watchin' the house." Reba wrung her hands.

"I came through the woods out back and down the old path. Nobody saw me. How is he?"

"Pretty good. Lately he's lost his appetite. But other than that, he's fine."

"And he doesn't know anything about—"

"No, thank the Lord. I been keepin' him watching them cable channels that don't have no news programs. He ain't even missed it." Reba patted her son's arm. "Go on in there. He gone be so glad to see you."

"Hi, Papa. You looking better every time I see you." Paul kissed his forehead.

"Hey, boy. You know you lyin' to me." Charles laughed in spite of himself. He sat in his favorite overstuffed recliner. He was dressed in a light blue sweatsuit. Gunfire came from the television as an old western played.

"You something else, looking all sporty." Paul tugged his father's sleeve playfully.

"Yep, your mama got me four or five sets of these. At first I told her I wasn't gone wear 'em. But shoot, they is some comfortable, yeah. See here?" Charles worked his left arm, flexing it out and back.

"That's great, Papa. You'll be out fishing in no time."

"I got news for you, me and your brother Sheldon already plannin' to go after some sac-a-lait at False River. Now, how you gettin' along? Got what you wanted outta that trip?"

"Yeah, I learned a lot. Kuwait is a testing ground for some of the most innovative technology dealing with chemical clean-up."

"That so. Ain't that somethin'? Still didn't tell me how you doin'."

"I'm okay."

"Okay?"

"Yeah."

"Tell me, you think I'm senile?"

"No, of course not. Why—"

"You think I'm stupid?"

"Papa—"

"Well, answer me."

"No, Papa. I do not think you are senile or stupid."

"Then talk to me like it. Claude Trosclair is dead an' they think you did it. Now, I ain't faultin' your monmon or your sisters and brothers. They was tryin' to protect me, thinkin' I was too sick to take that kinda news. That's all right. But I'm doin' a whole lot better, you just got back home, and I want you to tell me 'bout it." Charles waited patiently, watching the internal conflict of his son play itself out in his facial expressions.

"Since it's obvious you know and it hasn't caused a setback in your recovery, I might as well be truthful. Right?" Paul sighed. "But tell me, how in the world did you find out?"

"Your mama forgot about them news updates. Even the cable channels in other cities are carryin' 'em. Local news from a New Orleans station is comin' on that all-news channel now. One day she went to answer the phone and left the remote control where I could reach it."

"Oh, yeah. Damn, I should've thought about that."

"That don't matter. Tell me what happened."

Paul began hesitantly, afraid of the effect discussing Claude Trosclair would have on Charles. But Charles listened to his story impassively. Paul described his last meeting with Claude in detail as Charles broke in occasionally to ask pointed questions.

"When I left him he was alive. That was the last time I saw or talked to him." Paul rubbed his neck.

"Paul, you don't have to tell me you didn't kill him. I know all my children. Not one of 'em could or would intentionally hurt another human bein' on this earth. 'Course now, Sheldon might rough a man up bad if he insulted your mama."

"Now, that's the truth, Sheldon's got a temper on him." Paul chuckled.

"But I know you didn't kill that man." Charles still refused to call Claude his father. "If anybody in this family could, it would have been me." He clenched his right fist.

"Don't say that to anybody else." Paul stroked his hand until it relaxed.

"Hey, they done already checked up on me. You can b'lieve that, yeah. They know I been in and out of the hospital. Hell, I been so weak I couldn't swat a fly. But you in serious trouble."

"Since you know so much, I guess you must know about the private detective." Paul raised an eyebrow at him.

"LaMar Zeno. His daddy went to prison for killin' a

man. Got stabbed and died in Angola State Penitentiary.
They found out a year later he was tellin' the truth all
along. He hadn't killed nobody. LaMar been on a mission
ever since, when it comes to innocent folks bein' accused.
He may be a little, well, strange—but he good. And knowin'
he workin' for you makes me feel it's gone be all right."

"Sam thinks so, too. I hope you're both right." Paul
clasped hands with his father.

The light from the late-evening sun was nothing more
than a pale glow brushing the very tops of the trees as Paul
moved through the woods behind his parents' home. The
old path he and his siblings had used so frequently was
now much overgrown with vines. The once-bare dusty lane
was now covered with a carpet of grass reaching up to his
knees. He stood for a moment, remembering. To his left,
past a huge pecan tree, was the way to their favorite fishing
pond and swimming hole. To his right, the woods had
stretched on to become a place for hunting. In the last six
years, housing developments had cut into the wild countryside. Still, he found it little changed from his childhood.
How they had relished the freedom of summers spent
here! He could almost hear the voices of his sisters and
their friends, squealing in pretend fright as one of the
boys found some harmless snake to shake at them. Or the
shouts of joy when one of them caught the biggest fish.
Feeling his shoe strike against an object, he smiled upon
pushing aside weeds to find a child-sized canteen. Obviously a new generation had discovered his old playground.

Shaking himself out of his reverie, he continued toward
the small road, now paved, that bordered the eastern edge
of the woods. The hand in his pocket fingered the keys to
the rental car as he emerged from a stand of wild honey-
suckle bushes.

"Stop! Walk slowly toward the car, hands held high!" a
male voice shouted from somewhere to his right.

Instinctively, Paul began to turn in the direction of the voice.

"No sudden moves! Walk straight ahead to the car! Now! Do it!"

Louisiana state troopers dressed in dark blue surrounded him. Sheriff Triche and one of his deputies stepped forward. When he reached the car, Paul was shoved face down onto the hood and handcuffed. While one trooper patted him down roughly, another explained his rights. Sharply pulled upright again, Paul was put into a patrol car.

"Good capture, boys. Real good." Sheriff Triche grunted with satisfaction as he leaned down to stare at Paul.

"So, I figure Claude Trosclair went back to his office and was killed there. Quentin and LaShaun are strong suspects. They had more to lose than your friend Paul. As for Kyle Singleton, he's had his hand in the profits, covering gambling debts. Maybe the old man found out about him, too." LaMar sat back dressed in khaki work clothes, a plastic hardhat on his knee. He was the epitome of a working-class man.

"Well, Savannah, what do you think?" Charice poked Savannah's arm.

"I admit, it's interesting."

"Interesting!" Sam and Charice yelled together.

"We got at least three people with motive enough to waste a whole town, and all you can say is, 'It's interesting'?" Sam said.

"You are unbelievable!" Charice said.

"All right, okay." Savannah held one hand. "Chill, y'all. Let me think a minute."

"We need to be over at the sheriff's office, telling him all this stuff." Sam stood up.

"No, we got to prove one of them did it. Get the evidence on him." Charice chewed on a fingernail.

"No. We don't need to do either one. We just have to present enough evidence to create reasonable doubt. LaMar, they don't have a witness or physical evidence linking Paul to the murder, do they?" Savannah, still calmly seated, turned to the private detective.

"No." LaMar flashed a smile.

"People have been convicted on circumstantial evidence, but not often. Police usually count on a suspect making a slip during questioning, or even a confession."

"Right." LaMar's eyes had a gleam as he regarded her with increasing interest.

"Since he didn't do it, he has nothing incriminating to let slip and reveal. And nothing to confess, either."

"You got it."

"I'm no criminal lawyer, but the case against him is dripping with reasonable doubt." Savannah took a deep breath. "But I do think he's going to wind up on trial."

"You don't think the district attorney will decline to prosecute since the evidence is circumstantial?" Sam sat down heavily.

"Sam, both he and the sheriff are elected officials. Claude Trosclair was a rich, powerful man from a rich, powerful family. What do you think?" Savannah said.

"Damn! No way could that be kept from Paul's father." Charice sat down next to Sam and held his hand.

"Yeah, and he was doing so well, coming back from his stroke and all." Sam looked dejected.

"I didn't know." Savannah went to the picture window of Charice's living room. The lush green growth of late spring was everywhere.

"I know what you said about circumstantial evidence, but there are thousands of brothers in prison as a result of less than what they've got on Paul." Sam let go of Charice's hand to rub his eyes. A vein stood out on his neck.

"Cheer up. Somebody might just confess, you know."
LaMar, standing at the door, tipped his hardhat to them
all before striding out to a full-sized tan pick-up truck with
a tool kit across the back.

All three stared at him, then at each other, mouths
hanging open, eyes wide in astonishment. They were like
statues, unmoving for about thirty seconds.

"What the hell!" Savannah rushed to the door only to
watch the tailgate moving down the street.

"Honey, don't try to figure it out. I gave up the second
time I met him." Charice patted Savannah on the back.

They stood at the door as the truck turned a corner. A
grinning LaMar waved at them before the truck was lost
from view. The phone began ringing behind them.

"Hello. Oh, God." Charice closed her eyes. "Okay.
They're here. Yeah, thanks for calling."

"What is it? Not the kids?" Sam's brows drew together
in concern.

"No, that was Mr. Antoine. Paul's been arrested."

Savannah had calmly discussed the possibility that Paul
would not only be charged, but put on trial. Goosebumps
spread on both arms as the cold reality of the danger he
faced washed over her. All three came to stand close to
each other, huddled for warmth.

"Gentlemen, please. Circumstantial evidence is all
you've got." Gralin eyed the district attorney, Morton Daniels, and Sheriff Triche. Paul sat next to him.

"We found a button matching one from a jacket your
client owns at what we believe is the crime scene." Daniels
held up a sheet of paper from a folder in front of him.

"Which could have been dropped at any time since Mr.
Honore has admitted being in that office. He met with
Mr. Trosclair a number of times at that location."

"Your client left the country. Went to one of them Arab
places."

"Kuwait. And we have ample evidence to show this trip had been planned for months. Look, let's stop this game. We all know the reason the judge released my client on bond is because of the flimsy case you have. Taking this to trial is a waste of taxpayers' money."

"Our investigation is continuing. There are certain promising leads. It might be to your advantage to tell us what really happened. We might even be willing to discuss involuntary manslaughter," Daniels said, taking the tone of a solicitous uncle.

"And we might even consider not filing a wrongful prosecution lawsuit when this is over. Goodbye, gentlemen," Gralin said. He and Paul left.

"Well?" Sam and Charice hovered around them as they exited the courthouse.

"They won't budge. Can't afford to give up their only suspect and admit they've got no real leads. Hang in there, Paul." Gralin shook his hand before going back into the courthouse.

"At least he thinks it looks good for you." Charice tried an encouraging smile, but failed.

"I've been wracking my brain trying to come up with something, anything, to prove I didn't go back to that office or see him again," Paul said.

"Come on, let's get some coffee."

"What y'all staring at?" Charice faced down the other patrons at the doughnut shop. "Idiots," Charice muttered, when they averted their eyes self-consciously.

"Take it easy. This is a small town. Not only is it the first murder in six years, but he was the town's richest citizen." Paul sipped his coffee.

"I hate small towns," Sam grumbled to no one in particular.

"So, is Savannah okay?" Paul played with a paper napkin.

"Fine. She would have been here, but—" Sam stammered, looking to Charice for help.

"You know, she—had stuff at the shop. Man, since they went on television, business has been just—taken off. I mean, she is working constantly to keep up." Charice's voice trailed off lamely. She gave Sam a helpless shrug.

"Yeah, that's great." Paul took another sip of coffee.

"Why don't you give her a call?" Charice said.

"Nah, not a good idea." Paul stirred his coffee needlessly.

"Go on. She's over there now." Charice pulled his hand as if trying to tug him out of his seat.

"She doesn't think you did it," Sam blurted out.

"But she's not exactly a fan, either. I understand."

"Paul, really, she—"

"It's okay, Charice. Drop it. Hey, thanks for everything. I'm going to the office. Might as well catch up on some work, right? See ya." Paul left.

"Will you talk to her? She's your friend," Sam said.

"I've tried, believe me. There's nothing else I can say. Why don't you talk to him?"

"I've tried. He won't even call her on the phone."

"Well, that's it, then. It really is over, I guess." Charice chewed a corner of a doughnut.

Sam nodded.

"I'm through with it." Charice said.

"Me, too."

"They're grown, and you can't make grown folks do what they don't want to do."

"You're right."

"I have no more to say. I'm not wasting my breath on it anymore. She doesn't have to worry about me bringing it up." Charice waved her hands for emphasis.

"I agree totally." Sam slapped the table.

"This is crazy, Savannah." Charice threw up her hands in frustration.

"Charice, leave it alone." Savannah tied a white ribbon around a gift basket filled with Tante Marie's pralines and spices.

"Number one, you agree that he didn't do it." Charice held up one finger.

"Right."

"Number two, you say you understand why he didn't tell you about his grandfather being Claude Trosclair." Charice flipped up a second finger.

"Sort of." Savannah raised an eyebrow at her.

"And number three, you even understand him getting upset about Devin." Charice held up a third finger. "Three, count 'em, *three* good reasons to get back together with the man."

"You want to keep those fingers, you'd better quit waving them in my face. Now, you listen. Number one, I agree that he's no murderer. I had my doubts before LaMar Zeno gave me his information just because no matter how angry he'd made me, Paul is not a violent man. Number two, though I understand his secrecy, I still think we had become close enough that he could have trusted me. And number three, it wasn't so much his objection to my seeing Devin as some of the things he said to me in anger over it."

"You are some kind of stubborn."

"Besides, he doesn't want to see me. I mean, he hasn't broken his neck getting over here, now, has he?"

"But what if he *did* come over here?"

"He won't."

"He might."

"Have you talked to him? If you've been talking to him about me, I'll strangle you, so help me." Savannah moved toward her menacingly.

"No, no! You know I wouldn't do that after you told me not to. Um-humm." Charice back away.

"See that you don't." Savannah resumed her work on the basket.

* * *

"Call the woman, man!" Sam thrust the telephone receiver at him. They sat in their Lafayette office.

"Forget it. The last thing I need right now is rejection." Paul plowed into the mound of papers on his desk.

"She'd love to hear from you."

"Yeah, that's why she rushed over to the jail to stand by me. Right?" Paul snorted.

"Well . . . maybe she's hesitant to approach you, knowing how you'll react. Y'all didn't part on the best of terms, you know."

"I guess—"

"She is kind of upset about some of that stuff you said about her and that guy Devin." Sam spoke haltingly, testing the waters.

"Maybe I overreacted." Paul looked up, sighing.

"So call her. Better yet, go by the shop. Go on. I'm telling you, she'd like to see you."

"Wait a minute. Have you been talking to her about me?"

"I, uh, well, er . . ."

"Have you?" Paul rose from the desk, scowling at his friend.

"No, man. You know me better than that!" Sam held both hands out, palms up.

"Keep it that way if you wanna stay healthy."

Chapter 17

"Isn't this great?" Charice kept craning her neck to look around.

"It's a gorgeous day." Savannah sighed as she adjusted her sunglasses.

They sat at a table on the combination boat landing and café at the edge of Bayou des Glaises. At Charice's suggestion, they'd packed swimsuits, sunscreen, and a radio and left right after Sunday mass. Charice left her girls happily playing with a large group of their cousins at her mother's house.

"Yes, just us grown folks. That's one thing about being a single parent, you're always alone with your children. Plus teaching twenty kids all week. There are times I catch myself telling Sam to eat all his vegetables when we're out on a date." Charice started to giggle, then sat up suddenly at the approach of a car. Seeing the red convertible with a group of college-age kids, she eased back in her chair.

"Why do you keep bouncing up every time a car passes? And what is this about?" Savannah swiveled her head around in an exaggerated fashion to imitate her.

"Hey, I'm curious, okay? Just looking around." Charice grinned.

"Nosy is more like it." Savannah leaned back in her lounge chair.

Savannah was enjoying the scenery in spite of herself. The warm breeze rippled the water. Both wore swimsuits under shorts in case they wanted to swim or wade. They waved at waterskiers zipping by, recognizing a few friends. The radio played New Orleans boogie music from a station in Breaux Bridge. Savannah kept glancing at Charice, who seemed to be making a supreme effort not to peer around.

"I'm telling you, we never came here to go fishing. What is up with you today? Dragging me out here when we could have just as well gone to Bayou Teche." Paul's voice came from behind them.

"Look who's here!" Charice yelled, waving at them eagerly.

"Yeah, what a surprise to you, I bet," Savannah hissed under her breath. "Hello." Behind the dark glasses, her expression was unreadable.

"Hi." Paul came to a halt, shifting his feet awkwardly under her inscrutable gaze.

"Say, Sam, want something to drink?" Charice jerked her head toward the café. "They've got a wide variety of cold drinks."

"Yeah, yeah. That sounds good." He followed her inside, neither of them daring to look back.

"Take a good look at her. This is the last time for a long time you'll see her without bruises all over her butt." Savannah stared after them.

"Well, I guarantee they'll be a matched pair when I get through with him." Paul tapped his thigh with a clenched fist.

"You, ah, doing okay?" Savannah cleared her throat. She couldn't help but notice the way his yellow cotton knit shirt stretched across his chest or the way the navy blue shorts showed off his muscular brown legs.

"Under the circumstances, okay." Paul tugged at his collar, shifted to the other foot, then cleared his throat. "You look good—I mean, you look fine—I mean—" Paul forced his gaze away from her legs.

"Sit down," Savannah finally offered, after long, silent minutes had stretched between them.

"Yeah, uh, sure."

"Sorry about everything you're going through."

"Thanks."

"LaMar Zeno seems to be on it, though," Savannah said, twirling the straw in her soft drink cup.

"That's what Sam tells me. I haven't talked to him yet."

"Really? You're in for a treat. He's different, that's for sure."

"Oh, you've met LaMar?" Paul turned to her.

"Sam and Charice got us together."

"I see."

"Arresting you was ridiculous. They haven't got a case." Savannah waved a hand dismissively.

"You've kept up with it?"

"Yeah, sort of," Savannah said with an embarrassed smile.

"I didn't think you cared. After, well, you know. . . ."

"Yeah."

They both stared out over the water, not speaking.

"I said a lot of stupid things in my life, but I topped myself that day at the courthouse." Paul looked at her.

"I guess I should have told you I'd be seeing Devin."

"Telling you about being related to the Trosclairs scared the hell out of me."

"I wish you had, though. Still," Savannah quickly added, hearing him suck in a deep breath, "you were right. No way would I have trusted you after that. You know how I am. But you can't choose your relatives. If you could, I know I'd be less about five of my cousins." Savannah gave a short laugh.

"My dad—"

"I know. Sam told me."

"I really want to make things right with us. I've missed you." Paul got up to kneel beside her.

"Me, too." Savannah took off her sunglasses.

Savannah wrapped both arms around him. Pulling him close, she tasted the kiss she'd craved for weeks. Deeper and deeper she allowed his tongue to explore until they were both gasping, clutching each other excitedly. "Whoa!" Savannah yelled. With a loud crack, the lounge chair collapsed beneath them. Her giggle was cut off when his mouth covered hers again.

"Oh, no! Who gonna pay for ma chair, huh?" The owner of the café, a dirty white apron stretched across his pot belly, pointed at them from the door.

"I will!" Charice and Sam said. Grinning, they shook hands.

The foursome spent the rest of the afternoon together enjoying the splendid weather. They even went for a ride in a rented bâteau. Sunlight made the water of the bayou sparkle as though diamond chunks floated in it. Savannah held on to Paul's hand, letting go only when absolutely necessary. A tingle of pleasure and anticipation spread through her whenever they touched. His laugh was the most beautiful sound she had heard in weeks. Watching him move as he walked toward or away from her transformed the tingle into shock waves of desire. Throughout their day on the bayou she thrilled at finding his eyes on her, a glint of passion adding fire to his almond brown eyes.

"I haven't enjoyed myself like this for a long time. Actually, I know precisely the date and time I stopped enjoying much of anything." Paul reached out to touch her hair as they sat alone on the landing. Orange washed over the sky as the sun set.

"I'd guess the same day everything I had enjoyed up until then lost its flavor." Savannah tilted her head back, savoring the way his hand moved in her hair.

"Hey, you two, ready to head out?" Sam called. He and

Charice, arms entwined, came back from a leisurely walk along the levee.

"Yeah." Paul's hand trailed down Savannah's shoulder to take her hand in his. "I've got an idea. Why don't we go pick up my car? It won't take but twenty minutes to get there from here." His eyes never left her.

"Good idea, my brother." Sam pulled Charice closer to him, grinning.

"Let's not ever be apart like that again." Paul rested his cheek on the top of Savannah's head. They sat in the cypress swing on her front porch.

"It was awful, not hearing your voice or being able to touch you." Savannah breathed deeply of his sweet, woodsy scent.

He lifted her face to his and kissed her long and deeply. Savannah strained to him as his hands sought those familiar places that caused her to vibrate in his arms. Cupping one breast, he gave a short grunt of delight as her hands moved all over him.

"Whew! Isn't this where we started?" Paul asked, sitting back to catch his breath.

"Right on this very porch, cher." Savannah gave him a playful pinch on the arm.

"Have I told you how good it is to be with you again?"

"Yes, but once more won't hurt." Savannah rested her head on his shoulder.

"I want you. Nothing is more important than that. No silly argument, for sure."

"Same here."

"I'd better be getting on the road. I'm staying with my parents for a while. I want to help Mama with Papa. Give her some relief, you know? Wish I still had that trailer here in town." Paul put his hand on her thigh.

"There'll be time enough for that, time enough for all that." Savannah moaned faintly as he began moving his fingers across her flesh. "You'd better leave before we embarrass ourselves out here on this porch."

As she lay in bed later, Savannah wasn't the least bit sleepy. But this night it was for a totally different reason. The great aching emptiness that had gnawed at her had vanished. Those cold, miserable weeks without him had convinced her she did not want to live without his love. She no longer feared giving herself completely; she reveled in the joy of it. Smiling in the darkness, she imagined the time when they would be alone again. The way she would feel, the things they would do.

Dixieland jazz blared away. The band had the select crowd of well-to-do businessmen and their mistresses snapping their fingers in time with the music. Singleton sat at a corner table with a pretty young woman. Her long black hair was held perfectly in place. Stiff with hair spray, it did not move even as she tossed her head back to laugh at something he whispered to her. They had been at the New Orleans club for over an hour, drinking, laughing, and teasing each other. After whispering again in her ear, Singleton gestured to a waiter. Paying the bill, he took the woman by her hand, leading her to the door.

"Cab, sir." The driver of a white Chevrolet Lumina with "Mack's Cab Service" in black lettering on the side called to him. He was parked several feet from the entrance to the club.

"Le Crillion Hotel, please," Singleton said, only after making sure the car was clean inside.

Singleton walked several paces behind the woman, trying to relight his cigar. From the shadows between buildings, a man stepped out, blocking his path. The pretty woman melted into the crowd upon seeing him approach.

"Gimme your money, man."

"What?" Singleton froze.

"Give it up!"

The sharp tat-a-tat of automatic gunfire burst forth, causing bystanders to scatter for cover. Screams ricocheted through the air from all directions. Singleton lay on the pavement, his arms covering his head. Blood spattered his jacket.

"Man, I'm hit! Oh no! Ahh—ee!" The would-be robber rocked against a wall, holding his arms.

"Get in the car!" The cab driver began dragging a still cowering Singleton across the sidewalk.

Throwing him onto the back seat, the driver leapt over the car hood and slid behind the wheel. With the tires screaming, he took off. After driving for six blocks, he pulled to the curb on a dark side street.

"Let's see if you've been hit. No bloodstains, all in one piece, eh?" The cab driver checked him over with quick, efficient hands.

A silent figure stepped forward seemingly from nowhere, handed the cab driver a set of keys, then melted back into the night.

"It's quite all right, sir. Come with me and you'll be fine." The cab driver spoke calmly as he led a dazed Singleton to a light blue Plymouth.

"But who are you? Listen to me, take anything you want, but please don't hurt me." Singleton took out his wallet and began removing his Rolex watch.

"This isn't a kidnapping, Mr. Singleton."

"How do you know my name?"

"Oh, I know quite a lot about you, sir. Just relax. You're safe with me. I have something to show you."

"If you want to help, why don't you take me to the police? My God! Someone tried to kill me!"

"All in good time, sir. All in good time."

"LaMar always was weird, even in high school. Why are we meeting him at our office? It's after midnight." Paul had been complaining ever since Sam had picked him up.

"Savannah is meeting us there, too," Sam said.

"She shouldn't be out driving alone this time of night."

"She made me swear to call her when anything serious went down. Besides, Charice is with her. She's out of school for the summer and the girls are spending the night with their cousins."

"Great. They could both be stranded on a dark highway if they have car trouble." Paul glared at Sam.

"Will you stop acting like a nervous grandmother? Savannah has her car phone. They can call us or the state police in an emergency. Take it easy."

"Okay. Why are we going to the office again?" Paul's fingers made a rapping sound as he tapped the molded plastic on the passenger door.

"For the third time, LaMar wants us to meet him there. I don't know why. Yeah." Sam answered the car phone. He listened for several minutes. "We'll start on it. Forty-five minutes, got it. That was LaMar. How are your hacking skills, brother man?" Sam clapped Paul's shoulder.

They pulled into the parking lot of their suite of four offices. Located in a medium-sized complex near the Evangeline Thruway, the lobby was well lit. Waving to the night security guard, they bounded up the open stairway to the second floor.

"Now, do your thing." Sam sat back with his feet on another chair.

"Well, being suspected of murder makes illegally accessing another company's computer files seem minor." Paul laughed as he began the task of outsmarting security codes.

He worked intently for twenty minutes, not even noticing when Sam left. Sam returned with Savannah and Charice. They cut off their chatter so as not to disturb his concentration. Watching in fascination, Sam whispered explanations while Paul's fingers moved rapidly across the keys, trying different patterns.

"When we were in school, we got into some of the best

online systems. The research we accessed was fabulous. Like who had time to hang in the library all night, or the money to pay for all those services?"

"But isn't that considered a form of stealing?" Savannah gave him a disapproving look.

"Hey, we didn't take anything but a little information. And we didn't do it for long, anyway. Besides, we got busted by the dorm counselor and he confiscated our modem."

"Lucky you didn't get tracked down by the FBI." Charice pinched his right arm.

"Or kicked out of school." Savannah pinched his right arm.

"Oww! Cut it out." Sam massaged his arms.

"Shhh!" Savannah and Charice said at the same time.

"I think I've got it." Paul spoke over his shoulder. "Damn, not yet." He paused for only a few seconds before continuing.

The other three began to get worried as five, ten, twenty, then thirty minutes passed. It was hard for them to keep still and quiet. They snacked on chips and soft drinks from the vending machine down the hall. Sam took them on a tour of the office suites, then the rest of the complex. Upon entering the office again, they were surprised to find Paul sitting, wearing a self-satisfied grin, with his feet up on the desk.

"I'm in."

"Why am I here? What do you want with me?" Singleton blinked as he looked from one to the other.

"I think you know these gentlemen, Mr. Singleton." LaMar took off his black cap, throwing it on a nearby chair.

"Hey, man. What's happening?" Sam waved as though they were being reacquainted at a party.

"Hi again." Paul nodded.

"And this is Ms. St. Julien and Ms. Collins. Friends of Paul and Sam." LaMar sat on the edge of a desk.

"I don't understand any of this. Some mugger tries to kill me and my cab driver rescues me, then changes cars and drives me out of New Orleans. Is this a kidnapping?" Singleton wiped sweat from his chin with a linen handkerchief, his hand shaking.

"Certainly not, Mr. Singleton. May I call you Kyle? After all, we've been through so much together. Somehow, 'Mr. Singleton' sounds so formal. Kyle, I hate to tell you this, but that was no mere mugging." LaMar sighed.

"No? How do you know that?" Singleton stopped mopping his face.

"I'm a private cop. My investigation of you and Quentin Trosclair has led me to some interesting people."

"I don't know what you mean." Singleton's eyes slid sideways.

"Sources on the street are my lifeline, sir. And those sources told me exactly when that so-called mugging would go down. That man wasn't there to take your money."

"Uh-uh, my man." Sam shook his head slowly.

"Afraid not," Paul said.

"What are you saying?" Singleton's breathing became audible.

"We're saying he was sent to kill you, Kyle. You see, your partner in crime doesn't like the changes you've made at Batton Chemical. He is seeking to dissolve your partnership." LaMar leaned toward him.

"I—I don't what you mean by 'partner in crime.'" Singleton's gaze moved around the room.

"Quentin doesn't intend to give up money or power to you, Kyle. You know too much about his activities with company funds, about Claude Trosclair's death. You have to go, Kyle. Plain and simple." LaMar popped a mint in his mouth and flashed his teeth in a wide grin.

"But he demanded my money."

"Only as a cover for his real purpose. After all, folks are killed during robberies every day. Routine police paperwork. But not a professional hit of a respectable businessman. That would cause too many questions, too much heat," LaMar said.

"You're lying! You're just trying to get me to confess to something, get him off the hook." Singleton jabbed a finger at Paul. "Well, it won't work. Now, I demand that you take me home," Singleton blustered.

"Have you got it?" LaMar turned to Paul.

"Right here." Paul held up a long computer printout.

"As you can see, according to these documents, you have been embezzling company funds. See there? Your access code. And here, it clearly shows that you have profited greatly at the expense of one Señor Juan Carlos. Señor Carlos is an import/export entrepreneur, his main product being cocaine. Quentin gave this information to him. Señor Carlos is a little angry with you, Kyle."

"But it's not true! I'll tell him it's a lie."

"That kind of man is impulsive. You won't have time to try and convince him, Kyle—trust me. And he's got proof." As LaMar reminded him of it, Paul shook the printout.

"Oh, God." Singleton began to shake as he read the printout.

"We can work it so he gets his money back." Paul held up the keyboard to the computer.

"Unfortunately, for men like Señor Carlos, that's not enough. An example must be made to discourage others from such actions." LaMar's words caused the beginning of a hopeful look to fade from Singleton's face.

"A matter of honor and respect." Sam folded his arms across his chest.

"Oh, God, you can't let them kill me! What am I going to do?" Singleton began to snivel. Large drops of sweat poured from his face and stained the underarms of his jacket.

"It just so happens we know exactly what you should do," Paul said, slapping his back as three smiling faces beamed at him.

* * *

"Ain't dis one helluva mess!" Sheriff Triche wore an expression of disgust. Leaving his office, he pulled the door shut with such force the glass rattled.

"Damn! This is all I need." Daniels came from the opposite office. He took out two antacid tablets and chewed them. A pained frown twisted his face as he clutched his stomach.

Without speaking to each other, they both heaved a sigh. Sheriff Triche led the way down a hall to another office. Opening the door, he allowed the district attorney to go first. Savannah, Charice, Sam, Paul, and Gralin looked up expectantly.

"Did they talk?" Paul sprang from the metal chair.

"They talkin', all right. How we gone sort dis out I don't know." Sheriff Triche rubbed his unshaven jaw. "Quentin sayin' him and Claude found out Singleton was stealin' from the company the day before the murder. Says he thinks maybe Claude confronted Singleton and Singleton killed him. Claims he been suspectin' Singleton killed his grandpapa but was too scared to say so. He claims we oughta examine Singleton's office for evidence." Sheriff Triche looked up at the ceiling.

"Singleton says he found out Quentin was stealing from the company. He claims Claude found out, too. That Claude confronted Quentin and Quentin killed his grandfather. He says we should check the floor in the rear of Quentin's car for bloodstains." Daniels sat down heavily and began to rub his temples.

"And Miss Rousselle say dey did it together is how she figure. Quentin told her dey didn't have to worry 'bout the old man no more. Says he told her, 'We took care of it.' She ain't had no idea he meant he'd murdered the old man. She say she was too scared to talk 'cause Quentin beat her. Showed Deputy Arceneaux bruises on her body to prove it. Say we oughta check the trunk of Quentin's car if we don't believe her," Sheriff Triche said.

"What do you think, Sheriff?" Savannah stared at him, then at Daniels, when he didn't answer.

"We don't know what to think at this point. But we've got a real complicated situation to sort out," Daniels said in a tired voice.

"What about me?" Paul glanced from the sheriff to Daniels.

"You not the only, or even the best, suspect now. The strongest evidence we had was motive and your finger-prints. All three of those characters had a motive and their fingerprints were in Trosclair's office, too." Daniels stood.

"Lord, I can see now we gone be working into the morn-ing impounding cars, collectin' carpet samples and the like. Might as well call Clotilde now and tell her not to expect me home tonight, either. Better get movin'." Sher-iff Triche walked out. Shortly they heard him irritably barking orders to his deputies.

"Sorry for any problems all this caused for you, Hon-ore." Daniels gave a clipped nod before leaving.

"Man, let's get out of here. This place is depressing." Sam put one arm around Charice's waist.

"I'm more than ready." Paul pulled Savannah to him.

On the way out, they passed the offices where all three were being questioned separately. Quentin, his back to them, gestured wildly. A deputy sat in front of him with a tape recorder and tablet, scribbling furiously. Singleton sat slumped, head down. His expensive suit was crumpled, giving him the look of a bedraggled drunk-driving suspect. Noticing them walk by, he turned vacant eyes to them.

Savannah felt a tiny twitching sensation at the back of her neck. She swung around to find LaShaun standing a few yards away, between two deputies.

"Un de ces beaux jours, Savannah. Yes, yes. One of these

fine days." Though LaShaun spoke softly, her voice carried through the noisy station room. Her eyes flashed hatred.

Turning away, Savannah shook her head in a pitying dismissal. LaShaun let out of stream of obscenities as she was half carried, half dragged away.

"Some night, huh?" Savannah said. They sat in Paul's car in front of her house. They left Charice and Sam still affectionately teasing each other at Charice's house.

"Amazing." Paul smiled shyly.

"Bet your parents were thrilled to hear you're not a murder suspect now."

"Mama screamed and dropped the phone." Paul laughed.

"Poppy told me to give you a hug for him, and Tante Marie couldn't stop crying. She says she's going to start organizing a big celebration party."

"That'll be great." Paul looked at her, then quickly away. He chewed his lip in silence.

"Guess I'll go in." Savannah put her hand on the door handle.

"Wait. We haven't had a chance to really talk. I know I've made some mistakes. Even though I acted so—stupid, I still care about you very much. What I mean is, I love you, Savannah."

"Me, too."

"But I guess after everything that's happened, it might be a good idea to take it slow?" Paul asked, looking to take her lead.

"Maybe we should. I mean, talk about some of the things that made us act the way we did." Savannah fiddled with her purse strap.

"Sure. I, uh, could learn to open up and share my feelings more." Paul's fingers traced an invisible line around the rim of the steering wheel.

"And I could be more willing to trust, maybe, not so quick to judge." Savannah moved a little closer to him.

"I could let my guard down more, too." Paul's hand covered hers.

"This is a good start. Not moving too fast."

"I agree."

"See you later?" Savannah eyes searched his face.

"Yeah, later."

"Bye." Savannah did not make a move to leave, but instead moved closer.

"Bye." Paul leaned toward her.

"What a wonderful idea." Savannah wriggled against him as Paul wrapped his arm around her. Head tilted back, she moaned softly as his lips found hers.

"Great way to celebrate our engagement," Paul mumbled.

"I have to agree."

"Besides, it was the only considerate thing to do. It was bad enough we woke up your father and aunt at three-thirty in the morning to tell them the good news, but to have you go home so late, bumping around the house? That would only disturb them further." Paul spoke between kissing her face and neck, and, after pulling her blouse over her head, her shoulders.

"So, checking into a fancy hotel in Lafayette is really for them." Savannah began to unbutton his shirt.

"Absolutely." Paul unhooked her bra.

"For their own good."

"They need their rest."

"That's what I love about you. You're so unselfish." Savannah began walking to the bed, pulling him with her.

"That's the kind of guy I am," Paul said, his body covering hers as they slipped down onto the bedspread.